NOCTURNE

HE PULLED THE monster around in circles, hacking off chips of chitin with a broad crescent-shaped blade chained to his wrist and forearm. He went in low beneath its guard, dragging a bloody gash across its ribbed belly and drawing another agonised wheeze as the beast felt the wound bite. For Helfist, it was exhilarating. His hearts were beating like forge hammers in his chest and above him the tumult of the crowd was growing. It had been a long time since he'd felt this vital, this strong, this invincible. He liked the sensation – it was addictive.

Seven gladiators had died to this beast: seven hard men with warrior-spirits and wills of iron. Helfist was taking the scorpiad apart like it was nothing.

A WARHAMMER 40,000 NOVEL

NOCTURNE

Nick Kyme

BLACK LIBRARY

For Shakespeare, king of the awesome dudes.

A BLACK LIBRARY PUBLICATION

First published in Great Britain in 2011 by
The Black Library,
Games Workshop Ltd.,
Willow Road, Nottingham,
NG7 2WS, UK.

10 9 8 7 6 5 4 3 2 1

Cover illustration by Cheoljoo Lee.

A CIP record for this book is available from the British Library.

UK ISBN: 978 1 84970 088 7
US ISBN: 978 1 84970 089 4

See the Black Library on the internet at
www.blacklibrary.com

Find out more about Games Workshop
and the world of Warhammer 40,000 at
www.games-workshop.com

Printed and bound in the UK.

IT IS THE 41st millennium. For more than a hundred centuries the Emperor has sat immobile on the Golden Throne of Earth. He is the master of mankind by the will of the gods, and master of a million worlds by the might of his inexhaustible armies. He is a rotting carcass writhing invisibly with power from the Dark Age of Technology. He is the Carrion Lord of the Imperium for whom a thousand souls are sacrificed every day, so that he may never truly die.

YET EVEN IN his deathless state, the Emperor continues his eternal vigilance. Mighty battlefleets cross the daemon-infested miasma of the warp, the only route between distant stars, their way lit by the Astronomican, the psychic manifestation of the Emperor's will. Vast armies give battle in His name on uncounted worlds. Greatest amongst his soldiers are the Adeptus Astartes, the Space Marines, bio-engineered super-warriors. Their comrades in arms are legion: the Imperial Guard and countless Planetary Defence Forces, the ever-vigilant Inquisition and the tech-priests of the Adeptus Mechanicus to name only a few. But for all their multitudes, they are barely enough to hold off the ever-present threat from aliens, heretics, mutants - and worse.

TO BE A man in such times is to be one amongst untold billions. It is to live in the cruellest and most bloody regime imaginable. These are the tales of those times. Forget the power of technology and science, for so much has been forgotten, never to be re-learned. Forget the promise of progress and understanding, for in the grim dark future there is only war. There is no peace amongst the stars, only an eternity of carnage and slaughter, and the laughter of thirsting gods.

Have you ever been to our benighted world?

Its name literally means 'night', but we do not dwell in darkness.

Hell comes to our cities and our peoples,

it visits upon the earth such ravages as to make the sky black as sackcloth and the ground spew red, molten death.

It is not a hospitable world, this world,

for monsters lurk in its fuliginous depths and death is but a slip away for the careless, the unwary or the simply ill-fortuned.

It is not a populous world because much of it cannot be populated.

The mountains are bleak, craggy places, their summits wreathed with poisonous fumes.

The deserts are many, and they are desolate, unforgiving plains of ash.

Our few rivers are veins of acid and alkali, tainted by the sulphurous earth.

We have no forests, save for the petrified groves that lurk in the hot shadows of our tallest peaks.

Our fauna takes to the air on leathern wing or hunts the dune with tusk and claw.

It is serpentine and reptilian; chitinous and saurian.

But it is home, this broken land, and we defend it with our blood and breath.

Woe betide any who come here seeking to put it asunder.

They will find it a terrible place, a very terrible place.

– Unknown Nocturnean tribesman
of Themis

PROLOGUE

BLACK AS OLD night, the giant asteroid hurtled through the void. Trailing cosmic wake, this harbinger had come far. It careened through space lanes, circled gravity wells, coursed alongside refulgent suns and past barren moons. Dead stars witnessed its passage, a seemingly random trajectory, but there was nothing random about fate. It skirted the atmosphere of a dozen backwards worlds, its potent magnetic field wreaking cataclysm and consigning to oblivion a host of lesser races whom the universe would never know and so never mourn.

It was immense, a terrible gnarled orb, fanged with crags, colonised by hungry craters and possessed of a seeming sentience. Contrails of persistently clinging dust shadowed it like gossamer-thin fingers attempting to seize upon its celestial coattails. Dark splinters shed from its mass into an even darker plane, like jagged knives of night. It was inexorable, but when the warp swallowed it only to disgorge its unholy form back into reality, its journey was nearing its end. A world hung in its path, red and hot against the benighted canvas of space. It was a world of burning skies, of jet black mountains and deserts of fire.

Centuries earlier, the Black Rock's erratic course had been set. The Architect's own clawed hand had put it into motion. Those with the *sight*, who could perceive the grand conjurations of the galaxy, would behold the strands of fate pulling it towards the red world, presaging apocalypse. They had but to look upon it.

The Black Rock had seen much, and borne many travellers upon its ancient back over the years. The last had been tenacious, slow to die even when exposed to the cold grip of the void. Entire systems had fallen prey to its destructive appetites, devoured in the wake of its passing like tiny archipelagos erased by a violent tsunami.

It was destiny. It was doom.

The red world loomed before it, ringed by a haze of pyroclastic cloud.

A fiery hell world, a furnace of the universe where civilisations were forged.

Nocturne.

CHAPTER ONE

I
The Killing Place

THIS PLACE WAS death. Its shadow clung tenaciously to every alcove, every column. It lurked beneath every archway and crept inside every antechamber. Whispering like the husk of a corpse, it was the final exhalation of dust swathing the cracking brick in a patina of age and melancholy. The very air reeked of it, flavoured with copper. The gummy rime underfoot that softened his boot tread was further evidence, so too the redness of the walls. Fear came with it and laced the atmosphere with a greasy pall. He could feel it trying to adhere to his bare skin: fear, and anticipation.

Darkness only partially hid the crumpled forms of those that had come before him. Some had been dragged back into the barracks, broken and only half resembling men. Others had been recovered with shovels or would later be sluiced from the ground in a manky fluid.

Many found it was the waiting that was worst. Brutal warriors became gibbering wrecks in the quietude before the killing-time, where all they could hear was the roar and the scream. *He* was not shaking; *he* barely moved at all, except to breathe. His time had come, the one before him had been ended.

How many did that make for the beast? A tally of seven?

An auspicious number, he thought, rising from his haunches.

He'd seen some fighters clasp their hands together before going to their deaths, their lips mumbling oaths and promises in the hope of fortune. Others seized fists of earth as if tasting the battlefield and reading its ebb and flow. Such things were distractions only. They merely delayed and deluded. When he got to his feet, he rotated his arms in their sockets, and cracked his knuckles. His piecemeal armour *clanked* lightly as he did it; the chain attached to his weapon rattled dulcetly. He closed his eyes and peered through the narrow slits of his helmet a different being. To be a warrior was to be protean, the transition of one aspect to another. Mastery of both was the doorway to harmony and martial excellence. To embrace anything other was just reckless. For if a sword remained forever unsheathed it would eventually cut something for which it was not intended. When he opened his eyes again, his world was limned in crimson and he was of the killing mind.

I am Helfist. I am gladiator.

He climbed a sandy incline to the chorus of his chinking gladiatorial panoply. It was mainly leather, armour of the Old Ways as was tradition, but included some plated elements by way of aesthetic flourish. At the end of the ramp were a gate and a pair of grim-looking guardians festooned in metal from head to toe. Hulking, tall and muscular as if genebred for the very vocation, they still needed to look up as *he* strode past them.

Through the metal-banded doors, through the slim gaps in their bars, he could see the killing place. It was sand, it was blood-scent and it was torture.

He heard the screaming, the broken ones that pleaded and the baying of beasts...

Slowly but inexorably, the doors opened. Hollow skulls strung to their bars added a jangling refrain to the heavy creak of the iron.

Sunlight washed in, as red and visceral as the walls of the passageway.

He let it bathe his half-naked body before running the rest of the way up the ramp that led into the killing place. Ignoring the crunch of bone beneath him, Helfist stepped into the arena and listened to the adulation of the crowd.

His eyes never left the arena floor. There his fate was all too easy to see in the corpses of the other combatants. Men lay without limbs in drying pools of their own blood, or with heads cut from bodies and left to fester in the sun, or bloated with gangrenous poison, their eyes bulging and their appendages in the final throes of nerve spasm. Such were the destinies of all warriors in the end.

We are all merely ash on the wind, waiting to return to the mountain.

A brother in arms had said that to him once, before war had crippled him and turned his friend from poet to cankerous recluse.

A roar met his arrival in the arena, but the gladiator of Themis was unmoved. Let the mob bay and take their fill, it mattered not – his mind was on survival. Helfist adjusted the visor of his helm and peered through an aperture of pitted iron at the monstrous creature dominating the arena with its size and violent presence.

Scorpiad.

It was finishing the last morsels of its meal, another gladiator partly dissolved by intestinal acid from the creature's ruddy maw, when its attention turned to Helfist. Anticipating carnage, the belligerent crowd quietened to a dull murmur.

Dropping its half-eaten feast, the scorpiad advanced with clicking, syncopated movements.

A dirt-dweller, the creature had tiny insect eyes that glittered like a pair of black pearls in its crustacean-like face. Overlapping bone plates formed a chitinous shell that shimmered like umber carapace over its snout and back. Its eight limbs were gnarled, but scaly rather than shelled, and its ribbed underbelly was thick and leathern.

Due to their subterranean natures, scorpiads were not easy to catch. Groups of nomadic Ignean trappers went out onto the Arridian Plain in packs, tempting the creatures with sauroch carcasses, drawing them from their greasy burrows with the overwhelming promise of blood. Pay from the Themian Gladiatorial Guilds was high for any monstrous bounty brought intact and capable of fighting in the arena. It was just as well, for hunting the scorpiad came with a high mortality rate.

Helfist could well appreciate that as the monster shifted its bulk towards him. It was massive, dwarfing even the giant gladiator and many times heavier. He drew back as it came on, eliciting some derisive goading from sections of the watching crowd. Behind their high walls and glass domes, looking down onto the anachronistic arena, what did they have to fear? They desired battle and death, not posturing.

Helfist gave it to them.

Goading the scorpiad with shouts and threats, he let it attack first. It lunged with a blood-crusted claw, which he ducked then rolled under to ram a fist-spike into the fleshy part of the monster's limb. Its cry of pain manifested as a disconcerting wheeze from its puckered maw, where its mandibles clacked in agitation.

Scuttling back, it dived down at him with its other claw like a spear, but only managed to impale dirt. Helfist yanked out the spike and a gushet of ichorous green fluid came with it. The acerbic stink of bile-acid burned at his nostrils and the weapon came out slightly corroded. He leapt to avoid the sweep of the scorpiad's legs as it turned, and came up out of another roll just in time to see its barbed tail whipping towards him. Helfist parried using the glove of his fist-spike but felt the impact all the way to his shoulder. In seconds, the metal guard was rotten with venom from the scorpiad's stinger, so he discarded it and left the weapon to slowly dissolve on the ground behind him.

As he ranged around to the creature's blindside it followed, scuttling sideways around its core, pummelling at Helfist as it moved. Dust was kicked up in the wake of the frenzied claw attack that also sent bits of dead gladiator spewing upwards like aerial chum. Helfist ducked and weaved, sprang back and bounded forwards again foiling every hammering impact of the scorpiad's pincers. Hungry and becoming increasingly agitated; it combined thrusts of its tail with limb-slicing snaps of its claws. A spurt of acid from its fanged, tubular mouth left a burn scar across the sand but Helfist dodged that too. He pulled the monster around in circles, hacking off chips of chitin with a broad, crescent-shaped blade chained to his wrist and forearm. He went in low beneath its guard, dragging a bloody gash across its ribbed belly and drawing another agonised wheeze as the beast felt the wound bite. For Helfist it was exhilarating. His hearts were beating like forge hammers in his chest and above him the tumult of the crowd was growing. It had been a long time since he'd felt this vital, this strong, this invincible. He liked the sensation – it was addictive.

Seven gladiators had died to this beast: seven hard men with warrior-spirits and wills of iron. Helfist was taking the scorpiad apart like it was nothing.

The monster thrashed at him as he came from beneath it and this time he lashed out with his blade, cleaving a gore-slick wedge in the tail. It reared up on its hind legs, turning swiftly, its claws snapping impotently at the air.

Helfist looked up at it, a sneer just visible below the visor of his helmet.

'You are an ugly brute,' he told it in a deep, chasmal voice. He released the grip on his forearm blade and it dropped to the ground like an anchor, the chain around his wrist unfurling as it fell.

Every link was serrated like a knife-edge and as the scorpiad came thunderously back down Helfist yanked the blade up from the ground. As it cut through the air, it gave off a high-pitched keening sound before wrapping around the monster's left foreleg.

Helfist tugged and the serrated links of the chain drew taut and began to saw. The scorpiad stumbled, a panicked bleat issuing from its bubbling mouth. He heaved again and the chain came loose as the limb broke away from its host in a welter of greenish blood.

It barely had time for a weak and flailing riposte before Helfist swung again, this time for a rear leg, and tore off another limb. Spewing dark and viscous fluid from the ruined stumps of its missing appendages, the scorpiad slumped down onto its belly. The tail whickered out as Helfist came on but he countered with a lash from his chain-glaive and the barbed tip was sent bundling across the arena floor, separated from the rest.

A healthy sweat sheened the gladiator's body, helping to define his immense musculature, and his chest heaved with a deep but strong rhythm. The cured black leather of his armour blended perfectly with his slab-like skin, and the sun made it shimmer like oil as he went down on his haunches to look the monster in the eye.

'This was never a fair fight,' he said with quiet solemnity. Some of the scorpiad's blood had sprayed the bare flesh of his arms, adding to the many scars they already carried. 'It will be quick,' he added, rising.

Helfist let the crescent-blade fall from his grasp as he reached up over his hulking shoulders to retrieve a long-hafted hammer. It was a magnificent piece of artifice that gleamed brightly in the light. Pistons worked in the weapon's head, increasing its power and impact.

Hefting it two-handed, Helfist split the scorpiad's mewling face in two and ended its suffering. He turned and held the gore-slick piston-hammer aloft in salute of his opponent and his triumph.

The mob roared.

WHEN HELFIST RETURNED to the barracks someone was waiting for him.

'I thought I would find you here in these… *pits*.' He spat the word as if it left an acrid flavour in his mouth.

The figure was almost as tall as Helfist, clad in bulky green armour. Ribbed servos linked the joints between each concomitant plate and whirred as he moved. He still wore his battle-helm, which was white as opposed to green as was his right shoulder pad. The left guard bore the image of a snarling orange drake head on a black field to signify his allegiance.

Helfist was carefully removing his leather hauberk and scraping the blood from his body with a sharp-stone. A robed and hooded serf waited in the shadows behind him with its head bowed.

Overhead red sunlight hazed in, cut into grainy shafts by the barracks' lattice ceiling. It illuminated suits of armour of all stripes and eras, and copious racks of war gear. There was a surgery too, its doorway shawled by a sheet of darkly spattered leather. Another gladiator, a survivor of the scorpiad, was inside laid up on the slab for the medicus to do his gruesome work. Underfoot was grit and sand in homage to the Old Ways. The air reeked of metal and sweat.

Helfist answered without looking up from what he was doing. 'You don't approve of the Themian hell-pits then, brother?'

'No. I simply object to having to come all this way to track you down.'

There was bitterness in the other's voice that Helfist found hard to reconcile. He kept his eyes on his labours though, unclasping one of his vambraces and dropping it into a barrel of oil to soak. 'Keeps the leather supple,' he said, 'so it doesn't crack in the heat.'

The reply was caustic. 'I know how to tend armour, even those barbaric trappings.'

Helfist met the other's gaze. His eyes burned like red furnaces. 'It has been so long since I saw you with bolter and blade in clenched fist that I thought you might need reminding, Emek. How long since you graced the training cages or the arenas?'

The Apothecary, Emek, didn't answer. He stepped forwards. It wasn't a deliberately aggressive gesture but Helfist turned his shoulders towards him and squared his body ready for a fight.

Emek scoffed, 'You've been in these tribal slums too long, Ba'ken.'

Ba'ken scowled and clenched a fist. 'These are your roots, brother. Too much time spent secreted in darkness on Prometheus has made you forget!' His anger ebbed and he relaxed. 'It's time you took your head out of Fugis's data-slates and rejoined your Chapter.'

The Apothecary was much changed from the brother Ba'ken had once known. He was seldom seen without his battle-helm these days and rarely removed his armour on account of the horrific scarring on his body. These weren't honour marks, earned proudly for battles won; they were a painful reminder of an aborted mission on the stricken hulk *Protean* and the psychic attack of a xenos creature he had fought there. Emek limped where once he had stridden; he was weak and hollow where once he'd been strong and vital. This was a ghost Ba'ken beheld before him, a shade of the Space Marine the Apothecary had been.

Hope, which Emek had once been so full of, had died within him on that ship.

Ba'ken realised his anger was at that, not at his brother. Relenting, his shoulders sagged and he lowered his voice.

'I apologise. The heat of the arena still fuels my blood.'

With the hiss of the gorget clamps depressurising, Emek removed his helmet. His face was *ravaged*. His burns hadn't healed well. Some supposed it was on account of them being caused by psychic lightning. Overlapping scar tissues knotted and scalloped in places, giving Emek an almost patchwork appearance, as if his visage was comprised of not just one face but many. His left eye was dull and grey, whilst his right blazed with a bitter flame.

The Apothecary breathed in deeply and the sound rasped up his throat.

'Accepted, but I have important work to perform in the Apothecarion. Just because its progenitor is dead doesn't mean I should ignore Fugis's labours.'

'He is not dead, brother.'

Emek raised an eyebrow. It was an ugly gesture. 'He took the Burning Walk, Ba'ken – he's dead.'

To fight such pessimism was pointless; Ba'ken had tried at length to do so. He sighed instead and went back to tending his armour.

'Your wounds look well healed, though,' Emek added, casting an appraising eye. He paused, as if deciding his next course carefully. 'When I saw you after the Firedrakes returned from the Volgorrah Reef, I thought the worst.'

Ba'ken touched his chest at a lance of phantom pain. The wounds inflicted in the dark eldar frontier enclave, the so-called 'Port of Anguish', were gone but the memory of them lingered. So, too, the betrayal of Iagon.

'I was lost to darkness, but relieved when I awoke to find I wasn't in a metal tomb,' he said.

Emek laughed, but it was an empty gesture. 'The bioscan made for grim reading, I will tell you that. But you're a stubborn bastard, Ba'ken.'

'No more than any Salamander.' He looked over at Emek. 'Promise me this, brother: if I am ever beyond help and that the only recourse is to be interred within the dreamless sleep of the warrior-eternal then administer the Emperor's Peace and reclaim my genetic legacy for the Chapter. I have no wish to become like Amadeus or Ashamon.'

'Most would consider becoming a Dreadnought an honour.'

'I do not. Promise me.'

Emek held Ba'ken's gaze for a few moments before nodding. He then nudged at the chained blade hooked on the weapons rack. '*Helfist*, eh?' Something approaching a smirk crept into the corner of the Apothecary's mouth as he tried at levity, a thing he used to be skilled at.

Ba'ken's eyes narrowed. His joy at the flicker of humour in his brother's voice outweighed his embarrassment, but he showed neither.

'I heard the crowd chanting,' Emek explained. 'Didn't think you went in for theatrics, brother.'

'The arena *is* theatre. It's not like fighting against the anvil, in the fires of battle.'

'Still, you have some pretty scars.' The caustic demeanour returned again.

Ba'ken stared. 'Some scars cut deeper than most.'

'Indeed.'

And like the wind snuffing out a flame, the warmth between them dwindled into smoke. Ba'ken found he'd had enough.

'Why are you here, Emek? I assume it's not to discuss old times.'

'Why are any of us here on Nocturne? It's *him*, Ba'ken. He wants to speak with you.'

Ba'ken lowered his eyes. His voice went barely above a whisper.

'We have not spoken since his return...'

'Perhaps he wants to confess.'

Ba'ken's head came up sharply, his jaw clenched in anger.

'He was your friend, Emek. We both were... *are* still.'

A tremor of something registered below the Apothecary's left eye. It might've been because of the nerve damage he'd sustained. Ba'ken hoped it was regret.

Emek turned without reply, replacing his helmet as he did so.

'Be quick about it,' he muttered through the vox-grille.

Ba'ken called out as the Apothecary neared the way out.

'Why you of anyone, brother?' he asked. 'Why did you come to summon me?'

Emek stopped for a moment but then carried on without uttering anything further.

II

A Return

THE NOMAD'S FINGERS were curled into claws and his skin was dry as parchment as he putrefied in the hot sun. A sa'hrk worried at his leathern flesh, stripping back the toughened layers to get at the softer meat beneath. Above the lean-bodied predator, a flock of patient dactylids were disturbed in their circling by an immense shadow growing overhead. Emitting a panicked screech, the winged carrion-eaters scattered into a bank of ash cloud.

A tumultuous belt of sound preceded the shadow, which was spreading like a wave across the Scorian Plain. The earth vibrated, collapsing dunes and opening sand fissures that swallowed entire tracts of desert. Nictitating, the sa'hrk turned its ruddy snout to the heavens as the rolling darkness engulfed it too. Bleating in sudden terror, the creature took to claw, its meal forgotten. Muscular hindquarters bulged in its frantic efforts to escape, but the shadow was vast and consumptive. Over a dozen miniature suns opened up in the darkness, which reeked of oil and metal and incense. No sooner had they dawned than the miniature suns went supernova, spilling fire onto the sand, turning it to glass with the heat of their arrival.

The sa'hrk was rendered to a fire-black carcass that disintegrated as the collector ship touched down. Descent thrusters on the vessel's hull burned for several minutes after making landfall. Their powerful backwash drove furrows into the sand bars around the collector ship's crystallised contact point, unearthing further bodies the immolated sa'hrk had missed. These men and women were Ignean traders too, but the savage wounds that had killed them were caused by an entirely different breed of predator, one that carried sickle-wire, barbed falchions and serrated knives.

IT WAS LIKE a thick wedge of crimson-plated metal, blocky and functional. Even from across the Acerbian Sea, the fishermen in their tiny metal-bellied skiffs stood up in their boats to look. Riggers on the multi-limbed oil trawlers, trains of nomads and Themian hunter packs ranging the Arridian Plain, rock-harvesters out in the mountains all witnessed the vast ship's arrival.

So too did another. He adjusted the focus on his magnoculars, allowing for the lens scarring caused by the Pyre Desert's intermittent sandstorms, and recognised the ship's particular iconography. He panned along its flanks, observing the many storage vaults and collection vats, the paucity of defensive weaponry and the thickness of the armour. A freighter, not a warship. Having seen enough he shut off the scopes, letting them hang by a leather strap around his neck as he pulled down a pair of sand goggles over his eyes. A long drover's coat protected the rest of his equipment and a rugged-looking boonie hat with a wide brim and a mesh flap kept his forehead and neck in shade. As he got to his feet, he pulled the scarves he wore up over his nose and mouth until his face was completely obscured.

He'd left a sauroch in the desert basin below and clutched a fistful of rope he'd tethered to his kill. As he came back down from the dune, he realised he wasn't alone. At the periphery of his vision a pack of sa'hrk were creeping up on him, intent on his meal and his flesh. Leaving the long rifle secured on his back, he pulled out a dulled blade from the scabbard on his leg instead and let the predators come...

It was over quickly.

After wiping the blade clean, he sheathed his gladius. Then he headed off into the deeper desert, dragging along his earlier kill and leaving the dead sa'hrk behind. He still had a long way to go.

NOCTURNE BRED SURVIVORS. Ever since the ancient days of the tribes when the earth shamans founded the sacred bedrock upon which to establish their settlements, its peoples were hardy. But endurance and a wary respect for the elements was not enough to sustain a race on a volcanic death world. Technology gave them a crucial edge, the means to harness void shields to protect their cities, advanced seismographic warning systems and medical facilities that could withstand atomics. All of this and more besides was made possible because of the tithe.

Standing on a low ridge overlooking the landing site, Forgemaster Argos turned the piece of crystal he held over and over in his gauntlet. It shimmered beautifully in the sun, an ultra-rare chunk of stone unearthed after the last quake.

'Such riches she yields,' he muttered.

'When the earth splits and fire rains from the sky,' Orgento concluded the litany as he came shoulder to shoulder with his master. The ocular scope on his bionic eye trained on the crystal shard in Argos's hand. 'A rare specimen.'

Their voices were cold and mechanical, though Argos's carried a deeper resonance with a faint machine hum underlying it.

'It is why we're here,' the Forgemaster said to the other Techmarine, his gaze moving to the sand plain.

Orgento followed him. 'The pact.'

'Indeed, and thusly are our void shields kept strong and our armouries full.'

'Do you feel a longing for it, master?' asked Orgento as a depressurisation cloud engulfed the bulky collector ship in front of them. 'The red planet and the Martian fraternity, I mean.' The Mechanicus sigil was clearly emblazoned on the vessel's armoured flank: a bifurcated skull, one side bone and the other machine, encircled by a cog. Thick wedges of red and black plasteel covered the vessel in a pitted carapace. It was ugly and functional.

Argos shook his head, prompting the servos in his neck and head to grind. 'This is my home, Orgento. It is the fiery skies of Nocturne that I long for when parted from them. You and I, our brother Techmarines, we share a unique understanding amongst the Chapter but we are Salamanders before we are servants of the Omnissiah.'

Orgento bowed at the Forgemaster's wisdom and followed him as he leapt down onto the sandy plain below. As they arrived at the threshold of the landing site the two Techmarines were joined by a pair of tracked hauler-servitors, and were just in time to see the vessel's massive embarkation ramp lower amidst a secondary cloud of pneumatic depressurisation. Stepping out of the shadowy confines of the hull was a red-robed creature wearing a talismanic cog on a chain around his neck. His hands were clasped across his chest, just below the icon, but hidden within the folds of his robes. A thick cowl occluded most of his face and the telltale shine of cybernetics was only just visible in the shadows it cast. Much like Argos, the Adeptus Mechanicus magos travelled with an entourage. The meeting of pallid-fleshed, cyborganic creatures at the foot of the ramp was a bizarre one.

Argos inclined his head, setting the servos in his artificer armour whirring again. Unlike the Martians, the pair of Techmarines wore a lustrous green battle-plate. Only their right shoulder guards were red, as was Orgento's battle-helm, to show their affiliation with the adepts of Mars. Argos went unhelmed. Half of the Forgemaster's face was obscured by a plate with a firedrake symbol seared into the metal. A bionic eye glared coldly from the socket where the organic had once been. Snaking wires tracked from the device and terminated in plug-like implants in his cranium.

'Greetings from Mars, Adept Argos,' said the enrobed magos. The 'voice' came from a vox-amplifier in place of the creature's mouth. Shiny metal tendrils clicked either side of the grille-speaker in tandem with the diction. 'Praise be to the Omnissiah.'

Argos made the symbol of the cog out of respect. 'Welcome back to Nocturne, Xhanthix.'

The magos nodded, replicating human affectation. 'It has been almost two centuries, one hundred and eighty-six point three four Imperial years to be precise. You have embraced the Machine-God greatly since last we met,' he added, eyeing the Forgemaster's facial cybernetics.

'Necessity, rather than by choice,' Argos confessed, 'though I welcome it.'

First in the sewer hives of Ullsinar and then again on the desolate moon of Ymgarl, Argos had lost his face. Both times the alien species known as tyranids, specifically a sub-genus designated 'genestealers', had been responsible. Part of his skull and, in addition, his brain had been interfaced with the bio-cybernetics that replaced his face. It had saved his life, but altered him in other ways. An odd quirk of memory sometimes stirred his olfactory senses to recall the stench of bio-acid and burning flesh even when locked in the solitorium. It had once been disconcerting; now it was merely *interesting*. This reaction, or lack thereof, prompted another line of reasoning for Argos that had no clear resolution.

When not engaged in rites to the Omnissiah and the arcane litanies used for awakening the machine-spirit, Argos wondered if his loss of physical identity had removed him one step further from humanity. Certainly, he was more aloof than his Salamander battle-brothers, perhaps more so than Orgento or the other Techmarines of the Chapter. The thought did not concern him; rather, it was a conundrum that could not be solved with logic. In a Chapter concerned with humanity, both literal and figurative, it was a curious position to hold.

He brandished the crystal open-handed to Xhanthix.

'From our mines,' Argos explained, 'a strong harvest for the tithe.'

Mandible-like mechadendrites extended from within the magos's hood, twitching as they closed on the crystal. 'Flawless…' he breathed, describing its atomic composition rather than its aesthetic quality. As the multi-jointed instruments caressed the crystal's surface, feeding back information regarding its mass, size and geological properties, there was the lightest connection between the mechadendrites and the haptic implants in Argos's hand.

Even insulated by his gauntlet, the Forgemaster felt a jolt of data transfer that manifested as painful static in his head. He grimaced as Xhanthix took the crystal, drawing the attention of Orgento.

'Master?' asked the Techmarine.

Argos recovered, shrugging off the sensation. 'It's nothing, a synaptic quirk.'

Xhanthix barely noticed; his cohorts stared ahead blindly, even less affected. The magos was engrossed by the crystal, seeing within it all the possibilities for technological invention.

'Your forge-ship,' said Argos, 'it is docked at Prometheus?' He referred to the Salamanders' moon bastion, a sister celestial body to Nocturne that was responsible for the planet's tectonic fragility. Principally a space port, Prometheus was also a vault for the Chapter's relics and its hallowed halls were the domain of the Firedrakes, the Salamanders' elite First Company.

The magos finished his appraisal before answering. 'Yes, the *Archimedes Rex* and the rest of its crew are aboard at your stronghold preparing for my return.'

'*Archimedes Rex*?' In a rare expression of emotion, the right side of Argos's lip curled into a scowl. 'That vessel was wrecked. I know, for I saw it when it was recovered from deep space. The Marines Malevolent pillaged it.'

'It was reclaimed by the Adeptus Mechanicus then restored.'

'That I also know. I saw to its return to the Martian priesthood, not so long ago in fact.'

As far as his facial muscles were capable of it, Xhanthix frowned. 'I do not see the relevance of the spurious time period. It was one year and three point six months according to standard Imperial units of time, to be precise. I was the one responsible for its restoration. Despite its time adrift in the void, the damage it sustained was not irreparable.'

Argos felt an unfamiliar sensation filling him, rushing the blood around his body, fuelling him with adrenaline. 'But its crew were. I have seen the evidence of it. I even burned the remains of those creatures in our furnaces.'

Orgento shifted a little, eyeing the magos's servitors with sudden suspicion as his hand strayed to his sidearm. He didn't know what was happening or why his master's demeanour had changed so abruptly but reason wasn't necessary in this situation, only the readiness to act.

Even unencumbered by his massive servo harness, Argos was a huge and imposing warrior. He dwarfed the diminutive magos. 'They were tainted, Xhanthix. Homicidal, in fact. One of your Martian brethren who was aboard, a magos, went insane and tried to kill my battle-brothers.'

'*They* were also your brothers,' Xhanthix replied without recrimination.

'You know what I mean.'

'No, I do not. What is your meaning, exactly? Your argument is not logical and probably being tempered by your human side. Perhaps you are not as one with the machine as I first believed.'

It was a close to an insult from an Adept of the Mechanicus as you could get.

Argos relented – he *was* letting his humanity govern

his emotional state. In a way he was glad of it.

'I am merely surprised you re-commissioned the ship,' he said. 'I fully expected it to be denuded of anything of technological value and then scuttled.'

'You held on to a ship awaiting its reclamation, believing it would be destroyed?'

'It was not our decision to make, whether or not the *Archimedes Rex* should be decommissioned.'

'The vessel was of technological value,' Xhanthix asserted in that same neutral tone. 'It would not have been logical to destroy it, not based on the evidence of a fault in a particular magos that was transferred to his subordinates. Machine corruption is not undocumented, and doctrina wafers are prone to degradation over time should the proper observances to the machine-spirit not be met.'

Argos saw no concrete line of reasoning to dispute that, but still asked, 'Why did you bring it back here?'

'I found the symmetry intriguing,' said Xhanthix. 'Something of a human predilection, I admit, but even so. Does that satisfy all of your questioning? Because I am keen to proceed. My vessel detected inordinately large levels of growing magnetic radiation in your planet's atmosphere and I would not wish for any unforeseen delay to affect my instruments.'

Argos had discerned as much himself prior to leaving Prometheus. Such fluctuations were not uncommon but he was monitoring them anyway. Xhanthix was also right, of course – magnetic radiation could falsify geological results in his codifying instrumentation. In the end, he nodded.

'There are samples waiting for you at the mines. We are here to escort you.'

Xhanthix bowed, indicating compliance before issuing a blurt of binaric machine code to his servitors who began to animate.

'Lead on.'

Argos turned in the direction of the mines. It wasn't far.

Orgento fell in next to him as they led the group.

'Master, I am troubled,' he confessed. 'What just happened there? For a moment, I thought–'

'As did I, brother,' Argos said, interrupting him, 'as did I.'

They fell silent, but the veil of static remained.

CHAPTER TWO

I
Nulls and Fetters

DAK'IR WAS ALONE. He was stripped of his armour, only recently given, and rank. He was a Lexicanum no longer, the heavy collar he wore only emphasised that fact. Hard bands enclosed his wrists. The metal from which they were forged was black and dense. It was a 'null' collar, the bracelets a part of the ward, an unassuming but arcane device that inhibited the use of psychics. The one fastened tightly around Dak'ir's neck and wrists was dialled up to its most potent setting. They had even taken his force sword, *Draugen*, though he'd surrendered it willingly. He had been bonding with the blade, shaping its energy and spirit to his will. Thus amplified, he could've shattered his fetters and unleashed his power on the penitarium, breaking free of his enforced detention.

Instead, he felt a latent susurrus of the warp whisper across the collar's dull black surface and chose not to nurture it.

He had gone without a fight or much argument. Tu'Shan himself had given the order, and he would not go against the will of his Chapter Master. For many months, he had dwelt in the darkness of his cell awaiting the long judgement of the Pantheon Council. Dak'ir's eyes stung from the effort of keeping them open for several hours at a time. Whenever he closed them, he saw… *fire*. It was the flame that burned within him, the Ferro Ignis or Fire Sword as prophesied by Promethean lore, whose conflagration would rise up and consume all of Nocturne.

A low-born, one of the earth, will pass through the gate of fire. He will be our doom or salvation.

As revealed in the armour of his ancient forebears, the survivors of Isstvan, these fated words had haunted him for the last four years. As of yet, their meaning was unclear. He *had* passed through the gate of fire, besting the legendary drake Kessarghoth to do it. Visions of a dead world, Moribar, had assailed him and there he and Pyriel had discovered the plan of the Dragon Warriors to destroy Nocturne. Dak'ir's role in that prophesied cataclysm was unknown. That was for the council to deliberate and ultimately decide. It was a decision which could result in his death.

In this and so many other ways, Dak'ir was alone. Even surrounded by kin, he felt isolated. It had always been this way. He consoled himself with the knowledge that this was merely a part of the Promethean Creed, that which preached the importance of self-reliance and self-sacrifice in all Salamanders.

Even amongst such august brothers, Dak'ir was unique. Some believed he was an aberration. The only Salamander not to hail from a Sanctuary City, he was an Ignean, one of the nomadic tribes who had crawled from the darkness of his cave dwelling and reached up to grasp the heavens and become 'of the stars'. He had once believed his humanity defined him, that his uniquely human perspective gave him an empathy his brothers lacked.

Skin of onyx black and eyes as red as fire gave the sons

of Vulkan a diabolic appearance. A battle scar earned several years ago and a quirk of melanochromatic degeneration had left Dak'ir with a patch of skin that was pale and vital like human flesh. He'd taken it as a symbol of his believed empathy and even went as far as to forge a mask that concealed the hellish aspect of his visage. His battle-helm bore a simulacrum of that mask.

But I am not human, he thought.

Saviour or destroyer: that was the fate Dak'ir was consigned to. Both were heavy and unenviable mantles. Even his fellow battle-brothers looked upon him with suspicion and wariness. As a figure of prophecy, something unknowable and even potentially omnipotent, how could he share empathy with any human being now? As he lamented, Dak'ir touched the old scar upon his face. It was like connecting to a lens through which he could observe a piece of time, and he was briefly transported back to the Aura Hieron temple on Stratos where Ko'tan Kadai had lost his life and he himself had been grievously injured.

It all began with Kadai. His death was the spark that lit the flame of our vengeance against the Dragon Warriors.

'A death for a death.' Dak'ir spoke the words out loud.

Kadai for Ushorak.

'Reliving old dreams, brother?' asked a deep, comradely voice.

In his introspection, Dak'ir hadn't realised the door to the holding cell was open. The giant form of Ba'ken stood stolidly in the doorway.

'Unhappy ones, I'm afraid,' Dak'ir said but then smiled, the darkness vanishing from his face as he added, 'You look well, sergeant.'

Ba'ken was wearing his full war panoply, power-armoured with his battle-helm in the crook of his left arm. He carried no weapons, however, and behind him Dak'ir caught the vaguest psychic trace of his master, Pyriel, watching the exchange.

'Better than you.' He laughed but it was short-lived,

tainted by regret. Ba'ken's expression, crag-like but leav-
ened by a fading smile, darkened. 'I wish I had been
there at the council. It is difficult to…'

'To understand,' said Dak'ir. 'I know, brother.'

Ba'ken's jaw clenched, the impotence of the gesture
obvious. 'This is wrong, to treat one of the Chapter's
heroes like a traitor. Our efforts should be bent towards
Nihilan and the Dragon Warriors and all the deeds for
which they must be made answerable.'

'I am a threat,' Dak'ir replied simply. 'Until that can be
measured, I must remain here.'

'You look as you ever did to me, brother.'

'But I am not, Ba'ken. Not any more.'

Silence filled the cell, desolate, desperate and deafening. The anguish the sergeant fought within him was
etched upon his face as indelibly as the honour scars on
his body. A particularly harsh, almost blade-like, brand
crept up to the base of Ba'ken's throat and was just visible above the lip of his gorget. It represented the dark
eldar and his survival of the terrible wounds he'd sustained at their hands.

'What happened to you beneath the mountain?'

'I felt… *fire*. Not only literally, but on a deeper subconscious level. It was a pure and destructive flame,
Ba'ken, and it was in me. I *was* the flame.' Dak'ir looked
away, into the darkness but his senses had taken him to
another place far beyond the holding cell. 'Such fury…
it was incandescent, world-consuming even. The *Ferro
Ignis*…'

Ba'ken scowled. 'It sounds like you crave it.'

Dak'ir snapped to and met the sergeant's gaze.

'I do. It is incredible, but also terrifying. For the first
time since I assumed the black carapace, I feel fear. Not
of my enemies, but of what I might become.'

Ba'ken looked suddenly uncomfortable. 'Emek said
you brought me here to confess.'

'That I am the destroyer of Nocturne?' Dak'ir laughed.
It was altogether chilling. 'I have no idea what I am

supposed to confess to.' His truculence ebbed and he asked, 'How is our erstwhile squad brother?'

'Bitter.'

'I am sorry to hear that. When I learned of what happened to him on the *Protean*, I was already in this cage. Besides a brief exchange during his cursory examination of me in this cell, I have yet to speak him properly, since... since his wounding. I almost didn't recognise him.'

'Few do, who knew him before.' Ba'ken hung his head and his bulky frame sagged as if all the troubles of the Chapter had been levelled atop his shoulders, a problem for him and him alone to negotiate. 'By Vulkan! The anvil has been testing. It has beaten us to breaking point, tempered the steel that binds us until it cracked. Agatone tries to rally the Third, return to them their honour but we've laboured under long shadows, heavy with age.'

'And yet we stand,' said Dak'ir. 'Lift your eyes, brother.'

Ba'ken did. 'Why did you bring me here? I am supposed to join Master Prebian in the Pyre Desert in initiating the aspirants, my time is finite.'

'I cannot think of a better tutor for them,' Dak'ir allowed himself a wry grin, 'or should that be task master?' Despite the levity, Ba'ken's question lingered in the eye like a blade unsheathed and close to the neck. 'Emek told me you very nearly died on the Volgorrah Reef.'

Ba'ken snorted derisively. 'Not so moribund that he holds his tongue, I see,' he muttered.

'I wanted to see that you are alive and unscathed, brother,' said Dak'ir. He raised an eyebrow. 'At least part of that is true.'

Ba'ken protested. 'I am re-forged and ready for my duties to the Chapter.'

Dak'ir waved away the unintended insult. 'No offence was meant, but you are not fully recovered yet. But that's not why I requested your presence. I wanted to look you in the eye and ask you something.'

Ba'ken's anxious silence bade Dak'ir to continue.

'What do you see?'

Ba'ken frowned, not understanding. 'I see my brother, I see Dak'ir.'

'Look deeper.'

'I don't know what you are asking me to–' And then he saw it, roiling within Dak'ir's eyes, tiny pits of hell and damnation.

'I see fire,' said Ba'ken, and his voice was hollow and cold. 'All I can see is fire.'

Dak'ir nodded solemnly. 'Now you know why I must remain in this place. Find again your purpose, brother, and let your troubled thoughts rest upon me no longer. It is the anvil, and I am merely being tested against it. That is all.'

'Yes, but what if it should break you?'

'Is that what you believe?'

'I don't know what to believe. It broke Emek.'

Dak'ir sighed, abruptly melancholic. 'Yes… I think it did.'

II
Deeper Scars

JAGGING CLAW MARKS ravaged the interior of the Apothecarion's isolation chamber. Emek had put its inhabitant under with a potent blend of sedatives and anaesthesia. The doses were in extremely high concentrations in order to bypass the multi-lung's resilience to toxins. As an expert in Space Marine biology he was well suited to the task.

Divested of his power armour and other trappings, Emek's subject was crouched down in one corner of the chamber, sullen but dormant. A thick wall of ferrocrete with a single rectangular observation portal stood between them. As of yet, the Apothecary had been unable to draw any significant conclusions concerning Zartath's aberrant physiology. All attempts to make contact with his Chapter had also, thus far, been unsuccessful.

'I am a prisoner in this hole,' he growled, slurring his words only for them to become muffled by the armaglas.

Emek looked up from the data-slates and parchments scattered on the medi-slab in front of him. 'You recovered from that last belt of sedative much more quickly than the previous strain. I'll increase your dosage next time.' He went back to his studies.

'Release me,' Zartath snarled.

The light in the Apothecarion anteroom was subdued. Emek found the harsh surgical glare of its lamps painful and dulling them helped. The half-illumination hinted at medical paraphernalia – philtres, salving agents, coagulant-gels and other remedies – as well as a vast complex of corridors, infirmaries and surgeries where the Chapter Apothecaries could conduct their vital work. In the lower levels were the gene-banks where recovered progenoids from fallen Salamanders waited in frozen stasis. They represented the Chapter's future, its legacy after the warriors that once carried them were burned to ash and given back to the earth.

It was part *Codex Astartes* doctrine as laid down by Primarch Roboute Guilliman in ages past, and part Promethean lore as handed down by the tribal kings of ancient Nocturne. Rebirth and reincarnation were a core tenet of the Creed, the great Circle of Fire through which each and every Nocturnean, human or super-human, moved. A sacred flame was a means of providing transition, the earth the great cosmological forge to which the essence of the dead could be returned so that they might live on. Literal, puritanical, interpretations of the Circle of Fire hailed from Nocturne's ancient ages and were outmoded after the birth of Vulkan and the coming of the Emperor, but some still clung to the Old Ways. Veneration and remembrance were important.

Emek held on to a position of rationality and enlightenment. The ancient beliefs and prophecies were just that – *archaic* and no longer relevant. He wondered if his 'friend' beyond the armaglas thought any differently. The isolation chamber was only a small portion of the Apothecarion, one cell amongst many. Currently, Zartath was the only occupant.

'I will not be caged!' the warrior persisted.

Annoyed at the constant interruption, Emek glared and his still functioning eye flared brightly in the gloom.

'You were held prisoner on the Volgorrah Reef for six years. Who can really say what effect the tortures of the xenos, losing your battle-brothers like you did, had on your mind?'

Zartath bared his teeth. 'I am *still* a prisoner!'

Ignoring him, Emek went on, 'And then there is your mutation to consider…'

Little was known about Zartath, save that he was once a Space Marine in the Black Dragons Chapter. It was amongst those ill-fated brotherhoods referred to as the 'Cursed Founding' – although such terms varied according to the speaker – that the Black Dragons had come into being. His physical deviancy was obvious. Bony growths jutted from his head and forearms. When Zartath was roused to anger, they would become like ossified blades punching straight through flesh and skin. The savaging taken by the isolation chamber's internal walls was evidence of that.

Despite the sedatives plaguing his system, Zartath was belligerent. It was part of the reason he was still incarcerated.

'Face like blackened coal and eyes like embers, and you speak to me of mutancy.' He sneered, showing off his needle-like fangs. 'Let me go, hypocritical dog.'

'There is also the matter of your heritage.' Here, Emek pressed against his barely veiled contempt. For was it not Ushorak of the Black Dragons who had infected Nihilan with his canker, and ultimately brought about the creation of the Dragon Warriors and the death of the Salamanders' beloved Captain Kadai? His vitriol passed quickly but Emek left room for a final bite. 'Let us not forget your mental state, either.'

Zartath stood, although he should not have been able to, and charged the armaglas. 'Release me!' The bone blades *sniktd* from his forearms. Soon the view into the isolation cell was occluded by raking claw marks and flung spittle.

Unimpressed, Emek nulled the chamber. The raging became mute and the observation portal turned to black.

'Beast.'

'He is,' answered the darkness, a chill entering the room along with the voice. 'A real vicious bastard, too. He held a blade to Sergeant Ba'ken's throat and would've cut it if he'd thought we meant him harm.'

Elysius stepped forwards into the wan light cast by the dulled lamps. 'But were it not for him, we all would have died in that place.'

Armoured in black battle-plate festooned with talismans of purity and devotion, including a holy relic of the primarch, Elysius was a Chaplain to his icy core. Since his visit to the Volgorrah Reef his frosty demeanour had thawed somewhat. He entered the Apothecarion unhooded, his battle-helm mag-locked to his thigh. There was a time when he would not have done so. Contrary to a once-held belief, Elysius was not hideous or war-scarred, horrifically burned or twisted in some way. He was handsome for a Space Marine; his skin was unblemished, his features strong and even.

Only his left arm showed evidence of permanent wounding. The limb he wore was artificial, a bionic replacement for the one he had lost on Scoria fighting the ork. During campaign, he would affix a power fist to that arm instead and his debilitating injury would be turned into crushing martial advantage.

Elysius gestured to the blank slab of armaglas. 'I can't imagine he has taken to examination well.'

'He hasn't.' Emek didn't bother to look up. 'It requires heavy sedation every time I must take a dermal bio-scan or extract a marrow sample. Caged drakes are easier to handle.'

'You are as stern as your predecessor, Brother Emek.'

The Apothecary continued to be absorbed by his data-slates. 'I am merely being prudent.'

'Are those his notes you are researching?' Elysius asked, though he didn't pry. He didn't need to. He knew Fugis had a dossier on Dak'ir. It was obvious the notes in front of Emek pertained to him.

The Apothecary stopped what he was doing to face his Chaplain.

'Yes. Combined with the regular examinations I must conduct on the Black Dragon, I have little time for distraction.'

'Like visiting the hell-pits at Themis, you mean?' There was no trace of accusation in the Chaplain's tone, no reproach. He was merely asking the question.

'I meant by unannounced visitors.'

'I know what you meant. You are spending overlong in the Apothecarion; you need to be back amongst your brothers again. Your meeting with Sergeant Ba'ken suggests you realise that too.'

Emek's retort had barbs. 'Are isolation and self-reliance not a part of the Promethean Creed?'

'Not when they are bent towards self-destruction.'

Scowling, Emek returned to his work but Elysius wasn't done with him. 'You have a patient, not a prisoner. Your treatment of him suggests an imbalance in your humours, brother.'

'Until he can be reclaimed by his Chapter or my assessment of him deems his stability, he is too dangerous to be on the loose.'

'I agree. It is your harsh judgement of our distant brother that I question, Apothecary.' The Chaplain maintained a carefully neutral expression. 'It wasn't Zartath aboard the *Protean*.'

'So we get to the truth of it at last,' Emek sneered.

'I am responsible for the spiritual wellbeing of this company. You expect me to ignore this shift in your demeanour?'

'I was once whole, now I am not. The anvil has tempered me and I shall bear its judgement with the stoic pragmatism of my Chapter. Is that what you want to hear?'

'I hear only your bitterness, brother.' Now Elysius showed his anger. 'On the Volgorrah Reef, in the Razored Vale as my brothers died around me, I felt a darkness encroaching. It was a malaise of the spirit, a tempering against which I was to be measured. I witnessed much horror and death there, but here I stand. As warriors we are made whole by our bonds of brotherhood, by war's purifying flame.' He gestured to his bionic arm. 'On Scoria did I not lose a limb to the Great Beast?'

Emek clenched his fists as the rancour poured out of him. 'But you can still fight. How can I return to battle?' He met Elysius's gaze and in Emek's eyes were pictured all of his faded hopes. 'This ague plagues me, Chaplain. I am a cripple because of it!'

'Don't let it consume you,' said Elysius, lowering his voice. Realising his arguments went unheeded he turned and stalked from the Apothecarion.

Emek watched him leave.

'It already has,' he muttered to the dark.

CHAPTER THREE

I
Legacies

THE HOUR WAS late but the sun never set over the Pyre Desert and glared down on the aspirants with an oppressive heat.

Master Prebian was observing the summit of the Cindara Plateau. Though old, even for a Space Marine, he needed no magnoculars to find what he sought in the haze.

'Who is that?' he asked, in a gritty voice.

For over four centuries, Prebian had served the Chapter as Master of Arms. As de facto captain of the Seventh Company, a rank he had held for just over four decades, he had a small but august legacy.

Ko'tan Kadai had been one of Prebian's most celebrated pupils, his own legacy of honour lasting three centuries before his untimely demise; Elysius, now of the Reclusiam, had learned hand-to-hand fighting techniques from the master, so too Pyriel and Veteran Sergeant Lok. Countless other captains and Chapter luminaries had benefited under his esteemed tutelage.

Since the death of Zen'de, the Chapter's previous Master

of Recruits, Prebian had stepped into the breach but was looking for a successor. Only sixty Scouts comprised the full fighting strength of the Seventh, a throwback to the devastation wrought during the ill-fated Isstvan V assault that nearly destroyed the Legion as it was then and was still felt some ten thousand years later. A consummate drill-sergeant and expert in close-combat techniques, as Master of Arms, Prebian was needed by all Salamanders companies, not just the Seventh. The captain's mantle was his only to bestow upon another.

Sol Ba'ken squinted. Prebian was venerable, but his eyesight was certainly undiminished.

'He is called Val'in,' the sergeant said. The aspirant's name prompted recall for Ba'ken. Val'in was descended from the survivors of the 154th Expeditionary ship the Salamanders had found in the subterranean depths of Scoria. It was one amongst several other revelations, the substance of which currently resided in a vault on Prometheus. As for the boy, Ba'ken had been his rescuer after he'd guided the Salamanders through the myriad cave systems beneath Scoria's surface. Val'in and a few others had been taken off-world and brought back to Nocturne. Unlike some, who found life on the death world too harsh to survive, Val'in had adapted well and been chosen as an aspirant.

It was the tenth ascent without rope or pick up the crag-shawled flanks of the Cindara Plateau. It jutted from the ashen sands like a ruddy spike but with a flattened peak that was its namesake, and it sides were riddled with geyser holes. Scalding steam vented from the invisible fissures in the rock at sporadic intervals, making an already treacherous climb deadly. Many an aspirant had lost his face or worse to that unpleasant fate.

For the tenth time, Val'in conquered the summit before any of his would-be brothers. He stood on the plateau itself, breathing hard but triumphant.

'He's strong,' said Prebian.

'Determined too.'

'Indeed. Not unlike the warrior standing beside me.' He looked askance at Ba'ken. 'Let us just say that not everyone could have come back from the beating you took.'

Before reaching the pits of Themis, Ba'ken had spent hours on the Arridian Plain hunting leo'nid as the Master of Recruits put him through his paces. Like the sergeant, Prebian also hailed from the City of Warrior-Kings.

The armour he wore was slightly archaic, one of the Mark V suits created millennia ago but possessed of incredible artifice. In many ways, Prebian was an anachronism too and drew much of his fighting techniques from old tribal methods used by the first Nocturnean chieftains. He carried several blades about his person as if to emphasise his martial prowess. A saw-toothed spatha was strapped to his leg and a shorter gladius was scabbarded next to his left hip. On the opposite side was a holstered melta-pistol. Prebian's bolter, racked next to his armour's power generator on his back, completed the deadly ensemble.

Prebian folded his arms, his mind decided.

'Bring them in, those that remain.'

The rest, the dead or those too injured to continue, would be left to the desert.

Ba'ken felt no remorse. It was as it should be, as laid down by Promethean law. To an outsider it might seem contrary to the humanitarian beliefs of the Salamanders but nothing could be further from the truth. Strength and endurance were vital if the Chapter was to fulfil its duty to the Emperor and to its home world. Protection of Nocturne's citizens was one thing; gauging the suitability of aspirants by hammering them mercilessly was quite another.

A dull or weakened blade is as dangerous to its wielder as its enemy, so philosophised Zen'de.

Bellowing, Ba'ken summoned the aspirants to fall in.

By the time they had descended the rock and met with their masters on the desolate plain, there were nine left from the original twenty-three that had been chosen. The rate of attrition was not unusual.

Despite the fact he'd had to climb back down from the plateau summit, Val'in was the first to return.

Ba'ken nodded as they came back. The stern-faced Prebian loomed behind the sergeant, arms still folded. The arsenal he carried clanked as he shifted in his armour. The effect was deliberately off-putting for the aspirants, who wore simple fatigues and carried only las-carbines and Themian hunting knives.

By contrast, Ba'ken carried a bolter and his piston-hammer. The latter was a bespoke weapon of his own forging, as much a part of him as an extra limb.

'If you are to become Fire-born then you must learn endurance, you must learn how to survive. Our mistress,' Ba'ken gestured to the desert all around them, 'is cruel and unforgiving. She will temper you well for the challenges to come.'

One of the aspirants – he appeared almost broken – dared to spare a glance at one of his fellows who'd collapsed before reaching the masters and was slowly dying from the heat.

'Don't look at him!' Ba'ken snapped, coming forwards and using all of his bulk and massive size to intimidate. 'Heed *me*, aspirant. My instruction and your will are all which stand between you and that same fate. He returns to the earth, sundered by the anvil.' He went down on one knee to scoop up a handful of earth. 'This is what should concern you, what is real and tangible. This desert is your enemy, it wants to kill you. It *will* kill you if you do not respect it.'

Val'in's concentration never wavered. He followed every move of Ba'ken, who allowed no trace of their history to affect his manner. He was just another aspirant, albeit a seemingly gifted one.

Having undergone several stages of biological implantation associated with ascending to the lowly rank of Scout, Val'in was a boy no longer. None of them were.

Already, his skin was beginning to show the melanochromatic degeneration that would see him become like his full-fledged battle-brothers.

A mutation in the Salamanders genome meant their pigmentation reacted more aggressively and irreversibly to the implantation of the melanochromic organ than other Space Marines. Meant as a safeguard against ultra-violet and radioactive exposure, it actually *reacted* with the unique radiation of Nocturne's atmosphere to create onyx-skinned warriors. It also affected retinal cells, and the glow about Val'in's eyes was almost fire-red. His bulked-out musculature showed a strong response to the introduction of the ossmodula that enhanced bone mass and durability, as well as ossifying an aspirant's ribcage into a solid plate.

Ba'ken knew they would need all of these biological advantages if they were to survive the trials ahead. He also realised that for some this would not be enough.

Val'in met his gimlet gaze and didn't flinch.

You are a tenacious one, he thought with silent approval.

'Out there…' Prebian took over the oratory, pointing to the deeper desert, 'lies a heart of fire. You will march into it, to the hunting grounds of the sa'hrk and the dactylid, and you will do so without water or provisions.'

Ba'ken took the aspirants' canteens. Several licked their lips longingly at the disappearing vessels. His voice was low and forbidding as he then confiscated their stubby carbines. 'A warrior must know how to fight with blade and fist.'

Ignoring the looks of dismay on the faces of some, he gestured to the hunting knife of one aspirant. 'A sa'hrk's talons are both longer and sharper.' Then he pointed to his head. 'Here is where you must defeat its low cunning.'

Prebian came forwards. 'You have three hours. Bring trophies back with you.'

At Val'in's urging the nine ran off into the desert, following the Master of Recruits' direction.

When they were out of earshot, Prebian asked, 'How

many do you think will survive the trial?'

Ba'ken was staring into the horizon. 'This one? I see strength enough in eight to succeed and live. By the time we are done?' He let the question linger, before answering at length, 'Just Val'in.'

Prebian nodded slowly, following the sergeant's gaze.

'Soundly spoken,' he said then added, 'I am recommending you for promotion to Master of Recruits, Captain of Seventh.'

Ba'ken was taken aback at his abruptness. Prebian was not one to waste time with idle preamble and epitomised Themian directness.

'I am just a sergeant...'

'You are a veteran, a sergeant long before you ever carried the rank. Your campaign experience is almost peerless and you have an affinity for training. I see a Master of Recruits before me, even if you do not.'

'It is an honour, but–'

'And not one that you can refuse, brother,' Prebian cut in. 'I need to appoint a captain for Seventh – you are whom I will put before the Chapter Master for consideration.'

Ba'ken bowed his head. 'You humble me, lord. I am deeply–' He paused, looking up as something out in the desert caught his attention.

Prebian's hand strayed to his holstered pistol. The Pyre was a dangerous place even for a Space Marine. Monsters roamed its plains, in addition to numerous environmental hazards.

'What do you see?' he hissed, scanning around.

Ba'ken relaxed, but not completely. 'A feeling...'

Prebian tried to pinpoint it too, but saw only a featureless desert baked by the sun.

'Like we were being watched.' Ba'ken cursed under his breath and dismissed it. 'Paranoia,' he muttered ruefully. 'It's been a while since I was in the field.'

Prebian clapped his shoulder paternally. 'The dusk-wraiths have long talons, brother, and they sink deep.

It will be a while before your wounds heal fully. But if it makes you sharp, then embrace it.'

Ba'ken scoffed, but without humour. 'I think all of Third is on edge. Being recalled, Dak'ir and the prophecy... I want war to be simple again.'

'You'll fight your enemies soon enough. This...' said Prebian, slapping his spatha's blade, 'and this...' he added, touching the stock of his bolter, 'are the tools that will help you find your focus again. Be patient. Agatone was right to bring the Third back. Geviox... Scoria and Stratos,' he said, naming the worlds where N'keln and Kadai had met their respective ends, 'have been hard on all of you. To lose two captains in just a few years is tough on any battle company.'

'We must re-forge in the fires of war.'

'You will, brother. In time.'

'In time...'

Prebian turned. A Land Speeder hovered a short distance behind them, engines idling with a dulcet hum.

Ba'ken stashed the carbines in the vehicle's webbing, while Prebian climbed into the pilot's seat. Speeders were rare in the Salamanders Chapter but not unheard of. This one had a heavy bolter mounted on a rack and slide. Its muzzle was tipped downwards and off-centre. Ba'ken was about to get into the gunner's seat when he paused, one foot on the embarkation stirrup.

The paranoid sensation he'd felt earlier returned, but then quickly dispersed again like smoke on the breeze. He climbed aboard and Prebian gunned the engines before they roared off to follow the progress of the aspirants.

BA'KEN AND PREBIAN weren't the only ones observing the aspirants.

The strangers moved like shadows across the sun, defying the light and the brightness to stay undetected. Sinuous, graceful but also deadly, they left a trail of dead Ignean nomads in their wake. The poor traders had been unlucky. At least their deaths had been swift. The strangers had wanted to prolong their demise, to eke the hapless natives of all their suffering and pain, but discipline had surpassed desire. They moved on, burying the dead in shallow graves. Their landing ship was hidden too, cloaked with infernal technologies. They had used the magnetic interference from the Black Rock to bypass the enemy's wards. Their infiltration was perfect, their appetite for torture never slaked.

The armoured giant was aware of their presence, but its brutish wit was too dull to realise it.

Eyes narrowed against the sun, his cruel blade held close, the leader kept the boy-soldiers in his eye-line.

'Mon-keigh...'

The time to strike was nearing.

He hissed an order at his cohort to remain still until the ugly flying vessel had passed.

Then silently, the strangers followed.

II
Devotion of Another Stripe

THE UNDERDECK OF the *Hell-stalker* echoed with the sound of screaming.

'There's more for you to bleed...' promised a voice like cracking magma.

It took Tsu'gan a few moments to realise the screams were his. The blade embedded in the nerve cluster in his leg had brought him around. He couldn't remember how long he'd been out – it could've been seconds or hours – or how many times he'd gone under.

A taste of leather and copper tarred his palate. His tongue felt as if it were laced with crushed glass. Then he realised he had a strap across his mouth. He'd been gnawing on it when the pain got too much. Tiny slivers of leather stuck between his blood-rimed teeth.

'Open your eyes,' growled the voice again. It was deep

and resonant, sulphurous too – the stench of his torturer's breath was acerbic. It was also familiar.

A hard blow to the kidneys brought Tsu'gan's eyelids fluttering. They snapped open and he beheld the face of his tormentor.

Ramlek.

Nihilan's lapdog seldom went without his battle-helm. During the first few days, after they'd 'softened' Tsu'gan up in the arena-pits, the renegade had explained how it physically *hurt* to remove it. He said he wanted 'the whelp' to see his face as he applied the knife.

As his blurred vision began to sharpen, Tsu'gan noticed other things.

The torture chamber was small, its heady atmosphere cloying and hot; blood permeated the air and adhered to every surface, including the Salamander's skin, in a greasy residue. It resembled a workshop. A large recyc-fan with serrated blades, embedded in the left wall, spun lazily. Its droning was mocking rather than dulcet: *whomp, whomp, whomp,* ever turning, fanning the stink of death.

Ramlek had made his grisly work into an art form. All manner of tools hung on racks or were suspended from the ceiling on barbed chains. Some of them were bespoke, fashioned by the torturer; all were sharp and well-used. Tsu'gan could well imagine Nihilan offering scraps from the ship's serfs to satisfy Ramlek's sadistic tendencies. It was not so different from throwing cast-off meat for a dog to savage and devour.

The renegade drank deep, almost inhaling his victim's pain, as he returned with a fresh implement.

'I will peel your noble flesh…'

A cloud of ash and cinder escaped the Dragon Warrior's lips. They were black, as if smeared with soot. As he spoke, Ramlek exposed his fangs in a subconscious feral display of dominance. Dark veins running from the corners of the renegade's ugly mouth webbed his scaly cheekbones. Ramlek's left eye was red but the cornea wept hot, acidic fluid that left raw marks down his face. The right was like solid stone, unblinking. So ravaged, it was hard to tell which tortures he had visited upon himself and which were Chaos mutation.

Tsu'gan was no stranger to masochism, the self-punitive purity of it had been like a salve during his darker moments, but this was mutilation.

He laughed inside.

Darker moments.

It was hard to think of one blacker than that which he currently found himself in.

Ramlek was about to start in again, eager to re-anoint the leather apron he wore in place of his armour, when a voice stopped the paring-blade centimetres from Tsu'gan's skin.

'Heel.'

The tone was rasping like old parchment being crushed, but dominant.

Nihilan.

Ramlek snarled, but backed off.

Good dog…

Tsu'gan couldn't see the sorcerer but knew he must be looking on. Nihilan continued.

'That's enough for now.'

Despite himself Tsu'gan felt relief, even satisfaction at Ramlek's obvious displeasure.

'Raise him and let him speak.'

The voice was coming through a vox-unit. It must have been slaved to the cell to allow two-way communication between it and some adjacent antechamber.

A low grinding of gears presaged jerky movement in the slab that Tsu'gan was strapped to. It was forged of pitted iron and abraded his bare back. The clasps around his wrists were wrought from a similar material but had tiny spikes on the inner surface that dug into flesh. Belatedly, he became aware of the rust-grit under his fingernails from where he'd clawed the metal.

Pneumatic pistons, old enough to have been from

before the Scouring, were angling the slab to forty-five degrees. Tsu'gan grimaced as the magnesium lamps burned his eyes.

Then there was merely darkness in front of him and the pistons stopped.

'I had to hurt you, Tsu'gan,' Nihilan's disembodied voice issued from the formless void. 'If I had not let Ramlek play with you, he would certainly have tried to kill you.'

The dog was nodding. Tsu'gan sneered derisively as he thought of a wagging tail instead. There was a sudden jolt of fresh agony, and he realised the leather gag was being removed. His mouth was numb. It took a while to get the feeling back before he could speak.

Tsu'gan laughed. It was a cracked, unpleasant sound.

'You think that was pain? You know nothing of pain,' he slurred.

Ramlek went for a saw-blade but a shout from Nihilan froze him solid.

'Like I said,' the sorcerer went on when his hound had been verbally leashed, 'it was for your long-term benefit.'

'You should kill me now,' Tsu'gan told him, trying but failing to get a fix on his nemesis in the darkness. He suspected his sight was shadowed by warp sorcery. 'Because if you don't, I'll break free of this trap and kill your dog. Then I'll come for you, and the other one who's standing next to you right now. You, *Iagon*,' he snarled the name, 'you, I shall save for last.'

IN THE ANTECHAMBER, Iagon seethed.

'When Ramlek is done, I want my chance to cut him.' Spittle flicked from his perpetually sneering mouth as he looked into the torture cell. It hit the dark glass and smeared.

Iagon was gaunt and slight for a Space Marine, and in his time aboard the *Hell-stalker* his back had started to bend so he walked with a stoop.

He wore a renegade's panoply now. Gone was his

Salamanders armour, butchered and ground down, the raw metal splashed blood red and banded black in the colours of the Dragon Warriors. Chains and spikes blighted the once noble curves of a First Founding Chapter's ceramite. Random knife gashes marred the battle-plates. Some of the strokes were frenzied, others careful and considered, echoing the renegade's pathology.

His transition from loyal servant of the Emperor to traitor was both swift and easy. Nihilan was surprised to discover he found it distasteful.

'The power for you to make demands exists only in your own mind.' The sorcerer glared at him, feeding a little of his psychic will into the gesture. Iagon blanched but held his ground. 'You have yet to gain my trust or my counsel,' said Nihilan. 'Be grateful that I am even allowing you to witness this.'

Iagon had lost none of his oleaginous diplomacy and was instantly contrite. He even bowed.

Nihilan turned his attention back to the prisoner.

'I believe you would kill us all, Tsu'gan. Your rage is… *incandescent*. I can visualise its aura suffusing you.'

Tsu'gan spat a gobbet of blood at the darkness, earning a hard slap from Ramlek. 'I hope you choke on it,' the Salamander growled.

'Do you want to know why I am keeping you alive?'

'Because you are prone to repeating mistakes? You should've killed me on Stratos when you had the chance.'

Nihilan ignored the gibe, but he remembered Stratos fondly. Kadai had died on Stratos, the first link in the ever weakening chain around the Salamanders' unity and strength eroded by a multi-melta's beam. Tsu'gan had felt the loss acutely. Some damage, Nihilan knew only too well, was irreparable.

A captain for a captain; Kadai for Ushorak. It was balance, a way of redressing the scales. Vengeance, but only in part.

'No,' he said, 'you are far too valuable for that. I see

such potential in you, Tsu'gan, such bitterness.'

'You are deluded.'

'Am I? Are you sure it isn't you that serves the wrong master?'

Tsu'gan laughed. He laughed loud and raucously, so hard it brought agony to his battered body as he shook with the sheer violence of it.

Able to pierce the veil, Ramlek looked into the darkness for direction but Nihilan merely glared.

'You are a fool,' Tsu'gan said at length. There were tears streaming down his face, not of joy but derision. 'Did you bring me here to make me traitor? Idiot. I am not as weak-willed as that wretch who cowers in your shadow. Have the dog gut me or cut me loose; either way you won't get what you want.'

Nihilan delivered his retort with a smile. It pulled painfully at the scar-tissue around his face.

The armour he wore was old and the colour of incarnadine blood. A curved horn arced from either shoulder, and it was adorned by scale and chain burned black from exposure to fire. It carried the actual scars of campaigning, rather than the petulant marks inflicted as a result of petty rages. There were graven sigils and unholy talismans too that attested to Nihilan's mastery of warpcraft.

His crimson-lidded eyes glowed flame-red. 'Truthfully, I would have been disappointed had you yielded easily. At least now I know you are worthy of all this attention. It is interesting, though...'

Tsu'gan didn't bite so Nihilan went on. 'It is interesting that you think you have any choice in this. There is no choice. Even Horus Lupercal could not resist the lure of Chaos. Is Zek Tsu'gan mightier than the primarch of the Luna Wolves, the Warmaster of the Great Crusade?' he scoffed.

Tsu'gan responded with flippancy. 'Just like a servant of Ruin to refer to ten thousand year-old myth. Get over it, the Long War is done.'

'It is *never* done until Terra burns and that rotting corpse upon his Throne is put out of his misery.'

'I find your histrionics hard to swallow, witch. The only Legion blood in your line is the same as mine.' Tsu'gan grinned, showing bloody teeth. 'Save your pantomimes for the puppet you have beside you, dangling on a traitor's strings, and know this: I am Fire-born, true son of Vulkan and warrior of Nocturne. You reneged on your oaths, sorcerer. You showed your weakness to the galaxy. I will not turn as you did for promises of false power and hollow glory. I spit on your creed, scum.'

Another blood-veined gobbet of phlegm speared into the formless darkness.

'Leave me to your butcher's cleaver; at least I can ignore his inane babbling.'

Nihilan's fist was clenched when he shut off the vox-unit.

Iagon decided to fill the silence that followed.

'Lord, I meant no offence earlier. If I overstepped my bounds it is only because I am eager for him to suffer.'

Mastering his emotions, Nihilan swept out a desultory hand towards the grim vista in the workshop. 'He suffers. Was he not your sergeant once? Have your bonds of devotion been so utterly broken, Iagon?'

Iagon scowled, looking askance at Tsu'gan strapped to the torture slab. His voice was low and dripped with malice. 'I worshipped him. Even removed those in his path that sought to prevent his destiny.'

Fugis, *N'keln*, *Koto* – the list was growing…

He paused, letting his fanatical anger subside. 'In the end, I was betrayed.'

Under torture and mental conditioning, Iagon had revealed everything – every dark deed, every dishonourable act, all the secrets of the Salamanders that he'd been privy to. Most of it was useless; strategies would have already changed, battle plans and formations likewise. It was the personal details that Nihilan found interesting.

His psychological analysis of Iagon's behaviour, his

manias and paranoia, was well within the realm of the psychotic. Indeed, he was surprised that such an individual had lasted as long as he had without discovery or self-awareness of his deviant nature. The mind was such an intriguing construct; the slightest upset to its perceived idea of order could throw a fragile one into turmoil. Nihilan had yet to find Tsu'gan's mental pressure points but that was for later – let Ramlek have his fill for now. He'd earned it.

Nihilan adopted a more forbidding tone as his burn-ravaged face took on the dark light of unpleasant memories. 'Oh, I am familiar with the concept of betrayal, as was my master. We are both very familiar with that.'

'You mean Ushorak?'

Nihilan struck him, hard across the cheek. His clawed gauntlets raked an ugly gash in Iagon's face. 'You may not speak of him,' he declared with a terrifying coldness. 'Your tongue is unworthy of it.'

Iagon quelled his indignation and rage, bowing instead. 'I have sacrificed,' he went on. 'I can still feel the pain sometimes…' He worried at the bionic hand he wore in place of the organic one he'd lost.

Nihilan came in close. He was about to rebuke again but the words he'd planned to say were usurped by others, as were his emotions. 'Does the greenskin knife still hurt?' he breathed instead. There was a resonance to the cadence of it. Something inside him, buried deep beneath the surface but rising was influencing him. 'You had best get used to pain, for there is much more awaiting you. Much more. You are on the path now, Iagon, and you stand to lose more than merely an appendage or limb. But for the price…' Nihilan exhaled in lascivious pleasure, '… the rewards are beyond comprehension…' His expression changed again and the voice that came from Nihilan's mouth did not sound like his own. '*How I long to taste the world again…*'

Excitement and fear warred over Iagon's face. Nihilan

clutched his brow. He stepped back, shaking his head as if to cast off some invisible pall that had surrounded him. 'You know nothing of sacrifice...' He sounded drunk. When he lifted his face again, Nihilan's demeanour had changed back. He looked Iagon in the eyes.

'Wait here. Watch if you so choose, but nothing more.'

Beyond the shadows the torture slab was lowering again.

Nihilan left the chamber, as Iagon eagerly looked on.

IT WAS PROBING at his resilience, Nihilan knew this. To invite something in, as he had, was to become its host, but guests needed boundaries too. His was becoming restless. Nihilan needed a vessel for it, and soon.

He was walking the shadow-dark corridors of the *Hellstalker* by instinct. Few ventured this deep, even fewer stayed for more than moments at a time. The *things* that lurked in the undercrofts, the catacombs of the ship, were always hungry but they feared Nihilan and so he was left alone. There was a curious solace to the act of touring these seldom-trodden passageways. It was an old affectation from when he'd been part of a different order that he still sometimes indulged. Ushorak had shown him *truth*. He'd opened Nihilan's eyes to the lies of the False Emperor.

Not that he really cared about the Long War. In that at least, Tsu'gan had been right. His goals were much more realistic and infinitely more personal. Let the corpse rot upon his Golden Throne, what was that to Nihilan? In the Eye, he'd met and killed several petty warlords and chieftains who'd been slaves to that goal. They were blind fools who acted out of some misguided, millennia-old instinct. Now their warriors swelled his warband and gave him fealty.

A warrior who lives in the past shall die by the unforeseen hand of the future.

Ushorak had taught him that.

The terrible sanctity of the place Nihilan now walked

and its fell denizens were precisely the reasons he had chosen for the Chaplain's shrine to be here.

Nihilan uttered a word of power, one spoken to him and him alone during the 'day of enlightenment', and a fissure in the iron slab before him broke apart to reveal a small, dark chamber hidden within the bulkhead.

The scent of old death assailed him as he entered, head bowed, and the bulkhead closed behind him with a dull *clang*. Even the Glaive, Nihilan's inner circle, were not permitted into this unholy sanctuary. He knelt before a pedestal upon which a gauntleted finger, desiccated, burned but somehow still bleeding, rested. Above it a torn and rotten banner seemed to float suspended in mid-air. It was not, of course, but the visual illusion created by the conditions of the shrine-room was very convincing. A Chaplain was depicted on it, crozius aloft, a battlefield behind him engulfed in holy fire. His black power armour was resplendent and carried the image of a white drake coiled in upon itself. Gore-slicked bone blades raked from the demagogue's vambraces.

'*Ushorak…*' Nihilan intoned. The speaking of the dead Chaplain's name was akin to an invocation. The hot air inside the chamber grew cold until hoarfrost limned the edges of the sorcerer's armour. Some anima of the old, dead Chaplain still lingered.

Upon the ragged banner, the image shimmered. To Nihilan's eye, the battlefield was moving again, its players animated as if part of some incredible theatre acted out for his edification. It was not merely limited to sight, either. Nihilan heard the crash of bolters, the war cries; he smelled fire and smoke, tasted blood on a breeze that did not really exist.

It was *real*, and it was all taking place within the torn banner. A light *pitter-patter*, *pitter-patter* arrested Nihilan's attention until he realised it was blood, but blood that was dripping off the battlefield with every stroke of Ushorak's mace. The visceral tapestry even appeared to exude smoke and the heat of incendiary fire.

An explosion bloomed behind the Chaplain, slow to expand, with detail threaded as if it was being stitched in at an exponentially rapid rate.

Bowing his head in deference, Nihilan closed his eyes and allowed his other senses to dominate.

'We are close, my lord,' he whispered. 'Our vengeance draws near and so too your glory. I await your–'

You made a pledge to me…

The disembodied voice of his dead master rang aloud in Nihilan's mind, interrupting him.

That had never happened before. Ever.

Had all of his blessings and beseeching finally penetrated the veil? Was such a feat even possible? Nihilan dared to hope… 'Master?'

You made a pledge to me…

'Lord Ushorak, how is this–'

And I have maintained my part in the pact.

Nihilan scowled.

It was the *other*.

'Why do you come upon me in this sacred place?'

To remind you of our bargain and your part in it.

His skin was crawling as if thousands of tiny hands were pressing on the inside trying to get out.

'*Desist!*' He snapped, resisting the urge to use his warpcraft and inadvertently empower the *other* further. It was straining, Nihilan could feel it. Like a foetus grown too large for the womb, it wanted release. The pressure in the sorcerer's gut was incredible.

'*Desist…*'

The pain subsided and Nihilan could breathe again.

We creatures of the void are older than time. Our memories are long and we are patient. I am particularly patient but my sanguinity has reached its end, mortal.

'You will have your vessel. Everything is in–'

Did I not massage the skeins of fate to your desire and gift you with prescience for your war? I pressed weapons into your hands and manipulated allies towards your cause. All of this I did because we had an agreement forged in souls and blood.

It is burned upon your heart, mortal…

Reflexively, Nihilan clutched his chest.

…Even now I see the mark I made there. It is long and dark, jagged and black. It is eternal, Nihilan.

His voice returned as the pain in his chest dissipated.

'As I was saying, everything is prepared. You will have what you want.' Aeons were like moments to the thing crawling around inside him. A few more hours hardly mattered. It was merely playing with him, asserting its mastery. Who was Nihilan to defy it?

Images flared hot and agonising in his mind. The pain was excruciating, as if the grainy scenes had been inserted into his consciousness by a burning needle. He beheld fleets of ships, the *Hell-stalker* amongst them along with several renegade frigates and the strange vessels of the xenos with whom he was forced to join swords. There was a giant asteroid too, following an inexorable trajectory towards Nocturne, the huge swathes of magnetic radiation throwing off its core masking the approach of his armada very well. Like a doomsday clock counting backwards from the final minute to the moment of its inception, the last image was of a blocky forge vessel.

Cause and effect, a string of events had been set in motion and the moment of their fruition was almost at hand.

Every action has consequence.

How true those words were and would prove to be.

The *other* had influenced these events, it had bent fate and defied destiny to bring about this confluence. Nihilan had much to be grateful for, but he also loathed his benefactor for he knew it would exact a telling price for its boons.

He was about to try and placate it further when he realised the *other* was gone.

'What dark dreams must you entertain in your hellish slumber,' he muttered as a sudden sense of relief swept over him. He realised there were potent entities beyond the veil that would regard him and his petty concerns as the merest speck on the galactic canvas. Always pressing, ever pushing against reality; mankind would be driven to madness should it ever become aware of such fell intelligences.

Nihilan left the shrine, resealing it behind him, and then reactivated his armour's vox-feed. It was less than a few seconds before Ekrine contacted him.

'We have broken warp and our armada is in readiness, my lord.' His warrior's voice was sepulchral and reptilian. 'The xenos are also aboard.'

Nihilan was walking swiftly, only peripherally aware of the slitted eyes in the *Hell-stalker's* undercroft that followed him. Since transition into realspace their hunger had lessened. 'I'm on my way. Hold our ships in formation.'

CHAPTER FOUR

I
Needs

THE HANGAR WAS crude and ugly. It drew a sneer of barely veiled contempt from Archon An'scur. Like so many of the things he'd endured to maintain his millennia-long existence, he found the alliance with the mon'keigh distasteful but necessary.

If they ever found about it, they would hunt him down for this. His eldritch cousins in High Commorragh would see him flayed and eviscerated, and that would be but the appetiser to a much longer banquet of suffering. For what the sorcerer was promising, it was worth the risk. He had not lived as long as he had without knowing which bargains to take and which to refuse. This particular gambit was on the threshold between. Besides, An'scur had felt a creeping ennui of late. It manifested as a shadow on the edge of his vision, a sliver of darker black against the benighted corners of empty corridors… haunting him. He needed to escape the frontier lands. Too long had he been confined to the sub-realm of the Volgorrah Reef.

Eternity was a long time, he'd decided. It wore upon

him, draining the very sustenance from his body so that replenishment was needed frequently. The shadow knew, and it hungered for the day when restoration would no longer be possible for the archon. It waited, for death eternal was a patient mistress.

An'scur did not form attachments to those beneath him. Helspereth had been most literally beneath him, and he had bonded with her despite his better judgement. She had been a singular creature when it came to the reaping of souls. Of all the dark eldar at the Port of Anguish, she knew how to extract every iota of pain and suffering from her victims. They'd bathed in it, An'scur and his favourite wych.

Now she was dead, killed by a primitive's hand. And though it went against his nature, he wanted vengeance for her death. An'scur would derive much pleasure from exacting agony upon the one who took her, the one in the black.

She had been beautiful and terrible at once, the perfect female specimen. Her lovemaking was torture and ecstasy in unison – many of the nobles she'd bedded hadn't survived the experience. Her loss had left an ache inside An'scur, which surprised him. It had not come straight away; it was only later in solitude that he began to feel her absence. Perhaps that was why he'd dispatched Malnakor; the little bastard had coveted Helspereth's pearly skin and supple frame. He had also attempted to kill An'scur on more than one occasion. Retaliation against the upstart dracon was inevitable, albeit conducted via conspiracy and treachery so as to bypass the burden of proof and the tedium of recrimination.

An'scur's distracted musings ended when the sorcerer entered the hangar. He strode through a dank corridor of pitted columns and ugly ships, passed by grotesque and toadying serfs and menials unfit to even lick at a lowly dracon's boot heel. He was flanked by a cadre of armoured warriors, red and black like the rest. These

three praetorians joined the sorcerer upon his late arrival
and were just as imperious as their master.

An'scur fought his arrogance down and surreptitiously
checked the device on his wrist. The *Eternal Ecstasy* was
still docked with the renegades' flagship. Against his
better reasoning, he had come aboard with only two servants. One was a simple sybarite who kept his eyes low
and carried the archon's weapons. An'scur was paranoid
enough to keep various murder-devices concealed about
his person that only he knew about, lest the retainer turn
on him or they become separated. The other servant was
a haemonculus: a desiccated, patchwork creature with
a bent back and a stitched-on face, who was an artist
in torture and resurrection. As his former haemonculus
Kravex's successor, Lyythe was not to be wholly trusted
but had honoured the pacts of her old master.

An'scur would have preferred different company and
more of it, but his bodyguards were back on his own
ship to deter any potential mutiny in his absence. The
incubi had a remarkable ability to dissuade certain loy-
ally ambiguous subjects from doing anything rash. A
pity Malnakor had not learned that lesson.

The plunder in slaves and materiel that the sorcerer
offered was enticing, status-altering even. It would
enhance An'scur's fortunes greatly and cement his grip
on the frontier territory of Volgorrah. With a little bar-
ter and a lot of murder, it might even buy him passage
into High Commorragh. For that reason alone he had
acquiesced to the sorcerer's summons in person. But he
refused to cower before this overlord, no matter how
much martial strength he had amassed.

He bowed, maintaining a benign expression even
though he was scowling inside at being forced to show
deference to a being that was barely centuries old and
from a backward culture of hairless apes.

As the sorcerer approached, An'scur noticed something
different about him. All of the enhanced giants had an
aura of the warp about them, but this sorcerer was like a

burgeoning chalice. At once, the archon suspected a hidden power behind the renegade's throne.

'Your gathered armada is not entirely unimpressive,' said An'scur. The archon was lithe, even in his segmented armour, but tall. He met the sorcerer eye-to-eye.

'I suppose that is as close to a compliment as you'll give. Let us make this quick.'

An'scur smiled, but it was closer to a sneer. 'I am in agreement with that at least. Your feral language offends my superior tongue.'

The archon was amused when the silent praetorians bristled at his last remark. He knew he was putting himself in genuine jeopardy when he made it but could not resist. Apes dictating to an older, nobler race – it bordered on the ridiculous, but needs must, he supposed.

'Keep wagging it in that manner, xenos, and I'll see it cut out.' The sorcerer's eyes roamed to the craven figure of the haemonculus. 'Is this it?' he asked.

An'scur nodded. 'As requested, however irregular.' His black, pupil-less eyes narrowed. 'What *exactly* is it you want the creature for?'

The sorcerer's gaze didn't move as he appraised the xenos torturer. 'You know all you need to.' He looked back. 'What of your scouts?'

'Several days ahead of the fleet. My nightfiend assures me they will be positioned auspiciously by the time the main assault is launched.'

'See that they are.'

An'scur wanted to strike him for his insolence but fashioned a thin smile instead. 'But of course,' he purred.

The sorcerer turned on his heel, and An'scur had to fight the urge to rip the sword from his retainer's grasp and ram it, hilt-deep, into the sorcerer's back.

'Thark'n, Nor'hak… Bring it with us,' the renegade said idly to his cohort.

Two of the giants came forwards, their eyes burning with anger and repressed violence. An'scur glared defiantly, willing the apes to act on their obvious desire.

'She is to be returned to me, sorcerer,' he called. 'Without blemish, as we agreed.'

The sorcerer's voice was becoming increasingly distant, his mood dismissive. 'You're being well compensated for the *loan* of this wretch. Be thankful I do not alter our arrangement. Now,' he added, 'get off my ship.'

An'scur clenched his fists as the haemonculus was led away. It was a risk, the creature had value, but the dividends would be worth it in slave-stock alone. He bowed and backed away.

'Lyythe has the arcana she requires?' he asked of his retainer in a whisper, never deigning to make eye contact.

The sybarite nodded. 'Yes, my lord. We can extract her via the *Ecstasy* easily enough.'

'Good,' he hissed, not bothering to tell his retainer that no such rescue would be taking place. He gave one final glance to the disgusting hangar. To think such a brute race held dominance over the galaxy. It made An'scur want to kill them all and bathe in their inferior blood.

'We are treating with swine,' he said, as they entered the *Eternal Ecstasy's* docking portal.

Needs must.

EKRINE LED THEM down to the gun decks in the direction of the *Hell-stalker's* prow. The air was thick with the stench of blood and oil. Sulphurous soot clung to vast arching stanchions ribbing the corridors. Creatures, blind and decrepit, snuffled in the darkness. It was hot in the gun decks and the *chug-clank* of munitions being slowly prepared kept up a steady, mind-numbing refrain. Slave masters, hulking and gene-bulked brutes, worked the ratings harder and with greater cruelty as their overlords passed them. The screams of these unfortunate swine rang out in a pitiable chorus as their overseers beat them, while the dead or broken were shovelled into the furnaces as blood-fuel.

It was a hell-realm, this blackened forge in the bowels of the *Hell-stalker*. It was a place for the forgotten and the insignificant, human meat for the vast mill that could never have enough grist. Flesh and bone kept it turning, blood on blood and the constant sacrifice of innocent souls.

The quartet of Dragon Warriors ignored it.

The haemonculus had since departed, escorted by a cadre of armed serfs to a holding cell; Nihilan was alone with his inner circle. Only Ramlek, who was busy brutalising their prisoner, was absent.

'The xenos is arrogant,' said Nor'hak, radiating iron-hard coldness. He had a fat-bladed paring knife in his hands and was sharpening it against the plates of his armour. Unless he had a weapon in his hands to field strip, modify or fire his fingers twitched incessantly. Ramlek had once plunged a bayonet into either hand in an effort to still them when the affectation had begun to grate, but it failed. Nor'hak had later stabbed him in the shoulderblade with one of his longer blades in retaliation and it was considered evens.

Thark'n merely nodded, his gorget creaking at the strain put on it by his muscular neck. He spoke seldom. His tongue was a nest of barbs that hooked into the roof of his mouth, and to use it was excruciatingly painful. A more useful boon from the Eye was his behemoth-like frame. Even for a Chaos Space Marine, Thark'n was big. It made toting heavy arms easy. He'd hung the belt feed for his reaper over his neck like a chain. Bandoleers of grenades *tunked* loudly against his armour in the quiet passageway.

'It is a racial predisposition,' Nihilan explained.

'Can it be trusted?' asked Nor'hak, absently sharpening a different blade to keep from trembling.

'Of course not, but by the time it decides to betray us we will have what we came for.' Nihilan called ahead to Ekrine. 'Anything from the warsmith?'

'Nothing unforeseen.' His head jerked left to right with the syncopated motion typical of a reptile. Scales colonised much of his skin. They were just visible above the neck, suggesting a larger infestation beneath his armour plate, and patchy over his face and head. The flesh there had begun to flare outwards, becoming like a serpent's hood. In keeping with his snake-like aspect, Ekrine was fast. It was what made him such a good pilot.

Nihilan had taken much time and effort to acquire the clandestine lore that had put the planet-killer in his hands. Tougher still was forcing the Iron Warrior to serve him. The alliance on Scoria was to their mutual benefit, but even that had not been easy to broker; this was different again.

The end of the passageway opened out into a massive vaulted chamber. A metal gantry clanked loudly with the renegades' heavy footfalls. Seen through the lattice floor was a pair of immense capacitors. Menials, servitors and other debased creatures busied themselves in the darkness far below with the radiation and the heat. A low hum was coming off a bank of power coils that bled into the capacitors and flanked a large fusion reactor with refined fyron powder at its core. The machinery fed into an immense segmented barrel etched with graven runes that was only partially visible. The rest protruded into the void from the *Hell-stalker's* prow like the ram on an ancient sea-faring vessel.

Ironically, the weapon actually *was* archaic. At least, its standard template construct was. It had originated from an age before Old Night when all the many secrets of the universe had been lost. Through his patron and the obsession of the dead technocrat Caleb Kelock, Nihilan had wrested one of those secrets back from obscurity. Even witnessed in part, the seismic cannon was a thing of terrible beauty.

'Our Spear of Retribution,' he announced, as if blessing a fledging ship before its inaugural voyage.

Nor'hak's hands stilled at the sight of it. Thark'n wept.

Only Ekrine, who had kept a close eye on the weapon's construction, maintained his composure. He called to the creature performing the final pre-firing rituals.

'Warsmith...'

An armoured beast turned slowly at the calling of its name. It was clad in grey metal, its yellow and black chevrons described in scuffed paint. Hulking shoulder guards protruded with spikes. Rusted rivets held much of the panoply together. Old hate flared in its eyes as it regarded the four renegades, but like a flame about to snuff out. Much of its form was mechanised and it whirred and ground robotically as it moved.

Necrotic breath to match the condition of its pallid flesh washed from the Iron Warrior's ugly, slack-jawed mouth. It struggled to speak. Its tongue was black and lolled like a fat torpid slug between its teeth.

'*Allll issss reeeeady...*' it slurred.

Nihilan's eyes narrowed approvingly. 'Fascinating...'

Several devices, esoteric and alien in origin, were implanted into the Iron Warrior's skull. An ankh-like rune glowed dully upon the surface of one. It helped to conceal the fact that much of the back of the creature's head was missing, so too the bulk of its brain-matter.

'Reconstitution was not easy,' Ekrine hissed, 'but Ramlek managed to fashion something to animate it at least.'

'Is it fully revivified?' Nihilan asked as the creature stared and drooled.

'No. This is a husk with some remembered behaviours for our purposes. It is not unlike a servitor, except its protocols were slaved solely to the construction of the weapon.'

Nor'hak scowled. 'It smells foul.'

'That's because it's dead, you moron,' Ekrine snapped and there was a flash of potential violence between them.

Nihilan's voice quelled it. 'Is its task done? Do we require this thing further?'

'No, my lord, it is–'

The thunderous report of a bolt pistol ended Ekrine's reply.

Nihilan holstered his sidearm, looking down on the headless Iron Warrior.

'I have need of the mind shackles your dead-man is wearing. Sieve them from whatever brain chunks are left and throw the bodily remains into the furnaces.'

Ekrine bowed and swiftly dispatched a pair of nearby menials to the task.

As he returned down the corridor, the others followed Nihilan without word or complaint.

'Our dawn is coming,' he told them. 'It will be savage and drown all of Nocturne in blood.'

II
Secrets of the Earth

VEL'CONA TURNED THE pages with slow deliberation. Each was heavy with the weight of ages. Together they carried the fate of an entire world.

'*Doom or salvation…*' he muttered, fingers tracing the sigils for the hundredth time or more. '*So begins the Tempus Infernus… The Time of Fire comes to Nocturne, and all trials before shall seem as nothing to this.*'

The light in the vault came from the glowing veins of ore lining the cavern walls, just bright enough for the Chief Librarian to require no further illumination. Vel'cona had doused the brazier-lamps, finding solitude in the natural semi-darkness of Mount Deathfire's under realm. This place was a temple, a sanctuary of Vulkan, and should be treated as such.

He turned the page again, this same passage over and over as he tried to ascertain its true meaning. '*One will become many.*'

That seemed to suggest dissolution, a breaking of the Chapter, or a breaking of a world. He had pored over these symbols for many days without rest, entering almost a meditative state to better unravel them.

'*The Ferro Ignis shall emerge from ashes cold and wreathe our world in conflagration. He is the Fire Sword. He is our doom.*'

Vel'cona stared at the page, as he had done for the last few hours. Over and over, he turned the prophecy in his mind, trying to fathom the message within it.

Fire.

Doom.

The consequences were certainly dire, but the conditions required to bring about such a cataclysm were still veiled.

It was as much as the Chapter knew. Alone, it wouldn't save them.

'Why show us this?' he asked, turning a fresh page. 'What secrets lurk beneath the earth?'

His aura of solemnity was only broken as another entered the vault with him.

'Innocuous enough, isn't it?' he said without looking up.

The shadows answered. 'Most extremely dangerous things usually are. The same could be said of a virus bomb.'

'Justly spoken, Epistolary.'

Pyriel stepped into the light, wearing a suit of blue power armour. Arcane devices attached to the battle-plate showed his affiliation to the Librarius. A psychic hood arced around the back of his neck. His battle-helm was mag-locked to his thigh, allowing the shadows to pool in the grooves of an unremarkable face. A line of shaven white hair divided his onyx-black skull down the middle like an arrow.

Vel'cona traced the tips of his fingers over the edge of the page. 'There is much here still beyond my reach.'

'It was written by the primarch. What greater hand, save that of the Emperor, could have weaved its mysteries?' He came to Vel'cona's side, his noisy battle-plate disturbing the atmosphere of serenity in the temple.

Thusly armoured, Pyriel dwarfed his kneeling master who was dressed in a supplicant's robes. Vel'cona's presence, however, was still undeniable.

'None, Pyriel,' he said flatly.

The book before him was ancient, millennia old in fact. It had a simple drake-hide cover with a dark gold clasp and sat upon a humble pedestal of onyx.

'Doesn't look like much, does it?'

Pyriel came closer, but only a step. It was almost as if he dared not approach within the book's invisible aura.

'Our fate is really decided by what is in those pages?'

Vel'cona laughed. It seemed like an incongruous thing to do in a temple.

'I hope not. Even with Lord He'stan's help, we've uncovered almost nothing of its secrets.'

'Yet it was left to us by the primarch. His sigil opened this vault, a place that had been hidden from even our sight for millennia.'

'Perhaps. Certainly, it is of the Tome of Fire.' Vel'cona straightened and lifted his eyes from the page. 'I believe the wisdom within is veiled by the sigil-language of ancient Nocturne.'

'The dialect of the earth shamans?'

'Precisely. It is so old that much of the lore needed to read it has been lost. None alive can speak it.'

'Do you think that Vulkan could?'

'Yes. I believe he found something during his time on Nocturne, before he was reunited with us, and committed it to these pages.'

'Will it bode ill for Dak'ir?'

As he faced Pyriel, Vel'cona's expression was accusatory. 'Whatever fate awaits your old acolytum is etched in stone. I warned you long ago of the danger he represented.'

Aware of his master's rising anger, Pyriel chose his next words carefully. 'I could not abandon him. Nor do I believe he is this world's destroyer.'

'Your *beliefs* in this matter are of no consequence. Truth is truth; it will come out in the end. There is knowledge within these pages. Some of it may be of help to our cause, but there is much that is still concealed from my sight.'

'Enlighten me, master. What have you learned?'

'That your impertinence hasn't changed,' he scolded, a flash of cerulean blue flaring in his eyes before it dulled and they were ember-red again.

Pyriel went down on his left knee and bowed his head, contrite. 'Apologies, master. I overstep.'

'Yes, you do, but as my second you should know of what I've discovered.'

Lifting his eyes, Pyriel waited like the eager student to receive the knowledge of his master.

'Do you believe that the dead can come back?' Vel'cona asked.

Pyriel was nonplussed. 'I have seen battle-brothers at the brink of death or lost to suspended animation coma, only to return against the odds.'

'No, the dead, those beyond hope of healing.'

'There are... plagues. I have heard of the slain brought back, but they are misshapen things, flesh-craving horrors...'

'You misunderstand my meaning.'

'Because what you suggest is impossible, master.'

Vel'cona gestured to the book. 'Within these pages ancient rituals are described of an earth culture, the progenitor of the Promethean Creed by which we all abide. They preach of the returning of the dead.'

Pyriel frowned. 'A resurrection cult?'

'Of a kind, I suppose, yes.'

'And this was condoned?' His tone suggested the idea beggared belief.

'As far as I can tell, which isn't very far at all, it was *condemned*... by the tribal kings and their earth shamans. These were arcane rites, brother, practised by graven men. To call it by its proper name, it was sorcery.'

Pyriel was shaking his head. 'Why would Vulkan commit such blasphemies to parchment?'

Vel'cona shrugged. 'As a warning, or a means of simply passing on knowledge. These were the records of his culture, perhaps he wanted to preserve them. It should not surprise you. Nocturne has seldom been a world at peace with itself. Before Vulkan united them, the disparate tribes fought tooth and nail for the "sanctuary rock, where the earth's fury could not split the land" – meaning the seven sacred sites where Nocturne's Sanctuary Cities now stand. According to the book, a struggle for land was not the only war of survival. It also speaks of a conflict before Vulkan's coming against a corrupted brotherhood, the resurrection cultists and the casting of these *corpsemancers* into fire.'

'Into the mountain? Into Deathfire?'

'I suspect so. They were hunted down and killed as pariahs. The rest I have yet to discern.'

The revelations disturbed Pyriel, who knelt unmoving and unblinking as he considered them. After a few moments he asked, 'But what purpose does this knowledge have? How does it concern the prophecy?'

Vel'cona got to his feet and smoothed down his robes. 'It doesn't as far as I can tell.'

Pyriel wore a pained expression. 'I am deeply troubled, master. These feel like ill omens.'

'It is merely history, Pyriel, and ancient history at that. Much of what I've learned here is open to interpretation and conjecture. Nothing is certain.'

Pyriel regarded the book as it sat open upon the pedestal. To his eyes, the writings were meaningless, described in a form and code he could not understand.

'Why keep it here and not within the Pantheon Chamber like the rest of the Tome of Fire?' he asked.

Vel'cona closed the covers reverently and reattached the book's clasp.

'Vulkan put it in this temple for a reason, as inscrutable to us as that may be. Here is its place and here it will stay. Is our Lord Chapter Master ready for us?'

'The council of tempering is convened, yes. But I still do not see why Dak'ir must be measured like this. He passed his trials and endured the gate of fire–'

'Only the Pantheon can decide that. All of us, our trials

are different. This is merely the path Dak'ir must follow. We, the entire Chapter, are bound to it to whatever end.'

'Then I hope for a favourable resolution.'

The two Librarians then left the chamber, the door closing behind them. Revelation would have to wait a while longer. A Thunderhawk, its engines idling, was standing on the surface above. It would convey them both to Prometheus and the Pantheon Council.

CHAPTER FIVE

I
Savage Meat

TSU'GAN WAS HURTING. He felt like tenderised meat. He'd lost a lot of blood and several of his bones were fractured, some broken. It didn't need an Apothecary to provide diagnosis. His sternum was cracked; he had a fractured clavicle; carpals, metacarpals and phalanges were all traumatised to the point where it hurt to tense let alone grip; the ulna and radius were fractured; three ribs, fused together in his ossified torso plate, were broken; he also had minor breaks in his left tibia and right femur. That was without even mentioning damage done to muscle tissue, ligaments and tendons.

Ramlek had been thorough and had laboured hard, indulging his every sadistic desire, to inflict pain on his prisoner. He wanted to break him, to bring Tsu'gan down where he'd crawl on his belly and swear loyalty to the dog's master.

Begging in front of a dog? He was not about to give his torturer that satisfaction, for Tsu'gan knew something that gave him a distinct advantage.

Ramlek couldn't kill him.

For whatever reason, Nihilan needed Tsu'gan alive. Drawing him out, turning Iagon in order to capture him, the sorcerer had gone to great lengths for his prize. He wasn't about to let some unhinged lackey undo all of that careful planning. Tsu'gan suspected that was why Ramlek had showed restraint.

The beatings had stopped. It had been a few minutes, or as close as Tsu'gan could guess. It was difficult to tell how much time had passed. The ringing in his head and the blood in his eyes and mouth impaired his concentration. Ramlek was searching for something amongst his tools. He was muttering to himself, the words lost in the low *thwomp-thwomp* of the recyc-fan. Tsu'gan could just see it blurring around, every rotation exacerbating the mortal stench alive in the workshop. The muttering continued. He suspected it was little more than inane rambling.

Ramlek was insane. Utterly and blissfully unhinged, but not in a demonstrative, obvious way; rather his mania was the quiet, dangerous kind, the kind that often erupted without warning. If Ramlek got carried away, his word to his master might not be his bond. Tsu'gan knew he had to escape.

The brief respite gave him some encouragement. The last hammering he'd taken had loosened one of the clasps around his right wrist. In his frenzy, Ramlek hadn't noticed. Frustrated that his 'art' wasn't having the desired effect he'd ventured off to find something sharper and more unpleasant to cut his prisoner with.

Tsu'gan tested the clasp's strength. Nothing happened at first, but then… a little give; a slight bending in the iron. Salamanders knew metal well; they worked it in their forges, understood its strengths and flaws. Just by the feel of it, the way it moved under the tension exerted by his wrist, Tsu'gan knew he could break the bond. His hearts started to beat faster, flooding his system with adrenaline to overwhelm the pain. Twisting his wrist, he managed to lever the clasp a little further. It was wide enough to slip out of. A nearby surgical table lay strewn with some of Ramlek's failed implements. They were bloody and gore-slicked. Dark splashes coloured the tarnished metal. Tsu'gan noticed something else too, an operation unit for the recyc-fan. It was a small and dirty rectangular box. A simple icon increased the unit's speed; another reduced it. The cable feeding it power from the *Hell-stalker's* reactors was entwined around the legs of the table. By pulling on it Tsu'gan could drag the tray of cutting tools within his grasp.

He just needed someone to stab with them.

'Dog...' he rasped.

Ramlek was engrossed, throwing saws and blades around as he sought for just the right one.

'I said, dog.' Louder this time, with more aggression.

Ramlek stopped what he was doing and turned.

Tsu'gan scowled. 'You are by far the ugliest bastard I've ever had the displeasure of sharing air with. You stink, Ramlek, did you know that?'

Ramlek snarled. 'Be patient, flesh. I shall return with more pain very soon.' He was about to continue his search when Tsu'gan's voice stopped him.

'Tell me something: does Nihilan feed you scraps from his table when you've done as asked? Does he make you perform tricks for his amusement? Which is it: fetch or roll over?'

Ramlek snapped a blade he was considering in his clenched fist and threw down the broken remains. Ash and cinder gushed from his mouth, signifying his rage.

Tsu'gan smiled.

Come to me, you brutal bastard...

'Or perhaps it's play dead?'

'For you it will not be play, flesh,' Ramlek declared. 'I am my master's loyal subject.' He'd abandoned the tools and decided to batter the prisoner with his fists instead.

'A dutiful hound, for sure,' Tsu'gan goaded. 'Let us just say I have never seen one renegade scratch another's balls, but in your case–'

Ramlek roared.

A dog was always so protective of its master.

Tsu'gan ripped his hand free seconds before Ramlek thundered into him. In the same movement, he yanked on the cable and pulled the surgical table into the renegade's path. Unable to stop his momentum, Ramlek careened into it, sending hooks and scalpels scattering across the room. Enraged, he wrenched the table aside. The blow lifted it off its feet and cast it against the wall where it lay in a bent and crumpled heap.

As he fixed his meaty hands around Tsu'gan's throat a flash of dirty silver caught in the lume-lamps above. Ramlek screamed as the paring knife was lodged, hilt-deep, into his eye. His cornea bubbled over the blade, corroding it, but he held on.

'Took my eye!' he raved.

Under Ramlek's iron grip, Tsu'gan felt his throat constricting. 'You'll lose more than that,' he promised, ripping out the paring knife. A jet of blood gushed from the eye socket at the same time as a howl of agony tore from Ramlek's mouth, before the blade was jammed it into his neck. Tsu'gan pushed it so hard that the ragged tip punched through the opposite side.

Spitting blood, Ramlek loosened his grip.

'I told you…' Tsu'gan snarled through gritted teeth, getting up in the renegade's face, '…you should've killed me when you had the chance.'

He snapped one of the clasps around his ankles, bringing his knee into Ramlek's gut. It broke the renegade's hold and Tsu'gan followed up with a heavy kick that propelled him across the workshop floor. Belt grinders and glaiving-blades burred dangerously close to the renegade's face as he stumbled. He was blind, but came at Tsu'gan with unerring accuracy. The Salamander tore off his other wrist clasp and smashed the last one holding his other leg with his heel. He was hurting, but he was also extremely angry.

He used his forearm to block Ramlek's wild overhead

swing and palm-smashed his solar plexus in retaliation. If the renegade had been power-armoured, even whilst blind, the fight might have gone a different way. As it was, Tsu'gan felt the rib-plate shielding Ramlek's vital organs crack. He still had the recyc-fan's control box in his hand and thumbed up the speed. The rotor cranked around at a punishing rate, flecking off chips of caked-on viscera. It turned into a billowing, rust-coloured cloud.

Ramlek staggered, one arm held protectively across his chest. That last blow had wounded him. Before the renegade could return the favour, Tsu'gan dropped the control box and vaulted off the torture slab. His momentum carried him forwards, two-footed, into Ramlek who was flung backwards into the whirring blades of the recyc-fan…

Tsu'gan turned his cheek just before it was spattered with gore. It was hot and viscous. He was careful not to get any in his mouth or eyes, but didn't recoil. He wanted to see it, see his tormentor's demise. Cracking bone and chewing meat overwhelmed the ugly grind of Ramlek's tools for several seconds. The renegade didn't scream. Tsu'gan fought hard not to respect him for that.

He sagged, fell to one knee and then stood up again quickly. A stink had started to permeate the air, fouler than a xenos abattoir.

'Can't say I never gave fair warning,' he said, spitting on Ramlek's headless corpse. It was still twitching. 'Least I've improved your looks.'

Tsu'gan grimaced as his injuries flared afresh. Biting pains jabbed into the balls of his bare feet and hands. His limbs throbbed like he'd been running for months without rest, but it was the dull ache in his chest that concerned him. He suspected internal injuries and knew that while his enhanced physiology would repair some damage, he needed an Apothecary for the rest. The renegade had battered him, torn him up like savage meat and hammered his war-weary body to its limit. He looked around the workshop, feeling his strength ebbing even as his will screamed for him to endure.

Ramlek had not just been a butcher; he saw his given vocation as craft.

'Where is it?' Tsu'gan slurred, fighting back the dark flashes impinging on his vision. He tossed over a bench, sending a grinder clattering. Another, he upended, tipping barbed needles and fingernail daggers to the floor. He was about to rip up a third when he found what he was looking for.

It was a small lozenge-shaped container. It looked hermetically sealed.

What does every interrogator worthy of his art require?

He unclasped the container, its lid flipping back as a hiss of pressurised air escaped from the padded chamber within.

A means of keeping their victims alive and awake.

There were chemicals inside, vials and philtres, small ampoules of mottled liquid. Not all of the solutions were medicinal, he guessed. Time was against him. Tsu'gan took a handful of vials and sniffed at the contents, even tasted them. His enhanced olfactory senses, combined with the neuroglottis, allowed him to filter out the toxins and find what he needed. Casting the other vials aside, he kept one and grabbed a syringe that was secured in the base of the container. His fingers were shaking as he filled it with what was in the vial. He'd need a large dose.

As he primed the syringe, Tsu'gan was put in mind of the chrono-gladiators that fought in the underhives of numerous frontier worlds. For a while they would be unstoppable, their physiologies enhanced exponentially, but when the chrono finally ran out...

'Make me unstoppable,' he said, and rammed the syringe of adrenaline into his primary heart.

It was like fire running through his veins as a hundred suns exploded inside his mind. The effects were intense and instantaneous. Hearts thundering, breath hammering in and out of his battered lungs, Tsu'gan smashed through the door to the workshop and saw prey.

The first serf died before he'd realised what was going on. The second tried to raise an alarm before the Salamander snapped his neck. Crouched on all fours, Tsu'gan held the dead man down and became silent as he looked up the corridor. It was dark, but only dark.

He rose to his haunches and ran on.

Chrono's ticking.

II
Judgement

At first, the flame didn't burn. It was bright, luminous even, and roared like a primal thing.

Though it did not speak, it promised destruction. It needed no words, it was elemental, the spark to ignite the violent potential of the universe. And it was inside him, burning gently just below the surface.

Within his mind's eye, he tried to gauge its tides but the flame was capricious and defied all attempts at hubris. It didn't possess a pattern, some scheme which mortals could predict. It merely ravaged; the ultimate force of transition as old as the stars themselves.

The time of the burning came back, pressing at the barriers of his subconscious despite the psychic fetters. A conflagration to consume a planet rose up from nothing, tsunami-like in its fury. In that moment, he was struck by a terrible revelation – the flame was sentient, it wanted to be born.

Then it burned and the pain of it, coursing through his veins, shocked him to the core.

Everything burned…

His eyes snapped open. Dak'ir was back in the penitarium again. The long exhalation from his lungs carried a tremor. The faintest beading of sweat chilled his forehead as the tang of heat still lingered. He had relaxed his vigil for but a moment.

It was like scaling the face of a new-born sun, weaving through its fire squalls as they whipped off its core, coursing across molten oceans that stretched into infinity. It was the flame, and it had shown him its strength, learning Dak'ir's in return.

I am master, not the other way around.

A pity that declaration sounded so hollow.

Seconds later, and the door to the penitarium parted revealing Pyriel's armoured form.

'They are ready for you,' said the Librarian. Though he concealed it well, Dak'ir could sense the concern in his master. Pyriel must have felt some psychic echo of what had just transpired in the cell. He had seen evidence of the inner flame's power before, during the burning and on Moribar.

Dak'ir lowered his gaze, obscuring the cerulean glow that hadn't yet faded.

'Then let's not keep them waiting.'

CLAMPED IN CHAINS, Dak'ir awaited the judgement of his lords and masters in a small, austere chamber.

He'd been led from the penitarium by Pyriel and flanked by a squad of six Firedrakes wearing unmarked, saurian power armour. Each one carried a ceremonial chainblade and melta-pistol. Their identities were hidden from him by their draconian faceplates and none spoke nor would have uttered a word if spoken to. The procession from the penitarium rang with the uncomfortable silence common to an execution.

'Is this to be my last walk, Pyriel?'

The Epistolary hadn't answered, though the act of staying his tongue wasn't easy.

Dak'ir took that to mean it was entirely possible he was about to be killed. Idly, he wondered who would do it and how it would be done. A blade through the neck, the blow angled downwards to pierce the heart? That was a soldier's death, an honourable death, something likely favoured by the Ultramarines should such an unconscionable situation ever arise to require it. Perhaps it would be the cold, hard muzzle of a bolt pistol, pressed against his temple? That felt dirty, undignified, an end reserved for betrayers. Cast into the fire, back to the heart of the mountain, that was how he would want it to be. He would go willingly, should it be the judgement of the council; for their sanction was absolute.

Such morbid thoughts had dogged Dak'ir's every step since being escorted from the penitarium.

All was in readiness for him by the time they reached the chamber.

His ankles were shackled, the chains fed through a metal ring worked into the floor. The polished obsidian allowed Dak'ir to see his reflection in the black glass surface.

At least I look defiant.

His wrists were bound behind his back, the null bracelets unclasped and then re-clasped again quickly by his grim attendants. The collar around his neck had never felt so heavy. Surrounded by a refractor field with the energy wall turned inwards, every precaution had been taken with Dak'ir's imprisonment.

I feel like a traitor, but one without trial or evidence of betrayal against him.

Lifting his gaze, he recognised the faces of his judges.

Much like the Pantheon Chamber this place of deliberation and judgement bore eighteen seats, one for each of the vaunted masters of the Chapter. Several were empty, those belonging to the leaders of the battle companies in the field or those who were engaged elsewhere on Nocturne.

Captains Mulcebar of the Fifth and Drakgaard of the Sixth were present. Both wore artificered suits of power armour, the latter favouring a hood of chain instead of scale for the ornamentation of the shoulder guard. Their drake pelts were old and gnarled. Despite their reserve company status, each carried honour markings from Badab and Armageddon and wore them proudly. Drakgaard's 'souvenirs' from those campaigns extended to a crippling facial injury that had torn up his bottom lip, revealing one side of his teeth even when his mouth was shut. By contrast, Mulcebar was unscathed, but had a broad brow that shadowed his eyes and gave him a perpetually disapproving expression.

Their battle-helms were sitting on a stone table that arced around the seated area in a ring and stared coldly at the accused with dead lenses. The eyes of the reserve captains were equally stern.

The two captains were joined by another, Dac'tyr. The Master of the Fleet and Fourth Company appeared pensive as he regarded the prisoner. Like all of the Chapter's pilots he bore the honour-brand of the dactyl over his right eye, albeit this one's tail was longer and it had a greater wingspan than his comrades to denote his vaunted rank. Its meaning was 'Lord of the Burning Sky', and only the captains of Fourth were ever allowed to bear it. His left eye was augmetic, the bionic aperture tracking back and forth as if examining the accused.

Agatone was sitting next to Dac'tyr. His face was unreadable, though Dak'ir had heard about his fervent desire to bring glory back to the Third who had suffered so heinously in recent years. A former veteran sergeant who had served on Scoria, he was Master of the Arsenal now and bore the mantle with all the stoic pride he was famous for.

It left only two vacant seats for the company captains: Mir'san of Second, at large somewhere on the edge of the Uhulis Sector but otherwise in absentia, and Prebian, Master of Arms and acting-captain of Seventh, who was training aspirants in the Pyre Desert. Thus far, all efforts to reach Prebian had met with failure. Unusually high magnetic radiation was believed to be the cause.

As well as being Regent, Tu'Shan was also captain of the First, but sat alone. The Chapter Master leant back, chin resting on his massive fist, deep in contemplation. It was hard to discern the details of his finely wrought armour but Dak'ir knew it was magnificent. Curls of drake scale unfurled from his back and draped over the granite steps of his throne. His bearing was not unlike the tribal chieftains of ancient Nocturne.

At his right hand was Praetor of the Firedrakes. The bald-headed veteran sergeant was armour-clad like the rest. Unlike the other masters, he was ramrod straight, his thunder hammer and storm shield within easy reach. Perhaps Praetor would be Dak'ir's slayer then? Should something go wrong and the other Firedrakes fail to act in time, the veteran was the contingency. He'd see it done; see the accused dead before he could become the destroyer they were all so wary of.

Dak'ir thought that assertion to be optimistic, even slightly naive. The slightest mote of arrogance pushed the thought into his mind and he wondered briefly if his will was actually his own. Ever since Moribar, that first fateful visit over four decades ago, he had felt a design at work in the shaping of his destiny. Perhaps the flame had always been within him, merely flickering at first but now ablaze. He marshalled his thoughts, suddenly aware again that the eyes of the Chapter were upon him.

Elysius sat to the Chapter Master's left. The Chaplain wore his skull-plate for the occasion, armoured in the black of the Reclusiam. His fingers were steepled, gauntleted digits overlapping bionics. No one had been as battle-ravaged as Elysius. He'd lost his arm during the battle for Scoria and nearly his faith out on the Volgorrah Reef, if rumours were to be believed. The Chaplain had endured all trials and appeared stronger than ever.

I pray to Vulkan that my will is as strong.

All the Masters of the Forge were absent so the positions normally occupied by the Armoury went empty, which left only the Librarius.

Dak'ir's gaze fell on Vel'cona last of all. He saw nothing in those pitiless orbs, an utter void of emotion. Pragmatism ran through the Master Librarian's veins like floes of ice. During the burning, Dak'ir had felt Vel'cona's disapproval towards him. It was only through Pyriel's dogged insistence that he become his master that Dak'ir had survived at all.

Even through the psychic wards, he could sense the Epistolary's unease. Alone of the entire council, Pyriel was standing. He had vowed to do so, to be at Dak'ir's shoulder or as close to it as his confinement allowed.

Why does it feel like I am in need of more allies?

Vel'cona's voice, given by unmoving lips into his mind, made Dak'ir start.

All of us here are your allies, Lexicanum. His face never moved. There was just the faintest glow of cerulean blue in his eyes to give him away. *This is not about you, Salamander. It is for the preservation of Nocturne that we convene and make council.*

Dak'ir nodded, shamed by the master's wisdom and his own arrogance. Selfishness and ego went against the Promethean Creed. Whatever the Pantheon Council willed he would have to abide by it, even if that meant his destruction.

It had taken a year for the masters to be assembled, for Tu'Shan to deliberate on the mysteries of the prophecy. It had been a slow, methodical process – it was the way of the Fire-born. But that time had ended and the decision would soon be known to Dak'ir, as the last member of the congregation entered.

Even arrayed in his power armour, Emek seemed like a withered version of his old self. The Apothecary was stooped and carried a limp. He held his left arm close to his body. Under the right he had a batch of data-slates.

Dak'ir tried to make eye contact with his old friend but Emek was studiously avoiding his gaze. That didn't bode well.

The circular ring of stone that delineated the council seats had a break in its circumference where its artisan had fashioned a raised dais and lectern. Emek took it, laying the data-slates on the flat surface. In ancient days, tribal chieftains of Nocturne had assembled in similar circular councils when the deed was sufficiently great as to not be the concern of a single tribe. The chamber on Prometheus echoed and honoured that tradition.

Dak'ir exchanged a concerned glance with Pyriel. The Epistolary's expression hardened.

When he was ready, Emek looked to the Chapter Master who gave the barest nod to proceed.

'I have before me the Apothecarion records of Brother Fugis, comprising both private notes and a medical assessment written for the attention of the now deceased Captain Kadai. They concern the prisoner, Dak'ir.'

The prisoner. It was a barb Dak'ir would not quickly forget.

Now the Apothecary made eye contact and there was a gulf of ennui contained in his gaze. Suddenly the comradeship of battle-brothers seemed very long ago.

Emek went on undaunted.

'Aside from the fact that Dak'ir had been singled out by the then Apothecary of Third Company for...' he paused to read from a data-slate, '... "special examination", there is documented evidence of "somnambulant visions" during battle-meditation in the solitorium. Initially these were described as traumatic memories and later became apocalypse dreams.'

Captain Drakgaard learned forwards in his seat. His voice was raking, like bone claws across scaled hide. 'I fought with Kadai at Ullsinar. He was sound of judgement in all things. I would know his reaction to his Apothecary's assessment of the prisoner.'

Emek obliged, reading directly from Fugis's transcripts. '"Dak'ir's spirit will be cleansed in the crucible of battle; that is the Salamander way. Failing that I will submit him to the Reclusiam and Chaplain Elysius for conditioning." According to our Brother-Apothecary, these were the captain's exact words.'

A quiet but commanding voice spoke up as Dac'tyr addressed Elysius. 'Brother-Chaplain, was such a concern known to you?'

Elysius shook his head. 'Dak'ir's spiritual guidance was no different to the rest of his brothers. He has only ever fought with honour under my eye.'

That was unexpected. Dak'ir had thought the Chaplain would be the most punitive of the assembly.

Drakgaard turned to Agatone, with whom he shared a strong bond. 'You were his company-brother, how would you gauge his humours?'

Agatone's jaw unclenched. He cleared his throat, unfolding his arms to brace them against the table. 'All I see before me is my brother in chains. Dak'ir was no more troubled than the rest of us and I am of the belief–'

Mulcebar cut in. 'But you acknowledge a shadow lies upon Third and there is the legacy of Nihilan to consider.' His eyes invited a comment from Vel'cona.

'A known traitor and renegade, your point being?'

'That precedent exists for enemies guised as allies, especially in the midst of our Librarius.'

The captain of Fifth was a staunch traditionalist whose views on psykers and use of the warp were scathing at best. A diligent historian, in more partisan crowds he occasionally made reference to the ten thousand year-old sanctions laid down at Nikaea. It was ancient history to most that now walked the Chapter's halls, but Mulcebar had determined its ideals would not die out completely.

He continued. 'I know that Master Argos shares my concerns in this regard.'

'A pity then that he is not here to voice them,' Vel'cona replied.

A stern rivalry existed between the Armoury and Librarius. Like that between the Sanctuary Cities and their respective companies, it was encouraged, but on occasion it spilled over into something more confrontational.

'Regardless,' Mulcebar continued doggedly, 'the very fact that Dak'ir could be prey to the warp should not be overlooked. This combined with his... *unusual* behaviour gives me cause for concern.'

Vel'cona's riposte had a little venom in it. 'Are you pushing a different agenda here, captain?'

Mulcebar waved away the spurious remark as if it were beneath comment.

Drakgaard, who had maintained his neutrality so far, considered his fellow captain's last point. 'Apothecary Emek, does Brother Fugis's report make mention of further testimony?'

'No, but I have some of my own.'

Dak'ir's eyes narrowed as his former friend spoke to him directly. 'Just scrap, you told me,' he said. 'Do you remember?'

It took a few seconds for realisation to occur. Before Scoria they had met in the low-forges. The resonance of Stratos still lingered, his wounding still fresh-felt. Dak'ir had created something which he later destroyed in the furnace. 'The simulacrum mask, you saw it, didn't you?'

Emek nodded as an interested murmur passed around the room.

Agatone looked deeply uncomfortable. 'What mask? What is the meaning of this? What possible bearing could it have?'

'Facial scarring,' Emek began, gesturing to the injury Dak'ir had suffered on Stratos, the patch of cellular degeneration inflicted by a renegade's multi-melta. It was the same blast that had killed Ko'tan Kadai. The entire council could see it. 'Dak'ir fashioned a mask in secret, like the one that adorns his battle-helm. He made it to occlude his genetic heritage, to conceal that which makes him one of us, a Fire-born.'

'You saw this, and yet you said nothing,' Elysius challenged him.

Emek turned to face the Chaplain. 'At the time I thought it meant nothing–'

'And now you do?' Elysius interrupted. 'Believe it has meaning?'

'In light of Brother Fugis's notes, I do. At the very least it demonstrates a flaw in character, a lack of trust. Was Nihilan not condemned to his fate by such minor defects?'

Vel'cona answered. 'Nihilan's was a bitter seed, and he had help in the reneging of his Chapter oaths and his betrayal of the Librarius.' He shared a glance with Pyriel, who knew full well the extent of the Dragon Warrior's treachery. 'He craved secrets and power, misguided by the whims of a dark master.'

'You speak of Ushorak...' Mulcebar's assertion drew protest from Agatone.

'Do not utter his name!' he snapped. 'We waste our tongues on it. Even dead that traitor's legacy has damned the Third.'

Mulcebar held up a hand to show no offence was meant.

Minor outburst over, Vel'cona went on. 'Dak'ir *has* power. I have witnessed it first hand, felt it. But know this: I do not believe he is Nihilan in another guise, but he is dangerous. His presence, his continued existence troubles me greatly.'

'My lord–' Pyriel started to interject.

'You have seen it too, Epistolary,' said Vel'cona, admonishing. 'A prophecy that foretells the coming of a destroyer, he that is the Ferro Ignis – we had, all of us, best be mindful or that flaming sword will ruin all of Nocturne.'

'So you would kill him then?' asked Elysius.

Vel'cona's eyes blazed with fierce determination. 'I would have done so long ago had I known of the potential threat we now face, but such measures passed out of these hands long before it was my place alone to pass judgement.'

'And what of Gravius,' Elysius replied, 'our venerable brother discovered in the bowels of Scoria, whose gene-seed even now is harboured in our vaults? His signal, some ten thousand years old, was discovered by Dak'ir on the *Archimedes Rex*, was it not?'

'A hell-trap that almost killed the Fire-born who went aboard,' was Drakgaard's retort, though he uttered it without accusation.

'And who without being so imperilled would never have discovered Vulkan's mark and our ancient brother's existence,' added Pyriel, finding some traction in the Chaplain's arguments so he could at last mount a defence. 'He inscribed armour that led us to the missing volume from the Tome of Fire.'

'This,' said Mulcebar, 'the very armour that foretold of the doom prophecy we are discussing here in this council.' He shook his head. 'I am of the same mind as Vel'cona. Whether he is conscious of it or not, the Lexicanum represents too great a risk.' His eyes saddened as he regarded Dak'ir. 'For what little worth it is, I am sorry, brother.'

'I cannot–' Pyriel began but was silenced by his master's obvious displeasure.

Elysius saw the exchange and reacted. 'Speak! Vel'cona has no rank over you in this place.'

The Chief Librarian glared thunderously at the Chaplain but didn't intervene.

Pyriel licked his lips, abruptly aware of the dryness in his mouth. The tension in the chamber was rising as all present began to feel the gravitas of the decision facing them.

'Dak'ir passed the trials. True, I saw him display psychic mastery no Lexicanum has any right to possess. But it saved my life on Moribar. I see in him the potential for terrible deeds, destruction on an incredible scale, but it is tempered by a noble will. If that power can be honed and bent towards a righteous cause...'

Vel'cona scowled. 'It changes nothing.'

'I agree,' said Mulcebar.

'As do I,' Drakgaard concurred. 'This risk is too great for any of us.'

He was losing. It did not take great wisdom to see that. Dak'ir felt the grains of his life like desert sand, straining through his nerveless fingers. His only regret was that he wouldn't get to see Ba'ken one last time. His gaze fell upon Emek, and he hoped that his brother would cast off his bitterness and find peace.

Elysius addressed the entire council. 'I beheld a miracle

on the Volgorrah Reef. It was fate that I survived, that the sigil be returned to us and our father's secrets unlocked. I am convinced of that. There is a destiny unravelling here and Dak'ir is part of it. Whether that bodes for ill or good, I cannot say but we should not act out of fear.'

His declaration was met by silence. Irritated, he went on.

'Is it to be death then? Shall we condemn this son of Vulkan and cast his ash to the Arridian Plain? Brothers! Do not act in haste. There is more here than any of us can see. I sense Vulkan's hand in this.'

Tu'Shan stared pensively. The scales were evenly matched. In the end it was another voice that answered.

'As do I.'

All eyes went to the shadowy figure sat back from the rest, removed from the circle just as he was removed from his Chapter by the necessity of his sacred mission.

Vulkan He'stan spoke and all heeded him.

'*A low-born, one of the earth, shall pass through the gate of fire. He will be our doom or salvation,*' he said, reciting part of the prophecy. 'What if it is salvation?'

CHAPTER SIX

I
Carnage

AT FIRST HE had tried to hide his kills, used stealth to cull the unwary or alone. Now Tsu'gan had left a trail of carnage behind him. Once he'd penetrated far enough into the ship, he'd left warnings. Corpses were pinned to the walls by their long-blades or slit from ear to ear and propped up in groups as if sleeping. Others he hung with cables or spools of wire and let them swing like metronomes. After a few hours, by the time that word and fear had spread, it had the desired effect.

The terrified serfs now roamed in packs as they tried to apprehend him. It only played to Tsu'gan's advantage. Larger groups simply meant less patrols. Evading detection suddenly became much easier.

In the section of duct where he was crouching, he heard an explosion. Shrapnel, both bloody bone and metal, spumed into the junction he was watching.

A feral smile pulled at the corners of his mouth.

With the greater freedom of movement, he'd had time to fashion improvised booby traps. Simple trip-wired clusters of frag grenades were easy to miss when scared.

He was trying hard not to enjoy it too much.

His other pursuer was less affected. Tsu'gan could hear it coming in the wake of the dead and maimed serfs. It stopped to gnaw on the wounded, and he heard a plaintive wailing abruptly cut off. Bounding up on his feet, he moved on.

Rounding a corner, Tsu'gan nearly ran into a Dragon Warrior headed for the hangars. It must have been a late-comer. His skills at evasion were good, Prebian had taught him well, but Tsu'gan was grounded enough to realise that if Traitor Space Marines had been a part of the hunt he wouldn't have lasted this long. The entire filthy order was preparing for war. Nihilan had issued his call to arms. That's why none were chasing him, that's why they'd sent *behemoths*. He considered rushing the renegade. If he found the gap between helmet and gorget with his stolen blade, both larynx and throat were viable targets. Bring the knife up and with enough force it penetrates the skull, cuts the brainstem. Killing blow.

In the end he decided against it, and bled back into the shadows. The corridor split in three. He couldn't go back the way he'd come, the behemoth was close, so he took the third route. He went low and quiet, hugging the walls of the benighted ship. Structurally, the *Hell-stalker* wasn't so different to an Adeptus Astartes battle-barge. Tsu'gan even noticed some tell-tale Imperial markings that had been half-scoured or obscured by manic over-engineering. He suspected the vessel was once loyal and wondered briefly how the Dragon Warriors had come upon it. At the very least, it meant he was partially familiar with the probable layout. A schematic unfolded in the abstract of his mind, his superior tactical acumen plotting potential courses, gauging where vulnerable systems might be situated.

Nothing was certain, of course. Modifications had likely been made, but even a renegade warship, especially one stolen from a loyal Chapter, would have some sense of order. As far as he could tell, he was on a sub-level, possibly between decks. Workshops, even those utilised for interrogation and torture, tended to be near the enginarium or munitions decks.

His musings ended when a patrol of serfs, tooled up with auto-carbines and serrated swords, hustled into view. Tsu'gan retreated into an alcove, avoiding contact with the hot iron of the corridor's stanchions. They were in a hurry, probably after him or maybe even avoiding the behemoths, so he let them go.

Tsu'gan had no real illusions of escape, though the audaciousness of such a feat appealed to his ego; he would try and find something useful instead, something vital he could sabotage. As missions went it was purely spiteful rather than strategic, but then spite was all the Salamander had left.

A dirty, snuffling sound issued from the corridor behind him.

It had his scent.

Thought delays action, trust instinct.

Zen'de's wisdom. Between them, the two combat masters had moulded scores of fearsome soldiers.

Tsu'gan ran. The adrenaline in his system was still boosting him, but on the wane. Barrelling straight into the patrol, he wrestled two of the serfs to the ground, before gutting a third and throwing his sword like a dagger into the face of a fourth. The rest opened fire. White agony erupted in Tsu'gan's shoulder where the round clipped him. A second ripped open his leg, just a glancing blow.

The serfs were wearing dirty charcoal-grey fatigues, not unlike boiler suits, with a leather cuirass and greaves over the top. So when Tsu'gan punched the first shooter in the torso, his chest caved. Something splashed against the mouth-plug he wore as part of a leather fright mask. He was dead before the Salamander had swung his corpse around to act as a human shield. Solid shot *smacked* against the meat. It jerked and shook in parody of life with the last serf's desperate salvo. Tsu'gan crouched into

it, head against the meat sack, body sideways to present
a smaller target. When he was close enough, he threw
the corpse into the last shooter and ran like hell just as
the behemoth scuttled around the corner.

It was massive.

Flesh-pink, dewy-eyed and sweating, the behemoth
was a wretched and muscular thing. Its eyes were tiny, as
if it lived much of its life underground or in abject darkness and had devolved accordingly. A flared snout with
broad undulating nostrils dominated a brutish face. Bul-
bous growths mutated its already overdeveloped limbs
and back. Its neck was thick and brawny. Though it carried no weapons, its fists were like piston-hammers and
its malformed skull like a battering ram capable of dent-
ing tank armour.

The serf mewled as the behemoth crashed into him.
He turned to paste, ground beneath its monstrous bulk.
It barely noticed. It didn't even slow down.

Tsu'gan flung himself down the next corridor. Merci-
fully, it was empty. Hammering a door rune, he passed
through a ragged archway and found he'd reached the
gun decks. Ramlek's workshop must have been close,
situated on a sub-level between the gun deck and whatever was above it just as Tsu'gan suspected. He couldn't
remember heading down and he'd never used a stairway
or lifter, but somehow he had found this place. It would
have to do.

It stretched before him, a vast metal plaza of mesh
decking with a ribbed ceiling. Chains dangled from the
vault overhead, hung with hooks or skeletal bodies.
Darker than the outer passageways, it had a visceral cast
to it. The air was an oily fug that greased the skin upon
contact. Heat, cloying and oppressive, radiated off the
vast banks of gun batteries where the emaciated deck-
hands toiled under the gaze of bloated overseers. For
now their hatches were sealed but ammo hoppers and
vast crates of munitions were being gathered in readiness.

It was an engine room of sorts, colonised by gears of flesh and blood.

Sweating ratings, the flesh-branded slaves of the under-decks, paid him little heed as he hurried past them. Even so, Tsu'gan kept to the shadows. He was looking for a weapon, something more potent than his stolen blade. Auto-carbines were no use; their human-sized grips were too small for his fingers. He needed something bigger, maybe a belt-feed or sentry cannon. He could tear it off its mountings, use it low-slung, hard into the shoulder to absorb the inevitable kick.

Screaming echoed behind him and knew the behemoth had followed. Overseers watching from above either laughed or got clear before the monster decided to tear down their gantries and feast on them too. It wanted Tsu'gan and only killed what got in its way.

He ducked down a side corridor; the gun deck was a labyrinth of conduits and tunnels, antechambers and sub-levels. Trying to throw it off was pointless. He needed to kill it.

A heavy kick caved the door to a weapons chamber. Its guard had already fled. He slipped inside and looked around. There were dozens of boarding weapons, large tracked cannons and belt-feeds. Booted feet rattled on the deckplate outside. Something with authority was trying to restore order.

Tsu'gan seized an auto-fed cannon. Someone had left a drum in the breech. He estimated over four hundred rounds.

'Praise Vulkan,' he whispered, taking the cannon off its mounting tripod. It was hefty, but wieldable.

'Just like being back in the Devastators…'

The patrol reached the munitions locker before the behemoth. Four serfs carrying studded body shields made cover for four more toting heavy carbines.

Foolish…

Triggering the cannon, Tsu'gan filled the doorway with noise and fire. The serfs were rendered into ruddy chunks in a matter of moments. Others on the periphery, not in the direct line of fire, took shrapnel hits or were felled by the sheer explosive force of the attack.

Muzzle flare lit Tsu'gan's face as he pressed ahead, jaw clenched with the recoil, his already bruised shoulder and torso taking further punishment with every *chug* of the barrel.

He moved legs spread, body open with his free hand outstretched for balance. In face of such incredible fury, the intervention by the *Hell-stalker's* armsmen was abandoned. As he came into the main deck corridor again, Tsu'gan noticed the gunnery-slaves were in full flight. Then he noticed the behemoth.

Men were strewn around it, serfs with goads and electro-pikes. They were dead, crushed and maimed by a beast that didn't want to be caged.

It wanted its prey.

Tsu'gan was glad to oblige.

'This way, ugly…'

Heedless of the auto-feeder, the behemoth charged.

Tsu'gan felt the momentum of it all the way up from the balls of his feet, across the length of the gun deck.

'Far as you go,' he growled, and unleashed what was left in the cannon.

It got another few metres before it slumped and died. The behemoth's grotesque body was riddled with bullet holes and drooling blood from countless wounds. Tsu'gan was gasping at the end of it, the auto-feeder whining empty long before he'd released the trigger.

There was no time to celebrate. Shouts echoed behind the slain monster, coming from further out. They must've been waiting for the behemoth to kill or be killed. Now the reinforcements were headed his way.

Tsu'gan dumped the cannon. There wasn't time to grab another. He'd got lucky with the first anyway; others might not be loaded. Time was running down at last.

You'll have to catch me, you bastards.

He went deeper.

Scattered packs of bone-thin ratings and gunnery slaves huddled together at the periphery of the deck corridor, willing the red-eyed demon to pass.

Tsu'gan glared at any who wandered into his path, acutely aware of his grievous injuries. As pain returned, his chemically-enhanced prowess ebbed at the same time. He was limping, his arm tucked into his body. Sweat poured off him but he wouldn't give up. Not yet.

Vision fogging, he reached the end of the long corridor and emerged into a large vaulted chamber. It was curiously empty and silent. Even the sound of his pursuers had ceased. Tsu'gan's laboured breathing was louder than the sounds of the ship at that moment.

He recognised the vast weapon before him. He had seen it before; at least, he had seen its design. On Scoria. It was the exact imitation of the seismic cannon, only several times bigger. A phrase sprung to mind, unbidden, as he beheld it.

Planet-killer.

'Death of Nocturne…' The words slipped from his mouth, rasped, disbelieving. Nihilan had found a way to kill their home world. *This* was his ultimate vengeance upon the Chapter that had spurned him.

Heavy footfalls that could only belong to power-armoured warriors resounded against the deck behind him. Tsu'gan turned to face his aggressors, only just realising he had taken several steps towards the vast gun.

'The chase is over,' uttered one of the Dragon Warriors. In either hand, he carried a spatha and gladius. Their edges were keen and serrated. He looked eager to put the blades to use as they twitched in his gauntleted grip. Though his horned helm was sealed, Tsu'gan caught a flash of malice in the renegade's eyes.

He was joined by two others, armoured in black and red, scaled and dressed with chain that hung like a metallic web across the spikes. This had been power armour once, worthy of the name. It was a recent mark, not like that of the old traitors, the ones who still thought of themselves as Legion.

Tsu'gan wanted to gut all three just for defiling sacred battle-plate.

Of the others, one was broad and generally huge. His size rivalled that of Ba'ken. The second was sinuous and fidgeting, as if ill at ease in his own skin.

'Three against one,' Tsu'gan rumbled. He was almost done. 'I don't like your odds very much…'

The blademaster came closer. 'Fortunately for you, our master wants words.'

The arrogant smirk on Tsu'gan's face changed to a scowl. 'I recognise you…'

Then the world around him grew dark and he felt a strange lightness affect his body.

'Not again,' he growled, but knowing that translation would be harder on him if he resisted it. 'Nihilan, you bastard…'

It felt like falling.

II
Proposition

THE ROOM HE emerged into was dark. Even Tsu'gan's occulobe failed to pierce the gloom and he realised it was warp sorcery that hampered his vision. He was crouched on one knee, and chose to stay like that until the effects of teleportation faded. There were no doors he could detect, just bare metal walls in every direction. Even that he wasn't certain of. It could be a vast, echoing chamber or an oubliette. Without anything spatial to gauge it by, the room's exact dimensions were a mystery. He only thought it was metal because of how the ground felt beneath his feet.

'Is this your plan?' he shouted at the dark. 'Do you mean to bore me into submission?'

Silence answered. Not merely quiet, but the total

absence of sound. Were it not for the solidity underneath him, Tsu'gan might have believed he'd entered some sort of oblivion or nether realm.

'Nihilan!'

A *whoosh* of flame broke the silence and illuminated an alcove in front of him. A brazier burned above a bulky form beneath, casting flickering shadows over a suit of armour.

It was power armour. Tsu'gan recognised scars in the battle-plate that no amount of beating or re-fashioning could wholly erase. Geviox and the perfidy of the dark eldar were mirrored in the dents and scratches. He knew them as intimately as he knew his own face. It was his armour. He'd not seen it since his capture. Even in the shadows, it looked no different to the last moment he had worn it.

Without knowing why, he rose to his feet and approached the empty suit. His fingers were about to touch it…

'Are you sure that is the choice you wish to make?'

Tsu'gan turned around, a stolen blade in hand.

Nihilan was standing behind him.

'I am unarmed, Tsu'gan.' He widened his arms, opening his body to a kill-thrust. 'You may slay me if you wish.'

Tsu'gan stepped forwards.

'But is it really me that you are angry at?'

'Stop speaking in riddles, renegade.' Tsu'gan eyed the darkness, expecting an ambush. 'If I killed you now, what is to stop your warriors rushing in here and killing me?'

'Nothing.'

Nihilan paused. The fact he had survived this long showed he had Tsu'gan's attention. Inwardly, he smiled.

'I wish to know something, Tsu'gan. You are an intelligent warrior. You know there is no way off this ship. Even if there were, your brothers would suspect you tainted. An entire year to be broken down and remade by the enemy? At the very least your status as a Firedrake would be withdrawn. At worst, Elysius would have you at the not-so-tender mercies of his chirurgeon-interrogators. So, why then do you still try to escape?'

Tsu'gan was lowering the blade. 'Because I must.'

'Ah.' Nihilan smiled. It was an ugly expression. 'The legendary tenacity of the Salamanders. Such an over-rated trait. No cause is ever lost, no battle ever done until Vulkan decrees it.' The sorcerer's mood became rancorous. 'Where was that attitude when I awaited rescue on Lycannor? As my brothers lay dead and dying around me, where was that tenacity then?'

Tsu'gan had no knowledge of Lycannor. Few did, save Kadai and he was dead.

'Why have you brought me here, to whine and bleat? Don't you have servants who can listen to your interminable whimpering?' he asked, throwing down the blade. It would be of no use here. Nihilan wasn't about to let Tsu'gan gut him. 'If it is to kill me, then do it and end these games. They're tiresome.'

'Always so fatalistic, brother.'

'You are no brother of mine!'

'But I could be. Tell me, how long is it before the pain comes back? When you have the brander-priests carve into your flesh to obscure the agony in your soul, how long before it returns? A day? An hour?' He came closer, lowering his voice. 'A minute?'

He had no answer. Tsu'gan was powerless.

'It is a sickness, Tsu'gan. You've kept it hidden so far, but your masters are intolerant. Strength and only strength is what they respect. Weakness… well…'

Tsu'gan snarled. 'I am not weak!'

'Kneel.'

He rebelled, but Tsu'gan obeyed Nihilan's command. The sorcerer looked down on him as king to vassal. His voice was deathly calm.

'Your *brothers* abandoned you on the Volgorrah Reef. They left you for dead, assumed you were lost without even a shred of evidence that pointed towards your demise. Where was Nocturnean tenacity then? It was outweighed by Nocturnean pragmatism.'

A thick vein in Tsu'gan's forehead throbbed. He fought but could not rise. Nor could his leaden tongue make him speak.

'I told you once of your destiny, and who stands in your way.'

'Dak'ir...' The word was rasped.

'Nocturne's chosen son, the reason you take blade to flesh and cut. You cannot excise him, Tsu'gan. Not that way.'

A second brazier flared into life, illuminating another alcove alongside the first. Within was a suit of armour, just like before. Only this time, it was in the black and red of the Dragon Warriors.

Still cowed by Nihilan's sorcery, Tsu'gan was incredulous.

'I said you had a choice,' Nihilan told him. 'This is it. Search your desires. I know of the pain, of the yearning for retribution.'

From above there came a shaft of hazy yellow light, like the crack in a coffin lid. It speared down to rest upon an eviscerator.

Tsu'gan saw his reflection in the dull metal housing for the serrated blade. A glabrous onyx skull with a red spike of beard jutting belligerently from a noble face looked back. The patrician lineage of the kings of Hesiod was echoed there.

I am unworthy of it.

The two-handed chainsword was immense. Its monomolecular teeth could even cut adamantium apart.

Somehow, Tsu'gan had got turned around. He was on his feet, though he didn't remember getting up.

Nihilan looked on in silence, though his voice drifted into Tsu'gan's subconscious.

'Make your decision.'

Tsu'gan took up the eviscerator. The grip was leather-bound, solid and weighty. It took all of his fading strength to lift it above waist height. Fate was pulling him. He had come so close to a reprieve. Vulkan He'stan had very nearly saved him, but the masochistic craving was coming back. He could feel it under his skin, the desire for pain to smother pain.

'I am already damned,' he whispered and hacked into his power armour.

Chunks of green battle-plate were hewn from the venerable suit, the line from its previous incumbents broken in an orgy of destructive self-hatred. By the time it was done, a ragged mess remained where once had been a proud relic of an even prouder Chapter.

Tsu'gan's back and shoulders were heaving. It was hard to breathe. Sweat glistened on his naked body.

'I must confess,' Nihilan began… just as Tsu'gan turned and drove the still-churning eviscerator at the sorcerer's face.

Tsu'gan grimaced in expectation of flying bone chunks and flesh, but the keen blades whirred impotently a fraction from Nihilan's misshapen nose.

Even exerting more pressure, Tsu'gan couldn't push the eviscerator closer. A kine-shield was blocking it.

'You do not disappoint,' said Nihilan.

The chainblade was edging away, against Tsu'gan's will, getting closer to his own face and body as his hands betrayed him. He fought, but was already weak. There was no escaping it.

'I expected this,' said Nihilan, an outstretched hand acting as puppeteer for Tsu'gan's rebellious limbs. 'Your traitorous brother said you would capitulate, but I know you better.'

'Iagon…' The name came out as a growl.

'You truly are a defiant bastard.'

Tsu'gan stopped struggling, closed his eyes.

The churning blade ceased. It dropped to the floor from his numbed fingers.

'Kill me!' he roared. 'Kill me then if that is my fate.'

Nihilan slowly shook his head.

'No.'

'Then what is it? What is it you want from me? I am not Dak'ir. I am not chosen by Vulkan. I am–'

'Exactly what I need,' Nihilan cut in. A device had appeared in his left hand. It was fashioned from silver, but the surface seemed to flow like mercury. Initially ovoid in shape, its form changed when three pairs of talon-like appendages snapped out from its body. Now it resembled an insect with limbs and a carapace. Upon its back there glowed a tiny sigil like an ankh.

Tsu'gan frowned at the device, knowing it was alien in origin but no more than that. He felt the urge to resist anew but was at the limits of his endurance.

'Keep that filth away from me…' he slurred.

'I lied too, Tsu'gan.' Nihilan was impassive as he advanced on him. 'There was never any choice.'

As the door parted to the antechamber, Iagon was afforded a tantalising glimpse of Tsu'gan in the throes of agony. The scrape of the knife against his already butchered vambrace quickened.

Unlike the one Ramlek had subjected him to, this was torture of the mind and a place where the broken Salamander was so much weaker. 'I want to watch him suffer again…' he rasped. The door slid shut as the knife blade stuck in the groove he'd made.

'No,' said Nihilan simply. 'You've seen enough.'

'I *need* this…'

Iagon started towards the door, but Ramlek stood in his path. 'Shall I kill him, my lord?'

Nihilan shook his head.

'You really are twisted, aren't you?' he said.

Iagon backed off from the brutal Dragon Warrior to plead with Nihilan.

'I was supposed to ascend,' he said. 'Here!' He brandished his augmetic gauntlet, the one he now had in place of a hand since he'd cut it off in a fit of deranged devotion. It was slashed to hell and back with knife scars. 'See what I gave? My flesh and bone. And he…'

Iagon pointed to the door. 'He left me behind. Betrayed me and discarded me like I was nothing.' His face darkened, the mania parting to reveal something altogether more homicidal. 'I am not nothing,' he muttered in a throaty whisper.

Nihilan appeared to consider this.

'Tsu'gan is loyal to his Chapter and places that above all else. I believe he saw what was truly inside you, Iagon, and it disgusted him.'

Iagon shrieked and, twisting the knife around, came at Nihilan.

Ramlek's meaty fist seized him. His own blade was immediately at Iagon's throat.

'I could remove his head,' he offered.

'There has been enough of that already.'

Almost instinctively, Ramlek stretched his neck where the regenerative tissue still irritated him.

Nihilan waved him down and drew closer despite the fact Iagon had just tried to stab him.

'You do not disgust me,' he said in a conciliatory tone. 'I know you are not "nothing". I shall make you into something more. Would you like that, brother?'

Iagon lowered his blade and nodded slowly. 'I'm listening…'

Nihilan held up his hand.

'Then come forwards,' he said, 'and embrace me as your liege-lord.'

Something in the strained smiled on the sorcerer's face should have warned Iagon, but his sense of self preservation was blurred by overwhelming ambition. He did as requested, kneeling and taking Nihilan's outstretched hand.

Unseen by Iagon, Nihilan's expression changed as the supplicant's gaze went to the floor in deference. Hatred filled his eyes and his smile turned into a thin line expressing his grim satisfaction.

CHAPTER SEVEN

I
Infection

THE DOCKING GATES opened up chasm-wide in the
scalloped flank of Prometheus, admitting the *Caldera*
into Hangar Seven. A cloud of venting pressure was
released from the hold prior to atmospheric stabilisa-
tion, becoming particulate upon contact with the void.
The gunship ghosted on low thrust across a vast floor,
its fuselage lamps hinting at tracts of cable, maintenance
pits and access hatches, until reaching its holding bay.
Landing stanchions mag-locked to the deck once it was
in the delineated safety zone and secured the Thunderhawk firmly in place. It joined several others that were
all awaiting launch or undergoing routine inspection.

Hazard strobes continued to flash intermittently
throughout the landing, washing the expansive hangar
in grainy amber light. It did little to alleviate the dark,
vapour-clouded environs, but warned servitor crews that
a second vessel was incoming.

This was no gunship.

The Adeptus Mechanicus collector ship followed in
the *Caldera's* engine wash, its massive thrusters vibrating

the walls. The shock-dampened glass of the command station overlooking the hangar trembled before the larger freighter set down. Its hold was full with the mineral tithe from the Nocturnean mines and it would need prepping and readying for return to its forge-ship.

As the docking gates closed and atmospheric integrity was restored, the forward embarkation ramp of the *Caldera* slammed down onto the deck.

Orgento was first to descend the ramp. His bionic eye relayed data back to his frontal cortex concerning temperature, pressure, oxygen saturation. A system-failure icon flashed up briefly but then disappeared. He put it down to a glitch and scheduled the augmetic for re-sanctification at the next available juncture.

Several landing crews wearing atmosphere suits were already en route to the vessels, accompanied by technical servitors. A grim host of cyber-skulls hovered in the air above them. They were the remains of serfs long-dead, immortalised in reliquary so they could continue to serve the Chapter.

The crews parted before the Techmarine like a flock of dactylids interrupted in flight by a larger predator, only to reassemble once he had passed. Ritual flamers doused the hull in his wake as the crew overseers spoke rites of function over the gunship.

'Promethean Creed meets worship of the Omnissiah,' he remarked to Argos who had followed on behind him. The Master of the Forge saluted to their pilot, Loc'tar, who would report to the solitorium for fire-cleansing, before answering.

'The *Caldera* will be all the better for the twin baptism,' he said. 'As to its effects on *that* vessel, I am unsure.'

Attached to the hangar's exterior docking spine was the impressive forge-ship the *Archimedes Rex*. It loomed through a vast portal of clear armaglas that was durable enough to withstand meteor strikes and starship barrage.

Argos had been on Nocturne ensuring the mineral tithe was ready when the Martian delegation had arrived.

It was the first time he'd seen the ship since it had been salvaged from deep space.

Its flanks were still scarred from long exposure to the void. Asteroid erosion marred the armour plates and there was staining from the effects of solar wind. Much of the Martian red in its paintwork was scored to the bare, grey metal beneath. The machine-cathedra, the mech-temples, data-shrines and factorum of the immense forge-ship appeared rusted, almost fossilised against its craggy hull. Jutting laser batteries and macro-cannon turrets slumped lazily at their stations. The entire ship seemed to exude malaise. The *Archimedes Rex* was a goliath and even outside its presence dominated the hangar.

After the ship, Argos was drawn to the battalion of Martians standing in its shadow. A cadre of servitors, genetors and lesser adepts were ranked up awaiting the return of Xhanthix.

The magos and his cyborganic cohort had recently disembarked.

'What is the meaning of this?' Argos asked as the Martians joined them on deck.

'I was granted permission to visit your forge-ship. I believe the designation given to it by your Chapter is *Chalice of Fire*. I am intrigued by its manufacturing process and would data-log with my own mechadendrites.'

Out the corner of his eye, Argos noticed the vast security doors to the hangar were opening. Closed, they sealed off the rest of the space port and Prometheus's inner halls, including the route to the *Chalice of Fire*. A five-man welcoming party from Fourth, bolters clasped across their chests, was standing to outside the doors.

'There are over fifty–' A jolt of painful static made Argos wince. His Lyman's ear was suddenly filled with white noise.

A warning rune flashed up on his bionic eye. A message scrolled across the retinal display in binaric. It took a fraction of a millisecond to translate.

++Infection detected… Infection detected++

'Who…' The word crackled out of his mouth, as if from interference. He had seen the warning, deciphered its meaning, but cognitively could not react.

Orgento's voice was broken, distant as if it needed tuning in.

'M…as…ter…'

The security doors were almost fully open. Something was happening to the Martian cohort. Red lights flashed up on their diodes and optical units. Tracked servitors went from docile to manoeuvre-ready, rising up on their hydraulics. It took another second to realise they were armed.

Argos was almost on his knees, his eyes flicking from Xhanthix's dumb expression to the Martian cohort that was steadily weaponising.

++*Infection detected… Infection detected*++ slid across his view, mocking him.

'Orgento…' It was like speaking through a broken vox-impeller.

His eyes went to the ugly, lumpen thing at the end of exterior docking spine of Hangar Seven.

There was something wrong with the ship. Whatever had afflicted the *Archimedes Rex* wasn't gone. It was merely dormant, waiting for a synaptic trigger to release it.

Xhanthix had primed it, inloaded some crucial data-packet out on the dunes.

The corrupt data was within him, running rampant within his cybernetic implants, virulent as a contagion. A binary compound, he was the reactant to its catalyser. Alone, each component was harmless; together, they were lethal.

Terrible knowledge unfolded in Argos's brain slowly, too slowly.

I am the trigger.

Like a sluggish data-file that had finally inloaded, Argos realised he had been compromised. Something had happened to him when he'd first interfaced with the forge-ship; something so powerful and invasive that it could overrun an entire Martian complement. It had done so before, turning its denizens homicidal. The signal was strong; he'd felt its resonance even on the surface of Nocturne when the *Archimedes Rex* was at dock on Prometheus. It had been dormant for several years. Logically, it was the only way it could have escaped detection. Otherwise, it would have been isolated, quarantined and neutralised during one of his sanctification rituals.

'Enemies inside perimeter...' He was reaching for his bolt pistol as the main hangar lights hummed into life. He felt his hearts beating in his chest as the biological part of his body struggled to react to what was happening to the inorganic part.

The security doors were disengaged. Five warriors came striding through them.

Orgento's face creased into a scowl as he went for his own sidearm. His body was shielding Xhanthix from view but as he turned Argos could see beyond the Techmarine. A data-light was flashing inside the magos's hood. It was a countdown, about to reach its terminus.

'Get down...' Argos growled, knowing it was already too late.

Three high-pitched bleats emitted from Xhanthix's vocaliser, synchronised with the data-flash, before he exploded.

The deck fell away beneath him – or rather, he was lofted above it by the intensity of the blast wave. His retinal senses were immediately overloaded by the angry flare of light. Temperature gauges red-zoned as the tolerance levels of his armour reached their limit. He was spun in slow motion, rotating through a hundred and eighty degrees, limbs flailing. Hot frag launched from ground-zero with the velocity of bolter rounds, shredding hapless crewmen and tearing servitors apart in a welter of oily blood.

Argos's roar merged with the cacophonous explosion until it became one agonised sound. Seconds seemed to stretch into minutes as furious incendiary waves rolled out across the hangar.

He hit the ground with a jolt, ripping off a shoulder pad and scraping across the deck for another ten metres before finally coming to a stop.

A buzzing sensation muddied his hearing, but Argos was wary of using his other senses. He'd shut down his bionic eye. The left side of his face felt numb from deactivation. Staggering to his feet, he found his bolt pistol and aimed it at the smoke roiling over the hangar.

'Orgento!' It was like shouting under water.

There were fires, bodies strewn between them. Some were badly burnt; others writhed in agony, speared by shrapnel. He heard shouting and then the steady staccato of automatic weapons fire. He could see no enemy, only the dead and dying. Dull muzzle flashes coloured the gloom but it was hard to tell how far away or pinpoint their precise origins.

Klaxons screamed, echoing off the hangar walls which were washed red by hazard strobes warning of depressurisation.

'Orgento!'

Argos was bleeding. The servos in his right leg were damaged and it didn't move as easily. Every third step he had to drag his foot. The static in his head was fading, becoming more like a dull ache. He risked reactivating his bionic eye. A heat spectrum overlaid his vision. Bio-scanning matrices identified Orgento's signature to Argos's left. Only a few metres separated them.

The Techmarine had flat-lined.

Orgento was dead.

His power generator was torn up along with most of the cuirass protecting his back. One of his arms was missing, the blood clotting but not enough to save him. Massive internal haemorrhaging registered on the scan. Several organs had been liquefied as poor Orgento bore the brunt of the explosion.

'Vulkan guide thee…' Argos muttered sadly and made

the Circle of Fire. His grief was postponed by a bulky silhouette coming out of the dissipating smoke.

His targeting systems were still inactive, so he snap-fired and tore a line of sparks from a servitor's weapon mount. It returned with an auto-cannon salvo but only succeeded in raking the deck. Argos put three precise rounds in its torso and the cyborganic split apart with the mass-reactive detonation. Its tracked impellers ground forwards another half-metre before coming to a final stop.

More of the creatures were emerging from the gloom. Some were engaged with unseen opponents attacking from other directions. Argos advanced towards the ones zeroing in on him.

A burst of solid shot ripped into his exposed shoulder, forcing a grimace. Argos replied with a two-round headshot, before swinging in the opposite direction and putting down another servitor.

Despite the vastness of the hangar, it was not unlike guerrilla warfare, stalking through the smoke and killing whatever came his way. He ambushed one cyborganic. It was eviscerating a crewman with a rotary saw. Grisly work. Argos slipped a vibro-knife from a sheath fastened to his chestplate and severed the thing's thorax cabling. It struggled for a few seconds, whirring plaintively, before he cut the head from the neck entirely and ended it.

Minor skirmishes were breaking out across the hangar, but bereft of cohesion. As logic took the place of instinct, Argos tried to determine the purpose of the enemy's plan. It was an attack, designed and premeditated, but it didn't make any sense. Even with the route to the inner halls open, it should require a considerable amount of force to gain entry. The automated defence systems alone could repel a sizeable invasion party without the need for additional reinforcement.

Argos dispatched another servitor and swung around to engage the next opponent, but stopped a fraction of a second before pulling the trigger.

The battle-hardened form of a Salamander of Fourth Company greeted him.

'Master Argos, praise Vulkan you are alive.'

Argos analysed the warrior's unique facial signifiers to ascertain his identity.

'Status report, Brother Ak'taro.'

'Hangar Seven is contained. Ek'thelar and Rodondus hold the security gate. I came to look for you on Brother-Sergeant Kel's final order.'

'Final order?'

'Brother-Sergeant Kel is dead, my lord.'

Argos nodded. The firefight was starting to ebb as the Space Marines and human armsmen reasserted control. Scattered gunfire still rang throughout the hangar but it was spaced further apart and no longer sustained. Dac'tyr's troops had reacted swiftly, but Argos was still troubled.

He eyed the *Archimedes Rex*.

'Nothing enters or leaves that ship. Lock it down; lock this entire area down.' Emergency crews had succeeded in activating stasis shielding to prevent further venting and were re-pressurising the hangar. The security doors to the inner halls beyond the space port were still being worked on. Until that was done, fortification would have to come from Ak'taro and his men.

'Aye, my lord,' the now acting-sergeant replied.

Argos gave a last look to the forbidding forge-ship. 'In fact, assemble crews and weld shut any access hatches, conduits or pipes.'

Ak'taro tried not to blanch. 'On a vessel that size that is a considerable undertaking, my lord.'

Argos was already on his way. He needed to interface with one of Prometheus's control hubs, find out if the infection from whatever scrap code the *Archimedes Rex* harboured had penetrated further than Hangar Seven.

'Then you had best get started,' he said.

It was still unclear what the purpose of the Martian sabotage had been. Efforts to penetrate the inner halls

had failed but the security door was compromised and
so too the docking gate into the hangar, which had
suffered badly in the explosion and was ripped open.
Stasis shielding would keep out the void and maintain
structural integrity but it could not prevent any enemy
ship from landing.

'We are vulnerable,' he said to himself as he passed
beyond the threshold of the security door. He still carried the limp. Fixing his armour servos would have to
wait. He shut down a part of the mechanism, which
increased the drag but abated the hydraulic pressure
release and stopped the sparking.

Labour crews and squads of armsmen Ak'taro had
summoned to secure and stabilise the hangar gave
him a wide berth as they hurried in the opposite direction. It was like wading against the tide, but with Argos
slowed by his injuries rather than an imaginary current.

He reached a second security door. This was also
being kept open while the serfs were needed from
other parts of the space port. Ahead, he knew there
was a control hub where he could assess the extent of
the damage done by the scrap virus. The other direction led deeper into the complex and would take him
to Prometheus's core defence system.

An unsettling thought entered his mind as he
stopped at the junction.

I cannot move.

It wasn't the servo. Even unassisted, he could force
his power armour's motor-function. It was just more
difficult.

The static returned, invading his senses and infil-
trating cognition. The human part of Argos's brain
rebelled as it realised it was being manipulated, whilst
the machine part had already surrendered to it.

He seized the arm of a passing serf with his last act
of free will.

'What is your name?' Argos barked the question, his

voice resonant with tension and mechanical interference.

The startled labour serf balked and stammered at the cybernetic giant that had grabbed him. 'S-sonnar, my liege.' He looked old but had recently received juvenat treatments. Some of the aging in his body had been regressed, restored to beyond its prime. As the impromptu bio-scan concluded, Argos realised that he knew him.

'Sonnar Illiad,' the serf said at last.

'Get help.'

His heart rate was well above normal. Illiad was terrified. Pupil dilation and increased respiration were rapidly logged and recorded as Argos desperately tried anything to stave off the harmful code infecting him.

'My liege?'

'Our deep space augurs have been off-line for the last twenty minutes and… I… I am not myself. Do it now!'

Illiad stumbled down the corridor without looking back, headed to the hangar where he knew Brother Ak'taro was waiting.

Argos was moving again, though not entirely of his own volition. Mechadendrites sprang from their housings in his gauntlet. The haptic implants interfaced with the door controls, locking it in an open position. Only another Master of the Forge could override it. Then he turned and made for the core defences, ignoring his original destination of the control hub.

As he sealed the door to the other corridor shut, a single compulsion repeated within his mechanised subconscious.

He was headed for Vulkan's Eye, the immense defence laser that protected Prometheus from orbital assault. It came from a forgotten age of technology. There was no other weapon system like it that still functioned. It had never failed the Chapter.

Until now.

* * *

II
Preyed Upon

HUGGING THE DUNES, the Land Speeder barely kicked up a sand cloud as Prebian minimised the engine wash. Its repulsor plate that reacted to Nocturne's gravity was kept low. They were stalking the aspirants and he wanted to observe them undetected. Even the rear thrusters that provided propulsion were baffled, so they could run silent.

Decreasing in speed, the skimmer crested a small dune before sinking into the deep ravine behind it. There they idled, engines humming with just enough power to keep them aloft, observing another dune some three hundred metres away.

Heat haze radiated off the baking desert floor and a sand squall was rolling in, driven by distant winds coming off the Acerbian Sea. It would blanket their position perfectly.

'Scopes...' Prebian held out a hand, taking the magnoculars from Ba'ken as they were offered. 'Should be coming over that rise any time now...' he muttered, half to himself.

'And if not?' Ba'ken asked. He was watching the sandy peaks at either side of the ravine, his earlier paranoia still lingering.

'Then they're lost in the Pyre and already dead.' Prebian handed back the magnoculars. 'Val'in has the lead.'

Ba'ken took a look.

The view was grainy and green-tinged, tracking data spooling across his view, but the aspirant stood out clearly enough. Hot winds were rolling in, kicking up a dust storm. Val'in kept his head bowed against it, leading with his shoulder and taking long strides through the gathering ash-sand.

'Head up...' Ba'ken knew the aspirant couldn't hear him but scolded anyway.

It was basic survival technique. Eyes on the ground

perceived nothing of the danger ahead. It was why so few military advances were conducted *against* a storm. Deserts were particularly hazardous. As well as equipment malfunction, which was common, there was also the heat and sun-glare to contend with. Sandstorms only added to the lethality of the environment. Survive all of that and in the Pyre there were still the sulphur drifts, ash-sinks and acid geysers to kill the unwary.

He increased magnification. The youth was glancing up intermittently, head low to keep out the worst of the storm.

Ba'ken smiled.

Though he looked tired, Val'in was making solid progress.

'Conserve your strength…'

The breeding grounds of the sa'hrk were close, and the monstrous denizens of the Pyre were just as remorseless as its other dangers. Val'in would need his Themian hunting knife and whatever was left of his wits very soon.

'Keep the blade close…'

'Your instruction will avail your protégé little all the way out here, brother-sergeant,' said Prebian.

Ba'ken lowered the magnoculars and secured them in the speeder's cockpit. It was a Storm-variant, with capacity for carriage at the expense of deadlier weapon systems. Any aspirant that survived induction would at least have a ride back to the nearest Sanctuary City. The Storm only had room for two crewman and five riders, which said a lot about Salamander pragmatism and the harshness of the trials.

'My apologies, master. It doesn't seem so long ago that I was out on the sands, hunting prey, earning my black carapace.'

Prebian grinned ferally and all his many years seemed to fall away.

'Stirs the blood, doesn't it?'

He gunned the engines and they drove out of the ravine at cruising speed.

As they were nearing the peak of the next rise, Prebian checked their coordinates on the map screen built in to the Land Speeder's console.

'Better get on that cannon,' he said, eyes ahead. 'Sa'hrk will be near.'

Ba'ken hauled on the heavy bolter, unlocking it and sliding the gun around on its mounting rail. He checked the load – a full mag of heavy mass-reactive. Any sa'hrk hit by one would be crimson mist.

Flicking up the iron sights, Ba'ken adjusted his aim by tracking along a distant ridge. A reflection, sun on metal, caught his eye. It was ephemeral but definitely not a figment of his imagination.

'Contact high,' he snapped, providing the bearing as he slung the heavy bolter round on the same line. 'Approximately five hundred metres.'

Prebian slewed the speeder around in a wide arc without hesitating, adding thrust to increase manoeuvrability. It brought the bearing Ba'ken had just given to their front aspect, where their armour was toughest and the cannon had the broadest arc of fire.

They slowed to a near stop, halfway up a rise, nose pointed at a distant ridge behind where the aspirants had come from.

Prebian was reaching for the magnoculars.

'Confirmation?'

'Nothing further,' Ba'ken replied, eye trained down the iron sight. He panned across the ridge, slow and steady.

'Is he following us?'

'Direction suggests yes.'

'Nothing on scopes.'

Prebian put the magnoculars down and waited.

Apart from the low engine throb from the speeder, the desert was quiet.

Ba'ken could feel his twin hearts beating. They were strong and steady, calm. His perspective condensed down into the circular world viewed through the heavy bolter's iron sights.

Dust motes curled lazily across the summit of the ridge but nothing else stirred. It was dotted with volcanic rocks, clefts and crags – plenty of places to hide.

'Keep the high ground covered,' said Prebian, getting out of the driver's seat. 'I'm heading for a closer look.' He unhitched a sniper rifle from the speeder's webbing and proceeded to stalk up the dune, his blindside facing away from the potential ambusher.

Ba'ken lost the Master of Arms beyond his peripheral vision but resisted the temptation to follow him. He stayed fixed on the ridge as Prebian went wide and low to outflank.

He caught a brief glimpse of the master again a few minutes later, much farther off as he homed in on Ba'ken's bearing. He was staying down, hugging the rocks. Whoever was following them would've seen him disembark; they would either attack or withdraw. Both actions would reveal their position to the Salamanders.

Prebian was using his sniper sight to get a bead on the summit of the ridge, looking through the scope exclusively as he advanced. As he crested the rise, coming in at an oblique angle, Ba'ken lost sight of him again. He felt a moment of tension in the intervening moments before Prebian's head appeared above the ridgeline and he waved the all-clear. Ba'ken switched to the driver's seat and gunned the speeder up the rise to pick him up.

'Whoever it was has gone,' Prebian announced when they were reunited.

Ba'ken frowned. 'I saw something. I swear it to Vulkan.'

'There's no need to do that, brother. I found this.' He held out his hand. In it was a dagger, but a strange jagged implement utterly unlike the heavy blades used by the Chapter or indeed anyone who had business roving the desert.

Old memories flared in Ba'ken's mind like raw wounds reopened in his flesh, and his face darkened. 'I know this weapon's provenance,' he said.

'It's a message.'

'Friend or foe?'

'Unknown.' Prebian climbed into the gunner's seat. 'We're not alone out here. Dark eldar are on Nocturne, abroad in this desert.'

Ba'ken gave the engine some throttle.

'Ease down,' Prebian warned. 'If they are stalking the aspirants, they might not have seen us yet or at least know where we are. Low and silent, brother-sergeant, but be ready to move.'

'You mean to use the aspirants as bait?'

'They are already bait. We are alone in this desert without reinforcement, against an enemy we cannot see and whose number we cannot yet ascertain. We must press our every possible advantage.

Ba'ken nodded, bringing the Land Speeder around and cruising slowly back down into the ravine.

Training was over. Either the aspirants would earn the right to become Space Marine Scouts or they would die.

LIVING IN THE caves beneath Scoria, Val'in had formed a healthy respect for dangerous things. As a boy, he was all too aware of the chitin and the threat those monsters represented to his way of life. He had become adept at avoiding them, at knowing when they were close. One might describe it as a sixth sense, though Val'in was certainly no psyker. Rather, he was simply accomplished at survival and had honed his instincts to a razor's edge.

He relied on that innate quality as he stooped beneath a craggy outcrop of volcanic rock and the hackles on the back of his neck rose. Val'in was not a native of Nocturne but he had lived on and endured the hell-world for over three years, learning much in that time. He knew of the leo'nid, apex-hunters of the Arridian Plain, and the sa'hrk that even now he hunted; he had seen what flocks of hungry dactylids could do to lone travellers and heard the bellow of the great fire lizards that lived beneath the earth. Nocturne was possessed of all these terrors and more besides, some of which had no names or had not been seen in decades; this however, was something different. He could not say why he knew that. It was just a feeling, a creeping sense of dread that reminded him he was still human.

Val'in had chosen the overhang as a good place to get out of the sun, whilst still making progress across the desert basin. It was firm underfoot, too. He'd never intended for it to become a haven from whatever was stalking them.

Blending into the shadows of the sparse rocks, he waited.

Heklarr was first through the opening, following the same logic and possibly the route of his fellow aspirant. As well as his tracks, he also found Val'in's knife at his neck.

He hissed for silence, even though a storm was blowing outside. An embryonic flash of fire-red lit Val'in's eyes as he let the other aspirant go.

'Who follows you?' he asked, cutting off any objection from Heklarr.

Heklarr scowled. 'What are you–'

'Who? Speak the names!'

Whether it was the tone of Val'in's voice or the look in his eyes, but Heklarr understand in that moment the severity of the danger they were in.

'Kot'iar, Ska'varron and Exor. The others, I don't know. Maybe they fell behind; maybe they're already dead.'

Val'in eyed the entrance, thinking. 'We'll have to assume they've taken them.'

'Who? What are we hiding from, brother?'

'I don't know, but it isn't the sa'hrk nor is it something devised by our training masters.' He quickly gauged the size of the overhang. It was partially enclosed, more like a cave. Only two ways in and out, but it was also long and narrow. Penned in at either end there would be little room to manoeuvre but being caught out in the open somehow felt worse.

'How do you know all this? Did you see something? Storms can play tricks on the mind.'

Heklarr was a native, born of Epimethus in the Acerbian Sea. He had seen countless drovers and whalers lose their sanity to the rough elements.

'I felt something. An instinct, like when you're being watched.' He eyes narrowed as he fought to remember the initial experience. 'It was almost as if it wanted me to know it was there, that my fear of it would give it power. No beast hunts that way, not even here.'

'What are you proposing we do?' Heklarr asked. He had spent enough time around Val'in to know his hunches were usually reliable. He gestured to his blade. 'The masters took our carbines. We are armed with knives.'

Val'in frowned, his plan not yet fully formed. 'Signal to the others. Bring them here if you can. Other than that, I suggest we try and survive.'

'*That's* your plan?' Heklarr was incredulous.

'You have a better one?'

After a moment, Heklarr went to the entrance and tried to find the others in the roiling storm.

HE'D BEEN WRONG about the others. They weren't dead, at least not yet.

Dukkar got as far as the basin of the sand valley before his body erupted in a shower of shredded gore. To Val'in, watching from the rocks and willing the others to reach them, it appeared like a thousand tiny splinters had exploded from inside the poor aspirant's flesh.

Ralas'tan had a different fate. He was slit groin to cranium as he crested the rise. The blade-wielder was unseen, as was the blade itself. It was as if he merely parted and his organs sloughed out of his body all over the ash-sand.

Of the stragglers, T'org came closest to salvation. The Themian had strong legs which he used to outpace the others. Heklarr, standing with Val'in at the entrance, urged him on. He outstretched a hand to pull him in,

when T'org became rooted to the spot. There was a look
of abject terror etched on his face that literally froze in
place as particles of hoarfrost coalesced around it. Ice in
the desert – the very fact it was anathema to the natural order sent flurries of dread rippling through Val'in.
He snatched back Heklarr's hand before the deadly frost
spread to him too.

'Retreat,' he hissed, barely daring to breathe let alone
speak.

The five survivors headed into the tunnel of rock. They
only got halfway before the shrieking began.

Something was moving outside, something fast and
black against the sun. Val'in saw it through the cracks
in the rock. It went on foot, or at least it seemed to; its
incredible pace and dexterity suggested an altogether
slicker mode of motion.

There was more than one, though the shadow-speed
made it difficult to tell just how many. Taunting, they
darted back and forth, running their blades against the
outer rock.

'Form defensive perimeter!' shouted Exor, who'd taken
it upon himself to act as leader.

The other four obeyed, though Val'in's eyes continued
to try and track the shadow-creatures flitting by outside.

'I have the north facing,' said Kot'iar.

'South,' added Ska'varron.

Their masters had trained them well. They were falling back on their lessons, applying well-honed tactics
appropriate to the situation. They would avail them
nothing against this enemy.

'I see something…' hissed Heklarr, pointing over
Kot'iar's shoulder to the north-facing entrance they had
just fallen back from.

It was sinuous, whatever this thing was that slid its way
into the tunnel. Scent-pits flared in its nostrils, almost
tasting them. The troglodyte thing was utterly blind, but
its other senses more than up for this deficiency. Grey in
pallor, it weaved towards them with a hungering gait.

Outside, the shadow-creatures had stopped moving.

They are watching this! Val'in realised with a terrified shudder.

'Vulkan's fire beats in my breast...' he began, trusting to the litany to galvanise him in the darkness as the grey whip-thin horror came closer.

Kot'iar broke. He roared, as fear overwhelmed him and turned into reckless abandon. He left the defensive cordon, deaf to the protests of his brothers, and threw himself at the beast.

The ur-ghul reacted faster. It bent away from Kot'iar's knife like a serpent jinking from a predator. A half-dozen shallow spurts of blood vented from the back of the aspirant's neck. It took the others a few seconds to realise the beast had plunged its spine-like claws into Kot'iar's vital organs. Even with the enhanced physiology of a pseudo-Space Marine, he was dead before the ur-ghul began to feast. Rows of its needle fangs ground poor Kot'iar's flesh, devouring it in succulent slivers. It took all of Val'in's resolve not to attack, and considerable presence to prevent the others from doing so too.

Further reckless action now would see them all dead.

This dread thing was beyond them but for now, with the shadows looking on, it was all the aspirants faced; together, they could kill it.

'Vulkan's fire beats in my breast,' Val'in began again, keeping the beast in his eye-line even though it disgusted him to watch what it was doing to his brother. 'Speak the oath!' he snarled at the others when met by their silence.

'Vulkan's fire beats in my breast...' he said a third time.

'With it I shall smite the foes of the Emperor.' They chorused in unison.

'Feed your courage, brothers.' Val'in was only just on the right side of sounding confident. 'We may not be full-fledged Fire-born, but we have strength enough to kill this wretched thing and avenge our fallen.'

They spread out, Ska'varron watching their backs as Val'in and the others crept towards the beast. Its grotesque head jerked up at them when they were close. It snarled, revealing blood-rimed teeth jammed with chunks of Kot'iar's flesh.

Exor lunged and the beast whipped aside as before. Its deadly riposte was prevented when Heklarr slashed its pallid limb. It lashed out in reply, but then Exor cut it too. The pain didn't seem to slow it, though its wounds bled freely and with a noisome stench. An angry bleat escaped its misshapen lips as it went to fight both assailants at once, before Val'in slipped beneath its guard and rammed his Themian knife into its screaming throat. He pushed the blade deep until it punched through the beast's skull. Still it fought, until Exor and Heklarr punctured its reedy torso.

There was no plan to it, no great strategy any of them could lay claim to. It was a desperate and frenzied thing, only successful because they'd attacked en masse. It was dirty and clumsy, the kind of assault Master Prebian would've chastened them for. But they were alive and the creature was about to be dead. The first true rule of hand-to-hand combat was to survive. In that at least they had achieved their lessons.

As it faded, all three aspirants gave in to aggressive fear and repressed grief, butchering the horror until it was little more than offal. To the observer far removed it would've seemed gratuitous; to the aspirants it was entirely necessary.

There was blood on Heklarr's face. He spat on the thing's visceral remains, beaming triumphantly. Relief flashed through the eyes of the others, but Val'in knew it was far from over.

'On your feet,' he told them. His gaze was locked on the north-facing entrance and the figure standing there.

It wore shaped leather, angular and sharp like blade edges. A segmented metal greave armoured one leg, where the other was bare and showed pale skin. It was the same with the beastmaster's arms, one of which was coiled around with a whip. A scalp lock scraped the dark, lustrous hair back and Val'in realised upon looking into its eyes that this one was female. She was fearsome, her laughter cruel and lilting. He felt pathetic before her gaze, insignificant.

Though he wasn't Nocturne-born, Val'in knew of the dusk-wraiths. Raiders, slavers and soul-thieves, they were the ancestral enemies of the tribes. The Salamanders Chapter knew them by another name: dark eldar.

The beastmaster said something in her language that was equal parts lustful promise and dire curse, before standing aside to admit her abomination.

This one was much bigger than the ur-ghul. It had a broad back with long, ape-like limbs and was swathed in a rough patina of fur. Muscular and brutish, it had the aspect of something lupine and chiropteran in nature. A corded tail that ended in a barb lashed about behind it, displaying the monster's agitation. In a mask of ruddy chitin was a nest of eyes, twinkling like malicious emeralds. Its slitted snout flared as it drank in the aspirants' fear.

Her eyes fluttering, the beastmaster seemed to echo the creature as the slightest expression of sadistic pleasure escaped her lips.

'Back up,' Val'in told the others. He didn't want to run. *They* wanted them to run, and a strong part of him desired to deny them that satisfaction. But to stay was death and, perhaps, in the playing of the dark eldar's game there might yet be a way out for him and his brothers.

'Ska'varron…'

'The way is clear,' the aspirant replied without needing to be asked.

'They will hunt us down out there,' snapped Exor. 'It was you who brought us in here in the first place.'

The fiend was stalking closer, filling up the end of the tunnel with its bulk and flesh-hunger.

'I was wrong,' said Val'in. 'In here we are good as dead already. At least out there we make them work for their slaughter.'

'Good enough for me,' agreed Heklarr and the four surviving aspirants fled, taunted every step by the laughter of the beastmaster.

The storm had almost abated as they broke through the other side of the partially enclosed outcrop and the sun was blazing overhead. Val'in winced as his eyes adjusted to the sudden, harsh light.

It was bleak and grey with a bloody orb pulsing in the fire-red sky above. Lightning cracked, framing the distant mountains as smoke billowed from their calderas in a pall. Vast and expansive, there was no refuge in the Pyre Desert, only death.

Ska'varron was first. Barely a few steps beyond the edge of the tunnel and he crumpled. Exor tried to haul him up but there were some kind of shards embedded in his neck and arm, weakening him. It wasn't mortal but it had made a mess of him and he was venting blood.

'Leave him,' snarled Val'in. 'We have to move!'

The engine throb of vehicles starting up hummed across the dunes. It went against his better instincts but Val'in looked back.

First he noticed the hulking fiend lope from the tunnel and seize upon Ska'varron. He balked when he saw the dozen warriors wearing black segmented armour, carrying serrated falchions and needle-like rifles. The beastmaster was amongst them and where she rode a sickle-bladed anti-gravitic board, the others were mounted on a long, barb-prowed skimmer-raft.

Somehow these creatures had infiltrated Nocturne; they had bypassed its defences for some unknown purpose and were eliminating anything that could betray their presence.

Val'in had been wrong. There was no hope out here on the dunes for them. But he would not be cut down like a dog. He stopped running. So did the others.

We'll stand our ground like Salamanders.

'This isn't how I imagined it to end,' said Exor as the

three aspirants came together. 'I wanted glory, not ignominy.'

'We all did, brother,' muttered Heklarr.

Val'in had nothing. No speech, no strategy. War and death – this was it, just as they'd been told in the lectoriums.

'At least we'll die on our feet.' It was all he could think of to say in the end, and even that sounded cheap.

The chase was done and with it the dark eldar's appetite for sport. The raiders homed in on the aspirants with purpose now, their taunting and cajoling over. Actual blades, not barbs cast by tongues, would do the wounding from here on out.

Val'in wondered briefly if they should slit each other's throats in preference to what the dark eldar were about to do to them, but dismissed the thought as ignoble.

We fight, such as it is.

They lifted their heads as one, defiant.

Exor spat a gobbet of phlegm onto the ground where it sizzled bitterly. 'To hell with this fate, and to hell with them.'

The dark eldar were unmoved.

Val'in, Exor and Heklarr prepared to meet them.

The dense bark of heavy cannon arrested their mordancy.

It struck the skimmer-raft in a whickering tracery, ripping the vehicle apart and tearing up its inconsequential armour plating. Like a vertebrate with its spine broken, the skimmer folded in on itself, engines exploding in a series of fiery blooms. They swept over the crew, devouring the screaming xenos in a burning wave.

Some of the xenos leapt clear, bringing up rifles and shouting obscenities in their raking tongue. Val'in followed their aim as another throaty report roared from the cannon. He saw a muzzle burst in the distance, like lightning on the sun. It spread out from a fat black barrel, a cruciform flare made from spikes of fire. Heat haze and the desert drifts made it hard to see what was coming. It was moving fast, tearing out from a ravine.

Heklarr cried out in retribution for Ska'varron as the fiend disappeared in a welter of gore.

Val'in's eyes narrowed as their saviours closed. He made out the sigil of the drake on the speeder's tail fin as a plume of smoke vented from the launcher under its flat nose.

Pushed along on streamers of fire, the missiles detonated amongst the scattered clusters of dark eldar warriors. The Cerberus launcher was usually employed as a stun weapon to disorientate the enemy. Prebian had had one of the Techmarines modify this one so it fired incendiaries instead. Out in the Pyre there were some large predators that a heavy bolter wouldn't scratch. A missile payload, however...

Bodies were tossed in the air along with thick geysers of ash-sand. Others were thrown by the blasts, landing twisted and broken next to fire-blackened corpses.

VOR'LESSH KNEW IT was over. She cursed her own stupidity for listening to Skethe. The bastard nightfiend had made careful assurance that the young ones were alone. Now she knew he'd betrayed her to draw out the warriors watching over them, bait atop bait. It was enough to make any predator choke. Her small cohort was dead or maimed. It was tempting to linger and taste their suffering, so sweet and fortifying, but self-preservation took over the desire for sadistic pleasure.

She fled, leaving the dying to their fate.

It ended before it had begun. She felt a sudden jolt beneath her as the skyboard achieved loft, and heard the hard bang of the ugly speeder's main armament. Spinning vertiginously without hope of realignment, Vor'lessh ditched in the gritty ash-sand of the mon'keigh desert.

As she lay in the gore of her own vital fluids she understood the reason for Skethe's betrayal. Death so imminent in her future gave her clarity. She'd discovered the nightfiend's fealty towards An'scur, their overlord, to be in question. He served another. A pity she had not learned whom before this unfortunate ending.

Vor'lessh tried to move but her body was shattered, impaled on a piece of capricious shrapnel. She laughed, spitting blood through snarling teeth, as the swarthy young one approached her with knife unsheathed. There was murder in his fire-red eyes – they almost burned. She'd witnessed the same look in her own.

This was a barbarous race, despite their intention to seem otherwise. These hairless apes were debased, cannibals dressed in cloth and nothing more. In the end, when the veil had fallen, they'd eat each other.

She tried to fight down her fear. It wasn't from the knife; She Who Thirsts was calling, promising an eternity of agony and not the pleasant kind.

Cut quickly then, whelp.

She spat a torrent of abuse, hurrying the knife along.

EXOR DIDN'T UNDERSTAND the beastmaster's barbed language but knew when he was being derided.

'Shut up, bitch.' He slit her throat, standing back to watch the life drain away.

'Brother!' Val'in pulled him back, a warning in his tone not to go too far. They'd all suffered but malice for its own sake was the preserve of the dark eldar, not the Salamanders.

The Land Speeder hovered into their collective eyeline, engines screaming. Heklarr had already climbed aboard, priming his carbine as he urged the others to join him.

'Mount up!' snapped Prebian, raking the heavy bolter aside so he could leap from the gunner's seat. The old master proceeded to track down every xenos survivor and execute them in turn.

'They're just scouts,' he said to the aspirants upon his return. 'More will be coming.' He got back into the gunner's seat and turned to Ba'ken. 'Hesiod is closest.'

'That's a ride of several hours.'

'Then we'd best get moving.'

Leaning back in the driver's pit, Ba'ken addressed the aspirants behind him.

'Hold on.'

Val'in gripped the nearest guard rail. Over the next rise he saw a vast cloud of dust. It was closing. There was something else too, something much closer. Despite the heat, a rime of frost crystallised on the speeder's vertical roll bar. It was just like outside the tunnel where T'org had died.

He praised Vulkan's mercy as the speeder tore away, bouncing along the dunes at full acceleration, and left whatever had caused the ice behind them.

'What's happening?' Exor had to scream to be heard above the engine noise.

'No enemy has ever set foot on Nocturnean soil unde-tected,' Prebian replied. 'This ambush precipitates an attack. Raiders do not do this – it is something more.' The hot wind rushing by almost stole the words but all aboard the speeder heard them.

'We have been invaded.'

CHAPTER EIGHT

I
Unbound Flame

NONE PRESENT WOULD ever doubt the sagacity of the Forgefather.

He spoke with Vulkan's wisdom, even shared his name. He was the living embodiment of everything it meant to be a Salamander. No one epitomised the values of the Promethean Creed better than he. Self-sacrifice, endurance, self-reliance, tenacity in the face of impossible odds. His quest for the Nine had taken him, and those who wore the mantle before him, across the galaxy and into the darkest regions of uncharted space. He commanded the will of the Chapter, should he need it. He'd given up brotherhood for a sacred calling. There was none more lauded.

And when he spoke everyone listened.

'It is our nature to mistrust that which is unknown,' he said. 'I don't know our primarch's mind, I merely enact his will. He is with us all. His words guide us, but they are incomplete. We must earn the wisdom intended for us. We Fire-born must decide his meaning.'

Dak'ir hoped this testimony would absolve him. He

had never met Vulkan He'stan, though he had heard of his deeds. He knew he was once a captain of the Fourth Company, but that had been long ago. From what little Dak'ir had garnered from Pyriel, he had only recently returned to the Chapter. His sacred journey had brought him far from Prometheus and Nocturne. It was either an auspicious moment or a terrible omen that he had chosen this time to return. Either way, it was definitely not mere coincidence.

It was Zen'de, the old Master of Recruits, who had first recounted the legend of the Nine. As he looked upon the shadowed outline of the Forgefather, Dak'ir found himself back in the lectorium when he had only just become a Scout.

'In ages past Vulkan hid nine sacred artefacts throughout the galaxy. His prophecies, buried within the Tome of Fire not only reveal where the artefacts reside but what form they will take.'

The words were as hot and clear as ritual fire within Dak'ir's mind.

'Of the Nine, as they are known, only four remain to be found. Three are borne by the Forgefather as his panoply of war, whilst the other recovered relics remain here on Prometheus.'

Zen'de referred to the *Chalice of Fire*, the forge-ship where the Chapter's armour and weapons were crafted, and Vulkan's Eye, a massive orbital defence laser that stood sentinel over the space port and Nocturne itself.

His eyes were the only thing visible of the Forgefather in the gloomy chamber, blazing like the molten core of the mountain, and they rested firmly on Dak'ir as if he had read his thoughts.

It was hard to meet his gaze, but Dak'ir didn't falter.

'I have been on a long journey. It has brought me back here to my brothers.' His sweeping arm encompassed the entire gathering. Some of the older masters nodded reverently at this remark. 'I rejoice!'

He'stan leaned forwards and the many whorls of

scarification were revealed on his face. He had a noble countenance, youthful but wise. Despite his obvious zeal, there was a hint of melancholy to temper his tone.

'But there is despair in my heart too, for I am a warrior apart, alone and without peer. This road I take, it only bears my footprints, but I do not believe it is random, that it would lead me here without reason.'

A hush descended as He'stan let the words sink in.

Elysius was first to speak. 'Noble Forgefather, do you counsel absolution for the accused, then?'

He'stan regarded the Chaplain curiously. 'Absolve him of what, brother? Of deeds he might yet commit or those he never will?'

'A threat to the very existence of our Chapter, of Nocturne, stands in our midst,' Emek cut in. 'We should not ignore that.'

When He'stan's eyes fell upon the Apothecary they were heavy with regret. 'Are you so bent on judgement that it has blinded you, brother?'

Emek went on undeterred. 'If we have an opportunity to avert cataclysm by taking Dak'ir's life we must do it! To risk otherwise is folly. What of the prophecy and the doom of which it speaks?'

'There are many prophecies,' He'stan told him. 'Few are easy to discern or possess clear meaning. Even then the outcome is seldom absolute. If we set aside our bonds of brotherhood we are as good as dead anyway. It is the anvil, brother. We must endure it, however harsh the trial.'

'And if it breaks us?' asked Mulcebar.

He'stan slowly shook his head. 'I see fear around this room and a willingness to believe in superstition over what we can see with our own eyes. We are warriors of the earth, that which is solid and tangible.' He clenched his fist. 'Not ethereal, ephemeral creatures – we are Fire-born, as unchanging as rock.'

Some of the masters shifted uncomfortably at the Forgefather's words. Others were not so easily shamed.

'I fear nothing, brother,' Drakgaard stated flatly. 'It is terrible, what we are countenancing here, but if we have to commit one heinous act to avoid a greater one taking place then we should do it.'

'I'm unconvinced by any of this, but can we really leave our existence to fate?' asked Dac'tyr. 'One life balanced against millions...' He tailed off, shaking his head.

The Master of the Fleet looked like he'd be a supporter. Dak'ir felt a sudden turning in the tide.

Vel'cona certainly advocated his destruction. Only his adherence to ritual and the Promethean Creed had prevented him from doing so already. Both Mulcebar and Drakgaard were of the same mind, pragmatism guiding them towards the safest path.

The swell had risen to Dak'ir's neck, it seemed. Pyriel thought so too; he could sense the resonance of the Epistolary's anxiety in the faint psychic aura that bled off his body. Within Dak'ir the flame stirred. It was just a susurrus of disquiet, a tang of burning on his tongue, the prickling of heat underneath his fingertips, but enough to make the Lexicanum want to close his eyes. In the end he clenched his fists and prayed.

'But does that not depend on how you bias the scales?' asked Elysius. 'If you execute Dak'ir and he is our saviour then you have condemned those very millions you are trying to save.'

Vel'cona scowled. 'Where is your conviction, Chaplain? I don't recognise the warrior before me.'

'Alive and well, Master Librarian, though your compassion is apparently lacking.' He turned on Emek, 'As is any hope you once possessed, Apothecary, or did the *Protean* cripple your spirit as well as your body?'

'Enough!' Tu'Shan's voice reverberated around the chamber as loud and rousing as a war horn, yet he didn't shout. He'stan was not the only one who needed to do little to be heard.

All parties bowed obediently to the Chapter Master.

'We are divided,' Tu'Shan continued after the three

had made gestures of contrition to one another and to him. 'Seeker,' he used an ancient term of address for the Forgefather, 'the winding path of the Nine brings you back to Prometheus. Tell us why.'

He'stan nodded to his Regent.

'There are four I seek,' he said. 'I speak of the Nine, the artefacts of Vulkan.'

All eyes were upon him now, watching silently.

'Here,' he declared, brandishing a gauntlet of incredible artistry emblazoned with the sigil of the drake, 'the Gauntlet of the Forge. I ripped it from the hold of the pirate lord Iath Bloodweaver. And this,' he thrust forth a spear in his clenched fist, 'Vulkan's Spear, whose burning blade never dulls. I wear Kesare's Mantle, the beast slain by our primarch.' He stood and a great scaled cloak unfurled from his back. 'Vulkan's Eye and the *Chalice of Fire* are the last,' he added, 'harboured here on Prometheus.'

A visceral fire ignited in his eyes, an old burning that spoke of the terrors he had seen and the darkness he had overcome.

'Four remain. Only their names are known. It has been this way for millennia. Many Forgefathers, and the Fire-born in their service, have died in search of them.' His eyes became calderas of flame-red as his fervour increased. 'Even the slightest inkling of their form would be progress the likes of which this Chapter has not seen in centuries. I don't believe we will ever know. I believe the path will only be revealed when it is already trodden.'

He'stan glanced at Elysius.

'Faith, brothers. Our belief in Vulkan's wisdom. What if we are on that path?'

'Enlighten us, brother,' said the Chaplain, his voice taking on a sense of awe. Something momentous was building. It would happen in this very chamber at this very time. Dak'ir found his hearts beating, a flicker of nascent fire clasped desperately in his hands.

I want to be born, the flame seemed to whisper – or was it some wilful part of his mind rebelling against its incarceration?

'The Song of Entropy, the Obsidian Chariot and the Engine of Woes are three,' said He'stan. He looked at Tu'Shan. 'You asked me, Regent, why I returned to Prometheus. At first I thought it was to help guide the Chapter through this time of reckoning, but now I am of a different mind. The path has brought me here, just as it brought me to Iath Bloodweaver.'

The Chapter Master's eyes widened. 'You come to us now…'

'Because one of the four is here,' He'stan concluded.

Vel'cona gaped. 'Not possible. I would have seen it.'

'We have all been blind,' said Elysius.

Drakgaard was incredulous. 'An artefact of flesh and blood?'

Every master present knew the name of the fourth of Vulkan's missing gifts. Only Tu'Shan had the courage to speak it.

'The Unbound Flame…'

All eyes went to Dak'ir.

II
Blinded

ARGOS SLAMMED DOWN the corridor like he was inebriated. Such a thing was nigh-on impossible for a Space Marine, the action of specific genetic implants would prevent it, but it was as close as the Master of the Forge could equate to how he felt at that moment.

He was… *aware*, but his movements were not entirely his own. Some external force drove him, an impulse, an infection in his psyche. He'd been unprepared for it and thus it held him fast in its tainting grip. Every step he fought it, the impulse that repeated like a distress beacon in his mind. But he was losing and the compulsion gnawing at him was getting stronger.

He passed servitors and half-human tech-adepts on his way to Vulkan's Eye. No one stopped him or queried his odd behaviour, nor could he signal for aid. No one was coming. The way behind him was shut and Ak'taro would not reach him. His own fight for survival was coming.

The great gated arch to the Vulkan's Eye chamber loomed in front of him.

Argos couldn't remember how he had got there. Lucidity flickered in and out like a damaged lume-strip in need of repair.

I am in need of repair…

It was a beauteous thing, crafted by Salamander artisan-smiths, as regal as it was forbidding. Argos saw none of the arcing filigree or the inscribed illumination around its edge. He failed to notice the image rendered on its plated surface of Vulkan and T'kell, the first Master of the Forge, together. It was a sacred place that the gate protected, a temple as well as a battle station, and Argos was about to defile it.

At a haptic command from his mechadendrites the barrier slid open. Such was the vast size of the gate, it happened slowly and with the grinding of tremendous gears. The rendering of Vulkan and T'kell split down the middle, one on either side as two halves of burnished metal were revealed and drew apart.

Before it had opened fully, Argos strode through the widening crack and stepped into a glorious light issuing from within. This too, he did not perceive or appreciate. It was as if he walked amidst a cloud of static, his perception lost to external interference.

Except, it is coming from within… from inside me…

He fought, but his feet were moving of their own volition like he was suddenly a puppet on another master's invisible strings.

Submitting to the machine, becoming one with the Omnissiah, had its sacrifices. They were payments of the

flesh, in trade for knowledge and understanding. Will
was not one of them. It had ever been the Master of the
Forge's greatest fear – the surrender of self. He might
become hardened to emotion, embrace the coldness of
metal, but he was always himself, the decision a conscious and well-reasoned one. This was nothing short of
abomination.

He was beyond the threshold of the gate now, the great
barrier resealing behind him. Teeth clenched he tried to
override whatever command was compelling him to do
what he knew he must not do. But it was evasive and
time was running short. Muttered litanies between taut
lips were all he could muster: rites of cleansing and
repair, of purging and function.

There were pipes and cabling, the churning of vast
machines. Incense overloaded his senses from braziers
swinging on chains strung across the vaulted ceiling.
Alcoves harboured relics and statues devoted to the primarch, to Masters of the Forge past and present.

This is a holy place and I am about to commit sacrilege.

The impression of the chamber became a blur as
Argos's optical senses betrayed him. Whirring plaintively, his bionic eye zeroed in on the armoured figure
slaved to the seat of the cannon. Not all of the weapon
was visible; much of the defence laser protruded outside
of a plated dome, its massive barrel pointed heaven-
wards.

*And so doth Vulkan watch over us, his eye unblinking
against the darkling night…*

It carried sigils upon its flanks and bore the mark of
master artisan-smiths of an elder age. Vulkan's hand was
evident in it, for it was he who had forged it in millennia past.

The figure joined to it via mental interface uplink did
not stir as Argos approached. He was intent on his duty,
his eternal duty. Servitors and lesser adepts roamed the
area too, consulting cogitators and examining streams of
data, or observing monitors and augur arrays.

Something troubled the seated figure. He was much larger than his cohorts, armoured in red and green plate, the sigil of the cog emblazoned upon his plastron. He was distracted. In his state of half-self, it took Argos a few moments to understand why.

The augurs were not functioning. Nothing was functioning as it should. He saw the interference addling his mind echoed on their fractious screen-slates, heard the white noise mimicked in their audio outputs. Argos tried to isolate that, to help him find where the rogue signal originated from, but he would be too late.

One screen remained. It was the largest and hung above the cannon like a vast piece of obsidian. An image had appeared in the glass-like plane of a huge asteroid, several thousand kilometres away but closing. The zoom adjusted, as if fast-forwarding the rock's trajectory. Sharp crags were revealed across a rough sphere wreathed in celestial gas. Its wake trailed like the tendrils of some ocean-born beast come to the surface in search of prey. And it was black, so black like the end of all things, a void against the void, dark upon dark.

Targeting data streamed across the visual in a series of runes and rapidly changing geometric diagrams. Some of the symbols flashed crimson as the weapon's crosshairs aligned over the sprawling rock's core. Adjustments were fed into the machine, subtly altering the prescribed position of impact.

Argos was close now. He staggered towards the armoured figure who was engrossed in his work, throwing aside a servitor that got in his way. The cyborganic crashed against a wall, leaking blood and fluid.

A message crackled belligerently on Argos's retinal display: INOPERATIVE.

He cut down another, this time a tech-adept who had deliberately tried to impede his progress. It was as if his mind was no longer connected to his body, that he was witnessing the event from outside it and crying out in impotent horror.

'Kor'hadron…' he slurred, and the machine voice was fraught with static and did not sound like his own.

Now the armoured figure turned. His baleful helmet lenses regarded Argos, lit by amber flame.

'Brother?' asked the armoured figure he had called Kor'hadron. His anger faded, usurped by confusion. Another question emitted from the vox-grille on his battle-helm. It was an ornate piece, just like the rest of his armour. Argos recognised it but couldn't quite place it, like a face just beyond his reach, like the salvation from this nightmare he couldn't quite touch.

Kor'hadron's words were lost to the static, rendered down into white noise as the Master of the Forge's lucidity failed again.

It must have been something in his demeanour or perhaps the tiniest mote of a distress signal that Argos managed to transmit before he was utterly lost that alerted the other Forge Master. For when he struck, Kor'hadron moved. Synaptic cables snapped loose with a flash of angry sparks, a hiss of steam whipping them about like agitated vipers, as the blow struck the shoulder.

The power axe dug into Kor'hadron's guard, cleaving it. There was a sudden cry of pain when the edge bit flesh.

Still reeling from the forced synaptic disconnect, Kor'hadron was slow and sluggish; whereas all of Argos's disorientation vanished in the face of a certain, homicidal drive. He hacked again, and cut the other master a glancing blow that severed the cog on his plastron and dented his battle-plate.

A punch to the side of Kor'hadron's head caved in the side of his helmet. One of the retinal lenses burst outwards in shower of super-hardened glass, revealing a bloodied eye wide with disbelief and rage.

He had no time to act on his fury as Argos pummelled him out of the chair and onto the deck nursing a swathe of energised cuts. A vicious backhand blow as he tried to rally smashed Kor'hadron off his feet and sent him skidding prone into the wall. There he stayed, unmoving.

Three more servitors, in an attempt to intervene, died quickly before Argos mounted the command chair to Vulkan's Eye and jacked in.

It rebelled at first, whatever machine-spirit possessed the artefact realising the caustic element in its new symbiotic partner. Whatever was driving Argos, the impulse he continued to fight so hard to locate and neutralise, overwhelmed it.

Data streamed into his compromised cortex. Targeting matrices and alternative firing solutions presented themselves in an unfettered blur of rapid information exchange. He and the cannon were now one. The mental interface was complete.

Subconsciously he adjusted the aim of the cannon, a vast and complex procedure that took seconds as it aligned over an immense distance.

A warning flashed up on the screen. The core of the asteroid was highly combustible. A direct hit would result in a chain reaction that would release an explosion of such force and magnitude as would be felt across several planetary regions. Prognosis for its effect on Prometheus verged on catastrophic.

A vestige of resistance surfaced briefly in Argos's mind. Kor'hadron, his fellow Forge Master, had intended to glance against the asteroid's surface and spin it off its current trajectory. The calculations streamed by, jettisoned in favour of a more direct and entirely destructive approach.

I am about to unleash hell…

It was like shouting inside a vacuum. The body did not react.

His fingers were shaking as he manipulated the controls for a core shot. Argos struggled, the tension manifesting in the ropey vein protruding from his forehead. He opened his mouth, releasing a stream of anguished binaric that echoed off the chamber walls…

…but the foreign presence within him would not be denied.

Firing codes populated the data stream scrolling across Argos's vision, the first act of an apocalyptic script set to the pages of fate over four decades before.

Vulkan's Eye beaded down on its prey.

Power coils embedded in the weapon's superstructure reached optimum levels as the artificial scream of capacitors at full tolerance drowned the chamber in ear-shredding noise. No human could bear it; even unaugmented Space Marines would experience massive auditory discomfort. This was a god-weapon, a slayer of monsters. In Argos's tainted hands it had become the monster.

In a shriek of venting energy the defence laser fired. The whickering beam coursed from the barrel at incredible velocity, impelled by semi-nucleonic fusion. Its retort was felt in the resulting shockwave that rattled instrument panels and caused tracts of cabling to quiver.

The heavens were scoured by the beam's passage, the Black Rock at its terminus impaled as if upon a lance of pure light.

Reaction was instantaneous as a second sun was born briefly in the void-night, its life expectancy cut cruelly short as it went from red dwarf to supernova in a matter of micro-seconds.

Argos perceived none of this – no one did. Only his mind's eye bore witness.

False dawn bathed all of Nocturne below.

Hell was unleashed.

CHAPTER NINE

I
Outgunned

As THE SPEEDER bounced across the Pyre, Val'in struggled to sight down his carbine.

The pilot rode it close to the desert floor, ripping through canyons of ash-sand and skirting over crag-ridged dunes at skin-stretching speed. It left little room for error. One slip, a jutting rock striking the propulsion plate, a miscalculated turn and it was all over.

The slant-eyed jackals chasing them would show no remorse with their knives and barbs if the Salamanders crashed.

Val'in saw them in grainy green luminescence, through the crosshairs of his lasrifle: three arrow-shaped skimmers that mirrored the one they'd broken earlier. Their segmented prows were armed with spiked rams that glistened in the sun. A cohort of warriors, clad in night-black, crowded each vehicle's deckplate, cackling and jeering.

And they were gaining.

Val'in fired and missed.

Exor and Heklarr had similar misfortune.

'It's like shooting Aethonian fire-serpents in the dark, one hand tied behind the back,' grumbled the former.

'Ba'ken, try and keep her steady,' Prebian shouted against the wind. They'd picked up further speed, ramping up the thrusters to maximum in the hope of losing their pursuers. All it had achieved so far was to hinder communication and make aiming more difficult. 'Have you ever tried skewering gnorl-whales in an Acerbian sea swell? This is tougher.'

Fire-serpents, gnorl-whales, all killers; even a pack of leo'nid or colony of scorpiad would be preferable to the hunters that closed on them as the sun painted the sky as blood above them.

It wasn't just the jerky motion of the speeder. The skimmers were protected by some kind of flickering field that masked their true movements and provided unnatural camouflage. Doubtless it was how they'd managed to infiltrate so far into the desert without detection.

Ba'ken kept his attention on the route ahead, switching between that and the vector map scrolling by quickly on the control console. The augur slate displayed a wiremapped version of the upcoming terrain, the contours described in hexagonal delineation so he could predict when to turn or how close they were to a ravine or ridge. The construct was a basic one but highly accurate.

But regardless of Ba'ken's desert-craft, his knowledge of the surroundings and the ear-pulsing acceleration of the speeder, he was not able to shake the dark eldar. He suspected they could catch them at any time but chose to torment their prey first. He dearly wanted to shut down the engines and meet them in honourable battle, but even that would be denied him. Without aid, outnumbered, outgunned, death looked certain. He avowed the savages would not torture him, though. He would not submit to chains or any other snare. Death in battle was the only outcome he would willingly accept.

I am Helfist. I am gladiator.

Even outside the Themian hell-pits, he felt the first

tendrils of transition brush across his psyche.

A whickering burst of dark energy lit up the side of the speeder in Ba'ken's peripheral vision, forcing him to swerve. He rode the move up a ridge of sharp rocks, propulsion plate shrieking loudly as it scraped over them. A second burst had him pull to the left, a jinking transition a Ravenwing would've been proud of, but it threw him into the path of a steeper dune.

'Impact!' he snarled, piling on as much loft as he could muster, as the nose of the speeder dug into the ash-sand and sent squalls of dirt rolling over the hull. Thickening cloud obliterated the view so Ba'ken relied on the augurs to navigate the blacked-out terrain. He managed to bring the nose back up, using the momentum of the thrusters to push them free of the dune. They were trailing fire and smoke. Several warning-runes flashed up on the control console in red.

'I know, I know,' he muttered under his breath.

Behind him, he heard Prebian curse as he and the aspirants struggled to hold on.

There was a brief sensation of weightlessness as they launched into the air like a mortar shell. The sharp parabola brought them down again within seconds, hard ash-sand rushing to meet them with bone-jolting force. They cleared the ridge, Ba'ken driving wild and on instinct at this point, and plunged into a deep canyon threaded with acid streams.

Instantly, the already acrid air became sulphurous. The speeder's green paintwork started to crack and peel away as it was eroded.

An acid-sink, even a shallow one, was no place to touch down. It was one of Nocturne's deadliest hazards.

Ba'ken had brought them here deliberately.

From the back of the speeder, Val'in watched as the first skimmer reached the crest of the ridge and dived down into the ravine. Its driver was unprepared for what lay beyond. The aspirant looked on in grim satisfaction at the sudden screaming, the dark eldar without helmets feeling the acid burn more acutely than the rest. It was unfortunate for them that the skimmer driver was vain enough to eschew any face protection. Still flickering with the action of its alien field generator, the craft turned and then ditched, burying itself nose first into a mire of sulphuric acid.

The stench of burning flesh resolved on the hot breeze, as did the wailing of the dying xenos.

As the speeder levelled out and cleared the ravine Prebian rose from a crouching position, one hand against the roll bar to steady himself. His face was untouched.

'We are born in Vulkan's forge,' he told the perishing eldar. Even the aspirants, not yet having reached their full apotheosis, only carried minor burn scars. 'We know what true fire is.'

It was only a minor victory. The other skimmers were wise to the trap and swerved around the ravine, leaving the dying to their fate.

'They are malicious bastards,' said Heklarr, tracking the pair of craft as they took opposite sides of the high ridge surrounding the drop.

'They will give us the same regard,' Prebian told them. He turned his head. 'Ba'ken, we have gained crucial minutes. Put them to good use.'

'We've taken damage. Our engines might not last out and the propulsion plate…' Ba'ken gestured to the control console awash with urgently flashing crimson.

'Unto the anvil, brother…' Prebian held his shoulder guard. 'Do whatever you can.'

The alien cannons started up again, dark-light raking the air next to the speeder. Ba'ken rode the gauntlet valiantly until a beam caught his tail fin and threw the vehicle off balance. They were careening down a wide plain of ash, shuddering violently. He fought the controls, trying to wrench the speeder back onto some kind of line, when the sky ahead burst suddenly into magnesium white. The flare of light roared across the heavens as a second sun blazed into life above. A blast wave came with it, the epicentre in deep space felt even on the surface. It smashed into the speeder like a god's fist, turning the vehicle over and tossing it desultorily across the ash-sand.

His harness kept Ba'ken seated, strapped into the rolling mass of fire and metal as the others were thrown painfully clear. He felt the wreckage close in around him as the flanks, hull and roof of the speeder bent and caved each time they hit the ground. He gritted his teeth, trusting to his genhanced resilience to save him.

Without knowing why, the words spoken to him earlier by Dak'ir returned amidst a flood of kaleidoscopic sensation.

I wanted to see that you are alive and unscathed, brother... At least part of that is true.

As Ba'ken's world broke down into slowly shattering fragments of light, sound and pain, he realised those words had been accurate.

I am not yet whole. I am not yet inviolable.

The world reached equilibrium again, time flowed as normal. Ba'ken could smell fire. He tasted blood. In several places he felt broken bone. Blackness took him.

Of the aspirants, Val'in was the first to rise. A moment later he realised he'd been hauled to his feet by Master Prebian.

'Take some cover,' he was saying, though he heard it as if through a dense fog that was slow to clear. He stumbled towards a small patch of rock, hunkering down as the dark eldar reaved in.

Prebian got Heklarr and Exor to the rocks before the shooting began. It was pinning fire, intended to herd not to wound or kill. Val'in saw him consider the wreck clutching Ba'ken in its metal embrace, but he couldn't reach it.

His breathing was coming hard and fast, partly a reaction to the sudden adrenaline rush from the crash and partly his genhanced physiology preparing him for imminent battle.

The skimmers slowed to a crawl, put up their guns and

then hovered in front of the beleaguered Salamanders, taunting them.

Val'in leaned on the rocks to steady his aim but then retracted his hand smartly as a rime of frost began to coat it.

'Master...'

Prebian's narrowed gaze roved over the gaps between the raiders and the shimmering dead space either side.

'They're called mandrakes, aspirant.'

He didn't elaborate further but Val'in followed his eye-line and made out the vaguest suggestion of something stirring in the long shadows cast by the skimmers. It flitted from the patches of darkness, itself a concomitant part of the shadow, darting almost imperceptibly between them until alighting in the one thrown off the rocks where the Salamanders were crouching. One shadow became several, like black blade slashes anthropomorphising in front of him.

'My lord...' uttered Exor. Hoarfrost crusted his vambrace and greave.

Prebian had seen it too. 'Withdraw,' he said in a low voice. 'Go to your blades.'

The aspirants drew their Themian hunting knives in a flat scrape of steel.

They were backing up, leaving the cover of the rocks behind them. The dark eldar didn't want to shoot them down like dogs; their mandrakes wanted to gut them like swine instead and wear their steaming entrails as a trophy.

'I cannot see them,' hissed Heklarr, glancing uncertainly in the direction of the waiting skimmers.

'They are close,' whispered Exor.

Val'in mimicked Prebian, staying silent and watchful.

'How can we fight something we can't even– *hurrlcch*!' Heklarr staggered forwards, spitting blood. The Themian knife slipped from his dead fingers, as a gore-slick blade resolved as from the ether jutting out of his back. In front of him, standing in the inky pool of his own shadow was a mandrake.

Lank, white hair cascaded from an alien skull. Its body was lithe, clad in rags and not entirely fixed in this plane of reality. It flickered in and out of resolution like a weak pict signal, syncopated and aglow with eldritch flesh-etched runes.

Prebian struck a second before Val'in. He drew a hollow shriek from the dreaded creature, whereas the aspirant only cleaved air.

'Open fire!' he roared, swinging up his bolter and spraying the area with shells. Poor dead Heklarr jerked and bucked with the explosive weapon impacts but Prebian was taking no chances. 'Watch your shadows,' he said as the two remaining aspirants opened up with their carbines.

Full auto raked the ash-sand, flashing between the darting half-glimpsed figures of the mandrakes as the rest of the dark eldar returned fire.

'Back, back!'

Prebian urged them to retreat but was careful not to let them give in to their instincts and flee. They were not yet Scouts, let alone Space Marines; their human predilections might still hold some sway.

Val'in took a splinter round to the shoulder, dropped his knife, but kept a hold of his carbine. The power cell was almost exhausted. He had another but wouldn't get a chance to reload. In the wake of the intense shooting, it seemed the mandrakes had withdrawn but that still left the pair of skimmers and the warriors aboard.

They were moving quickly now, accuracy sacrificed for rate of fire and speed. The wide ash plain narrowed into a tighter bottleneck of rocks and high ridges. It dipped into an unseen trench that had Val'in scrambling with the sudden shift in terrain. For a few moments they were screened from view by the high lip of the canyon's mouth. The short bout of speed it afforded got them to the middle of the basin before the skimmers came over the rise in single file.

Shadows prowled the smoke-wreathed summits of the

ridges on either side, but they weren't mandrakes. Even in obscured silhouette, Val'in knew sa'hrk when he saw them. He realised that in their haste to outrun the dark eldar they must have overshot the edge of the sa'hrk's feeding grounds and ended up deep in the creatures' territory.

'Master...' he began.

'Stay at the lowest point of the basin,' hissed Prebian. His eyes never left the approaching dark eldar but he knew the other predators were close. 'The ones on the ridge are not alone.'

Smoke lay in swathes at the nadir of the canyon. It had come as if from nowhere, funnelled down from the ash-drifts rolling across the plains above and creating thick and choking smog. The xenos tried to hover above it, but soon even they were forced into the grey morass to hunt for their prey.

'Ba'ken chose this route well,' muttered Prebian.

Val'in agreed but couldn't banish the fear that the sergeant was dead. Even if he'd survived the speeder crash, there was nothing to prevent the mandrakes torturing then executing him.

His morbid thoughts were arrested by a crewman on one of the skimmers shouting something in the barbed dark eldar dialect to his captain. Val'in saw him point to the high ridges. At a barked command a few of the warriors aimed then fired rifles into the smoke-shrouded rocks.

High-pitched impact sounds revealed a cluster of missed attempts, but the prowling shadows scattered. The crewman who'd spotted the roaming sa'hrk was laughing when a lean shape sprang out of the smog and claimed the skimmer's gunner. A half-choked scream echoed out of the smoke before xenos and beast were gone.

That was when the firing started in earnest. The warriors aboard both skiffs unleashed their rifles and assault weapons in a blurring fusillade that tore up the smog.

More shadows pounced from the darkness, one arrested in flight, transfixed by a dark-light beam; another bearing a xenos to the ground. Several of the sa'hrk landed on the skimmers' deckplates. They savaged limbs and torsos before being bought down by combined rifle fire or the jagged blades of falchions.

A steady stream of the creatures were spilling down the ridge-side now, curt, ululating throat-cries organising the pack. But these weren't Ignean nomads or even desert-weary Scout aspirants; they were also predators, albeit of a different stripe.

Weaving through the melee, the mandrakes returned. Val'in saw their outlines blurring in the smog. It was impossible to track them but no sa'hrk could lay tooth or claw on the apparitions and it was beginning to thin their numbers.

'Should we engage or retreat?' Exor sounded conflicted.

'Neither,' Prebian replied. 'Stay together, back to back. Form a circle.'

Val'in faced towards the dark eldar. It was hard to tell whether there were three or thirty mandrakes, they moved so swiftly and seamlessly. Distracted, he almost missed the sa'hrk running at them before a well-placed las-bolt ended it. The desert predators were non-discriminating and had no allegiance to their native-born.

But they were losing.

A deeper throat-cry from an unseen great sa'hrk signalled the retreat. The pack broke off, low against the desert basin, before scurrying back up the canyon walls to find easier prey elsewhere on the Pyre.

The dark eldar had been badly mauled by the ambush, their warriors stripped by over half in a matter of a few blood-drenched minutes. Unscathed, the mandrakes came on at last, having decided to claim the heads of the Salamanders for themselves. Whilst the others were still licking their wounds what appeared to be a female mandrake whickered into existence in front of the survivors. Her eyes were shrouded by her grey-white hair that seemed to ghost about her narrow face. Runes on her coal-black skin shimmered and a veil of frost preceded her, reaching for Val'in and the others.

'No point in running. This is as far as we go,' said Prebian, the hope dying in his voice. 'Stand your ground.' He triggered a burst from his bolter but the mandrake disappeared. By the time the muzzle flare had died she was within striking distance.

Prebian swung at her with his gladius but she bent away from the blow like a serpent, stabbing him through the shoulder with a thrust of her own blade. The Master of Recruits cried out in agony as the evil weapon penetrated his defences.

Val'in and Exor were only beginning to move when a second blade materialised in the mandrake's other hand, intended for Prebian's neck and a quick death. She got as far as the pull back before her head jerked violently and blood vacated the side of her skull in a red plume.

She flickered once in vain, mouth frozen in a silent scream, and crumpled to the ground.

A second shot – Val'in heard it as a *whip* of displaced air – took out the second skimmer's gunner, neutralising the dark-light cannons. By now the xenos had realised the sa'hrk preceded a greater menace and were scouring the ridgeline again. They should've been watching the mouth of the canyon instead as a stampede of sauroch came barrelling into it mewling and baying.

The foremost cattle-beasts were cut down by frantic, panicked shard-fire but the others behind them drove on, trampling the dead and then crashing into the skimmers. Sauroch were bulky, muscular beasts with hard, horned snouts and powerful forelegs. The skimmers were swept aside and broken apart on the beasts' armoured backs, their riders borne down and crushed beneath pounding hooves.

'Climb!' Prebian led the aspirants scrambling up the ridge. Some of the xenos tried to do the same but were either too late or picked off by sniper fire.

By the time the stampede had worn itself out, the skimmers were destroyed and the xenos were dead almost to an eldar. Some of the survivors made it back to the lip of the canyon and fled into the desert to be hunted down by the sa'hrk; the rest languished bloodily on their backs, impaled on wreckage or half-crushed to death.

One of the wounded tried to rise, reaching for his weapon. His head snapped back, venting crimson, before he had even touched the grip.

Val'in followed the shot's trajectory and saw a figure walking brazenly down the ridge-side, a sniper rifle held loosely in his grasp. He was large, broad around the shoulders too, and looked like a drover. With the scarves and boonie hat, it was tough to make out a face. Any detail was concealed. He moved down the mouth of the canyon where he'd started the stampede. Hitching the rifle onto his back where it hung across his left shoulder on a strap, he parted his long drover's coat and unsheathed a gladius.

That was the first thing that gave Val'in pause as he tracked the stranger through the sights of his carbine. The second came when he stooped to slit a dark eldar's throat and there was a brief flash of fire-red that lit the shadows beneath the hat.

Prebian was smiling as he pushed down Val'in's aim.

'Be calm, aspirant. You draw on an ally, though I can scarcely believe what I am seeing for myself.'

'Who is that?' asked Exor in a low voice as Prebian went to meet the stranger.

'I have no idea,' Val'in confessed, 'but I think I know *what* he is.'

They watched Prebian approach the drover, who had finished executing the wounded and stood up to receive him.

'Brother,' said the master in greeting.

The drover nodded, unravelling his scarves and

pulling back his hat to reveal a blade-thin, onyx-black face.

'Master Prebian,' he said.

Prebian laughed. 'Apothecary Fugis, I thought you were dead.'

II
Salvage

'I WAS NEVER dead, just absent,' Fugis said. He'd done all he could to help Ba'ken and was crouching down alongside him. Extracting the wounded sergeant from the wreck was difficult but not impossible. Fortunately, the dark eldar had left Ba'ken for dead. Either that or they'd intended to return for him later when they were done with the others. Fugis had put a sizeable crimp in those plans. Prebian was standing next to him, scouring the horizon line with the magnoculars. Besides Ba'ken, it was about all they'd managed to salvage from the speeder.

The aspirants were crouched down, clustered around a dully flashing beacon Fugis had speared into the ground as soon as they'd got Ba'ken loose.

'I'm sorry I couldn't reach you sooner,' he said, reviewing the injured Salamander's vitals. Without a bio-scanner he had to perform the medical analysis by eye and touch. There were some fractures, even possible breaks in the ossmodula skeleton and some internal bleeds. Ba'ken was unconscious but hadn't drifted into coma. It was a positive sign.

'I found the beacon in a crashed ship, deep in the desert,' he said, apropos of nothing. 'I didn't think the skeletal remains inside would need it.'

Prebian lowered the magnoculars. 'And you left us a message too.'

Fugis was still busying himself with Ba'ken's care.

'Ah, the dagger... Yes, I took that from a straggler

who'd lingered to torture a Themian desert trader. I couldn't save the human but I choked the xenos easily enough. They'd lost some warriors already to the Pyre. I didn't think one more would be missed. There is a hierarchy. Those on the lower rungs are given little regard.'

'How long were you tracking us for?'

'A while. I'd been following the xenos much longer.'

Prebian paused to think. 'Was that explosion something to do with them?'

'I'm not sure. Possibly.'

'I think there are more xenos at large in the remote regions, away from the scrying towers near the cities.'

'I agree,' said Fugis, 'but those we killed were the only ones I've seen. I believe this to be a larger incursion, the dark eldar merely the vanguard of a much greater force.'

Prebian nodded then looked down at him. 'What made you come back? Did you find what you were seeking in the desert?'

Fugis met his gaze. 'My Burning Walk was over. That ship I found didn't just have a beacon inside. There was something else too, a sign.'

'What sign? Could you discern its meaning?'

'I not sure yet, but I must speak with Lord Tu'Shan immediately. It's why I returned.'

Prebian frowned. 'You said you found this sign in a ship. Who did it belong to?'

Fugis smiled. The resulting tightening of his features only made him appear more intimidating.

'You wouldn't believe me if I told you.'

The hard drone of gunship engines getting closer forestalled further questioning as a Thunderhawk responding to the distress beacon came into view. They all knew it well.

It was the *Fire-wyvern*.

Val'in had listened to the exchange between Fugis and Prebian keenly, only trading occasional glances with Exor who was keeping a watch.

'Who is he?' Exor asked.

Val'in shook his head. 'An Apothecary that used to be part of Third, I think. I've heard his name mentioned before and he was on Scoria but that's all I know.'

'What did he mean when he said he'd found "a sign"?'

Gunship engines pummelled the breeze, creating hot vortices in their downdrafts. Both aspirants looked up as the shadow of the Thunderhawk eclipsed them. Landing stanchions began to extend as the embarkation ramp slowly opened.

'I know as much as you, brother,' said Val'in.

At the top of the ramp there stood a Salamander in artificered armour. Fugis recognised the suit and the warrior who wore it, even if the warrior did not recognise him.

He was an Inferno Guard, the broken command squad of Adrax Agatone and Third Company. The snarling orange drake head blazed proudly on his pauldron and a fanged battle-helm rested in the crook of his arm.

'You are a welcome sight, Brother Malicant.'

The Salamander bowed humbly.

'I am glad we found you when we did. Come aboard, my master, there is much–' He paused to look intently at the drover. He frowned, disbelieving and then…

'Kesare's breath. Fugis, is that you?'

Fugis nodded. He too had once been part of the Inferno Guard. It seemed so very long ago now.

Malicant came down the ramp and embraced him warmly. He clapped his hands on the Apothecary's shoulders.

'By the primarch, we all thought you were dead!'

'A common mistake, it seems.' He risked a wry glance at Prebian.

The Master of Recruits stepped forwards. 'We have wounded and must make for Prometheus at once.'

Malicant's face fell.

'What's wrong, brother?' asked Prebian.

'Prometheus has been badly damaged. It might not be possible to make dock.'

'An attack? So soon?' He exchanged a worried expression with Fugis, who remained stern.

Malicant was shaking his head. 'No, master. An explosion in deep space, but communication is down and details are slow to appear.'

The magnesium flare, Prebian realised. To be felt so egregiously on the planet surface, the magnitude of whatever combustion event preceded it must have been immense.

'Where is Dak'ir?' asked Fugis, his tone cutting.

'On Prometheus, brother. The Pantheon Council meets to decide his fate.'

'They must be roused at once.' He leaned in close, fire burning in his eyes. 'I cannot express how important it is that I reach Prometheus and Hazon Dak'ir. Nocturne's fate might well depend on it.'

SKETHE WAS ALONE when he returned to the canyon. He did so via the deepening shadows and the patches of darkness between the grey crags. Travelling as a whisper across the sand plain, he took great cares not to be spotted by the departing vessel. It was an ugly thing, flat-edged and clumsy-looking. The ship roared away on dirty jets, leaving the nightfiend to his task.

It had been close. The stampede was not entirely without cunning for a mon'keigh but a true servant of the old city was wiser. Skethe had survived where all else had perished. The ravening beasts of the desert killed the craven. It meant he wouldn't have to at least, and could delight in the psychic echoes of their suffering before She Who Thirsts claimed them.

The morsel was enough to stave off the soul-hunger for a while; certainly, it would sustain him until he reached his ship. The stripped down Razorwing was waiting nearby, cloaked with nightfields and other visual bafflers so as to defy detection. He had never intended to join the ground assault – let the genhanced mon'keigh and their cohorts die in that meatgrinder. Skethe wanted heads, lots

of them. He liked flesh-trophies, keeping the great many
he'd procured over the ages in a secret vault only he knew
how to locate that existed between dimensions. Tongues,
fingers, he had even collected voices and heartbeats across
the millennia of his existence. The damaged space port
carried an infirmary of sorts. There would be a great many
wounded in its halls very soon, all ripe for the edge of his
executioner's blade. He would do it to honour Kheradru-
akh, the great Decapitator. Perhaps one day, Skethe would
add the skull of his patron to his collection too.

Such vainglorious thoughts evaporated when he found
what he was looking for.

'Siliathe…' he purred in a susurrus that could just as
easily be mistaken for the turning of the breeze.

The dying woman turned. She'd blended into the shadows of a rocky overhang but Skethe perceived her easily
enough.

'Are you dying, sister?' he asked, supping up her pain
like it was nectar.

Siliathe's lips moved but she couldn't speak. She was
clinging to her soul with slipping fingers, but didn't plead
or beg. As a mandrake, she would have shown an equal
measure of pitiless disdain should their roles have been
reversed.

'She will come soon,' he promised. 'Your suffering will
be long, however, but I cannot stay to enjoy it. I must only
ask you this – does he know whom I serve?'

Siliathe's eyes widened but her feigned shock was far
from convincing even in her death throes.

'Do not lie,' he warned her. 'We three are coven, and
share our secrets.' The sigils carved into the flesh of
his half-naked body pulsed hungrily as they drank in
Siliathe's pain. 'Syarrth is dead, dwelling in eternal soul-
torment, so I cannot ask her. Tell me now: does he know
whom I serve?'

Slowly, almost imperceptibly, Siliathe shook her head.

Skethe smiled but there was nothing benign about the
gesture.

'Thank you, sister,' he said. 'I believe you.' The night-fiend leaned in close to the dying mandrake. 'And now a confession from me. I lied.' He placed his hand upon her chest. 'I will watch you die and take from you all that's left to give...'

Siliathe tried to breathe but she was already dead, her soul tumbling into an abyss of everlasting agony.

'Your final breath,' Skethe whispered, clenching his fist as if he held this last kernel of life force in his hand and devouring it. 'Delicious...'

He slid away like smoke on the wind, a half-remembered shadow, and made for his ship.

CHAPTER TEN

I
Absolution

A BOUT OF agitated conjecture became a clamour amongst
the gathering as they struggled to comprehend the magnitude of what the Forgefather was suggesting.

Tu'Shan held his hand aloft to restore calm.

'The Unbound Flame in a vessel of flesh and blood?
Are you certain of this?' he asked He'stan.

'Nothing is certain, but it is my belief.'

Vel'cona remained unconvinced. 'How can this be?
Vulkan hid his gifts almost ten thousand years ago, yet
Dak'ir has not even earned a single platinum stud.'

'Could the primarch have begun a confluence of events
that would reach their terminus at this point?' suggested
Dac'tyr. 'Could he have foreseen this, somehow known
a vessel for the Unbound Flame would emerge in this
time, at this hour of crisis?'

'It is ten thousand years ago, brother-captain,' said
Vel'cona. 'How can we possibly know? At best it is myth,
at worst it is maliciously false.'

'When we entered the *Archimedes Rex* and found that
casket with Isstvan's origination stamp, I thought we

had discovered something monumental.' Pyriel looked humble as he spoke, as if he realised he was part of something unfolding that was so much greater than him or any one of them. 'I thought we had found Vulkan, and that he was not dead but merely… *absent*. I do not know if Dak'ir is somehow the personification of the Unbound Flame but I believe he is a herald.'

'One of doom and destruction,' snapped Vel'cona, annoyed at his protégé. 'I knew you were an optimist, Pyriel, but I did not think you credulous. There are countless prophecies that speak of our father's return but we cannot trust in any of them to come to pass. We must look to ourselves, not fate ten thousand years old, for our survival. Vulkan is gone. Dak'ir is not the Unbound Flame, nor is he some kind of messianic figure, a deific artefact made flesh. He is a dangerous psyker, his strength unprecedented, but it is strength that he cannot marshal. I have witnessed it for myself and seen the world drowned in fire and blood.' He jabbed a gauntleted finger at Pyriel, 'So have you, Epistolary.'

Elysius raised his hands for calm. 'None of us here can see all ends, brother,' he said in a conciliatory tone. 'What of our bonds as Salamanders, our fealty to Prometheus?'

Vel'cona was quick to retort. 'Have you forgotten our pledge to the tribes of Nocturne, our sworn duty to protect the weak from any threat?' He gestured to Dak'ir. 'One stands before you, Elysius. If an unexploded bomb is in your midst, you do not sit back and hope it doesn't go off. You do something about it.'

'Dak'ir is not some piece of metal without breath or blood.' The Chaplain appealed to his Chapter Master.

Tu'Shan sighed deeply. The matter was not a simple one. He heard all testimonies, confronted with the incredible possibility that what stood before him in chains was no mere Salamander but an artefact clad in skin and wrought of bone, a legacy of his primarch.

'Answer me this,' he said. 'Who am I to trust? You are both my loyal servants and paragons of this Chapter, one who counsels with the mind, the other with the spirit. Even our Lord He'stan can give no clear answer.' The Forgefather had retaken his seat and nodded at this acknowledgement.

They had reached an impasse and were teetering at the cusp of an impossible decision that divided the masters of the Chapter down the middle as keenly as any blade.

In the end, resolution came from an unlikely source.

'Lords…' A stentorian voice, built to bellow not whisper, resonated around the chamber.

Praetor, who in his role as enforcer had remained silent throughout the proceedings, got to his feet. The veteran sergeant of the Firedrakes dropped to one knee, his head bowed.

Tu'Shan raised him with a gesture.

'Speak, Herculon.' He used Praetor's first name. Such informality was beyond the veteran sergeant of the Firedrakes, his temperament as stern and rigid as his appearance.

'Word from the outer defences breaches the sanctity of this chamber,' he said.

'It must be of dire import to interrupt a ruling of the Pantheon Council,' Vel'cona interjected, making his displeasure obvious to all.

Praetor looked askance at the Master Librarian.

'It is. A massive asteroid on a collision course with the planet has been destroyed in close proximity to Nocturne.'

'So the danger has been averted? I fail to see the threat here,' said Tu'Shan, but knew that no Fire-born would ever break the sacred vow of isolation imposed during a conclave of the Pantheon Council without reason.

'The asteroid was fashioned of a volatile core. The resulting explosion has inflicted tremendous destruction upon the space port. We are too deep and insulated to feel its aftershock.' Praetor's face darkened further, weary with loss for the deaths he had witnessed in recent times. 'Many are dying.'

Dismayed at this news, Dac'tyr asked, 'How was this even possible? Our deep space augurs would've detected the mass long before it could threaten us.'

'I do not know, Fourth Captain,' Praetor answered.

'What of Kor'hadron?' asked Elysius, 'and Vulkan's Eye? This rock should be dust floating in the void.'

'The Master of the Forge Secundus has so far been unreachable, a communication interrupt at Hangar Seven.' Praetor had heard this information only seconds ago and was being updated by a broken uplink to Prometheus's comm-feed. So far, details were vague but something had clearly gone wrong.

'Hangar Seven,' said Agatone, 'what do we have docked there?'

'Two squadrons of gunships in for refit and repair,' said Dac'tyr, 'and the *Archimedes Rex*.'

Pyriel spoke up. The tension in his voice betrayed him. 'The Adeptus Mechanicus forge-ship?'

'What of it?' asked Dac'tyr.

Agatone answered for the Epistolary. 'It's the self-same ship a strike-team from Third entered over four years ago. It led us to the prophecy.'

A resonant voice stole the attention of the chamber.

'It is the Black Rock, this doom that sunders Prometheus. We have seen it before, on the ash world of Scoria. It is a harbinger of death and blood, beginning the Time of Fire when a sword will be unsheathed and wreak conflagration on the world.'

Dak'ir only realised it was he that had spoken when the eyes of the entire congregation were upon him. Even Pyriel appeared disturbed by his pronouncement.

Vel'cona was quick to seize upon the moment. 'He is a prophet of doom to us. Condemned by his own words!'

'The apocalypse weapon, the attack,' said Pyriel in an urgent tone, 'it is happening *now*. This is merely the beginning. All of this,' he gestured widely with his arms to encompass the entire chamber, 'is but a distraction. Nihilan comes and he brings ships and a burning lance of light that will split Nocturne and this Chapter in half! A year has passed and our vigilance has ebbed. Our ships are back in their docks, our eye has wavered from the darkness around us, but it is here now – the Dragon Warriors are here. Now.'

Tu'Shan's face was ridged with displeasure. He gestured to Praetor.

'Show me my enemy, brother-sergeant,' he said in a low growl.

Praetor saluted to his Regent then took a holo-picting device slaved to Prometheus's augurs. With its destruction, the Black Rock's magnetic field was dissipating and the interference that had dogged the station's viewing arrays was alleviated. A grainy image fed from the small device in a reverse triangle of green light.

'East quadrant,' Tu'Shan ordered. An aspect of Prometheus that faced in the direction where the asteroid had come from resolved on the display.

A vast field of floating debris was revealed. Behind that there came a flurry of small vessels, each no larger than a frigate in size. The fleet was eclectic, consisting of both xenos and renegade ships.

Dac'tyr leaned forwards to inspect the image closer.

'War spheres and dark eldar escorts. There are some smaller gunships and fighters of non-specific design too.'

'Mercenaries,' Mulcebar spat with distaste.

'A vanguard,' said Tu'Shan.

'We are beyond these proceedings now,' Elysius told them all, 'and must look to the defence of Nocturne. It would appear we have already lost Vulkan's Eye, what more are we willing to sacrifice?'

'Our Brother-Chaplain is right,' said He'stan. 'Nothing we do here can alter fate now. It has begun. Our backs are to the anvil, brothers. Vulkan's judgement falls on us all.'

Another ship, coming in the wake of the smaller vessels, appeared on the holo-image. It was a vast, ugly thing; a bastardised Space Marine strike cruiser debased by the attention of traitors. A small flotilla of escorts surrounded it. The jutting prow lance of the capital ship was like nothing the Chapter Master had ever seen. This then was the apocalypse weapon Pyriel had warned them about.

'That vessel is the *Hell-stalker*,' said Agatone. 'Nihilan's flagship.'

'And it bears the seismic cannon as its main armament,' added Elysius. 'A scaled up version of the one we saw on Scoria.'

'We knew this moment would come,' said Pyriel, 'and have to stop looking for potential enemies within when faced with certain ones without.' His pleading gaze was for Vel'cona, who he hoped would understand.

Tu'Shan's face was a mask of barely restrained anger.

'Council is ended,' he announced flatly. 'All efforts must be made to help our beleaguered brothers. Marshal any and all forces you have at your disposal.'

All present nodded.

'Lord Dac'tyr...' he began.

'I have the *Firelord*, *Vulkan's Wrath* and *Flamewrought* void-anchored and ready to engage.'

Tu'Shan nodded approvingly. 'Your quiet wisdom humbles us all, brother-captain. Deploy your fleet and any others still docked that can be made void-ready. You can be certain our enemy means to press his fleet immediately within our defensive cordon. Since Vulkan's Eye and much of our orbital defences are no longer functioning we will have to counter it ship-to-ship.'

Dac'tyr made a curt salute and departed swiftly.

'All reserve and battle companies are to embark gunships and make for the surface at once. Even on his best day, Captain Dac'tyr cannot contain a fleet of that size. Landers will likely deploy in the deserts, which will be to their cost, but rest assured the traitors and their sellswords will be approaching our Sanctuary Cities en masse. Fortification of any land-bound settlements is our priority here,' Tu'Shan ordered. He turned, 'Praetor...'

'Ours is the void-war, my lord.'

'Indeed.'

Praetor slammed a fist to his plastron and went to summon the rest of the Firedrakes, accompanied by the masked guardians, as the other captains also made to depart.

He'stan was already gone, intent on his own mission.

Only five others remained with the Chapter Master.

One of them was Dak'ir.

'Brother, I do this because I know it is right.' Tu'Shan was looking at Vel'cona.

The Master Librarian was stern-faced. 'You are sparing him.'

Tu'Shan nodded. 'We need every bolter and blade,' he said, and turned to Dak'ir.

The refractor field shimmered and then collapsed at the Regent's silent command.

Pyriel stepped forwards to remove his nullifying bonds.

Emek was perturbed enough to speak out. 'But, my liege…'

Tu'Shan's glare in the Apothecary's direction was scathing. 'Concern yourself with the wounded, brother. There will be many already in need of aid. My decision is made, for good or ill.'

Emek gave no further dissent and bowed, leaving for the Apothecarion. Tu'Shan turned to Pyriel.

'Get him into his armour,' he said with a half-glance at Dak'ir.

'Take him to the Reclusiam, we'll do it there. It's too far to the armorium,' said Elysius. 'Besides, our wayward brother will be in need of some benediction.'

Tu'Shan nodded his approval.

'The time for debate is over,' he said. 'War calls and every Fire-born son of Nocturne must answer. We face annihilation and I will not submit to that fate without a fight.'

* * *

II
Unleashed

EMEK DID NOT reach the Apothecarion easily. It was carnage outside the confines of the chamber. A mood of barely shackled panic pervaded the space port as those aboard struggled to comprehend what had happened and how they were going to contain it.

Fires had broken out in several areas and entire sections were sealed off by emergency bulkheads to prevent atmospheric depressurisation. Many sectors were already registered as being breached. Secondary explosions, promethium reserves cooking off after the initial impact or as a result of slow structural degeneration, shook the station's chambers and corridors.

The hangars themselves had been the worst hit. Praise Dac'tyr for his foresight that there were any vessels left to launch. Though information was flowing painfully slowly around the stricken space port, it was clear that the great asteroid known as the Black Rock had broken apart explosively, unleashing a meteor storm upon Prometheus. Some of the slower-moving chunks, trapped in Nocturne's gravity well, had yet to impact. Others were hitting the station constantly in a barrage.

Emek was slammed against the wall as a particularly violent tremor hit and cursed his injuries for how they weakened him. They had made him into a ghost, confined him to his infirmary and the hollow halls of Prometheus. He was glad of it. To think of his brothers' pity made him sick. He had been a warrior once, on course for a glorious future. All of that had ended in ignominy the moment the psychic fire had half-destroyed him aboard the *Protean*.

Now all he could do was labour to repair others, spare them the same fate.

None should suffer like this, he thought bitterly, pulling himself back up.

These corridors were seldom trodden and the first serfs

he met were several levels up from the catacombs. With curt commands he directed them to the Apothecarion, gave instruction as to what to do with the injured and began to formulate a triage system in advance of his arrival to cope with the influx of wounded. Scores might already be awaiting him upon his return. If this was indeed an attack, there would be many more.

Emek entered the Apothecarion through a side chamber. A long corridor that reeked of counterseptic led to a smaller room that he used as his solitorium. He kept this place away from the death and suffering. Dismissing his brander-priest many months ago, he used the spartan chamber as a refuge to think, to train, to mourn.

There was a wooden statue, a bare-featured simulacrum of a man, in one corner of the gloomy solitorium, on which Emek hung his armour. He removed it himself, painfully, piece by piece. When he was done, the statue was armoured and he was naked before a tall slate of polished obsidian. He knew it was tantamount to a form of masochism, torturing himself with the mirror reflection of his ravaged body, but he couldn't help it.

A figure Emek did not recognise glared back. He was burned and scarred, this grotesque doppelganger. His entire left side was torn up and twisted. Knots of flesh and rough-edged skin described the years of pain he had endured but could not begin to articulate his suffering. Loss of self, loss of what it was to be a Salamander, a Space Marine, was the highest price Emek had paid aboard the *Protean*. An hour did not pass when he wasn't filled with regret about that mission. Talons of psychic lightning had left their indelible mark. He was half a warrior, so full of bitterness he almost choked on his own bile.

A face, once strong and youthful, was drawn and blasted. Having refused a bionic replacement, Emek's left eye was ruined. His mouth, now given only to the occasional sardonic smile, was pulled down at one corner as if a heavy weight attached to his lower lip was pulling and disfiguring it. His scalp, where once he'd worn three chevrons of flame-red hair, was reduced to a grubby patch of half stripes.

He was in pain, but a pain that went far deeper than any physical scar.

Emek also used the chamber as a gymnasium. Since sustaining the injuries aboard the *Protean*, he no longer trained with the others. His physical disfiguring meant he couldn't match the pace of his battle-brothers anyway. Various pieces of equipment were stowed away on racks at the back of the room. He hefted a light weight; it was shaped like an anvil and forged from a dark metal. The effort to lift it was excruciating. It felt like the sinews in his left arm were about to snap. Letting the weight *clang* loudly to the floor, he sank down into a crouch and closed his eyes.

'What am I doing?' he whispered to the shadows. There were those in pain who needed him. Now was not the time for indulgent self-pity. He remonstrated internally – there was *never* a time for that. He rose to his feet, pushing on the discarded weight for support.

Emek was dressing in a light robe and cowl when he heard a muted cry outside the sanctum. Averting his gaze from the aberration in the mirrored obsidian, drawing a veil of black cloth over it, he left the chamber and stepped into the corridor beyond. Passing through a shorter corridor, its walls harsh and white, he reached the main gate.

What greeted him when he finally stepped through the doors to the Apothecarion proper, into its wards and infirmaries, was a sea of blood and screaming.

Though principally a dock, Prometheus was so much more than that. Conservative when compared to the vast stations of Ultramar or Baal, it was still many levels deep and could comfortably make harbour for the entire Salamanders fleet. It also possessed secret places, ancient halls and crypts where the Firedrakes performed clandestine rituals and the masters met in private deliberation.

It had an entire barracks for the First Company, together with an extensive armoury.

The Apothecarion was at the centre of all this, located on a surface level to make conveyance to the facility easy for those coming from the planet itself. It had its own docking pad, which was small but amply appointed for Thunderhawks and vessels of similar size. So far it was empty, but it wouldn't stay that way for long.

It was just as well – there were many, mainly deck crew from Hangar Seven, that needed the Apothecary's attention.

Cadorian, a medicae and one of Emek's practitioners, approached him.

'Praise to Vulkan you're back,' he said, wiping a bloody hand across a sweating brow. It smeared a ruddy line, like war paint, across his weathered features. The man had a rude, irreverent disposition that suited the Apothecary. Better still, he could be left to his labours without continual instruction.

'We are already stretched but injured are still arriving from across the space port,' he concluded. Emek hobbled past him, picking his way through the forlorn wounded languishing in groups around the Apothecarion floor. Cadorian kept pace, shadowing Emek at his shoulder. The man was markedly shorter but betrayed no sense of intimidation towards the Space Marine. Emek liked that about him too. 'It's mainly burns, occasional lacerations and contusions from debris, some trauma.'

'There will be more,' Emek growled. 'Activate the rest of the medi-servitors and requisition any man that comes in here with experience in field surgery. Secure the gene-banks–'

'Already done. All is well.'

Emek glared at him. He pulled back his cowl with an agitated hiss. A scowling, scarred visage was revealed behind it.

'And clear this floor. Non-critically injured are to

return to their posts, the rest are to be warded. Anyone who cannot assist is to leave.'

He was headed for the isolation chambers, beyond the throng of the bleeding and dying. Emek was inured to their suffering, too preoccupied with his own.

The practitioner held back and Emek assumed he'd gone to his duties before he spoke up again, 'Apothecary...'

'What is it now, Cadorian?'

'That way has taken some damage. It's why we are so overrun.'

Now that he looked ahead, focused for the first time since re-entering the Apothecarion on his surroundings rather than Dak'ir's exoneration and his own bitterness, Emek saw that part of the complex was damaged. Several systems were red-lining, malfunction icons flashing persistently on a control slate set into the wall. He was standing before an adamantium door that stubbornly refused to open.

Cadorian was a few paces behind him.

'I thought it prudent to seal it.'

'Unseal it,' Emek snapped. 'There is someone in there. Do it now!'

Cadorian worked at the control slate, releasing the locks without question.

The door slid open halfway and jammed. The portal was wide enough, though, so Emek stepped through.

'I bio-scanned the entire section,' Cadorian was saying. He'd been deep in the gene-banks where the Chapter's legacy was secured when Emek had left for the council. 'It came back with no vitals.'

'Then one of two things have occurred,' muttered the Apothecary, snarling as he battered his way through the wrecked interior. Part of the ceiling had caved in and fires were still rampaging in the deeper areas. Armaglas carpeted the floor and various instruments and machinery lay smashed and destroyed. Debris was everywhere, barely visible through gouts of venting steam and clouds of smoke.

'He's either dead...' Emek bludgeoned his way to the

observation chamber, using a chainsword to cut through a fallen beam he couldn't vault. He unshrouded the viewing portal. A flickering light above revealed the isolation cell in stuttering white illumination. It was empty.

'Or he's escaped.'

IT DID NOT take long to call the Firedrakes to war. They came from their barrack chambers, solitoriums and shrine-holds quickly and efficiently.

Praetor had already seen to the sealing of the Hall of the Firedrakes where many of the Chapter's most hallowed relics were kept safe. Only two others had the authority to unseal it, the Reclusiarch and the Regent.

By the time they had reached the vicinity of the armorium, close to a hundred warriors of the vaunted First Company marched in lockstep with the veteran sergeant.

Word had been sent ahead. A veritable army of artificers and armourers were ready and waiting to festoon their lords in the trappings of war. A void-war meant only one attire was suitable and it was the sole honour of the Firedrakes to wear it.

They entered in robes or power armour and left as Terminators clad in Tactical Dreadnought Armour.

Rites and blessings were observed, battle markings made in flesh by the brander-priests. Before the end Praetor dismissed the human flock, his deep voice carrying throughout the massive armorium.

This last part would be conducted by them and them alone. It was only for the Firedrakes to know.

With his chosen warriors arrayed before him, their venerable green battle-plate gleaming, Praetor turned to Vo'kar.

'Ignite the flame...' he uttered.

Vo'kar nodded solemnly, swinging his heavy weapon around and releasing a burst of superheated promethium. A cradle in the centre of the room about which the Firedrakes had gathered roared into life. The fire clasped within its stone curves was vibrant and raging. It rose, becoming a mighty column that thrust into the air and almost touched the ceiling.

'First squad step forwards and receive the ritual fire.' At Praetor's order the warriors who had been to the Volgorrah Reef to rescue Chaplain Elysius came forth.

'Vulkan's fire beats in my breast…'

'With it I shall smite the foes of the Emperor,' they concluded the veteran sergeant's invocation together. They each then thrust their power fists into the blaze. Those without, the ones bearing thunder hammers and storm shields, let the tips of their gauntleted fingers blacken in the flame instead. It was a baptism of war, a transition into the warrior-state.

One by one the squads stepped forwards and the litany was repeated. It was done methodically, exacting and by rote until all of the Firedrakes were scorched.

'We are, all of us, born in fire,' Praetor told them, 'so do we wage war with it clenched in our mailed fists.'

'Unto the anvil!' the Terminators bellowed.

'An enemy has come to us,' Praetor said with the echoes of thunderous affirmation still fading around him. 'He is bent upon the destruction of our world. Many have died already in service to Vulkan. We remember them all.' He gestured to Persephion, a survivor of grim wounding at the hands of the dark eldar, who brandished his vambrace. Upon it, as with every Firedrake who mustered in the armorium, were inscribed the names of every fallen hero of the First.

Beginning with Persephion a name was uttered aloud, so that each of this vaunted brotherhood would be remembered before battle.

A great, long list of honour was recounted, each name given with zeal and fiery bombast. As was ritual, Praetor went last but spoke the final warrior's name with quiet melancholy.

'Zek Tsu'gan… Let him return to the mountain and the Circle of Fire be remade.'

CHAPTER ELEVEN

I
Old Friends

A PUNCH TO the jaw jolted Tsu'gan awake. He tasted blood in his mouth and spat it out before opening his eyes.

At first he thought he'd returned to Ramlek's workshop. The air was rank with the heady stink of copper and he'd been restrained on some kind of slab again. Something was different though. He was armoured this time. Tsu'gan could feel the heft of it, clad to every inch of his body except for his face. He wore no helmet, nor rebreather or faceplate, but there was something attached to his cheek. It sank tiny sub-dermal needles into his flesh and covered a quarter of his skull. He felt a throbbing there and the impact points of the needles itched.

It was cold, not a natural chill from standing outside but something more invasive. He realised it was void-frost and knew then that he was standing in the hold of a ship. Not the *Hell-stalker*. It was too small for that. Felt like a gunship.

Darkness surrounded him. It was thick and black, a shroud his eyes couldn't penetrate. He knew he wasn't

alone and not just from the violence to his face. There
were others, several of them ranked up and ready for battle.

Another punch sent his ears ringing.

'You're with me now,' snarled a familiar voice. Not a
renegade, though. Tsu'gan couldn't place it at first. He
smelled oil and solder, old metal and filing wire.

'Let me have a piece of him…' snapped a second voice.
It was greasy, insidious, affected by mild hysteria. He
sensed this one did not just mean him harm but wanted
to kill him. Tsu'gan knew the voice but he was having
difficulty forming his thoughts and the name wouldn't
come.

'*Curb your ire,*' uttered a third. The cadence was rasping
and seemed farther away than the rest, yet at the same
time much closer. '*Open your eyes, Tsu'gan.*'

He'd thought they were already open. The dark veil
lifted and he was standing in a crowded troop hold.
Dingy red light bled from flickering strip lumes overhead. A steady judder rattled the inner walls and his
view directly ahead was of the back of another warrior's
battle-helm. In the wretched light it was hard to tell the
warrior's allegiance.

'You are to be honoured,' the snarling voice told him.

'Hurt him again,' said the insidious one.

That sense of familiarity again. Tsu'gan wanted to turn
but his neck was rigid. His entire body was stiff as if
petrified into stone. He struggled. Veins bunched in his
neck, teeth clenched but achieved nothing. He managed
to work his lips. A croak escaped.

'Where… am I?'

'Amongst old friends,' mocked the snarling voice.

Tsu'gan wasn't attached to a torture slab; he was
cinched into a battered grav-harness. He saw motifs on
his armour, kill-markings he wasn't familiar with. Heavy
rivets bonded together some of the plates, which were
beaten up and re-sealed many times over.

This wasn't his old Salamander armour, but nor were

they the trappings of the renegades.

'What have you done to me?'

The snarling bastard was laughing.

A swell of anger possessed him and with a roar Tsu'gan threw off the grav-harness. It was old and decrepit, the metal yielding easily to his strength.

'I am no prisoner!' he bellowed, ripping the gladius from its sheath and ramming it deep into the snarling one's throat. Blood foamed the dying Space Marine's vox-grille as he scrabbled at his murderer with gauntleted fingers.

Tsu'gan tore the blade free, slashing it across the insidious one's throat as he tried to release his harness. There was panic in his eyes, weakness. Deep red fluid sprayed from the wound, showering the warrior's neutral armour.

Battered by the pitch and yaw of the descending gunship, Tsu'gan dragged his way through the troop hold to the vessel's cockpit. Behind him, he heard the others as they released their harnesses.

It was too late for them. Tsu'gan had already opened the door. Sweeping up a discarded bolter he raked the cockpit, ventilating the crew. Only the pilot hung on, his body half-draped across the controls as he attempted to make an emergency landing.

'I am death…' Tsu'gan plunged the gladius into the top of the pilot's skull and left it there. Then he turned the bolter around and used its heavy stock to smash the control console, pitching the gunship into a fatal dive.

The others from the troop hold had just breached the cockpit's threshold when he turned.

'None survive,' he declared, raising up the bolter as he made his last stand.

Their faces were formed of nondescript battle-helms without insignia or Chapter marking. All of them were laughing as the glacis plate burst and fire swept in.

'What is this?' Tsu'gan lowered the gun…

…and blinked.

He was still in the grav-harness.

'*The last vestiges of your will,*' the rasping voice told him. '*Your mind is strong, preconditioned to resist outside influence–*'

'Release me!'

'*I cannot. You are an integral part of my plan.*'

Nihilan… Tsu'gan's fists clenched despite the paralysis affecting his body. Something had been done to him; something added that was interfering with his neutral pathways, sub-diverting them to another's control.

'When will you learn, sorcerer, that all the methods of coercion at your disposal cannot compel me to do your bidding?'

'*What is your mind telling you to do?*'

'To kill every one of the whoreson-dogs on this gunship.'

'*And yet…*'

Tsu'gan's wrath was impotent, confined to a body that could not vent it. It was furious in his eyes and the tension in his jaw but the arcane device attached to his face kept him otherwise quiescent.

'*Nurture that hatred, all of your rage, you will need it to survive what's to come.*'

'I will find you, Nihilan,' Tsu'gan promised through ranks of teeth. 'I will pull your still beating hearts from your ribcage.'

'*I believe you, brother. But for now, I am far from your reach. Others, though, are not so distant…*'

Tsu'gan turned his head, vaguely aware that the impulse to do so was not wholly his own.

Iagon glared at him from the next grav-harness along. There was murder in his pitiless eyes and he worried at his right gauntlet, scratching it with augmetic fingers.

Tsu'gan laughed at him, the decision to do so entirely his own.

'I thought I smelled the stench of traitor filth. Are Nihilan's boots not yet clean of it that you must work your tongue a little harder into the grooves?'

'I am his equerry,' he replied with self-deluded satisfaction. '*You* are the betrayer,' Iagon spat, struggling against his better judgement not to put hands on his old sergeant.

A sigh of genuine regret escaped Tsu'gan's lips. 'The fact that you still believe that shows just how far you have fallen. Whatever promises he has made you to slake this desire for vengeance, will not come to be. You are a fool, Cerbius.'

'No, *brother*,' uttered the snarling voice.

Tsu'gan faced his other tormentor. Realisation crashed in on him in a wave of iron. He almost balked.

'You are the fool,' Sergeant Lorkar informed him. 'I said you were with me now, and did not lie…'

Tsu'gan's eye was drawn down to the armour he was wearing. It was painted yellow but chipped gunmetal grey from numerous battlefield repairs. The suit was old too – one of the antique Corvus patterns – and had an octagonal release clamp in the centre of the plastron instead of the Imperial Eagle.

Lorkar was smiling beneath his faceplate, though his eyes just visible through his retinal lenses were dead and cold. The mockery was evident in the tone of his voice.

'The sorcerer thought you'd take to this attire a little better than the trappings of a renegade.'

'I see no difference,' spat Tsu'gan.

'I don't care either way. You're Marines Malevolent now, and you'll be killing Salamanders before this is done,' Lorkar replied. 'Tell me, *brother*. What will your precious Chapter of mutants think of you then?' he asked, before punching Tsu'gan in the face and knocking him out cold.

IT WAS A loathsome task, and it took all of Lorkar's resolve not to order their guns open up on the xenos vessels alongside them in the vanguard. He knew the flotilla included dark eldar, kroot and a half-dozen lesser alien and mercenary ships. He wanted nothing more than to obliterate them from the void.

The crackling voice of their pilot came through on his helmet's vox-link.

'*Brother-sergeant, some of the dark eldar are peeling off from the first wave.*'

'The sorcerer has promised them flesh,' Lorkar replied. 'Keep them in our sights until they're beyond range. I don't trust the scum.'

He cut the link, and inwardly cursed the day they had ever set eyes on the *Demetrion*. Everything had changed after that mission. Lorkar was only here on this ship because of it.

It had not been difficult to join Nihilan's warband. The sorcerer's arrogance blinded him to the guile of true warriors. Lorkar would show him the error of that.

The title 'renegade' sat about his shoulders like an ill-fitting cloak. Lorkar did not think of himself thusly. To some, the methods of the Marines Malevolent might appear extreme, even excessive, but these were the failings of heretics and traitors, those who would shun the true light of the Immortal Emperor.

Lorkar knew better.

Despite what had happened to him and his warriors.

The ends always justified the means. Hate is the surest weapon. Never accept a slight without retribution – this was the creed of the Marines Malevolent and it was this last part of their warmongering mantra that saw him here upon this gunship, amongst enemies.

The equerry the sorcerer had sent was a poor excuse for a Space Marine. Lorkar could see the conniving look in his eye, the stoop in his bent back from listening at keyholes and other craven acts ill-suited to warriors. He remembered him vaguely, as one of the Salamanders his war party had encountered aboard the Mechanicus ship. That he had turned his back on the Emperor's light only further convinced Lorkar that the sons of Vulkan were indeed tainted. It also helped him reconcile with the deed he had sworn to commit.

Still, it was not his business to lay judgement. How could he speak of resisting the corruption of dark forces and not feel a tremor of hypocrisy? But the Salamanders were different. They bore their mutancy openly and with pride. They embraced it! Could he have put his sword to their necks, he would have. Vinyar's orders had been very specific when he'd learned of Lorkar's *malady*, as was the stipulation the captain not be implicated in any way. Loyalty to his Chapter overrode all else in Lorkar's mind. Promises had been made regarding his very public excommunication. What else could Vinyar have done but condemn? In private he had pledged his aid.

He opened up a closed channel in his battle-helm. Even those harnessed next to him wouldn't hear his next orders.

'Vathek, Rennard...'

Two warriors close by reacted with the slightest of movement. He'd told Vinyar back aboard the *Purgatory* when all of this was just still words, '*I'll need men I can trust...*'

All of those aboard the *Demetrion* had been sworn to his cause, even those who were unafflicted.

Lorkar's eyes narrowed.

'I don't know what the sorcerer has planned. The other one is nothing to us, but watch Tsu'gan. He is dangerous.'

Vathek and Rennard nodded as the scream of descent engines filled the hold. They had breached Nocturne's atmosphere. The ground assault was close at hand.

II
Wreckage

ARGOS STAGGERED THROUGH the burning debris. He'd blacked out for a few minutes and was struggling to remember what had happened. The static in his head had lessened with the execution of his mission. Seeing

Kor'hadron slumped face-down amidst the wreckage of the chamber brought it all flooding back.

All of the servitors and tech-adepts were dead. Argos had killed most of them, and the rest had died in the explosion. Vulkan's Eye had borne the brunt of the aster- oid's blast wave. It had overloaded and shut down their void shields, damaged the defence laser array so that it no longer functioned.

Heading towards Kor'hadron, Argos staggered and fell to one knee. It brought him face to face with a col- lapsed augur screen that had come back online. It was one of the few pieces of machinery that still worked in the devastated weapon's room. A vast fleet of enemy ves- sels was inbound. Argos saw smaller escorts forging a path through the debris field for the larger capital ships as they drove to the edge of Nocturne's atmosphere.

A vanguard was already beyond the beleaguered orbital defences and locked into descent trajectories. As he watched, several ships were breaking off from this flotilla and heading for Prometheus. Hangar Seven was gaping open like a rotting wound. Infestation would begin there first. Only just ahead of the scouts was another ship. This one had a Nocturnean signature and had come from the planet's surface below. Fire and smoke had taken hold in the room. There was no time to investigate further. He dragged himself up and went to Kor'hadron.

Argos tried to perform a bio-scan to ascertain the Forge Master's vitals but the interference in his brain was get- ting in the way of an accurate reading.

He stopped, performing self-diagnostics as he tried to isolate the source. Muttering machine-rites of cleansing and purification, he found the section of his artificial cortex where the debilitating code had embedded itself.

Without hesitation, he took a piece of shrapnel from the floor and rammed it like a dagger in his metallic cra- nium. He jerked and there was a final scream of static like a death cry before he got the spasming under control as well as his senses. It felt as if a heavy weight had been lifted from his back. Data streamed across the internal retina of his bionic eye. Some of his neural functions governing memory and targeting were damaged but otherwise he was fine. The static had abated. A piece of sharp metal lodged in his head was an inelegant solution but there wasn't time for anything more. Argos resolved to find something permanent later. More pressing concerns demanded his attention.

A bio-scan revealed Kor'hadron was alive but had slipped into sus-an membrane coma. Argos hauled him onto his back and made his way out of the chamber.

The damage was little better in the adjacent corridor. A firestorm had ripped through the door to the weapon room, tearing it from its bearings. Argos found it halfway down the corridor embedded in the scorched wall.

He reached another door, the one that led back into the main conduit and eventually Hangar Seven, but it was sealed. Code overrides didn't work and neither did brute force. Without substantial cutting tools, Argos couldn't get through.

After the destruction of the asteroid, levels of magnetic interference had diminished. Communication should be operable again.

He opened up a channel to Brother Ak'taro at Hangar Seven.

'Master Argos, when we lost contact I feared the worst.'

'The enemy's sabotage went deeper than we thought,' said Argos. 'What forces do you have in place?' he asked.

'Two squads of Fire-born and a small contingent of armsmen. Sergeant Balataro is in command. Do you wish to speak–'

'No. But tell the sergeant to prepare for an attack.'

'At once, Master Argos. Brother Draedius is also en route to you as we speak. A serf, Sonnar Illiad, passed on your message.'

Draedius was a Techmarine, one closely affiliated with Third. Argos would need his assistance to remove all traces of the scrap code if he was to employ Prometheus's defence systems without fear of corrupting them.

'I am on my way, but bearing wounded.'

Another voice cut in. '*This is Sergeant Balataro. We will provide egress for the wounded but can't reinforce the hangar further. Most of Fourth are heading to the surface.*'

'Then you'll have to hold with what you've got. I'm coming and will provide reinforcement of my own.'

He severed the link – it was causing havoc with the spar of shrapnel jutting from his skull – leaving Balataro to wonder at his meaning. Then he waited, Kor'hadron over his shoulder. After a few minutes, a tiny patch of superheated light appeared in the metal of the bulkhead. Draedius had found him.

THE FIRE-WYVERN TOUCHED down on the Apothecarion's landing pad amidst flaring stabiliser jets. It had been a rough passage through the floating debris field and more than one dent marred the gunship's outer surface.

A docking clamp extended automatically, pressing against the vessel's side embarkation hatch before maglocking to the hull. It slid open to reveal Fugis, still in his drover's garb albeit with hat and scarves removed, and Ba'ken aloft on a grav-sled.

Fugis turned back to Prebian as the interior lume strips started to light up the docking corridor to the Apothecarion.

'I can take him the rest of the way.' He glanced at Val'in and Exor. 'What will you do with them?'

'Take them with me to Hesiod and the rest of Seventh. We'll join up with the Third and protect the city. If you see Tu'Shan, tell him that's where I'm headed.'

Fugis nodded and was about to depart when Prebian's voice stopped him.

'Whatever sign you saw out in the desert,' he said, 'I hope it bears good omens.'

'So do I,' the Apothecary replied, turning. 'I have a feeling we shall be in need of them.'

He descended into the docking corridor as the *Fire-wyvern's* hatch closed. The way back was sealed behind him. Ahead was the Apothecarion.

'Hold on, brother,' he muttered. 'I did not survive this reunion just so you could die on me.'

Ba'ken was awake but in incredible pain. His weak smile quickly turned to a grimace.

The outer hatch to the Apothecarion opened, revealing Cadorian and a pair of medical-servitors. The practitioner bowed.

'Where is Emek?' Fugis asked curtly.

'Looking for an escapee,' Cadorian replied. 'Are you a… drover?' he asked, noting the obvious melanchromatic defects and burning red eyes of a Fire-born but matching it to the stranger's incongruous attire.

'I am Brother Fugis, former Apothecary of this station.' Ignoring Cadorian's shocked expression, Fugis gestured to Ba'ken. 'He needs urgent attention.' The medi-servitors were bringing the grav-sled inside. Fugis went with it.

'I… I heard you were dead,' said Cadorian, following them.

'I am alive,' Fugis replied unnecessarily. He laid a hand on Ba'ken's shoulder, muttering a litany of healing over the wounded sergeant. When he looked up at Cadorian, his eyes were hard. 'If Emek should return, tell him I have gone to speak with Lord Tu'Shan.'

'The entire council has just broken up. They were in one of the lower chambers. I don't know where precisely.'

'That's because it's not your business to know. Do your duty, practitioner. This is but a taste of what's to come. We are at war.'

Not waiting for a reply, Fugis stormed off. It was difficult entrusting Ba'ken's care to others but the need to speak with the Chapter Master was paramount. It could decide the fate of Nocturne.

CHAPTER TWELVE

I
Rally

THE DAMAGE WORSENED the closer they got to the docks.
It was a short walk made longer by the fact that sections
of the space port were closed off and the usual means of
conveyance were denied to them.

Praetor led close to a hundred Firedrakes down the
expansive corridors of Prometheus. They were not a full
complement. Costly missions to Sepulchre IV and the
space hulk *Protean* had taken a toll on the ranks of the
Firedrakes.

'I see the look in your eyes, Herculon.' It was Halknarr,
a brother-sergeant of First and one of the Firedrakes
who'd also been to Volgorrah.

'What look?' Praetor glanced askance at the old campaigner. 'There is no look to be seen.'

Halknarr gave a rueful smile that creased his already
wrinkled features. Age was evident in the greying around
his temples, the numerous lines around his eyes and
mouth, but experience had made him shrewd too. He
kept his voice low.

'Precisely that. You seem to be as stone, brother.'

Even Halknarr's trappings were vintage. His Terminator armour was of an ancient design, a previous
incarnation that was just as inviolable but bulkier that
operated an extended chainfist and a triple mag storm
bolter that was anything but standard.

'I am ready for war, Halknarr.'

'Then fill your gaze and heart with fire, for you'll
need it.'

Sacrifice and death were a warrior's destiny, but
Praetor had seen overmuch of that in all too recent
memory. It was part of the reason for the *remember-
ing* and the burning of the hand in the sacred flame.
None who fell in battle would ever be forgotten – their
legacy would live on. He vowed not to lose any more
so needlessly, but knew the perils of their present mission.

It had hardened him, near petrified his soul.

'*A warrior fights with heart and mind, as well as bolter
and blade,*' Praetor quoted Zen'de. 'Thank you, brother.'

Halknarr merely nodded. 'I need you angry. It'll be
my back you are guarding after all.' He smiled broadly
and they laughed together.

Behind them, Vo'kar laughed too.

Halknarr turned his head towards the heavy weapon
specialist.

'Do you even know what this is about?' he asked.

'No, but it seemed a good time for humour,' said
Vo'kar honestly.

Praetor laughed louder still, and left Halknarr muttering.

'Should keep his mind on igniting the flame and not
listening to the conversations of others…'

Wise, yes, but Halknarr was also cantankerous.

Levity, however incongruous, was what bonded
these warriors. Praetor knew they had shared blood,
honour, glory and defeat across countless battlefields.
Only now this was a war upon their own soil, on the
very earth they had sworn to protect. Unlike the other

Salamanders, the First did not live amongst the peoples of Nocturne. Some thought that meant they were
haughty, arrogant, uncaring of the plight of mortals.

Like *other* Space Marines...

It was not so. They knew of the horrors of the galaxy,
to a greater and more detailed extent than many captains. It was their solemn duty to gird mankind from
those horrors and that could best be achieved through
seclusion and isolation.

In order to conduct his sacred mission, He'stan had
to be estranged from his brothers, the Chapter he
knew; Praetor felt that way about his people, his earth,
but he could bear it because he knew it was necessary
to protect it. If anything should ever happen to change
that...

His mood darkened again swiftly as the names of
the fallen came back to haunt him even in his waking
hours. He focused on the march.

Deckplates shook beneath the Firedrakes as they
advanced and the walls trembled with their passing.
There were few serfs, save the armourers, this far down.
Most of the humans had been evacuated to saviour
pods or transferred to more secure areas of the space
port. It was a lonely walk but one conducted in determined silence the rest of the way.

When they reached the vast teleporter pad that
would take them to Dac'tyr's flagship, a lone figure was
waiting for them.

Every Firedrake in the company knelt as one when
they saw who it was. 'It is rare to see the entirety of
the Firedrakes so arrayed,' he said, gazing upon the
vaunted warriors with approval. 'But rise, Herculon,'
he added, gesturing for them to stand. 'Halknarr,
Persephion, all of my brothers, arise. We have fought
together before, and I would ask that we do so again.'

Praetor lifted his chin and rose noisily to his feet.
It was done amidst protesting servos and screeching
pneumatics. Terminators were not meant to kneel.

The others followed him, first Halknarr then
Persephion until a cacophony of grinding gears and
mechanisms filled the echoing halls and all the Firedrakes were standing once more.

'*Ask*, my lord? Vulkan He'stan need not ask the First
for anything. It is his.'

He'stan extended his hand. He was clad in his own
power armour, a finely wrought suit as potent as any
Tactical Dreadnought Armour.

'Even so... I ask.'

Praetor clasped his forearm in the warrior's grip. In
his Terminator suit he was a head taller than the Forgefather but still appeared humbled.

'It would be our honour.'

Halknarr nodded, pride overflowing.

'To war again then, Herculon,' said He'stan, appraising the others with a glance, and released his grip.

'In the fires of battle, where the stakes have never
been higher,' he replied.

All of First took up position on the vast teleporter
pad. Distant explosions from farther into the space
port boomed dully as if to emphasise the severity in
the veteran sergeant's tone.

'I had thought,' he ventured, 'that your place would
be with Dak'ir. If he is the Unbound Flame...'

Halknarr had begun the countdown to transition.
An automated voice rang out from the external vox-
hailers, issuing warning. Klaxons were sounding as the
chamber was sealed off from the rest of the station and
a temporary Geller field cocooned it. Magnesium light
dawned overhead like a new-born sun warring with
the red of flashing lamps.

'So had I,' admitted He'stan, 'but Unbound Flame or
not, Dak'ir's destiny is his own. I can play no further
part in it. Vulkan has guided me.'

The light overhead grew to blindingly bright levels.
Everyone standing upon the teleporter pad donned his
helmet and muttered a prayer to Vulkan. Those who

had been to the Volgorrah Reef remembered what had happened the last time they attempted complex mass-transition. They remembered Tsu'gan.

'Can you hear him, his voice?' Praetor asked barely above a whisper.

'I see his hand, his will, and know that we are not alone.'

Praetor was grateful for his battle-helm, and that it obscured the tears of fire running down his chiselled face. Halknarr had been right. Stone was not a fitting disposition for the heart before battle. An automaton could become stone; he was flesh and vital flame.

He'stan regarded the veteran sergeant through his retinal lenses. His voice issued through the vocalisers in his battle-helm but was no less sincere.

'My place is here,' he said, as the teleportation flare engulfed them, 'with my brothers…'

FROM HIS THRONE on the bridge of the *Flamewrought*, Dac'tyr surveyed carnage.

Prometheus had taken severe damage. Tiny fires guttered like dying candles attached to its surface and streams of atmosphere bled out into the void from hundreds of miniscule fissures like escaping breath. It made Dac'tyr think of a drowning man, doomed to the oblivion of the endless ocean.

Several of the moon station's docking arms had been destroyed. The long drake-like necks were cut off at the jugular, spewing sparks and vapour. Fluids flash-froze upon contact with realspace, crystallising into banks of shards that broke upon the cold flanks of the dead ships severed from dock like icy surf.

Dac'tyr had yet to make an inventory of the vessels critically damaged during the attack. They'd lost many. More than they could bear. A conservative estimate put the fleet at around forty per cent. Nihilan's own armada would have outnumbered a full-strength complement but Dac'tyr would have wagered on them anyway. With these odds, the Lord of the Burning Skies was not so sure.

Shutting down the view of the devastated space port, he concentrated on the battle line he did have.

Flamewrought, so named for Vulkan's flagship back during the days of the Great Crusade, was flanked by the frigate *Firelord* and the strike cruiser *Vulkan's Wrath*. Two other strike cruisers, *Hammerforge* and *Serpentine*, joined the small fleet as well as a handful of lighter escorts and several squadrons of gunships that had escaped the destruction of their parent vessels.

He brought up the tacticarium and a cluster of crimson icons lit up on the display revealing enemy dispositions. There were twice as many capital ships and the same again in escorts and fighters. One wing, consisting solely of smaller gunships, broke off from the vanguard to deviate around the Salamander sfleet.

Dac'tyr hoped the defenders aboard Prometheus were ready for them.

Nihilan had arrayed his void-forces in two lines with the *Hell-stalker*, his flagship, in dead centre at the rear. Even at distance, too far yet to engage in meaningful cannon exchanges, the manoeuvre planned by the traitor was obvious to Dac'tyr. Only the *Hell-stalker* mattered, the rest of the ships were fodder. Vessels in the centre of the line were pulling forwards, utilising their more powerful engines to get ahead of the rest, whilst the flanks kept steady pace. Evidenced by the tacticarium display, both lines were evolving into an arrowhead formation. It was a breaching tactic, intended to break through blockades. In this case it would try and scatter the Salamanders fleet, taking heavy damage in the process but delivering the core ship into position over the planet.

Nihilan only needed the *Hell-stalker* to get within range and he'd unleash the apocalypse weapon.

Dac'tyr had no intention of being rolled over by the vast enemy armada, nor would he submit without a fight. He raised the respective captains on the fleet-wide vox-band and ordered them to disperse. So arranged it

would leave them open to attack from multiple quarters, especially when the vessels closed, but weathering
a frontal assault, even a suicidal one, wasn't an option.
They would attack in two arms, either side of the enemy
line, leaving their centre open to advance but largely
impotent without targets to bear on. It would even the
odds, giving them a tenable possibility of victory without annihilation.

It left only one problem. Without opposition, the *Hell-
stalker* would breach easily. But Dac'tyr had a solution
for that too. An icon flashing on his tacticarium screen
told him it had just arrived aboard the *Flamewrought*.

There would be no time for greetings. The Firedrakes
knew what was expected of them. All of the boarding
torpedoes were prepped and ready for launch. Dac'tyr
just had to get them close enough to the *Hell-stalker* so
they had a fighting chance of surviving its anti-boarding
barrage.

He looked up from his strategising. The bridge was
plunged into darkness with only the light of consoles to
alleviate the gloom. Silhouettes of crewmen working dil-
igently at their stations were just visible. One activated
an alert that appeared on the tacticarium screen.

The enemy were within engagement range. Dac'tyr
gave the order to power all forward lance batteries. An
array of firing solutions materialised on a sub-screen.
One-by-one they were locked in as target acquisition
came online. The other large vessels in the fleet reported
similar states of readiness.

Before addressing his captains, Dac'tyr opened a channel to the torpedo deck.

'Brother-Sergeant Praetor, we are about to engage.'

'*The First are aboard and ready to launch,*' the crackling
reply came back.

A second sub-screen gave green lights for all thirty-two
boarding torpedoes in the breech and primed to fire. It
was ten more than required by the Firedrakes and their
'fire support'; the rest were loaded with anti-personnel

weapon systems but also functioned as slower-moving decoys to draw fire.

'I will get you as close as I can, brother-sergeant.'

'*In the Lord of the Burning Skies, I have no doubts. In Vulkan's name.*'

'In Vulkan's name.'

Dac'tyr closed the channel and switched the link to the fleet-wide band.

'Captains, you may begin your assault. Nothing less than the fate of Nocturne rests on our success here today. Our darkest hour is upon us all. Bring the light. Bring the fire of Prometheus to them.'

A series of affirmations was returned and Dac'tyr cut the link to concentrate on evasive manoeuvres.

'And may Vulkan watch over us all,' he muttered.

II
Bulwarks

TU'SHAN SPREAD HIS hands wide so they gripped the outer edges of the strategium table. Vel'cona had joined him in the throne room and was standing at the opposite side of the hololithic map that depicted the surface of Nocturne. An expansive view showed all of its Sanctuary Cities as well as minor settlements, oceanic platforms, watchtowers and remote defences.

'Who would come to hell with thoughts bent on invasion?' he asked the flickering green vista before him.

It was a deadly world. The ash deserts, the mountains and acid seas – all would be quick to punish an invader who was ignorant of the danger each presented. Not to mention its native fauna, the saurian beasts of the crags, the chitinous, subterranean horrors beneath the sands. Nocturne was not a place that welcomed outsiders.

Vel'cona answered. 'Nihilan does not want to conquer, he wants to annihilate us.' The Master of Librarians hadn't mentioned the Regent's decision to spare Dak'ir once. It was done and now they would endure the consequences of that, whether they were good or bad. It mattered only to serve his lord and protect the sanctity of his Chapter's home world with all the powers at his disposal.

'All of this for vengeance?' Tu'Shan shook his head slowly. 'It smacks of petty madness.' He looked up from the glow of the hololith map. 'Should I have hunted him down? Should I have scoured the galaxy for the taint of Vai'tan Ushorak and all his corrupt progeny?'

'That was Ko'tan Kadai's duty, one he fulfilled at Moribar.'

'And Nihilan?' The Regent shook his head again, his face creased with rueful anger. 'I should have purged this dirty aberration to our Chapter as soon as it was given birth.'

'No one, except Nihilan himself, will ever know the truth of what was spoken on Lycannor. They lasted several days in that city, lost many brothers and faced the prospect of death before being rescued.'

'Giving Ushorak opportunity to lay the seed of treachery in once noble hearts.'

'I do not think Nihilan's heart was ever noble, my lord. His was an addiction, I realised belatedly. He craved power, *craved* it! To Nihilan, no wisdom should ever be denied, no knowledge ever proscribed. He was censured but not nearly enough. Too late, I saw the danger. But it is past and we must look to this day, this hour, if we are to survive. Nihilan *has* come and brings with him an armada to destroy us. Will you yield to it?'

Tu'Shan scoffed at the last remark, as if it wasn't even a question.

'Of course not. I will break him and his renegades upon the back of my anvil with this fist,' he brandished it, 'as my hammer.'

'Then cast out these doubts and self-recriminations,' Vel'cona gestured to the hololithic rendering of Nocturne sitting between them, 'and defend us, my lord.

Defend Nocturne and cast this traitor to the flame.'

Tu'Shan looked down grimly.

'It will begin at Hesiod...' he said, marking the site of the city on the map with a touch of his gauntleted finger.

Subterranean beacons indicated multiple planetfalls coming from the direction of the Pyre Desert. The first Sanctuary City in their path would be the Seat of Tribal Kings.

'Themis will be next,' he lit up a second marker over the City of Warrior Kings, 'though they'll find the Arridian Plain tough country to negotiate.'

'All of Nocturne is "tough country", my liege,' Vel'cona interjected. 'The land knows when it is under threat. It will try to kill the invaders just as we shall.'

Tu'Shan smiled thinly over the grainy projection. It cast haunting shadows across the noble grooves of his face.

'Spoken like an earth shaman of old.'

'Am I not, albeit clad in armour and armed with the strength of my Emperor?'

'Indeed,' Tu'Shan conceded, and went back to the map.

Epithemus, the Jewel City, was situated in the middle of the Acerbian Sea and would only be vulnerable to aerial attack. A small attack wing of gunships held in reserve that had survived the devastation on Prometheus could protect it.

Heliosa and Aethonion, the Beacon City and Fire Spike respectively, would be defended by the reserve companies of Mulcebar and Drakgaard. That left only Clymene, the Merchant Sprawl, and Skarokk, also known as the Dragonspine. Both were at the remote edges of Nocturnean civilisation, bordered by the T'harken Delta and eastern Gey'sarr Ocean. So isolated were these regions that an enemy would be hard-pressed to mount an invasion there without first marching across vast tracts of inhospitable desert, and that was assuming they had already sacked Hesiod and Themis. If Nihilan managed to get that far all was lost anyway, so Tu'Shan focused on his first bulwarks.

'I will lead our armoured divisions across the Themian Ash Ridge,' he declared. 'Only Fire-born can navigate its crags. The peaks will provide natural cover from any gun emplacements Nihilan has brought to sunder our walls and void shields.'

He took up his thunder hammer from where it leaned against the table, appreciating its heft.

The weapon's name was *Stormbearer*. Rumour persisted around the Chapter that it was forged from the self-same metal as its ancestral twin *Thunderhead*, the hammer of Vulkan. Though none alive could refute or substantiate such a claim. In truth it was one of many hammers, blades and spears that Tu'Shan possessed in his armoury. As a master forgesmith, he had several weapons but *Stormbearer* was his favourite. There was no armour it couldn't break, or so the masters told the aspirants when recounting its legend.

'Then I shall await you at Hesiod where hell will fall hardest,' Vel'cona answered, also readying to leave. The time was long past when the lords of Nocturne should go to war.

Tu'Shan nodded and drew a line in the hololith between the two neighbouring cities.

'We'll break them here or not at all.'

'It might not come to that,' said another.

Cerulean fire dimmed in Vel'cona's eyes as he recognised the figure beneath the archway to the throne room. It lay open to all, and with the Firedrakes all aboard the *Flamewrought* was largely unguarded.

'You have looked better, Apothecary,' said Tu'Shan. 'I'm glad you've returned from the Burning Walk.'

'Unfortunately, to inauspicious times,' added Vel'cona, folding his arms with a nod of greeting.

Fugis bowed humbly to his masters. 'Perhaps it was to bring important tidings,' he told them, rising. 'Where is Dak'ir? I must see him at once.'

'The Reclusiam, readying to join our defence with Pyriel and Elysius,' Tu'Shan replied.

Vel'cona's eyes narrowed as the psychic glow returned. 'You saw something out in desert. What was it, brother?'

'An omen, one that could decide the fate of us all. '

'Then deliver it. Nihilan has assembled armies and brought them to our world,' said Tu'Shan.

'I have seen the dusk-wraiths in the desert.'

'Another vanguard to silence our towers and outer defences. They have prepared a landing zone for a considerable ground force. Vel'cona and I go to meet them.' Tu'Shan picked up his battle-helm and held it in the crook of his arm. 'I'd advise you to make it quick. The majority of the transports have left Prometheus already, and not all of us can walk through the gates of infinity.'

He gestured to a flickering light, clinging to the air like iridescent dust motes, where Vel'cona had been a moment before.

Fugis was nonplussed. 'Don't you wish to hear of it? What I have seen?'

'Take no offence, brother,' said Tu'Shan, moving around the table. 'I can either stand here, listening to talk of omen and prophecy that may or may not come to pass, or I can go to my people where I am needed.' He clapped Fugis on the shoulder as he passed him. 'Bring your message to Dak'ir. It is for his attention, not mine. You'll find me on the Themian Ash Ridge, shouting the primarch's name from the cupola of *Promethean*.'

Fugis nodded. 'I will join you as soon as I am able to, my lord.'

Tu'Shan left the throne room without another word.

Nothing more needed saying. They would fight and live, or they would die – Nocturne, the Chapter, everything.

CHAPTER THIRTEEN

I
Hangar Seven

A SWARM OF Venoms swept into the raw wound of
Hangar Seven, splinter cannons roaring. They emerged
from the void amidst an expanding pall of darkness
exuded from their insectoid hulls, and spread across
the deck like a contagion. The withering return fire
from the barricaded defenders was indiscriminate but
sustained.

Las-bolts and solid shot *fizzed* and *spanged* off their
alien hulls but achieved little more than metal-scoring
ricochets. The jet-skimmers were strafing fast across the
expansive hangar, hurtling around the burnt-out shells
of boxy gunships and other craft, making accurate targeting almost impossible.

The docking bay was a vast flat plate of metal scattered
with sunken maintenance pits and racks of machinery.
It was wide with plenty of open space for turning and
landing. Intended for vessels as large as escorts and
bulk-freighters, the blasted hangar gate was more than
wide enough to accommodate the dark eldar raiding
ships. It was twisted, the adamantium peeled back

from incredible explosive force so that it resembled a ragged, gaping aperture.

The defenders could not hope to protect every avenue of attack, especially from an enemy so swift, but they had tried hard.

Arrayed in four lines – utilising crates, wreckage and pieces of shattered gunship fuselage – the defensive barricades were improvised but not entirely ineffective. Semi-circular heavy gun emplacements were interspersed between ranks of crude laser rifles and noisy hand-held scatter cannons.

Despite their night shields, several of the dark eldar's transports went down burning. One, clipped by a missile burst, rolled across the hangar deck wrapped in fire. It screeched to a wrecked halt and exploded, killing the warriors aboard and spraying frag.

It was of little consequence as a second swarm hoved in after the first and then a third, followed by a fourth. Overwhelming force and a multitude of different targets made it difficult for the defenders to mount any sort of concerted defence.

An'scur was amongst the last to enter the hangar aboard the void-shrouded transports and watched with mild amusement as the mon'keigh's firing discipline became increasingly erratic. It was gloomy in the chamber and the muzzle flares from their brute weapons flash-cast the fear on their faces. Only the gene-bred ones, the armoured giants, maintained their resolve when confronted with horror incarnate.

Dispassionately, he observed the bodies of his kabalite warriors strewn around the deckplate like broken dolls. Their unwilling sacrifice had paved the way for the wych cults to leap over and amongst the first line of makeshift barricades where they could cut and cleave and kill for the mutual pleasure of all the dark eldar.

Reinforcements were piling in after them, dark lances and disintegrators ripping up the ramshackle entrenchments where the humans cowered. An'scur savoured their agonised deaths as his gaze turned to the wyches.

They were darkly beautiful creatures, but nothing in comparison to Helspereth. It provoked a sad memory that surprised him with its potency. The archon's melancholy soured to anger quickly and he armed himself with falchion blade and splinter pistol.

'Sybarite, stay close to me but within my eye-line at all times,' he ordered, sliding down the mask of his warhelm. A face as white as alabaster, narrow as a drawn blade with eyes of ash-grey, disappeared behind a daemonic visage forged from dark metal.

An'scur's blade-hand nodded slowly, and drew a long glaive from a scabbard of human skin upon his back. It crackled evilly as he fed a pulse of tainted light over its razored edge.

'By your will, lord archon,' he said, the husking voice obscured by a flesh-leather hell-mask.

An'scur did not reply. He began to run. Hot beams whipped past him, too slow to even glance his armour. There were approximately ninety-seven strides to the first line of barricades. The Venom could have got them closer but there was no thrill in that, no challenge. He leapt and rolled, a bark of heavy shell fire tearing up the deckplate where he'd been standing. Now there were only seventy-one.

Fleet-footed, the sybarite was his master's shadow. He moved in perfect symmetry, like he knew An'scur's movements ahead of time and could predict them. Weaving aside from a raking las-beam, snap-shooting the firer through the neck with a deft burst from his splinter pistol, An'scur considered the sybarite might be a little *too* good and began to formulate a plan to remove him.

After all, sell-swords, even those who styled themselves on the warrior kabals, were not to be trusted for any length of time.

Just thirty-three strides remained.

A Venom from the last attack wave pushed forwards,

hoping to slice a jagged hole in the heavier barricades towards the back of the hangar. Beyond this last redoubt was a fortified gate, which led deeper into the complex and towards An'scur's objective. The insectoid vessel was too aggressive and opened itself up to a gene-bred warrior who cut it apart with a salvo of hot light. It exploded, showering the area around it with fire and shrapnel. As it expanded, the burst engulfed An'scur and his lackey. Engaging his shadow field, the archon flew through the carnage, flickering out of existence briefly before resolving again on the other side. To his mild chagrin, the sybarite made it too, albeit trailing smoke, his Ghost-plate armour hazed with heat.

'At your side, my lord,' he rasped, with only the barest hint of sarcasm.

For a moment, An'scur thought he recognised the tone and timbre of it, but threats more immediate seized his attention.

At seven strides left, they vaulted the first barricade and set about them with their envenomed blades.

An'scur barely acknowledged the first cut. It sent a grubby mon'keigh's head spinning like a grenade into the deeper ranks, trailing arterial blood like red streamers. A thrust disembowelled a second then a series of blows, delivered at eye-stinging speed, slew a clutch of others. A ring of blood and dismembered limbs framed the carnage. Together, the archon and his sybarite leapt the second barricade.

AK'TARO KNEW THEY were being pushed back. The sheer number of dark eldar and their rampant aggression was proving too difficult to stymie in the massive hangar bay. The next fall-back point was beyond the gate behind them but he was loath to relinquish position.

Hold the line. Those were his orders. He intended to honour them.

At his left shoulder he heard Sergeant Balataro lauding another of his battle-brothers.

'Send them back to hell, Ikaron!'

The plasma gunner raised a fist in salute as the blazing enemy vehicle rolled in front of the first barricade in a storm of fiery debris.

Several figures that had yet to disembark were caught in the conflagration and staggered from the wreck aflame.

Ikaron took aim but Balataro stopped him.

'Let them burn.'

The plasma gunner switched to a fresh target, sending an energised bolt into another horde of warriors instead.

Ak'taro, who'd paused to reload, noticed something emerge through the fire and smoke of the broken vehicle. He pointed to it with a gauntleted finger.

'Brother-sergeant!'

Balataro followed his trooper's gesture and saw it too.

Two armoured warriors were coming at the barricades at speed. With hellish abandon they took the first barricade, advancing through a fusillade of las-fire and scatter shot, and cut down the armsmen behind it at will. Then they were in amongst the second, culling desultorily as before.

Lasguns pressed into the hands of deck crew, even highly trained combat-armsmen, weren't going to so much as slow these butchers down.

The sergeant drew his chainsword, thumbing the activation stud so the teeth-blades screamed.

'A lordling and his servant,' he snarled. Balataro was headstrong and not one to shirk from a fight. The rate of attrition was unusually high for squads under his command, perhaps part of the reason he would never rise higher through the ranks, but so too were the laurels.

'Combat-squad *Hyperion* with me,' he ordered, vaulting the barricade. Four warriors armed with bolters went with him.

Ak'taro was left behind, his own sergeant dead to Mechanicus sabotage, so he assumed command of his own squad's remnants and Balataro's leavings.

'*Apollus* and *Venutia*, close ranks and dig in!' he

bellowed, and the half-squads hunkered down. He
still had Ikaron's plasma gun so put some heavier fire
on the xenos pressing at the far right flanks of their
emplacements.

It took less than a minute for Balataro to reach the
lordling. Ak'taro heard the shout of Vulkan's name as
blades clashed and sparks fell as rain. It was hard to see
in the melee. Another fight had grown around it, dark
eldar warriors rushing in behind their nobles to exploit
the inroads they'd made.

Balataro's troops had formed a circle around him as
the alien lordling's reinforcements enveloped them.

Ak'taro fought the urge to advance and assist. He
couldn't level supporting fire either in case a stray shot
hit an ally.

Hold the line, he remembered, and snapped, 'Do your
duty!' beneath his breath.

Hand-to-hand fighting had erupted across the length
of the first two barricades. Through his retinal lenses,
the xenos appeared slightly altered. Their heat signatures
were different, colder. Men of Nocturne were dying in
their droves, the red aura of their bodies going dark like
candles slowly being snuffed out. Light was fading as the
dark eldar's noose tightened around them inexorably.

Ak'taro looked for Balataro but couldn't see him. For a
terrible moment, he thought the sergeant was slain but
then he appeared, bloodied and reeling.

THE GENE-BRED ONE was vicious but slow. An'scur parried
a clumsy blow, hacking into his shoulder with a deft
return. Spitting oaths that were little more than bestial
grunts to the archon's ears, the hairless ape came again,
swinging a bulky pistol around. An'scur stepped aside
from the barrage, the shells ripping first into air and
then the hapless kabalite warriors behind him. They
ruptured and broke apart from internal detonation,
showering the combatants with bone and gore.

Such loud, ugly warriors, he thought.

An'scur nodded to the mon'keigh, impressed at the savagery of his weapons. This gesture only seemed to further enrage the whelp, who charged in swinging. A brutal downstroke took a chip off the archon's lamellar shoulder guard, angering him. The upswing came late and laboured. An'scur weaved away from it and cut across, cleaving the churning saw-blade in two. Shadow-cloaked, he *flickered* through the storm of jagged teeth that spat outwards, embedding into flesh and metal.

The mon'keigh was digging one from his destroyed cheekbone, face painted in blood, when An'scur lopped off his wrist and drove the tip of his falchion into the opposite shoulder joint, severing a crucial nerve cluster. The broken haft of the mon'keigh's blade-weapon clattered to the ground from benumbed fingers. Disarmed, with one arm useless and another reduced to a wrist stump, the primitive drove at An'scur, head lowered like a battering ram. The archon took a second to marvel at the brute's tenacity before holstering his splinter pistol and drawing an agoniser that he lodged in the mon'keigh's screaming mouth.

Immensely painful death was not quite instantaneous. The mon'keigh's last expression was fashioned into a rictus of agony. A red rime coated his teeth from when he'd severed his own tongue.

Leaving the corpse still locked in agonised nerve convulsions, An'scur moved on with the sybarite in tow. The sell-sword had reaped a steady tally of heads with his glaive, and left a pair of wounded for the chasing pack to gorge upon.

An'scur smiled. Perhaps the warrior was worthy of being spared a little longer... The gate wasn't far now. The final barricade beckoned.

AK'TARO LOOKED ON in disbelief as the butchered body of Sergeant Balataro collapsed below the barricade line and was lost from sight. The xenos lordling had cut him apart, piece by piece. It was unworthy of the noble Salamander.

'Ak'taro…' It was Brother Rodondus. 'We must avenge him!'

The desire to do so was strong but a swift glance at the barricade line revealed it was breaking. Stabbing attacks had punched holes through barricade three, whilst two and one were completely overrun.

Terrified armsmen, far beyond the Salamanders' reach, were being rounded up and slaughtered. Over half the heavy gun emplacements were silent, either dry of ammo or their crews dead. No one ran. No one could run. The only way out was through the gate and the xenos were converging on that.

Ak'taro held Rodondus back. Every mote of his being wanted to charge, death or glory, into the enemy. Pragmatism and the knowledge it would be a life spent for nothing prevented him.

Hold the line, those had been his orders, but the line was gone.

'We fall back, corridor by corridor. Hangar Seven is lost.'

Rodondus looked like he was about to protest but conceded to wisdom.

Suppressing fire erupted from the Space Marines' ranks, as Ak'taro called the retreat. He raised Draedius on the comm-feed.

'Full retreat is in effect, open up the corridor and prepare for incoming. Keep the aperture narrow, enemy close.'

The reply was static-laden and hard to discern but a few seconds later the gate mechanism stirred into life, and began to part. Rodondus roared at the few human survivors as they pelted through the hydraulic pressure cloud, heads down. One unfortunate deckhand was clipped before he got through and fell bleeding. The others grabbed him but then a second man got his chest cavity vacated by a disintegrator prompting Rodondus to shout, 'Leave the wounded. Get through now. Go!'

Barring Ek'thelar, who was priming charges, Ak'taro was last to leave.

He turned for a moment, 'Twenty metres, hug the

walls and adopt overwatch pos–'

A brief stint as acting-sergeant ended with a splinter burst to the throat. Ak'taro's gorget bent and broke apart as a fountain of blood and shrapnel ripped out of his neck. He fell just as Ek'thelar was getting through the gate. It sealed behind him, locking Ak'taro's dead form in Hangar Seven.

With the closing of the gate silence resumed in the corridor, broken a second later by a dull explosion as the incendiaries placed by Ek'thelar went off.

Then they waited.

II
Siege

THE WALLS SURROUNDING Hesiod were thronged with troops. Since Captain Agatone had given his rallying speech, a quiet resilience had descended over the garrison that epitomised Nocturnean resolve. Militia, some soldiers, others who were rock harvesters or ash traders, stood shoulder-to-shoulder with Fire-born. United, they would cling to this city with tenacious fingers. They would do it to their dying breaths.

Behind them, clogging passageways and conduits, plazas and gantries were scared but stoic Nocturnean faces. Its peoples looked to the world's defenders, their thin green lines, and prayed to the Throne it would be enough.

Val'in was amongst the Scouts alongside Master Prebian, who surveyed the ashen plain beyond the walls through his magnoculars. They had not long returned from Prometheus aboard the *Fire-wyvern*. Emptied of its cargo, the Thunderhawk was headed towards Epimethus and the Acerbian Sea. Mercenary flyers had been sighted by the watchtowers, bound for the Jewel City. Squadrons of speeders and gunships had been sent to counter them. That any enemy force had managed to get so close to the

Sanctuaries prior to detection was testament to the dark eldar's infiltration.

Clutching a bolter close to his carapace plastron, Val'in regarded the approaching enemy ground forces with nervous eyes. All of the Scouts, even he and Exor as aspirants, carried bolters and other long-range weapons. Prebian had instructed the Chapter Bastion's armouries opened and its materiel distributed. The Master of Recruits had supplemented his already impressive arsenal with a chainsword that hung from a scabbard strap around his hip. There were heavy bolters and tube launchers amongst Seventh too, with drum-clips and missile crates close to hand.

'There's armour,' Prebian said to no one in particular, 'lots of it, coming from the west across the Pyre.' He lowered the magnoculars and gave them to Val'in. 'Here, see for yourself.'

Through the grainy scopes, Val'in saw a thick dust cloud presaging a host of armoured vehicles and infantry. There were tracked-haulers too, massive bulky things that dragged fat-wheeled artillery pieces behind them. The disciplined ranks of graven Dragon Warriors marched alongside an alien rabble: wire-limbed, avian creatures who rode along on brutish pack-beasts and in roofless rigger-trucks. Val'in was appalled to see other renegades amongst the throng. He knew they weren't Dragon Warriors because their armour was different, although they all bore Nihilan's mark of allegiance, but had no knowledge of these other warbands.

'There is a host of renegades, all wearing power armour.' Though he tried, he couldn't keep the fear out of his voice.

'Traitors, all the same,' Prebian replied. 'Nihilan has gathered strays and dogs from the Eye to swell his ranks. You'll be killing them soon enough.'

'How?' He'd never fought other Space Marines before. It had only just occurred to him that he ever might.

Prebian pulled down the magnoculars and pointed

at the ribbed joints between sections of his battle-plate. 'Here is where it's weakest, or if they fight without helm then aim for the head. Remember your rituals of accuracy. Use them.' He addressed both aspirants. 'Once they're beyond the void shields, no man-portable weapon can breach these walls. They'll need to climb. You'll have an advantage then. Keep your sights angled low, closer to vertical the better. A shell that penetrates something not fatal like a shoulder or kneecap will travel further. Hopefully it'll detonate around something important.'

He gestured to his hearts, throat and finally head.

'Killing shots,' he explained. 'No mercy, no quarter. This is the Great Enemy we fight. A Space Marine, even one corrupted by Ruin, can sustain a lot of punishment. Anything less and they'll be over these walls. That happens and it's over.'

Val'in nodded, and looked further.

Just behind the infantry, maintaining pace and coming in low, were the gunships. Unlike *Fire-wyvern*, these flyers were older, battered and of some antiquated design. The dark metal flock descended on contrails of fire and swathed the desert in their shadow. Buzzing around them like outriders were dark eldar riding jetbikes and a host of the skimmer-rafts he'd seen earlier.

This was but one army. Others would be gathering all around Nocturne and advancing on the cities. Hesiod, Prebian had told him, would be first.

Known as the Seat of Tribal Kings, it rose up on a mound of granite and backed against a broad shoulder of basalt that made its south and east aspects almost impossible to assault. It was to the north and west facings that Prebian had arrayed his troops. As the first line of defence, much of Third was also garrisoned here.

Val'in could not see his battle-brothers but knew they were ranked below, combat-ready. Some were also stationed on the north wall but were distant enough to be indistinct. He understood that a vanguard of assault troops was hiding in ambush amongst the dunes. Here they would harass and neutralise key targets to slow the advance, buying time for the defenders to hammer them. Thunderfire cannons had been brought from the armoury and were installed at intervals around the wall. Val'in had never seen one fired but knew they were deadly.

Although he'd only been an aspirant, not yet even a Scout, for a short amount of time, he knew this was not the Space Marine way of war. They were shock troops, fast-moving and adaptable, capable of achieving any mission in any battle zone. This siege had been forced upon them.

Prebian had stepped back from the battlements and was deep in conversation over the comm-feed. Val'in turned to Exor.

'I never expected to be fighting a war so soon,' he admitted.

While tactics and survival were Val'in's forte, Exor had excelled with weapons. He cradled a snub-nosed grenade launcher, a bandoleer of fat shells wrapped around his torso – it wasn't exactly standard armament but then this was far from a standard battle. He was checking the sighter sat at the end of the barrel when he looked up and met Val'in's gaze.

'Nor me. We'll earn honour for our Chapter this day,' he vowed, showing none of the other aspirant's anxiety.

'And retribution... for Heklarr, and Kot'iar, Ska'varron and the rest who fell to the dusk-wraith's blades.'

'For all of them,' said Exor, and held out his hand.

Val'in took his forearm in the warrior's grip and their pact was made.

'Retribution.'

'You'll have it, aspirants,' Prebian told them, unslinging his bolter, 'that and the black carapace if you survive this.' He racked the weapon's slide, checked the ammo gauge. 'Make your oaths to Vulkan. I've received word from Captain Agatone. We are to join in battle.' He gestured to the horizon where the first of the enemy's guns had begun to fire.

ACROSS THE LENGTH of the void shields the artillery barrage was like an iridescent lightning storm. The smaller shells created stabbing flashes in the shield's transparent membrane when they struck, whilst the heavier salvos erupted in vast eye-burning blooms that lingered for seconds afterwards like oil on water. Hot and stinking ozone raked the air, bringing an acerbic breeze to the wall as the defences were tested.

They were getting hammered with everything that Nihilan's immense arsenal possessed, but they were holding. For now.

Val'in ignored it and kept firing into the shadows below him. He was leaning deep into the crenellations, keeping the angle of his bolter low as instructed.

Void shields provided excellent protection against high-velocity shelling and turret-mounted energy weapons but were no barrier to slow-marching infantry. The first waves who'd survived the hell-storm beyond the shield threshold emerged like pale versions of themselves coming slowly into focus. They were scythed down mercilessly before they'd had a chance to charge the walls themselves.

Prebian and Agatone had arranged the defences so there was a 'kill box' between where the wall ended and the void shield began. Anything inside that zone would be slaughtered by close weapons fire. Meltaguns and flamers were particularly adept at this task and the ground below Val'in was clogged with smoke, and scorched black.

A burst jolted his shoulder with fierce recoil, but it was so numb and bruised that he could hardly feel it. Something screeched beneath him. It was an alien sound, slowly diminishing as it fell. A second burst, more measured to conserve ammunition, shot out its grapnel. The enemy infantry had weathered the barrage from the walls and were now making their assault in earnest.

At first only a few dregs had got through without being immolated in the kill box, the cannon fodder Nihilan was willing to sacrifice to blunt the defenders' guns, but now they were coming on in numbers. Renegades had joined the ranks in an elite second wave but these were still lesser warriors. So far none of the Dragon Warriors had committed to the fight. The last Val'in had seen of them before the crackling void shield obliterated his view was during the enemy's march to Hesiod.

Behind him, the Thunderfire cannons kept up a steady refrain that boomed across the battlements and threw up clods of earth, smoke and bodies in the middle distance. So loud was the barrage that Val'in almost missed the hollow *chank* in his drum-mag.

'Running low...' he warned, reading the gauge was down to single digits. A Scout, his name was Tk'nar, had just reloaded and took up Val'in's position as the aspirant went for ammunition. Resupply was strictly rationed. It had to last long enough to beat back the besiegers, break their will and send them reeling. So far, the enemy was proving tenacious.

In the brief respite from the wall Val'in caught a glance through the flickering void shields. Assault squads from Third were attacking the fringes of the enemy line, engaging isolated formations. In the few seconds of visual clarity, he saw angelic warriors clad in green battle-plate descend from on high and destroy a convoy of tanks that was repositioning. Before the infantry blocks protecting the armour could retaliate, the saboteurs were gone, buoyed aloft on streamers of oily flame, filling the air with jet-smoke.

To be amongst the Fire-born who waged war on wings of fire...

It was a glorious sight but one quickly lost as a missile salvo flashed angrily across the shield, obscuring the view.

Val'in returned to his post on the wall and the line

bunched together again, the bolt storm unceasing.

'Death to the traitors and all enemies of Nocturne!' roared Prebian, strafing a precise line along the base of the wall.

Exor was invigorated by his captain's war cry and pumped a barrage into the darkness. Multiple explosions lit up the shadows, churning up dirt and blasting bodies apart. Before the dust had settled, he went to release a second barrage when Prebian stopped him.

'Methodical, precise,' he warned. 'Conserve your ammo, it's not everlasting.'

Aggression when unleashed was hard to rein in, even harder to manage and direct. Val'in felt the surge of adrenalised abandon fill him too, a desire to kill everything in his sight, to revel in the power his genhanced attributes provided. But Prebian was right. Temperance, self-awareness and control – these were the traits that separated the loyal Space Marines from the traitors.

He heard the Master of Recruits on the comm-feed.

'We are holding, Captain Agatone, but have yet to engage any of Nihilan's elite forces.'

There was a brief period of silence as he listened to the distant commander. Prebian had his hand over one ear to try and block out the battle din.

'I agree, brother, the sorcerer is planning something. We can do little but hold them off for now. Tu'Shan is coming. We must become the anvil to his hammer.'

We are the anvil, the thought was like an island of calm amidst a sea of utter chaos. War was a brutal thing, without form, bereft of reason or even obvious purpose. There were those that lived and those that died, nothing in-between. It was changing him, Val'in realised. Bolter screaming, he felt it already with the iron in his jaw and the steel in his heart. In this cauldron, he would become Adeptus Astartes or he would perish.

Hundreds of bolters hailed hell down from the walls in a frenzied staccato of gunfire. A bass sound rumbled beneath their roar from heavy bolters and autocannon.

High-pitched missile bursts accented the brutal symphony as they vented from their tubes. Lower notes, the heavy *foom-thwomp* of expelled grenades, were interspersed between them. Deeper still were the *thund-chank-thud* of the siege cannons launching death and thunder into the heavens.

It became a cacophony for Val'in, blending together raucously in a belt of white noise without meaning, incapable of differentiation.

His bolter bucked and roared in his grasp like a sentient thing, craving carnage. Teeth gritted, he held it tightly until whitened knuckles could no longer feel and his hands became an extension of the weapon. With every violence-fuelled moment, he was changing. Val'in welcomed it, embraced it. He would need to evolve if he was going to live.

I will become the anvil.

The battle ground on.

CHAPTER FOURTEEN

I
Burning Skies

THE *FELLDRAKE* BROKE apart as a series of internal explosions rippled through its hull. The escort ship was easy meat for the bulky renegade cruiser, its shields and armour overwhelmed in a single destructive broadside.

Dac'tyr watched its destruction in enhanced magnification via the *Flamewrought's* main occuliport. Outgunned, outsized, the escort had stood little chance against the larger vessel. It was one of several. Despite the Master of the Fleet's pincer strategy inflicting tremendous damage on the enemy armada, the rate of attrition was catching up to his own ships.

He signalled to the *Serpentine* to converge with him on an attack heading.

The void was threaded with the long beam fire of forward lances and peppered with automatic bursts from cannon batteries. It rolled against the *Flamewrought's* shields, its own turrets swivelling to acquire fresh firing solutions. Fighters and lesser ships broke apart against the determined salvos, carving a path for the flagship to advance. It was a vast behemoth of a vessel that moved slowly across the scrap of space where the battle for Nocturne's upper atmosphere was being fought.

A pair of enemy frigates angled to intercept, pouring the forward momentum from their vast engines into a manoeuvre that would bring them both abeam of the Space Marine battle-barge, effectively creating a blockade. It would also bring their vastly superior broadside weapons to bear.

A pulse from the *Flamewrought's* prow mounted nova cannon tore one of the frigates apart and left it shedding fuel and atmospheric pressure. Its crew were expelled with it, jettisoned from the holes in the vessel's rent armour. A short burst of turret fire shredded most of them and left the rest flash-frozen by the void.

Serpentine removed the other frigate with a well-aimed lance strike, but not before numerous shield impacts registered on Dac'tyr's tacticarium screen from a bout of ineffective broadsides. A schematic of the flagship showed negative damage from the salvo, but elsewhere several decks were sealed off and engines were running at below capacity. So far, the nova cannon still functioned but it was taking longer to re-power after firing and a section of starboard broadsides was destroyed. Shields in that section were also displaying weakened energy returns. Overall, the voids and displacers were currently at around forty-seven per cent effective.

Four enemy capital ships, all cruiser classes, had been scratched already as *Flamewrought* and *Serpentine* had laid anchor on the port side of the enemy battle line. Their husks floated across the void, blank-eyed and silent. Emblazoned with graven images and fell statuary, they were not so different from floating tombs.

Across a distant gulf laced with wrecks, damaged vessels and intense battery fire, the *Vulkan's Wrath* and the *Hammerforge* racked up their own kills. So far the larger Space Marine cruisers were faring well but now the enemy vessels were gathering in attack formations and exploiting their greater numbers.

Dac'tyr had used enfilading fire with the *Serpentine* at extreme range to rip up numerous escorts and frigates too. These morsels were the first to burn, but represented little more than fodder. It had warmed up the guns but nothing more. In response, several vessels were peeling off from their previous attack vector and coming for the battle-barge. Draw them away from the *Hell-stalker* and Dac'tyr might be able to close enough for a boarding action, but it would take time.

Like all void battles, the conflict above Nocturne was slow and ponderous. A captain was not only required to think in terms of multi-dimensional space but he also had to predict and prepare. There was a sense of almost orchestral choreography in its complexity, where each instrument supports every other. In isolation each ship in a battle line was less effective than when combined and deployed in the right order at precisely the correct moment. Foresight was essential. If a hulking cruiser or battle-barge was in the wrong place, it would take a long time to move. Rapid manoeuvres in response to enemy tactics were simply impossible.

'All ahead full,' Dac'tyr ordered down the vox-feed to his bridge crew. In a few minutes they'd pass the debris field left by the sundered enemy frigates and bring their guns to bear on the renegade cruiser.

The battle-barge's cogitator banks identified it as the *Harganath*, an old Imperial vessel stolen by renegade pirates and put to the use of Ruin. Dac'tyr had no idea of who captained the ship now; only that it was an abomination that must be destroyed. Through the occuliport its hull appeared to be jagged and its serrated prow resembled the maw of some vast ocean predator. Dark slashes decorated its massive flanks like black blood.

Three more enemy vessels appeared on the tacticarium screen, forward arcs firing. A torpedo spread roared from each, intended to inflict critical damage on the *Flame-wrought* and *Serpentine*, which had just come abeam.

'*Deploying interceptors*,' the voice of Captain Sargorr'ath crackled over the external vox-feed.

Dac'tyr launched his own fighters too as a fourth ship ranged up onto his prow, alongside the more distant spectre of the *Harganath*. This was a lighter vessel with a flanged prow like a mace, spare with its weapons but carrying ranks of boarding claws along its flanks and underbelly.

To come into close proximity with a ship like that was to invite death by evisceration from its berserkers and breaching troops.

'Forward lances,' Dac'tyr roared, as an icon flashed on another sub-screen indicating the fighters had launched.

Shield impacts blazed across the *Flamewrought's* forward occuliport before its lances could retaliate. The tacticarium screen hazed and then blinked back, indicating they'd taken sensorium damage.

The lances powered and a salvo of deadly beams raked across kilometres of void-space to the aggressor ship.

'Torpedo spread, wide dispersal,' he followed, and the forward tubes were vented. Dac'tyr watched the tacticarium screen and the red icon representing the ship that had ambushed them. Forward lances registered several strong hits which downed the cruiser's shields momentarily. It was a calculated shot as the torpedo markers bypassed the overloaded defences and bloomed against the vessel's armour.

'Bring it up, full magnification.'

The overhead screen displayed a view of the cruiser, its prow wreathed in flames. Secondary explosions rolled up the hull as incendiaries and ammunition stores cooked off spectacularly. It was ailing, the damage inflicted by the torpedoes critical.

'Captain Sargorr'ath, she's yours to finish.'

'*At your word, my Fleetmaster.*'

A slew of lance strikes arrowed from the *Serpentine*, savaging the already stricken vessel. Without shields, the renegade cruiser was a floating powder keg primed for violent ignition. Its bridge was destroyed upon impact.

Several weapon towers went with it, collapsing and spearing into the superstructure below. Its engines capitulated against the strain of the attack and the cruiser fell from the void, set adrift and burning.

'*On our port side,*' Sargorr'ath returned.

The fighters had neutralised the torpedo spread but were still at large, attempting to regroup with their parent ships through a hail of flak. The trio of cruisers flanking them had closed their formation to better intensify the effect of their forward weapons. Desultory turret fire ripped into the plucky interceptors and barely half made it back to their launch bays.

Dac'tyr was focused on the *Harganath*. He had one eye on the nova cannon, which was close to full charge. Impact markers flared on the tacticarium screen as the *Serpentine* took a battering from the port side ships. It looked heavy as they all targeted the smaller strike-cruiser. Kill one and then they'd gang up on the larger battle-barge.

'*Serpentine*… Sargorr'ath, are you still with me?'

The return came back marred by static. Warning klaxons and the hiss of active fire-suppressant systems undercut the captain's jagged response. '*Taken… heavy fire… shields… almost out… lost port side weapon batteries.*'

The nova cannon was ready to fire. Dac'tyr could eliminate the *Harganath* but then Sargorr'ath was done for. His eyes scanned the tacticarium display, searching quickly for an answer.

Grimly, he hailed his helmsmaster. 'All stop. Bring us about, full power to port side aft to make her turn.'

'My lord, that will bring us abeam of the *Harganath*. Our starboard side batteries are unlikely to disable it and shields are already dipping below forty per cent effective.'

'Bring us about, helm,' Dac'tyr ordered calmly. 'Do it now, if you please.'

He raised the ship-to-ship vox as the rapid heading change went into effect. It was like turning the arm on a heavy crane, slow at first but quick to build as it accumulated momentum.

'*Serpentine*, this is Dac'tyr of the *Flamewrought*.'

'*I can see your heading, Fleetmaster.*'

'Very good, captain. The *Harganath* is all yours.'

'*I have lances powered and torpedoes primed.*'

'Vent it all, everything you've got.'

'*In Vulkan's name and for the burning skies,*' Sargorr'ath replied.

'Vulkan and the burning skies.'

The vox went dead as Sargorr'ath cut the feed.

Dac'tyr gripped the arms of the command throne as the bridge shuddered with the *Harganath's* assault on their broadside.

'How are those shields holding?' He had to shout above the sound of sudden warning klaxons and the perpetual tremors thundering throughout the ship.

The helmsmaster sounded fraught. 'Below thirty per cent, twenty-four, twenty-two…'

'Just keep us intact a little longer.' They were coming about. Ahead on the forward occuliport, Dac'tyr and the rest of the bridge crew could see the trio of advancing cruisers. Their front arc weapons were raining fury against the *Serpentine*, which had yet to release its own forward salvos.

'A little closer, Sargorr'ath,' Dac'tyr muttered, teeth clenched as a renewed bombardment brought fresh damage reports scrolling down a sub-screen.

'Eighteen per cent, fifteen…' The helmsmaster kept up the grim commentary.

Now the *Flamewrought* was taking fire to the front. The flanking cruisers must have seen what Dac'tyr was planning. None of them could break off; they were too close, any large manoeuvre would risk a catastrophic collision. Instead, they gave the front arc weapons everything, pouring hell and thunder against both Salamander ships.

Still a few degrees to go before the nova cannon could

be unleashed. Momentum from the aft engines was picking up. Dac'tyr estimated as long as a minute until they achieved the optimum firing solution.

'Nine per cent, six per cent...' The helmsmaster looked up anxiously from his station.

'Hold your nerve, helm. Bring us around... Just a little closer.' Dac'tyr's gaze was locked on the tacticarium. The *Serpentine* had just passed beneath them and closed to within lethal lance range. Markers indicated a torpedo launch from all of its bays. They streamed across the black void of the crackling display screen in formation, rendered as tiny dagger-shaped icons.

'Cut them open, brother,' Dac'tyr willed.

'Three per cent. Shield collapse imminent.'

'A few more degrees...'

'Starboard shields down, we're taking damage.'

Fire plumed across the bridge, engulfing several members of the crew. Others were thrown off their feet or clung desperately to their stations as the deck beneath them roiled.

Dac'tyr shut his mind to their screaming, to waver now and lose resolve would mean the end of all of them.

'Stay with me, helm!' he bellowed.

An explosion in his peripheral vision took out a bank of consoles, throwing bodies into the smoke-thick air. A section of the vaulted ceiling caved in, crushing a group of servitors who'd been attempting to get the fire under control.

'My lord!' The helmsmaster was bleeding and held himself awkwardly from some unseen injury.

Sixty seconds that had felt eternal in their passing finally reached a terminus.

The *Flamewrought* came about, bringing Dac'tyr's target to bear.

'Fire! Unleash the nova cannon!' he roared.

A coruscating beam thrust from the prow of the *Flamewrought* and coursed across the void. Hit with the destructive fury of a dying sun, the middle cruiser broke apart and shattered. Trailing fire and escaping pressure, she ditched at once, listing horribly to the port side. Motive power had failed utterly as sheer brutal momentum took the ship into the side of another cruiser which was attempting to move away.

The dead ship's spike ram tore into the fleeing vessel, ripping open its flank and spilling what was inside like guts strewn across the void. It drove on, pushing apart the other ship's inner decks and tearing prow from aft. The fleeing ship came apart and the two vessels, briefly entwined, exploded. The blast was immense. It rolled into the third ship like a tidal wave, heaving it over so its ventral section angled starboard. Turrets and cathedra towers came apart in the force wash as hundreds of small fires erupted across the hull like the sporadic colonisation of an ant horde.

Despite himself, Dac'tyr clenched his fist in triumph.

'Well done, helm.' His voice was a little strained. 'Well done.'

The fire was brought under control and auxiliary systems activated. Non-essential stations were shut down and crew re-appropriated across the bridge so the *Flamewrought* could still function.

Damage reports came thickly now. Dac'tyr processed each and every one, locking into his eidetic memory and deploying measures as needed. They were still combat-effective, which was just as well… The *Hell-stalker* had just appeared on tacticarium.

II
Stormriders

THE TREMORS BELOW decks subsided and Praetor whispered a prayer to the Emperor.

The launch bay was a vast space, but little more than bare metal with a strongly buttressed ceiling. A massive teleportation pad was well shielded towards the centre of the chamber where the Firedrakes had been received from Prometheus. It was dark too, lit solely by emergency lighting that ran in arcing lume strips halfway up the onyx-black interior. Both flanking walls were punctuated with circular docking hatches. Beyond each hermetically sealed, interleaved gate was a boarding torpedo. Thirty-two torpedoes were engaged for launch, each with a nose-mounted vulcan-drill capable of penetrating starship armour. The embarkation zone in front of each access hatch was delineated by warning chevrons. Currently, they were all occupied.

Praetor and a Terminator command squad were maglocked in one; Halknarr and his Firedrakes in another. All told there were twenty five-man units ready to breach and board. Most carried storm shields, thunder hammers and melta weapons. Vo'kar had his heavy flamer. A warrior in Halknarr's squad called Un'gar hoisted an assault cannon to bear. The deployment of even a solitary squad of the First represented a serious threat; to engage its entire complement for a single action smacked of overkill, but then their mission was one of necessity, survival for their Chapter its price. Overkill was what was needed.

'Trust in Lord Dac'tyr,' said He'stan. He had joined Praetor's squad and since translation into the *Flamewrought* had waited silently at the veteran sergeant's side.

'It is not my brother-captain that concerns me,' Praetor admitted. 'It is the vagaries of fate and the capricious nature of the void. I have fought in void-wars before and they have a habit of seldom running to plan.'

The comm-feed in Praetor's battle-helm crackled.

'At least we are still in one piece, a sign that Vulkan is with us if ever there was one.'

In the next embarkation zone, Halknarr held his chainfist aloft. A flash of fire lit the retinal lenses of his drake-helm.

Praetor replied. 'Why is it on campaign you are an obstinate, cantankerous bastard until faced with the prospect of imminent death, brother?'

'*I blame the years of my veterancy.*' He tapped the stilled teeth-blades of his chainfist to his forehead.

These are worthy warriors, all, thought Praetor. *Let me honour them; let us honour Vulkan and the Chapter this day of days.*

He looked up at the ready lights above the portal. One icon was lit green indicating that the boarding torpedoes were primed for launch. Two more were still dark.

'Give the signal,' he urged beneath his breath. 'Unleash us into the fires of battle…'

A second light joined the first and Praetor declared down the company-wide channel, 'All Firedrakes into boarding positions, mag-locked and harnessed immediately.'

The access hatches opened in quick succession. With a hiss of released pressure, the metal leaves retracted like an expanding iris that led into the darkened interior of the boarding pod.

Techmarines and their servitor crews wheeled the sentry weapons into the ten decoy tubes. The last two were occupied by Ashamon and Amadeus, hulking Dreadnoughts and warriors-eternal.

The massive war engines were equipped with seismic hammers. Where Brother Ashamon favoured a heavy flamer, Amadeus cycled an assault cannon through its pre-firing routines. Both were forced to stoop as they entered their respective tubes.

'In Vulkan's name!' they bellowed as one.

Praetor nodded to the venerable champions as the hatch closed behind him, shutting the launch bay off from view until only the inside of the boarding torpedo remained. Muttering litanies of activation, he flicked on a small targeting console affixed to the centre of the shallow strip of deck inside the tube. The simplistic display was rendered in blue and would chart their progress to the target. Icons represented the other vessels and debris along their trajectory to the *Hell-stalker*.

The mission objective required a very specific breach and insertion point. Margin for error was narrow, so he checked the small retro-jets fitted to the tube had manual power and enough fuel in case of course correction.

All was in readiness.

Praetor lifted his gaze to regard each and every one of the Firedrakes aboard with him. Gathimu... Hrydor... Nu'mean... he had already lost so many.

Who will bring back my corpse to the mountain? he wondered bleakly.

He'stan's hand upon his armoured shoulder removed all doubt.

'Vulkan is with us, brother,'

Praetor's grief was burned away by a righteous flame.

The third light inside the torpedo turned green.

They launched.

ON THE BRIDGE of the *Hell-stalker*, Nihilan consulted a hololith map of Nocturne's surface. His cohorts were engaged across two Sanctuary Cities. Themis and Hesiod would bear the brunt of the attack, for it was these bastions he'd have to raze first. As he gazed across a grainy projection of the ground assault, it was to the latter that he focused his attention.

Artillery was well entrenched and bombarded the Salamanders' void shields without cessation. Tens of thousands of infantry pushed up to the threshold of the shimmering barrier-fields as they fought to gain the walls. It was bloody, even from distance, and hundreds of the dead already clogged the base of Hesiod's defences.

Fire-born, he knew, were tenacious. They would hold until they no longer drew breath. A meatgrinder was where that trait came into its own. Nihilan had predicted the cities would not be easy to crack but that was not really his aim, and he had a solution for the defenders' obstinacy anyway.

Adjusting the pict-feed from the sensorium, he panned

out to a wider vista and then homed back in on Mount Deathfire, which shadowed both cities with its craggy flanks. Fumes spilled from the vast calderas. Nihilan could almost hear the lament of the firedrakes, wailing in sympathetic anger with the earth.

'She will be blighted before this is done,' he promised, his eyes alighting on a narrow aperture at the summit of one of Deathfire's peaks.

'Are you certain it is there?' he asked of the shadows.

A voice answered that only Nihilan could hear.

Drive your spear and you will rip out her still beating heart, drowning her children in blood.

It was more distant than before, as if only a relic of sentience remained. The crawling sensation beneath his skin was no more, the pressure on his mind absent. There was connection but it was no longer forged through symbiosis.

'My eternal thanks are yours.'

The pact is sealed, no gratitude is necessary. My hunger will soon be sated…

The voice drifted away as if carried on an unfelt breeze and Nihilan was alone again.

He straightened in his command throne, shutting off the hololith.

'Closing to within range, master,' growled the voice of his helmsmaster. The creature cowered in the gloom, head bowed with its claws wrapped around a control console.

Nihilan was pleased. The lesser ships had done their task well, occupying Dac'tyr and his fleet. He glanced at the tacticarium screen, noting the signatures of the *Flamewrought* and the *Serpentine* advancing upon them as well as a host of smaller escorts.

He leaned over to the ship's vox-feed.

'Ekrine, is the Stormbird ready?'

'And waiting, my lord.'

Thark'n and Ramlek were standing either side.

Kneeling before him was Nor'hak.

'You know what's coming for you?' Nihilan asked.

The supplicant raised his eyes to meet the sorcerer's. 'I will slaughter them all.'

In his Terminator armour his homicidal tremors were kept still. He had yet to don a tusked battle-helm, which he held in one hand and rested on his bent knee. His eyes spoke murder and a desire to inflict pain.

'It is difficult to say which one of you is the most sadistic,' Nihilan remarked with a glance at Ramlek. The larger warrior looked like he wanted to prove it even with his rival clad in Tactical Dreadnought Armour.

'Stop them, Nor'hak, that's all I need you to do. Do that and they will die on this ship. All of them, including the pilgrim.'

Nor'hak nodded and Nihilan arose from his throne.

'She's all yours,' he said. 'I need only to see one more thing before I depart.' He turned to the cowering wretch at the *Hell-stalker's* helm.

'The weapon is locked into position, master.'

Nihilan smiled, but the expression never reached his eyes.

When the order came it was given calmly.

'Then fire.'

FAR BELOW THE bridge of the *Hell-stalker* in the lower gun decks, the seismic cannon powered to life. The metals employed in its construction trembled as the mechanisms of its archaic design shifted like a slumbering titan, goaded into waking. It did not do so easily. This hand of gods, this weapon that had been dredged up after the aeons of darkness had buried it, stirred reluctantly as if it knew the devastation it could wreak.

According to the worshippers of the Omnissiah, the great Martian Machine God, every weapon has a spirit. It is this anima that must be soothed and placated in order for it to function. The seismic cannon possessed an ages-old sentience. It had the perspective of a terrible era when such apocalypse weapons existed that could erase entire races from being. Its spirit was malicious and terrible. It could not be placated, and was only capable of wrath.

The fully charged capacitors released a mournful whine as the fyron powder reacted in devastating molecular fusion. Energy coursed up the vast barrel, only barely contained. Upon reaching the mouth there was a flaring corona of power like a dawning sun that bleached the sky magnesium white.

Then it roared with a voice like crackling thunder and drove a wound deep into the heart of a world.

WITH HIS DEADLY cargo released, Dac'tyr prepared to withdraw and engage the rest of the enemy ships from distance. Through the forward occuliport he watched the *Hell-stalker* approach with disgusted awe.

It was immense, dwarfing even the *Flamewrought*. No weapon he possessed could stop it. Perhaps the nova cannon, if fired at close range and able to hit some vital system, might slow the behemoth down but this was a fleet-killer.

Dac'tyr had seen its like before but not for many years. It was a vessel built for crusading, so vast and powerful that it could take on opposing flotillas single-handed and run for centuries before needing to make dock.

It was once a true ship of war, but one whose noble lineage stood corrupted by Chaos. The vessel was bloated by additional cannons, torpedo tubes and fighter bays. Armour, thickened and re-bolted several times over, fattened its grossly cluttered flanks and underbelly. The *Hell-stalker* was an ugly thing, wrought for carnage at the sacrifice of speed and manoeuvrability. It would win simply by battering its enemy into submission, forcing him to empty his stores of ammunition until there was nothing left but desperation.

Then it would crush that too and spit the carcass back into the void to join the other lifeless, floating hulks.

And like the ship, its primary weapon was a spiked

and wretched thing protruding from its prow like a harpy's talon.

Dac'tyr was relaying evasive orders to the helm when he saw the crackling energy stir around the seismic cannon's immense muzzle.

He voxed the lead boarding torpedo.

'Brother-Sergeant Praetor, be advised something's happening...'

A pulse of light ignited from the energy flux. It held there, burning for a few seconds, before being unleashed in a single focused beam.

An escort in its path, attempting to come at the *Hellstalker* from beneath, was clipped. The ship disintegrated on contact with the energy lance uncoiling from the seismic cannon. A flash of light filled the *Flamewrought's* occuliport and when it faded the ship was gone. A squadron of smaller gunships, coming in the escort's wake but peeling away at the sight of the larger vessel's destruction, were swept aside by the blast wave. Their hulls were stripped back in seconds, the metal flayed off layer by layer until only atoms remained.

It hit the *Flamewrought* too and sent warning icons scrolling across the tacticarium display. Several lower decks had taken damage; the port sections reported it was severe.

If the Firedrakes were caught up in that...

Dac'tyr prayed that the boarding torpedoes were still flying within the umbrella of the flagship's void shields.

All comms snapped out, leaving a drone of static.

'Re-open a channel to Brother-Sergeant Praetor immediately!'

A series of dead returns came back.

THE BOARDING TORPEDOES sped from their launch tubes at incredible velocity into a mire of debris.

Praetor's leading torpedo, like the tip of an arrow, bore the brunt of it.

Broken sections of ship armour smacked loudly against

the hull, crates and drums disgorged from split cargo bays smashed upon its armoured nose, while the frozen bodies of dead crewmen simply bounced off. Every impact rocked the tube but failed to shake it off course. It was just chaff caught between the *Flamewrought's* void shields.

Using the guidance console to navigate, Praetor made small adjustments to avoid the larger pieces of floating wreckage. He burned the retro-jets sporadically, pulling the tube's trajectory to keep it steady.

Kilometres clicked by in one corner of the screen, counting down the distance to target.

They were approaching the edge of the void shielded area in a dispersed formation when the instrumentation across the entire spread overloaded. The torpedo shook violently and Praetor grimaced as a chain of sparks erupted from the console before it cut to black.

A secondary void-tremor slammed into the diminutive boarding vessel, spinning it. The shriek of protesting metal threatened an integrity breach. If that happened they'd survive but be cast adrift like all the other flotsam of space. The seals held but were under huge strain. Tiny fissures, venting minute pressure leaks, webbed the interior hull. Monstrous turbulence seized them and the torpedo trembled like a bunker exposed to a constant ordnance barrage.

'We cannot take much more of this,' uttered Persephion.

'Stand firm, trust in the primarch.' He'stan had his gaze fixed ahead, as if he could see through the drill-tipped prow to a point beyond the ken of his brothers. 'We must endure it.'

Praetor hammered at the darkened console, putting a crack in the glass.

'Navigation is out,' he muttered, as if it were a small matter.

The void-tremors were subsiding, signalling the return of comms.

Captain Dac'tyr's voice exploded through the static, fraught and over-loud.

'*...lkan's breath and all the damned hells of Nocturne!*'

In all the many years Praetor had known him, Dac'tyr had never once lost his composure. And here he was ranting like a zealot.

'Brother-captain...'

At hearing Praetor's voice, Dac'tyr's tone changed. Relief warred with shock for supremacy. '*Praetor! Brother-sergeant, they have fired.*'

'The weapon?' Even the stoic leader of the Firedrakes sounded anxious.

'*Hell-stalker has unleashed the seismic cannon,*' Dac'tyr confirmed. '*I have never seen...*'

'What is happening?' Praetor was struggling to concentrate. Though they'd ridden out the worst of it, the passage to Nihilan's flagship was still rough and, without guidance, uncertain. 'Speak to me, brother-captain.'

All aboard the torpedo were enrapt by the exchange. So far, the only known fact was that Nocturne had been hit by the apocalypse weapon. It was the very thing their intervention was meant to have prevented.

Silence.

'Dac'tyr!'

'*Hell and flame, brother, it was something terrible. Such power...*'

'What of our world, our home? Does she yet live?'

Shock turned into dour pragmatism. '*I cannot tell, brother. The augurs are damaged but Nocturne has been struck by the weapon. I saw it breach the atmosphere and lance the surface. I can't imagine what must...*' He trailed away. No one ever even countenanced such a doom, let alone expected to witness it.

Praetor was grimly taciturn. 'Then we must not allow it to fire for a second time.' He thumbed the retro-jets to maximum, intending to power through the wreckage field or die impaled upon it.

'We are upon the anvil now, brothers,' he told the rest

of his squad, shouting above the scream of the jets. Inertia shuddered the curved walls of the tiny hold as the entire vessel tried to shake itself apart.

He'stan was the only one to answer. 'Then let us show Vulkan we are worthy of its tempering.'

CHAPTER FIFTEEN

I
Destiny

APOTHEOSIS CAN BE a state of mind as well as body. Rebirth from what was to what is, a transition from one thing to another, begins with understanding identity.

Dak'ir had never been certain of that. Unlike his brothers, his memories of childhood hunting through the caves of Ignea were strong. In many ways they possessed him, became an aspect of his reality as it was now. Becoming a Space Marine had done nothing to clarify that; it had only left him conflicted.

How can I be humane if I am not human? It was not so long ago that he'd asked this question of himself. Upon his ascension to the Librarius and the rank of Lexicanum, his confusion had increased further.

I am a weapon, but then aren't we all? Over the last year, in the darkness and solitude of his prison, he had asked this too.

There were those that believed he had the power to doom or save a world. These were not idle-speaking men, nor were they credulous, paralysed by their own superstitions. They were vaunted champions, a council of elders whose wisdom was beyond question.

I am the Unbound Flame?

Was Dak'ir really expected to believe he was an artefact of myth given human form, an eternal fire anchored to flesh and blood?

Yet, there it lingered, this destructive force within him. He had kept it shackled within the bounds of his psyche. Through sheer will he did this, not through the null collars or the wards and sigils.

I am changing, he thought as the last of his armour was affixed to his body.

Apotheosis.

It felt good to become Lexicanum once more.

'Dak'ir…' Pyriel's voice brought him out of his reverie. The Epistolary was holding something towards him in outstretched hands. 'No Librarian should be without his staff or blade.'

It was *Draugen*, his force sword.

Closing his hand around the hilt, Dak'ir remembered the power it possessed and how to wield it with deadly purpose. The sword was like an extension of his being; without it, he was incomplete.

'Gratitude, my master,' he said, 'for this and your words during my judgement.'

'Besides angering Vel'cona, I achieved little. Be grateful for the wisdom of Tu'Shan and the expediency of the moment.' He paused, and took on a concerned expression. 'How do you feel?'

Dak'ir hooked *Draugen's* scabbard to his battle-plate.

'Better… worse. I feel as if I'm at the whim of some destiny I cannot shape or influence.' He took his plasma pistol as it was offered, holstering that too. 'The Time of Fire arises and yet here I am… *unchanged*.'

'Into the fires of battle, brothers,' Elysius, who was watching from the shadows at the edges of the Reclusiam, reminded them. 'War calls.'

Pyriel nodded to the Chaplain, before clapping Dak'ir on the shoulder.

'Whatever fate comes, whatever trial the anvil brings, we shall face it together, brother.'

The bonds of brotherhood burned fiercely in Dak'ir's eyes, 'In Vulkan's name.'

'Aye, in Vulkan's name.' Pyriel let him go so he could receive his benediction.

'Come forwards then, Hazon Dak'ir,' said Elysius, brandishing his rosarius, 'and let the primarch see you.'

Head bowed, Dak'ir was poised to kneel in supplication when the ceremony was interrupted.

Framed by the Reclusiam's triumphal arch, a dishevelled figure whose attire looked utterly out of place admist the religiosity and statuary of the chamber stood and observed them. Despite the modest trappings, when Dak'ir saw him he recognised the figure instantly.

'Fugis…' The name, only scarcely given, made the others turn. Dak'ir was already rising. 'Brother, I thought… I saw…' During the Totem Path, the final stage of his Librarius training in the desert, he had received a vision of Fugis's death and yet here he was.

The Apothecary's reply was typically acerbic. 'I live, and stand here in the flesh of my earthly body to prove it. Why did so many assume me dead? I had hoped for greater confidence in my survival skills.'

Elysius nodded to him. 'Few survive the Burning Walk. Is your faith restored, brother?'

Fugis knelt before his Chaplain to receive benediction, which was muttered over his bowed head. 'I am whole again,' he said, standing, 'but have learned much out in the desert.'

'You return at an auspicious moment, brother,' said Elysius, 'though I suspect that is why you are before us now.'

'Indeed.' Fugis couldn't take his eyes off Dak'ir.

The effect was deeply uncomfortable. Pyriel noticed it too.

'What is it?'

The Apothecary's next words dampened the ebullient mood.

'I wish I could return in better circumstances, but I bear a message that cannot wait for heartfelt reunion.'

'Speak, brother,' Elysius urged him.

'I saw a sign, out in the desert.' His gaze alighted on the Lexicanum and did not waver for a moment. 'About you, Dak'ir, and your destiny.'

Pyriel stepped into Fugis's eye-line to get his attention. 'Then tell us quickly, brother. Nocturne is at war.'

'I know,' he snapped at the Epistolary. 'I have already been fighting in it.' When the Apothecary's gaze flicked back to Pyriel's old acolytum, his eyes lit with the fires of remembrance.

'I wandered the ash plains for years. It felt as centuries, brothers, roaming those trackless, grey wastes. I survived through dint of my gifts, the genetic heritage we all share, but I was forced to adapt. I learned the ways of the drovers and used them to hunt, to find shelter, to live as a nomad beyond the solace of the Sanctuary Cities. I did it because my mind was in turmoil, my spirit and belief battered.

'Each night passed much as the last. I killed and ate, lived in harmony with our terrible earth but could not find what I sought to salve my wounded soul.' His voice darkened. 'On one bleak evening I was out in the Pyre Desert, close to the Cindara Plateau. I had hoped a reunion with the place of my ascension to Space Marine would stir providence. It did, but not as I imagined. Upon the farthest dune, I beheld a column of fire pluming high into the bloody sky, coiling like a serpent intent on devouring the heavens. Rising from the peaks of the Dragonspires, it presaged a storm. It was utterly unlike anything I have ever known.'

Fugis's eyes went far away as he relived the events of the fateful night he was describing.

'I left my camp, my kills, the shelter I had made. For to be abroad on the Pyre when it struck would surely be my doom. I ran, taking what weapons and provisions I was able, not knowing where I was headed, only that I had to go.

'It began as a wind at first, a hot zephyr I felt upon my back despite the advantages given to me by my progenitor. Then it grew into a roaring heat, an almighty flame that rolled across the dunes immolating all before it. Spears of flame came with it, turing into firewyrms as they were cast down from the hell-red sky in a veritable rain of conflagration.

'The heat burned the clothes from off my back, turned them into dust. It blistered my skin. Naked and on fire, I tumbled down into a ravine not knowing how much longer I would survive. Blinded by smoke, the churning of the desert ash in my ears and mouth, I reached out and grasped something in the darkness.'

Fugis reached out during his recitation, seizing air as he mimicked his night of hell for his audience.

'It was a hatch, and the hatch led into a ship. With the fire only seconds from spilling down into the ravine and destroying me, I crawled inside on pain ravaged limbs, the hatch closing in my wake. I fell then – the floor, like the air inside, was cool – listening to the storm as it battered my sanctuary and surged across its hull.

'I heard the frustration in the fire's voice as I was denied to it. My mind drifted into a place of shadows, of earth that smelled like the grave and of great, sweeping ossuary roads that went on into forever. Behind my fevered thoughts, the flame seemed to linger, trying to find ingress into my tomb…'

Fugis paused, the memories coming slower as he reached the terminus of his experience. He clenched his fist, brought it to his lips as he tried to effect recall.

'I must have passed out for a time, for when I awoke I was healed. I arose to regard my surroundings. It was indeed a ship, but not one such as I had ever seen. Naked as an infant, I wandered its lonely halls in search of survivors, but wary of other denizens who might be waiting for me in the shadows with hungry mouths.

'For hours I walked, inside a ship so vast it could not have gone unnoticed even in the Pyre and yet…' Fugis shook his head as if the mystery of the ship's anonymity still vexed him. 'As I was giving up hope of ever finding anything or anyone aboard, I discovered a small campsite in some chamber whose use had been long forgotten. There I saw a drover's coat, his hat and supplies. I took them all, the material cold against my fire-cleansed skin. Amongst the absent drover's belongings was a beacon, the one I used to summon the *Fire-wyvern* to my aid and come here, but he had left me a message too, this ancient outlander.'

Dak'ir's eyes widened at this remark, his twin hearts trembling. He felt the flame within him become restless and fought to suppress it.

'I almost missed it, so dark was the room,' Fugis said. 'It was etched upon the wall, a simple tableau rendered in clay-wax and the embers of a fire. As I looked, I noticed a piece of wood at the base of the wall. It was sharpened like a quill, its tip flame-ravaged and charcoal-black. It was the image of a dark rock, headed for a red world. In the next I saw a warrior emerging from the earth. Then again, but changed. In his maw he consumes a hundred warriors and is wreathed in fire. With sword in hand, the flaming saviour is depicted driving off a horde of draconian beasts who fly on pinioned wing and are the colour of old blood. Then there is fire, only fire. The rest of the walls were covered in it, hidden at first by the shadows and only revealed by a lume-lantern's light.'

Elysius exchanged a concerned glance with Pyriel.

'It was a flame-eternal,' Fugis continued, 'a world fire, consuming all and everything before it.'

Pyriel's face had darkened. 'It bears more than passing similarity to the prophecy of the Ferro Ignis, the Fire Sword,' he said, suddenly acutely aware of Dak'ir's psychic presence.

The Chaplain's eyes fell upon the Lexicanum. 'A low-born, one of the earth... He who is our doom or salvation and will drown Nocturne in an eternal fire.'

'But I am as I was,' Dak'ir protested. 'Look at me now – I am no saviour, nor a prophet of doom.' He turned to the Apothecary, whose mind had not yet come back to the Reclusiam. 'Fugis, did it say how I was to become this... *Fire Sword*?'

Fugis looked up. Lucidity was slow to return. 'Many become one. I believe this is what catalyses the process of rebirth.'

'Rebirth?' asked Elysius. 'Into what, exactly? Are we sure we *want* to bring about such an apotheosis?'

Pyriel turned on him. 'You had fewer doubts during judgement, brother.'

'Sparing a battle-brother a pointless and ignominious death is one thing, taking part in some... *ritual* to bring about an ascension we know nothing about and have no control over is another.'

Fugis wasn't listening. He spoke to Dak'ir. 'Where is the ancient's gene-seed, the genetic lifeblood of Gravius? Do we still possess it?'

That got Pyriel's attention. 'It is in a vault which can only be accessed through the Pantheon Chamber, under lock and key. None save Tu'Shan can get to it,' he said before Dak'ir could answer.

'That isn't strictly true,' said Elysius.

Everyone looked to the Chaplain.

'It is only by the Chapter Master's authority that the chamber containing all the relics we recovered from Scoria can be opened, but Vulkan's Sigil,' he brandished the hammer icon that was once believed a part of the primarch's armour, 'will grant us passage to what we seek.'

Fugis was already moving. 'We must go there immediately.'

Elysius's outstretched arm stopped him. 'And do what? How can we be sure of any of this? You were delirious, brother, half-dead from whatever rigours your body withstood in the desert. This might all be madness.'

'The beacon was very real.' Fugis was indignant, bordering on violent. 'There was a time when this Chapter trusted my word and thought me valued counsel. Has that changed so suddenly?'

The Chaplain held up a placatory hand.

'None here doubt you, brother.'

'Where is *your* faith, Elysius?' Fugis asked. 'Don't you believe in miracles any more, or the possibility of divine providence?'

He did. Elysius had borne witness to it on the Volgorrah Reef in the Coliseum of Blades when the broken crozius had ignited and killed the wych queen, despite the fact it shouldn't have been able to. Because of that, he'd lived; because of that, his belief and purpose had been restored.

He'd said himself that he sensed Vulkan's hand in unfolding events. The Apothecary's return was a part of that design. Now was not the time to waver.

The Chaplain stood aside.

Scowling, Fugis made for the Pantheon Chamber.

'His epiphany in the desert has done nothing to improve his demeanour,' remarked Pyriel in a low voice.

Elysius watched him as he left. His gaze was as steel.

'It would seem not.'

His instincts told him to turn back, to stop this and make for Nocturne immediately. He quietened them with a thought. It was time to trust in faith.

II
Vulkan's Hand

THERE WERE NO guards, no wards of any kind. The way was open before the Chaplain and empty. It was a disturbing sight, of times changed and the closeness of a calamity that had surreptitiously closed around the Salamanders without them realising.

'I have never seen this place…'

…k'ir stood in Elysius's shadow, not daring to step …er. An overwhelming sense of reverence emating from inside the sacred temple held him back. He was awestruck and fought the urge to fall on bended knee in supplication.

'It has that effect on everyone the first time they see it,' the Chaplain muttered wryly. 'I still feel it and I am the bearer of Vulkan's Sigil, a relic keeper much like this place is a repository of relics.'

Librarium, reliquary, lodestone, the Pantheon Chamber held a great significance for the Promethean Cult and the luminaries of the Salamanders. It harboured the Tome of Fire, the wisdom of Vulkan as given unto his sons to guide them beyond his passing.

Around the temple's circular walls were arrayed the many tomes, scrolls and charts where the primarch had inscribed his writings. There were arcane devices, statues, metal sculpture, even weapons that all bore some element of Vulkan's fathomless knowledge of that a time that now only existed in faded tapestry or rumour.

Some amongst the Chapter believed that the primarch was long dead, slain on the battlefields of Isstvan V during the start of the Great Betrayal. Others thought him merely lost, a pilgrim roaming the edges of the known galaxy to one day return at Nocturne's darkest hour. Theories differed wildly and were prone to large amounts of conjecture as history over ten thousand years old had a habit of being inconclusive.

Gravius, the anachronistic warrior that Third had discovered on Scoria, was the closest existing link to that era. Now all that remained of him was his gene-seed.

Of all Salamanders Dak'ir had ever known, Fugis best exemplified the Chapter's pragmatism. His observances were swiftly done before he stormed into the chamber and stood before a vast plaque of red-veined rock.

Though the chamber was small by comparison to the other sacred halls, Dak'ir still nearly lost sight of the Apothecary in the gloom as he crossed to the other side of the room. Flickering torch light cast his long shadow upon the sigil of a gilded drake's head wrought into the floor. The ever-burning embers crackled in chorus to the heavy thuds of his footfalls.

'Here…' he called, his harsh voice echoing.

Great serpents and monstrous drakes glared down at the interlopers from huge menhirs of volcanic obsidian encircling the room. Carved between them were other artefacts of Promethean lore, the anvil, hammer and the forge flame. Each stood sentinel over a granite throne, eighteen in total, for the vaunted members of the Pantheon Council. Even setting foot in the chamber, Dak'ir felt like a transgressor.

'Come,' Pyriel urged him, walking softly into the room behind Elysius.

Fugis was crouching down and gestured to the floor as the others approached him.

'I can see an indentation.'

Up close, Dak'ir realised the lustrous plaque of rock was another of the menhirs. The head of a draconian beast stared down from its summit, jewelled eyes glinting fiercely in the torch light. He made the sign of the hammer.

With the grinding of ancient gears, a mechanism from the time of T'kell the first Master of the Forge, the menhir slid aside to reveal the door to a vault.

Elysius was rising to his feet, having recovered the sigil from where he had placed it in the floor depression.

'It is still sealed,' uttered Dak'ir, a sense of moment beginning to overtake him. For his entire life he had not known his place or purpose; now that was about to change, his destiny revealed to him. For a second he rebelled against it, fought to urge to run as far away as he could, to throw himself into battle, to forget the prophecy and all its bloody promises.

'Have patience, brother,' Elysius told him. 'The workings are old, from an era when we were still Legion.'

Gradually a crack appeared in the silver-grey surface of the door as it began to open.

'There…' The Chaplain smiled behind his skull-mask,

choosing that moment to remove his battle-helm and mag-lock it to his armour.

Low lume-light painted the vault in visceral red but was slow to lift the gloom. It cast the armour suits within in the hue of blood, limning them crimson.

Much like Gravius, there was something anachronistic about this battle-plate. It was darker; its design archaic and rarely seen during the 41st millennium.

'So old…' Dak'ir remembered them. They were as they had been when Third had recovered them on Scoria, the armour husks of the ancient's long-dead brothers, the ones he had devoured to preserve their legacy. The strain of the memories and genetic identity of all those warriors had destroyed Gravius – one mind, even a Space Marine's, was not meant to hold so much. It broke him mentally.

Each suit of battle-plate was engraved with a symbol, themselves each a piece of a larger mystery. They carried Dak'ir's destiny, one that had been more than ten thousand years in the making. Only Tu'Shan had seen it. The message there was meant for Vulkan's Regent and his Forgefather to discern, but others too had discovered it in time and all Fire-born were now aware of it.

Dak'ir reached out to touch one of the suits, his fingers agonisingly close to one of the sigil-scars that formed part of the prophecy but never making contact.

'It seems impossible that it has lasted.'

'I once thought a great many things impossible, Dak'ir,' said Elysius, gently pushing down the Lexicanum's outstretched hand, 'but my perspective has been changed.'

Pyriel pressed against a rune-plate in the wall. It was easy to miss, fashioned to resemble the marbling of the stone. The vault had a metal floor. A circular outline appeared within it. A dense pressure cloud was expelled from the groove. Through the dissipating vapour, a silver column resolved with a force-fielded dome at the summit. Within the crackling field there was an armourcrys vial that contained a translucent fluid. Inside the amniotic solution was a progenoid gland, the last remaining biological element of Gravius.

Fugis approached as closely as he could without being repelled by the force field. 'The solution has preserved it well,' he muttered, 'prevented necrotisation as I'd hoped.' He looked up at Elysius. 'How do we switch this off?'

Pyriel pushed another hidden rune-plate. The force field protecting the vial flickered once and then dispersed into motes of energy that quickly dissipated on the air.

Fugis reached in and grabbed the vial without ceremony, though he was careful not to breach it.

'Hard to believe it had endured this long,' he said to himself, scrutinising the vital organ. Then he proffered it to Dak'ir.

The Lexicanum flinched at first.

'That's it. I just eat it?'

'For one to become many you must consume the gene-seed,' Fugis explained. 'It is life, Dak'ir, legacy. Your destiny.'

Pyriel had moved to the opening.

'If anyone wishes to leave then do so now,' he said, 'but I won't do this and risk the sanctity of the Tome of Fire or the rest of the inner halls.'

'Perhaps we should adjourn to somewhere safer and less important,' suggested Elysius.

'If you can name a place then speak of it, for I know none,' snapped Fugis. 'There is no time, Brother-Chaplain. The moment is upon us, here and now.'

Elysius glanced at Pyriel for support.

'When sealed this vault will contain any fury we might unleash,' Pyriel said. 'I am staying here.'

'As am I.' The Chaplain descended to one knee, head bowed. Silently, he began reciting a litany of protection.

A wild fire flashed in Fugis's eyes. 'We are all bound to this fate, then.' He brandished the vial again as the door to the vault was closing.

Dak'ir was unconvinced. 'What if something goes

wrong? One of you should remain outside to summon help.'

'If we fail here,' said Pyriel, 'if all we believe is to be proven false, then it won't matter, Dak'ir. War is upon us. Our cities are enveloped by it, our skies thronged with it. Doom or saviour, here is where we find out for certain.'

Dak'ir looked down at the tiny vial in his gauntleted palm. It seemed so innocuous, such an insignificant thing, until he remembered the very fate of a Chapter was held within its glass walls.

'Blessed Vulkan, be my guide upon the ocean of fire...' he muttered, and devoured the gene-seed.

Silence reigned, charged with anticipation.

Nothing happened. An immense sense of relief and disappointment warring within him, Dak'ir opened his mouth to dispel the tension when a wracking pain seized his body. He fell, hitting the ground amidst violent convulsions. Thrashing, he felt strong hands try to hold him and keep his spasming limbs steady but he slipped their leash. Agony fed through his marrow like the passage of a red-hot needle, stitching fire through his entire skeleton. His hearts were thundering like the pounding of waves upon the Acerbian Sea, crashing against his chest with force enough to shatter them. Memories sped into his mind, sights of ancient battles, of days of Legion, of the Great Crusade and the coming of the father.

'*Vulkan...*' he drooled.

Too fast, too much...

Someone was shouting. The tone was urgent but the voice was not directed at him.

His spine arched as his chest thrust forwards, so severely it cracked the bone, and Dak'ir threw his head back in a terrible psychic scream.

The flame that had been kept quiescent for so long broke free of its shackles and poured from his eyes and mouth, filling the vault with conflagration.

CHAPTER SIXTEEN

I
Gaining the Wall

LORKAR EMERGED FROM a pall of dust, the gunship retreating into the air behind them on screaming turbo-fans.

Overhead, explosive blossoms clouded the sky and wracked it with their dull thunder. Heavy flak and tracer fire whickered in an enfilading lattice poured on from the high city battlements.

Slogging across the dunes, he scowled at the various wretches arrayed with them in the second wave. Lorkar had an excellent knowledge of xenos creatures. He knew a great many ways to inflict pain upon them and then dispatch them. Weakness was something he loathed to his core but knowing the chinks in the armour of others, his enemies, was infinitely useful.

He recognised the avian creatures to his right flank as kroot. They were mercenaries and no better than cannibals. Savage beasts, they crowed and shrieked as they were lost to war-lust and drove ahead of the slower Marines Malevolent advance. That suited Lorkar fine. Let the craven wretches be first into the Salamanders' guns, they would soon learn the folly of their wild abandon.

There were others amongst the alien throng too, hairy-backed kharateg and reptilian loxatl, the saurian galthite. Mercenaries, bandits and renegades all. Nihilan had put Lorkar's men amongst the dregs and was saving his own Dragon Warriors in reserve for when the defenders' fury had been well blunted by the rabble.

Penetrating the threshold of the void shield, the Marines Malevolent entered a killing zone into which the Salamanders were pouring their fire. The hard bangs of scatter shot merged with the flat *chank-rattle* of bolters and the throaty cough of rocket-propelled grenades flung from shoulder-mounted tube launchers.

They waded in a mire of the dead, a charnel field of festering alien corpses and the broken bodies of human renegades. Part of the second wave had gained sections of the wall and the barrage from the defenders above was lessening as some of the city's garrison were forced to stop and deal with the breaches in security.

Even still, it was intense.

Any ordinary warrior would have balked, marching into that cauldon. Lesser men would have fled at the very sight and sound, piss trickling down their legs, uniforms soiled as they screamed to their hollow gods for deliverance.

Some did, and Lorkar cut them down if they strayed too close.

'Craven scum…' he muttered, firing from the hip and shooting up a band of fleeing idolators whose resolve had broken.

Breaking into a powerful run as the ash-sand ground beneath his boots, Lorkar acknowledged he'd never considered himself ordinary. That fact was especially true now, ever since finding the *Demetrion* and all that had happened within its walls.

Shouting, he exhorted his warriors. 'Forward, in the name of the Marines Malevolent!'

They left the corpse field behind and entered a patch of open ash-sand.

His men too were far from ordinary, some of them at least. Like Lorkar, they clung to the trappings of their old Chapter. Like a tether in the midst of a cyclone it kept them grounded, kept the *voices* at bay.

Lorkar refuted them with all of his being and his will, but they had followed him here on the back of his deepseated hatred for the Salamanders and he'd been powerless to quieten them.

Though he dare not admit it out loud, Lorkar knew he was lost.

Thirty warriors comprised his warband, every soul who'd survived the *Demetrion* and some that had not but still walked and could fire a bolter. He glanced at Tsu'gan on his left. The once Firedrake was keeping a steady pace, his borrowed battle-helm obscuring the device that had bound his will to Nihilan's.

Throne knew where *that* bastard was and what he was doing. The sorcerer had allies from the Eye and despite his recent clash with forces of the ether Lorkar still hated him for it. He despised impurity, and so he also loathed himself. Perhaps he and Tsu'gan had more in common that he'd at first realised.

The other one, the turncoat, was with him too. Iagon kept to rear ranks, the only warrior not under the Marines Malevolent's direct command. He called himself equerry but Lorkar saw the lie in that immediately. Iagon was just a pawn. When the siege was done he'd already decided to kill the worthless dog and suspected Nihilan had left his little pet in Lorkar's charge because he knew the puritan Space Marine would execute him.

It mattered not. When he was free of the voices, Lorkar would have his vengeance on them all.

A hundred metres ahead of them, the walls of Hesiod were holding.

Blinking the magnification in his retinal display to maximum, he saw the Scout squads that garrisoned the battlements and the missile launcher aimed in his direction.

Holding up a clenched fist, he brought the warband to an abrupt halt and they went to ground immediately, taking refuge in the undulating ash dunes and battle debris as a rocket-burst *foomed* overhead. It threw up clods of earth and grit that washed across Lorkar's helmet lenses but left them otherwise unharmed.

Having found his range, the Scout was calling for another missile as he adjusted his targeter for a second shot.

Lorkar wasn't about to allow that to happen.

'Harkane!'

The Techmarine was already preparing the tracked Rapier-mount he'd brought with them. It was archaic, the gun platform hailing from several previous generations of Space Marine warfare. The track bed it rolled across the dunes on was built for heavy terrain and coped well with the rigours of the desert. It had even surmounted the mound of the dead. As Harkane manipulated the hand-held control console a pair of cannon-bearing weapon arms unfolded from the Rapier's central stock and cycled into position. Drum mags dropped either side of the twin autocannons, belt feeds unfurling like brass-shelled tongues from their breaches.

With the angry growl of protesting gears, the Rapier rotated into position.

Lorkar smiled as the Scout gave the signal to his loader that he was ready. The other one was still ducking down as the Marines Malevolent bellowed his order.

'Silence that launcher.'

Hard staccato gunfire *chug-chanked* from the twin autocannons, raking the battlements and turning the air in front of the Scouts into a gritty storm. After a few seconds and several hundred rounds, the Rapier's muzzle flare died off and the dust cleared. The Scouts were gone. Others around them were shouting, hauling something away that was lost beneath the lip of the battlements and closing up the bloody gap it had left.

The Marines Malevolent were well within the boundary

of the void shield now and in striking distance of the wall itself; there was no time to wait around.

Lorkar hailed his troops. 'Advance!'

They came forwards together in three lines, crouched low and firing up towards the hazy summit of the wall. Overhead the sky was gore-streaked and wreathed with pyroclastic cloud. It was a fitting omen.

Someone staggered then fell, Lorkar thought it was Rygor. Ignored by his brothers, the plasma gunner picked himself up and rejoined the battle line at the rear.

Rygor was strong, a true Malevolent. Unlike some, such as the infiltrator in their ranks.

Marines Malevolent did not stoop to pull their brothers up if they fell, but they would have stopped to end this one should he have faltered.

A pity the shot had not pierced *his* armour plate.

THE ITCHING HAD grown worse, so bad it now eclipsed the phantom pain Iagon felt in his missing hand. In the early days after he'd severed it to cast off the veil of suspicion surrounding N'keln's murder, a murder he'd committed in cold blood, the wrist stump had been agony. Cauterised, nerve endings dulled and sealed, it still hurt. Even now with an augmetic hand to replace that which he'd sacrificed, the pain persisted. It was psychology, some remnant of guilt or paranoia at being caught that dogged him so.

Tsu'gan was a masochist, he chose to flay and brand his body to scour away the pain eating away at him. Iagon could only do that by inflicting pain on others and so his damnation was assured. He had taken the mirror into his soul and turned it from his sight so that it reflected on others. A sadist then. He knew it, and didn't care. He'd only ever wanted to *taste* glory, even bask in the glow of others. And power, of course. Oh yes, he desired power above all else.

Self aware enough to realise he was not remarkable, Iagon had chosen to attach himself to others that were and ride upon their backs. Tsu'gan had risen, in recognition of his abilities. *He* was remarkable.

He had done so and left Iagon alone, embittered and without a hand.

Through the murky red of his retinal lenses, his eyes never left the betrayer's back. Even with the mind shackle, Tsu'gan was a formidable warrior. Iagon could not hope to best him with bolter and blade. But then so too was N'keln and he bled easy enough...

To think of all you sacrificed, he whispered to himself as the bombs came down and gunfire ripped up the ash-sand around them. It was like passing through a breeze to Iagon, so removed was he from the world.

It was the itching. It dominated his thoughts, feeding on his hatred, exacerbating it until...

He found a point of the betrayer's back. It was a heart strike, a killing blow.

All it would take is a little thrust.

A smile turned his perpetually sneering mouth, but as the itching persisted Iagon failed to realise that the voice inside was not truly his own.

II
Stranger's Skin

IT WAS LIKE being a prisoner in his own body. He could see it, feel it, his senses were as alive as they always were but it moved in a way that was alien to him. It did things, performed acts he had not told it to. It was as if his neural synapses had been re-routed and Tsu'gan was no longer in full command of them. His limbs moved now as if of their own volition. He had become like a puppet, dangling helplessly on Nihilan's strings. But that wasn't entirely accurate. Tsu'gan had heard of some psykers that could inhabit the bodies of others, using their will to impel their actions, effectively *wearing* them like a suit of battle-plate. Nihilan's mind shackle was not

like that. Tsu'gan could only liken it to the command
protocols given to a servitor via their doctrina wafers.
It was as if he'd been given a series of pre-set routines
and was now bound to follow them. But programming
like that was not infallible, it could be overcome. With
enough willpower, anything was possible.

Tsu'gan formed a grimace, the only evidence that he
was fighting to resist the mental bypass. His body was
still not his own.

He was running, snap firing at his brothers on the
battlements, his every instinct screaming at him to turn
his weapon on the traitors in his midst instead. Solid
shot *spanged* off his shoulder guard and plastron, and
he grunted. That at least had been of his own making.
Tsu'gan's return fire forced the shooter to cower, whilst
a second burst clipped him and he disappeared amidst
gouting blood.

Lorkar ordered the advance and was first to lead the
line. The renegade kept Tsu'gan close, perhaps to keep
an eye on him, or maybe he was considering trying to
slay him during the battle.

I am surrounded by enemies.

He wondered if his mind-shackled body would protect him, or would he submit to the murderer's knife
without resistance?

Another of the Techmarine's tracked engines launched
grappling lines up onto the crenellations. Six flanged
hooks bit hard and deep, burying adamantium teeth
into Hesiod's outer wall. He fired another six as the
machine's launcher recycled its cargo and the Marines
Malevolent sprinted to grasp the dangling wire-weave
lines.

An ambitious kroot went for Tsu'gan's line, but the
once-Salamander wrestled the alien off and snapped its
neck before pushing into the climb. Three of its brethren
shrilling vengeance went for his back. With one hand
wrapped around the wire, Tsu'gan swung out from the
wall and gunned them all down with his bolter.

Backstabbers dealt with, he continued his ascent in earnest.

Though he railed against every metre, Tsu'gan quickly reached the apex of the wall and was confronted by a pair of scouts. Too close for bolters, they went for their combat-blades.

'Die, traitor!' one of them yelled, trying to fix his gladius into the gap between rerebrace and plastron. Tsu'gan turned the thrust aside with his arm, the blade raking a groove along his gauntlet and vambrace, before punching the Scout in the face.

He shattered the neophyte's cheek, using the stock of his bolter to block the frenzied hacking of the other one. Tsu'gan shoved him back and stepped into the space he'd created, drawing his chainsword at the same time.

Traitor…

Tsu'gan was no traitor.

Heed me, brothers! he pleaded. *I am trapped by another's will. Help me!*

The screaming voice echoed within him but only Tsu'gan could hear it. Though his face was swollen and lathered with blood, the Scout with the shattered cheek came on again. This time, Tsu'gan batted down his clumsy thrust and swatted him so hard he fell off the back of the battlements and pinwheeled to the ground below. The crunch of bone was lost to the sound of combat.

Turning his full attention on the other one, Tsu'gan pushed the muzzle of his bolter into the Scout's chest and pulled the trigger. The close-range burst scorched his armour, turning it black from the discharge flare, but ripped open the neophyte's torso.

Tsu'gan let him crumple in a bloody heap as he went to engage the next combatant.

He was back-to-back with Rennard, a warrior of Lorkar's brood, who was crouched down laying incendary charges. It seemed the Marines Malevolent meant to forge a breach from the inside out.

Glancing at his retinal display, Tsu'gan noticed Iagon had gained the wall too. His ident-rune flashed red, unlike the others which were yellow. The traitor-dog was in his crosshairs now, but he was powerless to slay him. The only upside was several other warriors separated them so at least Iagon couldn't plant a blade in his back like he'd done to N'keln. Nine renegades had reached the summit of Hesiod's defensive perimeter and were fighting hard along it to make room for the others coming after them. Elsewhere on the wall there were similar breaches.

Impulse drove Tsu'gan on into the Salamander Scouts. Most mortal fighters, the troopers of the Imperial Guard, the crusaders of the Holy Ecclesiarch, would find even Space Marine neophytes tough combatants.

To Tsu'gan, it was like fighting infants. Having cut his way through the initial press of defenders, he found he had room to manoeuvre and could bring all of his ruthless combat-training to bear.

He cut down the first two Scouts that raced to oppose him with contemptuous ease, though his mind was railing at their slaughter and burning with impotent rage at what Nihilan's technomancy had forced him into doing.

A third took a bracing stance and swung around a heavy bolter to rake the gap between them.

Tsu'gan reached back and seized Rennard. The Marine Malevolent wasn't expecting the move and by the time he fought it he was being used as a meat shield and struck by mass-reactive shells.

The dense impacts rocked the warrior's body and Tsu'gan pushed forwards behind it all the way to his opponent, causing horrendous damage to Rennard in the process. At almost point blank the sheer force of the heavy salvo knocked them both off their feet.

Tsu'gan landed hard on his back but was quick to roll the groaning Marine Malevolent off him as he led with his chainsword. He rose from prone into a crouch just as the next round of shells came chugging from the Scout's belt-fed cannon. Tsu'gan threw his blade, hilt over tip like a hand axe. It embedded in the Scout's body, impaling him. Spitting blood, the neophyte stopped firing and collapsed to the ground.

Wrenching his chainsword loose with a dirty *schluck* of engrained gore, Tsu'gan thumbed the activation stud and leapt over the body. Blood was thumping in his ears, like a wave battering the shoreline. He heard his breath, rapid in his chest, not from combat-exertion but from his efforts to break the fetters around his free will.

This was Hesiod, once his home. These Scouts, they were the Chapter's lifeblood, its next generation.

And he was killing them.

Tsu'gan was weeping now, tears of fire running down his face inside his battle-helm, but he couldn't stop. Leaving Rennard to bleed out, he went hunting for more enemies. The hapless warrior's incendiaries went off behind him, issuing a defeaning boom and filling part of the wall with fire and frag.

He glanced back. It had barely made a crack.

Inside Tsu'gan, the part of him that was fighting the mind shackle scoffed at the idiocy of the renegades. Nocturnean stone, especially stone hewn for the Seat of Tribal Kings, was not so easy to break.

The troops on the wall were thinning out as they struggled to defend it with reduced numbers. Attrition for Nihilan's army had barely made a dent; every casualty was felt keenly by the Salamanders, though.

Ahead of him, Tsu'gan saw a Scout fumbling with a snub-nosed grenade launcher. He looked up, half focused on reloading and half on the warrior rushing him.

Another easy kill.

Tsu'gan fought it but his chainsword came around in a butchering arc just as the Scout was bringing up his arms to fire.

Sparks spilled off the grinding teeth as they whined and growled against a rival blade blocking the route to the neophyte's neck.

A bulky warrior in artificered battle-plate hauled the Scout aside, shouting something to him that Tsu'gan didn't catch. He then twisted his arm, pushing Tsu'gan's chainblade away and out, exposing his chest where he stabbed a spatha that had appeared miraculously in the veteran's other hand.

Pain made Tsu'gan back off, and the spatha's serrated edge chewed up flesh and battle-plate as it was forcibly withdrawn.

'Fight me then, traitor,' the Salamander veteran invited, adopting a fighting stance that Tsu'gan vaguely remebered through the mental fug of the mind shackle.

'Master...'

The words actually issued from his throat but were lost behind his battle-helm and the veteran's fearsome renewed assault.

Tsu'gan went on the defensive at once. He tried to bring up his bolter for a close range burst to wing his opponent but the flash of a spatha sent the weapon spinning from blade-stung fingers.

'You are strong and skilled,' said the veteran, pressing his advantage and pushing Tsu'gan back across the battlements to negate the gains he'd made.

He knew this warrior. He had learned from him, been his student.

Tsu'gan fashioned a riposte that cut into the veteran's shoulder guard, but was hacked in turn against his flank. He tasted blood in his mouth and knew he was hurt. It rimed his vision, the edges of his sight burning black and the darkness creeping closer over it.

Parrying an overhead from the veteran's chainsword, he aimed a punch at his head but missed and hit the upper arm. It was enough to loosen the veteran's grip on the spatha, which Tsu'gan exploited with a chainblade smash of his own, disarming him. He'd used the flat metal of the weapon's casing but it was enough to send the secondary blade clattering away uselessly.

'*Very* skilled...' the veteran corrected, taking his

chainsword in a two-handed grip. It was only then Tsu'gan noticed it was modified with a longer hilt and broader blade not unlike an ancient bastard sword.

Other trappings of the veteran's war panoply came into sharp focus too – his armour plate, the holstered melta-pistol and gladius; the saurian-styled helm and the timbre of his voice.

'Prebian…'

Tsu'gan was fighting the Salamanders Master of Arms. Small wonder he was losing. He blocked a heavy cut that staggered him. A shoulder barge to follow up dented his plastron and had Tsu'gan reeling.

'Prebian…' It was louder this time.

He parried, but the blow was so hard it went through his defences driving Tsu'gan's churning chainsword into his own face. Sparks and chips of metal spilled from his gorget but the spinning teeth went higher, scoring a jagged line into his battle-helm and putting out one of the retinal lenses. One half of Tsu'gan's tactical display was reduced to crackling static and for a few brief seconds he was blinded in one eye.

'Here is the taste you've been craving, hell-kite,' Prebian snarled, pressing the blade closer so it bit deeper into the ceramite. 'I'll see your face before you die,' he promised as Tsu'gan's battle-helm split apart under the strain and fell away from his head in two battered halves.

Prebian pulled up short, his mouth agape.

There was remembrance in his eyes and disbelief, visible even though his helmet lenses.

'*Brother Tsu'gan?*'

The momentary distraction gave Tsu'gan the advantage. With a roar, he threw Prebian off and brought up his partly blunted chainblade. The mechanism was churning hard, its servos straining from when it had cut into ceramite, but he could still use it to kill.

He wanted to resist, staying his hand and putting up his blade, but the mind shackle wouldn't let him.

Instead, he attacked with gritted teeth and rivulets of

sorrowful fire trickling from his eyes.

Please, they said, *please, brother…*

Against his will, he fought on.

Prebian fended off each blow, holding back as he realised what was happening.

'Fight it, brother,' he hissed, eyeing the alien device attached to Tsu'gan's face. 'Give me an opening.'

Tsu'gan understood. He bored deep within himself, tried to use anything as a bulwark to hold onto, a place in his psyche where he could stand his ground and fight.

He tried to remember his first kill, when he had brought a leo'nid pelt from the dunes as a trophy; the first time he had wrought a blade and wielded it in anger; he thought about his father, the Tribal King of Hesiod, and the day he had wept before his cold tomb in the undercrofts before being taken by Zen'de. But they were, all of them, imperfect memories from a time that seemed like it belonged to someone else.

Tsu'gan was losing and soon Prebian would have to fight back with all his skill. The Master would be forced to kill the former student.

Brotherhood, honour, glory to his Chapter – they all meant something to him, but none alone was strong enough to countermand the mind shackle. He needed to focus on something vital, something powerful.

He remembered Dak'ir.

Not since Scoria had he seen the Ignean, not since he had been taken by the Librarius and Tsu'gan had ascended to the ranks of the Firedrakes had their paths crossed. Dak'ir might have slipped from his mind, but the anger had not faded. He, the low-born of the prophecy, fated as saviour or destroyer, was still the source of Tsu'gan's distemper. He used it, fashioned his wrath into a spear and thrust its tip through the barrier between his mind and body.

He lowered his chainsword.

Do it, his silent lips told Prebian.

The Master didn't hesitate. He struck at the mind

shackle, hacking into it with his gladius and cleaving it down the middle. But as soon as the blade was withdrawn, the damage was undone. The device had repaired itself.

Tsu'gan sagged in defeat, feeling the numbness in his head again as the tendrils of bondage were remade. His brief rebellion was over. The mind shackle had reasserted its influence. He lifted his blade.

End my suffering… His mournful gaze spoke the words even if his lips could not.

Prebian defended a hail of attacks but wasn't ready to give in. Waiting for another opening, he thrust again recklessly with his gladius this time and impaled the device. Already the blade was being pushed out, the split it had carved reknitting as living metal flowed over it like sentient mercury.

'Strength of Vulkan,' he said through clenched teeth.

Dropping his chainsword, Prebian used both hands to push back. His breath came heavy through his fanged vox-grille as he pressed hard on the gladius's pommel with the flat of his palm. His grip, wrapped around the hilt, was like adamantium.

The alien metal was stronger.

'I cannot…' he gasped, holding on as the device excised his blade like a splinter pushed from a closing wound.

Prebian's eyes met Tsu'gan's as he realised he was going to fail and be left defenceless.

'Brother, try–'

Tsu'gan lunged with the chainsword still clasped in his hand, thrusting it all the way into Prebian's side.

'Where it's weakest,' rasped the Master, repeating the selfsame words he'd given to the aspirants on the ash plains.

Tsu'gan had been one of his best.

He fell back, first onto one knee and then the other. The sword still jutted from his body, his life blood pouring down his armour in a dark flood.

With Tsu'gan standing over him about to finish the

kill, Prebian reached for the clasps on his battle-helm and then removed it.

His old face was lined, the skin turning from onyx to a charcoal grey. His hair was silvern and thin. Fire burned in the Master's eyes still but it was fading fast.

'My last embers,' he said, looking up at his killer, as if he could read his thoughts.

Tsu'gan yanked the blade free, drawing a grimace of pain from Prebian. A welter of blood came with it and he held it aloft for the murder-stroke.

Horror filled his eyes as the sheer magnitude of what he about to do came crashing down.

I am no traitor…

In retrospect, it sounded like a hollow declaration now.

He was about to fell his old master in cold blood when a lance of light roared from the hell-red heavens like the voice of a god and turned the sky magnesium white.

CHAPTER SEVENTEEN

I
A Thrown Spear

NOCTURNE SCREAMED. THE earth cracked and like a beast with its flank skewered by the hunter's spear its blood poured forth. Deep in the bowels of the world, the lamentation song of the ancient drakes was drowned by the sound of tectonic plates breaking and grinding.

Presaged by the runnels of lava spilling out into the plains like fiery arteries, a cavalcade of massive earthquakes wracked the surface of Nocturne. Mount Deathfire bellowed, spewing up a vast pyroclastic cloud that fashioned night from day in a matter of seconds. The air thickened with ash as the red world fought to tear itself apart, thrashing and shouting with the pain of her wounding.

Crimson lightning split the smoke-drenched sky; the deep lava glow of the erupting mountain chains was like a firmament of hot amber stars in the blackness. Thunder rolled in belligerent salvos, speaking doom and an end to all things.

Chasms opened in the lands beyond the Sanctuary Cities. Entire settlements, the tented outposts of nomads, the subterranean domains of cave-dwellers were extinguished in moments. Those not smothered by ash were boiled with intense heat; the few that survived those trials were swallowed by the gaping earth or drowned in hellish lava.

A jagging line in the ground fed all the way to the gate-wall of Hesiod, thick enough to devour a gunship whole without it touching the sides. It struck the void shield first, which shimmered in a few seconds of valiant resistence before capitulating and collapsing. Then it roared on, smashing into the wall itself and sharpening its craggy teeth on the foundation stone of Nocturne. This was the planet's bedrock, one of the seven places discovered by the earth shamans of old and where the tribal-kings had founded the Sanctuaries that would later become city-bastions.

A fissure rode up the dark obsidian of Hesiod's boundary. It became a crack, widening farther as each second passed, tearing open the city's defences like they were naught but clay.

As the gate-wall parted, the warriors upon it cascaded down onto the courtyard below in an armoured rain, still battling as they fell. Bodies struck the ground with the impact of mortar shells, a flesh and metal barrage where the ordnance groaned and bled and died in the aftermath.

The crack only dissipated when it reached the threshold of the Chapter bastion, but by then it had wreaked utter carnage. Like a broken dam, Hesiod lay open and all of the cruel waters lapping outside it poured in unabated.

A scalding wind came in the wake of the blast, whipping across the ash-plain.

Val'in heard the cry of alien beasts, unprotected by their heathen armour, and knew that many had died. His skin was stinging from the sulphurous air, and only his genetic enhancements stopped him from choking on it.

He was still on the wall, though now a massive ugly gap yawned between him and his brothers. It took him a while to come around and realise he was prone. Val'in felt a strong hand grip his forearm and help him to his feet.

'Master Prebian has fallen. Get up!' Exor was bloodied, but alive.

Dimly at first but with increasing clarity, Val'in remembered crying out as the master was stabbed. He'd been coming to his aid when the lance of light had struck.

'Where is he, brother?' Smoke and heat haze were hampering his sight.

Exor gestured into a grey miasma. Where it thinned momentarily, Val'in could see the slumped form of Master Prebian. He was laying on his side unmoving, a pool of dark blood wallowing underneath him.

'And his slayer?' Val'in had found his combat-blade in the debris and was on the move, head low.

Overhead, scattered bolter fire and solid shot still rattled.

'We don't know he's dead.' Exor ran alongside him, cradling his grenade launcher.

Somewhere in the melee Val'in had lost his bolter and resolved to fight without it. He preferred close-quarter combat anyway, and excelled at it. Against the dazed renegades emerging through the fog, he'd need to be at his best.

They'd not seen Prebian's prone body. It was partly covered with debris and obscured by smoke. The traitors were staggering, obviously wounded, and had borne more of the brunt of the blast than the two Scouts.

None of them were the warrior Val'in had seen stab his master in the flank, though. That dog had fled.

One pointed, a drool of blood exuding from his sealed gorget.

They'd seen the Scouts.

Val'in smiled grimly. That was good.

Raising their jagged blades, the renegades stuttered

into a charge. A burst of bolt pistol fire chewed up a chunk of broken wall near Exor, forcing him into cover, but then the weapon *clunked* empty and was tossed aside.

Val'in had got ahead of his brother, rushing to put his body between the enemy and the slumped Prebian who incredibly stirred with life still. If either of the renegades saw that they would end him.

Something else stirred a hand's width away from the master too. It was a chainsword, an ornate blade Val'in had seen racked to Prebian's power generator. It was *his* weapon. Sheathing the gladius, Val'in reached the master's body and took up his sword. It was hard to wield, but the machine-spirit was strong and vital. It yearned for vengeance after its wielder had been put down. Nothing short of traitor blood would slake it.

Muttering litanies of cleaving, Val'in hefted the buzzing blade and prepared to meet the enemy. He dragged it low, such was the weight, like a master swordsman minus the finesse.

'In Vulkan's name!'

The renegades laughed in their battered armour. Up close, some of the plates appeared as if they'd been fused to the skin. The one carrying the throat wound actually looked like his helm was part of his mocking face.

They wouldn't be laughing soon.

Val'in leapt over a small crack in the battlements, chainsword low in a reverse two-handed grip, so heavy it threatened to leaden his arms fatally.

He let the first renegade swing. It was a lazy attack, overconfident and indulgent. No discipline. Val'in was able to dodge it, and kept running. Using his momentum he vaulted up onto a jutting piece of rock, leaping over a wild slash from the second renegade that was intended to cut Val'in's legs from under him. As he descended, Val'in drove the chainsword through the warrior's damaged gorget and right into his neck, ramming it in all the way to the hilt.

He let go and rolled, coming up behind the choking

renegade whose insides were being churned into mulch.

The other one had turned and was coming at him. Without a weapon to defend himself… wounded or not, the renegade would kill him.

A grenade burst against the warrior's flank, pitching him off the side of the wall where he disappeared in the darkness below.

Val'in saw Exor emerging from cover. He showed his hand in gratitude. Exor thumped his chest in the warrior's salute and went to Prebian.

'He lives,' he said when Val'in joined him.

His breath was ragged and the pulse in his neck erratic. Val'in cursed beneath his breath. 'For now.' He glanced around in the thinning smoke. 'We are far from allies.' The damage to the wall had left them isolated from the rest of the battle, like survivors shipwrecked on an island rock protruding from a grey, swirling ocean.

Exor thumped Val'in's carapace breastplate.

'In Vulkan's name, indeed,' he said, nodding with awe-filled respect.

Val'in frowned.

'That move you pulled off,' Exor explained, 'the neck strike? I've never seen anyone do that before. How did you?'

Val'in was shaking his head. 'I don't know. My instincts took over. The blade seemed… *lighter* almost.'

An explosion blossomed overhead, but the showering shrapnel from it was absorbed by what was left of the wall's defences.

Exor crouched hurriedly. 'What shall we do?'

Out beyond the walls, fire was engulfing everything. The land had become a lava sea, the pitted earth cracked open and bleeding. Through the clouds of smoke, Val'in thought he saw a ship descending. It was unlike anything he'd ever seen before and was headed for Mount Deathfire and the massive pillar of ash roiling from its wounded depths.

His answer when given was distracted. 'More will be

coming. We stay here, protect the master.'

No, it was definitely not a ship he had ever seen before.

It was ancient, something that had once been described to him in the lectorium by the Master of the Arsenal. He couldn't be certain but he remembered the name his teacher had used.

Stormbird.

LORKAR'S WARRIORS HAD been severely reduced in fighting strength. Some of their bodies were still laying in the debris from the shattered wall, crushed to oblivion, injuries from which even a Space Marine could not recover. Others had been slain in the ferocious fighting that led up to its destruction.

He half staggered towards Iagon, wrapping a gauntleted hand around his throat while the traitor was still only half conscious from the fall.

'Worm!' he snarled, tightening his grip. 'Did you know he possessed such a weapon?' He ripped off the traitor's battle-helm, leaving the clamps torn and broken. 'He used it to kill his own. You were in that blast radius too.'

Iagon scrabbled desperately at Lorkar's gauntleted fingers. He slipped a jagged knife from his belt but Lorkar saw the blade and seized Iagon's wrist. He twisted it until it cracked.

'I'm not some callow fool you can stab in the back,' he growled and threw him down.

Iagon grabbed the nearest weapon, a snub-nosed bolt pistol, and shot Lorkar in the face. The sergeant of the Marines Malevolent roared, clutching at his face as Iagon fled.

'Let him go,' he snapped, watching the craven traitor disappear into the smoke. Most of the battlefield outside Hesiod was swathed in the dirty black pall. It smothered the bodies as well as the screams.

It also clung around the massive breach in the wall where the rear battalions were currently clamouring to get in. The Salamanders defended it tenaciously, and

Lorkar saw gouts of flame, the sporadic flare of bolters, in the darkness within. They were holding but only just, the weight of the tide would eventually push them back if something didn't change.

Blood-stink was heavy on the breeze, so too the stench of putrefaction barely masked by the sulphurous air.

Lorkar was inured to all of it as he and his men moved against the tide. The wall was won; he had other prey on his mind. At least that's what the *voices* were telling him. Of much greater concern were the channels of lava erupting at random across the battlefield. In the short time since being thrown from the battlements, he'd witnessed an entire tank squadron devoured by spewing magma and whole regiments decimated by caustic acid-wind.

A scorch mark muddied his faceplate where Iagon's barrage had hit him, the only sign of damage he'd sustained thus far. It was a glancing blow that dented his armour and hurt like a bastard but little else.

His warriors, those that were left, put up their bolters.

A brief lull had descended on the far side of the wall. Within Hesiod, the courtyard was being fought for doggedly but that didn't interest Lorkar. What did was the fact that the Salamanders would not surrender one of their greatest cities without more of a fight. Reinforcements were certain to be on the way. He gestured to Brother Vathek. 'Scopes.'

Crouching down to where the smoke was thinnest, he peered through the magnoculars at the distant ash ridges. There was a dust cloud approaching, cutting through the lava trails. He increased magnification.

'Heavy armour,' he muttered, the sound grating, as he saw tanks.

He turned the dial to maximum and saw who was leading the column.

Beneath the damaged battle-helm, an ugly smile split his scarred face.

'Tu'Shan.'

Hearing the vague sound of engines through the chaos, he panned the view upwards.

The smile became a scowl when he saw the distant drop-ship in Dragon Warrior colours.

'You dirty little–'

'Sire…'

Vathek was gesturing to the hosts of Dragon Warriors withdrawing back across the ash plain.

'Where in the name of Throne are those scum going?'

Several renegade battalions were embarking onto gun-ships and headed back for the upper atmosphere. They'd been deployed as a show of force only, something to galvanise the fodder.

Lorkar's eyes narrowed as he looked back to the distant drop-ship, descending in the mountains.

'You needed their gaze elsewhere, didn't you? What's down there that you're after?' he muttered.

Nihilan had betrayed them all, it seemed.

When he handed the scopes back to Vathek, Lorkar was on his feet.

Sixteen of his men remained, amongst them Harkane with his tracked Rapier and Tsu'gan. Lorkar sneered with displeasure as he recognised this particular survivor.

He was on his knees and appeared almost shell-shocked.

Lorkar bent down to speak into his ear.

'Saw you cutting up your kin like you were butchering meat on the block, *brother*.'

He tapped the muzzle of his bolter against the silver-metal growth attached to his face.

'This thing will keep you honest, eh? I'm surprised the sorcerer gave you up to me so easily. I thought he wanted you for himself. Still,' he gestured to the carnage unfolding behind the wall, 'now you've had a hand in this you won't be returning to your Chapter again.'

A nerve pulsed in Tsu'gan's cheek. His wide eyes burned as they were turned on Lorkar.

The sergeant clapped him on the shoulder. 'We'll

make a Malevolent out of you yet.'

An eldritch wind whipping from the breach made Lorkar turn. Streaks of lightning crackled the air presaging...

'What the f–'

...an explosion of light that blazed into life inside the wall. It lasted only moments but was bright and violent enough to overload the Marine Malevolent's retinal display. Blinking back the harsh afterglare, he saw a hazed silhouette step from the psychic storm like a wayward traveller arrived after a long journey.

He was clad in blue ceramite and steeped in arcana. A drakescale cloak flared behind him and cerulean lightning coursed angrily across his eyes. In a clenched fist he brandished a skull-headed staff.

Lorkar sneered, 'Witch,' then recoiled as the first ranks of Nihilan's rabble were thrown back, maimed by the Librarian's onrushing flame wall. He stepped into the mouth of the breach, hurling fire and death from his fingertips as simply as if it were breathing.

Those dregs without armour to protect them burned, their hair and clothes and skin shrivelled and cooked in a terrible inferno.

Lorkar balked as the Librarian came on, the other defenders advancing in his wake, taking the fight to any of the renegades that had survived the flames.

Beneath his feet the earth began to tremble and crack.

Lava oozed to the surface, tiny rivulets at first and then gushing fountains of the planet's molten core.

He snarled to his men, 'We're done here,' then looked at Tsu'gan. 'Get him up. He's coming with us.'

Vathek and Morgak shouldered their bolters and went to pull the once-Salamander to his feet when a plume of fire speared from the earth and took Tsu'gan with it. A second column of flame followed quickly after the first, scorching Vathek's armour plate and drawing a curse from his lips. Then came a third and fourth. Morgak was immolated by the fifth. It cooked him inside his armour and fused the metal to his trembling body. The warrior's tongue was burned away before he could scream.

Columns of fire were surging up into the air across the ash-plain, pushed up through the cracks, impelled by the Librarian's psychic will and the disruption of Nocturne's tectonic balance. Erupting like geysers they choked the sky with smoke and flame, spewing lava in a flood.

Lorkar thought about going back for Tsu'gan. The once-Salamander was a distant figure, prone against the ash-sand, burned and unmoving. If nothing else, Lorkar could at least finish him off and exact a measure of retribution.

'Leave him,' he decided in the end, retreating from the deadly eruptions and the renewed fight for Hesiod's wall. 'He's probably dead, anyway.'

Inside his head, the *voices* told him what to do. They guided him gently towards his prey. This was Vinyar's command, wasn't it? He would fulfil it.

'Never accept a slight without retribution,' he muttered, in a voice not quite his own.

II
Mortal Wounds

TSU'GAN WASN'T DEAD. He rolled onto his back and opened his eyes to look up, and found a sundered sky staring back at him. It was black, thick with smoke and ash. It was almost like night. The clouds moved slowly, as if sticking to the air and reluctant to take their leave of it. A smear of red, like old blood, appeared in a break in the cloud bank as if an invisible hand had cut a wound into the blackness and let it bleed.

That's when he realised he was partially blinded. Something about his visual perception was wrong. Diminished, even. It lacked depth and the periphery of his sight was foreshortened. One of his eyes was gone, burned out by the plume of superheated fire.

Agony came with realisation and Tsu'gan roared to dull the blazing needles in his face. Pain brought clarity. Awareness of place, the memory of the battle came back to him in a disconcerting flood. He remembered the wall, the lance of light striking from the heavens and the blast wave that rolled across the wastes like a tsunami. Then he knew only fire and the cold tendrils of near death.

Nocturne was tearing itself apart and he'd been kissed by her haemorraghing vitae. It pitted his armour, the left shoulder guard eroded down to the mesh underlayer. Pieces of his plastron were stripped back to the bare metal and an entire section of the cuirass on his back was gone with the bare skin visible underneath. Even ceramite was poor protection against the earth's heartblood.

Crawling onto his knees, Tsu'gan found his strength returning. Tentatively, he touched his face. He felt bone, not skin or flesh. When he brought them back, his gauntleted fingers were shiny with gore.

I've survived worse, he said to himself and tried to believe it.

Peering through a haze of heat and blurred vision, he discerned the outlines of the Marines Malevolent leaving the battlefield. Then he saw the Third battling through the breach with Vel'cona in their midst.

The Master Librarian was blazing like a righteous torch, laying waste to the mercenary hordes and lesser renegades with contempuous ease. Not so long ago, Tsu'gan had been a part of that horde. He regarded the tattered remnants of his traitor's garb, fighting the urge to tear it off, every damnable plate, and felt ashamed.

Disgusted with his self-pity, he averted his eyes from the borrowed armour and caught sight of Captain Agatone urging the troops from the wall. Adrax Agatone was brave, if stolid, but fought with a fire in his soldier's heart. Tsu'gan had known him as a sergeant, an honourable and forthright warrior he'd greatly respected.

There was Malicant beside him; the venerable banner bearer had served Kadai too. So too what was left of the Inferno Guard, the captain's loyal retainers. During his service to the Third, Tsu'gan had only known two other captains and they were both dead.

Seeing his former brothers, knowing he could no longer return to their ranks, was more painful than the ruination of his face. In those waking moments, Tsu'gan considered offering himself up to their blades. At least that way he would die in battle and by a Fire-born's hand. Agatone would do it. He'd place the blade deep, a heart strike, giving him a shred of honour. Tsu'gan could embrace the mountain like that.

But that would achieve nothing, save his ignominious death.

He would survive instead and find the ones who'd done this to him. With clarity of purpose came another revelation. It was slow to form, dulled by his injuries, but unmistakable. The numbness in his head, the sense of disembodiment had faded. Tsu'gan, not the mind shackle, was governing his actions again. He reached up to touch the alien thing clinging tenuously to his cheek. The skin where it was pinioned was raw, down to the bone; the lava had dissolved it, but it had also severely damaged the mind shackle. Tsu'gan didn't hesitate. Life was pain. He ripped it off his face and took what followed with gritted teeth.

Agony already wracked his entire body, what did a little more matter.

White heat dying like the embers of a fire behind his eyes, Tsu'gan regarded the alien thing clutched in his shaking hand.

'Not much to speak of really,' he sneered, the breath catching in his throat.

Vulkan's Eye, it was torturous!

Tsu'gan crushed the broken silver beetle and scattered its remains.

Rise, he urged himself. *Get up… do it now!*

Every nerve ending was burning.

It was a strange sensation to be caught in the midst of a battle but waiting in the eye of its storm. Gunfire, clipped and sporadic, the clash of blades and the screams of the slain, surrounded Tsu'gan's island of calm but it would not last. To believe he was divorced from it was as certain to kill him as picking up a knife and turning it on himself. War spread, that was its nature. Islands were swallowed by growing oceans of violence. It was inevitable, not merely probable. He needed to move on.

Staggering at first, Tsu'gan got his feet. He slipped once on the ash and clattered back down onto his knees. Defiant, his facial injuries having lessened to a dull ache, he rose again. His enhanced nervous system was trying to compensate for the incredible damage he'd sustained, pumping his body with endorphins and adrenaline so he could continue to function. He couldn't operate like this indefinitely, but it might give him enough time to find Lorkar and kill him. There was also the matter of Iagon. He'd promised the dog retribution and Tsu'gan intended to deliver but he'd lost sight of him after he'd fled from the wall. The wretch could be anywhere.

Caught in the no-man's-land between the host of Dragon Warriors and the broken Hesiod wall where the Salamanders were making their stand, Tsu'gan was wracked with a final moment of indecision.

I am Fire-born, this is my place. It would be easy to proclaim his survival and return from the hands of the enemy. *The city of my birth is burning and I should defend it, but I have killed my own, my brothers.* It would be triumphant. *This is their blood on my hands.* Glorious. *How can I embrace them again with unclean hands?* But ultimately, it would be a lie.

Tsu'gan turned his back on his brothers, his Chapter, everything he had ever known and started to run away from the battle. Returning to the fold of the renegades was unconscionable too, not now his mind was again his own, so he followed an oblique line between Hesiod's wall and the now advancing renegades.

For the first time in his life Tsu'gan was uncertain of his path. It was a dark one, he was well aware of that, and it had led him to this crossroads but now he stood upon it he felt powerless to act.

The muffled sound of clanking armour as an ambusher sought to mask his approach brought Tsu'gan around to matters at hand. The lapping ocean had arrived sooner than even he had realised. He turned, catching the barest glint of fire on metal in the smoke, and dodged the frantic blade thrust of Cerbius Iagon.

The jagged edge of the traitor's knife scored armour plate and then cut into the mesh of the eroded sections, drawing blood.

Tsu'gan grimaced, but trapped Iagon's arm in the pit of his own and turned him. Scrambling, the traitor stumbled away with the impetus of his momentum and came up snarling.

'Betrayer!' Foaming spittle on his sneering lip gave him the face of a madman. It was an accurate description. A wadge of phlegm was clinging to his angular chin and drooled down, tarring his gorget. He didn't even move to wipe it away, just let it hang there.

Tsu'gan backed off, Iagon's outstretched blade keeping him at bay.

'Says the one wearing a traitor's colours,' he replied. 'You dishonour your forebears.'

'Always so righteous...' Iagon, making a tentative lunge like a huntsman trying to cow a vicious predator, became scornful. 'The noble lord of Hesiod, he who would be king.'

Tsu'gan avoided the blow easily, it was intended to goad not kill.

'Do you want for privilege, Iagon? Is that it?'

Iagon slashed wildly this time. 'I want only for your death and suffering.'

'Because I'm noble born?'

A desperate lunge made Tsu'gan sidestep. 'You'll need

to do better than that, brother,' he muttered, acutely aware of the stimulants in his body that were keeping him upright.

Iagon laughed. It was an unpleasant, mocking sound. 'Brother? What makes you a brother to me?' He brandished his augmetic hand, clenched into a fist. 'I sacrificed. I murdered for you…' A terrible ennui passed across his face, a coldness of spirit that had hollowed him out until only darkness was left. He grinned, and it was an altogether repugnant expression. 'But now there's blood on your hands too.'

'Just like your master, you are deluded, Iagon,' Tsu'gan told him, ignoring Iagon's clumsy attempts to lure him. But he was careful to maintain his distance. Without the weapons he'd lost in the blast plume, Tsu'gan was vulnerable. He knew he was weak too. There was a chainsword laying half-buried in the ash nearby but he couldn't reach it without dropping his guard. 'You have sold your soul to Chaos, Iagon, and the price was cheap.'

'I'll tell you what I am.' Iagon slammed a fist against his plastron. It was an act of petulance. 'I am a survivor. I will outlast you, brother. I will outlast all of you.'

The tremors were intensifying, so too the battle around them.

Tsu'gan had landed in a shallow ravine but could see the approaching muzzle flares of bolters as the Salamanders and Dragon Warriors closed on one another.

'If you are going to kill me, then do so quickly,' he said. 'For once they meet,' he gestured to the two battle-lines, 'there'll be no escaping the meat grinder for either of us.'

Iagon sneered. 'Are you afraid, brother? Scared you won't fulfil your grand destiny?'

Tsu'gan's voice was hard as iron. 'I know no fear,' he replied, 'as any *true* Space Marine should.' He'stan had shown him that, on the Volgorrah Reef. 'Tell me though, brother, have you ever known what that feels like? Have you ever truly been a Space Marine?'

Letting out a cry of atavistic rage, Iagon threw himself at his old sergeant. Slashing frenziedly with the knife, he lost his footing as another quake hit and stumbled.

Tsu'gan barrelled into him, seeing his opportunity. Feeling the jagged blade bite into his exposed shoulder, he endured the pain and barged Iagon to the ground. The force of his momentum kept him going far enough to stoop. His fingers closed around the chainsword's hilt...

In the meantime, Iagon had hauled himself to his feet and was a handspan away from sinking his knife into Tsu'gan's neck when he found a track of sharpened blade-teeth buzzing next to his side.

Crouched down, Tsu'gan held the chainsword firmly and up at an angle.

'Do you remember the promise I made to you when Ramlek was sticking his knives in?' he asked. 'I said I would come after you and that I'd leave you until last...'

Using both hands, Tsu'gan hacked into Iagon's flank so hard he cut legs from torso in a single furious stroke.

'I lied,' he said, Iagon's blood flecking his ravaged face and leaking all over the desert as the traitor fell into two halves. His expression was etched in genuine terror.

Tsu'gan didn't linger. He felt no remorse. Even if he could have stayed, there were others to kill. Like a chrono-gladiator whose dial was ticking, Tsu'gan felt the finite nature of the time he had left. It was short. He'd need to kill quickly. He spat on the corpse, excising the last of the bitterness he felt towards a warrior he had once counted as his own, and went after Lorkar.

As the Emperor's Angels, His champions and mankind's chosen protectors, Space Marines could withstand incredible amounts of punishment before they finally expired. It was not easy to kill one, and the sort of thing that could only be achieved by another Space Marine or some of the most dangerous alien species of the galaxy.

Iagon knew this. He knew because it had been told

to him by the masters of his Chapter, by those who had turned him from a lowly human mortal into a warrior-god. To become such a thing, to aspire to the ranks of the Space Marines and be so vaunted was the single most significant event of Iagon's existence. Only, he hadn't been alone in his apotheosis. He had walked with other warrior-gods too and their shadows were long indeed. Longer than his own.

Guile, however, was something Iagon had in abundance and ambition… *such ambition!* It drove him to do great and terrible things. If he could not attain the trappings of power and pre-eminence for himself then he would look to others to do it for him. He would stand in their shadows still, but at least he'd be closer to the sun.

But despite his machinations, so carefully planned, so fearlessly and oft literally executed, he was undone. As his lifeblood leaked from the ragged ends of his flesh, he did not feel inviolable, nor a warrior-god. He felt painfully mortal, as if his regenesis was coming undone at the genetor's brutally unstitched seams.

Punishment was a Space Marine's trade, dealing it out and taking it, but the distance between the two halves of Iagon's body may as well have been a gulf.

He had been transformed into a killing machine only to be slain by a better one.

As his mind was fading and the last worn threads of his life slowly frayed and snapped, a mote of something vital stirred between feelings of thwarted destiny. Another transformation was taking place within Iagon, one that turned his slashed intestines into groping tendrils and forced the two halves of his body to reach out for one another across the bloody ash-sand.

Disturbed and excited at the same time, he felt the organs meet and re-knit. As a winch being wound by some invisible crank-hand, torso and abdomen slowly drew together. Skin met skin and began to fuse. Flesh regenerated. Meat, chewed up by the vigorous chain-blade, was restored.

Sensation, gradually fading into numbed oblivion a moment ago, returned and brought with it renewed strength. Feeling came back in his legs and he managed to stand. He clenched his fists and saw the augmetic hand had gone, replaced by another.

'Incredible...'

The hot gusting of his breath brought a sulphurous tang with it, more potent than Nocturne's blighted air. Iagon felt... *greater*, but strength and stature were not the limits of his gifts.

He turned at some unknown sign and saw the first of the Dragon Warrior vanguard spilling into the ravine where Tsu'gan had killed him.

Iagon gazed upon them with his arms down by his sides, unmoving, not as allies or enemies but as lowly beings and with ancient eyes that were not entirely his own.

Five Dragon Warriors, little more than a scouting party, aimed through the iron sights of their weapons as if feeling the old malice within Iagon. It exuded from his skin in a necrotic musk, putting him in mind of boneyards and flayed flesh. For a moment, he caught a glimpse of another realm, where armies of the lost and damned were slaves to darkness. A chorus of thunderous bolter retorts and muzzle flares crashed into existence as the renegades unleashed everything they had to slay him. In a fleeting second of doubt, Iagon threw up his arms to ward off the fatal fusillade.

There was no second death, no chunks of hot gristle scattered across the ash-sand. Iagon was whole, untouched. He watched in mute fascination as the mass-reactive shells impacted harmlessly against his body in slow motion. Pieces of broken armour spun into the air in a languid storm of ceramite. But his skin was utterly unblemished. There was no scratch.

The renegades saw that too.

Close enough to try and gut him, three warriors drew blades and went in close. Iagon dispatched them with a sweep of his arm. The blow struck all three renegades at once, shattering armour and bone. Thrown into the air they disappeared over the dune amidst a hail of broken spikes, split links of chain and fragmenting plate.

He leapt on the fourth, who was hurriedly reloading his bolter, taking a full clip to the chest before he tore the warrior's head off. The last he impaled with his hand. Blade-like it slid through the renegade's power armour like parchment and came out clutching twin beating hearts.

Such power!

Iagon's dreams of ascension were coming true. It was not exactly as he'd pictured it but nonetheless…

'I am… *gnn*…' Steeped in genhanced gore, he revelled in his newfound strength but then, just as a candle is snuffed out by the breeze, his awareness faded to a splinter as another presence took hold, '…*reborn.*'

Engel'saak regarded the burning desert with hateful eyes. It quietened the terrified screams of the mortal, confined them to a black place where light never touched and none could ever hear. The vessel would serve… for now.

For millennia the daemon had dwelled in the ether of the abyss, with only its wrath and desire for vengeance to sustain it. Visits to the mortal sorcerer were petty amusements, his flesh little more than a lens through which Engel'saak could perceive the race of men. He was a gatekeeper and the flesh sacrifice he'd provided the key. Such bright little soulfires the mortals made and in such abundance – how it longed to feast upon them again.

Banishment had robbed it of earthly form. It could still remember the white heat of the warrior's hammer and see the forge fires raging in his eyes. This mortal was not like the others, there was something incandescent about him. Deific. He was earth and fire incarnate.

Engel'saak had been guilty of underestimating him. It would not make the same mistake with his lesser progeny.

The daemon was only vaguely aware of the shouting mortals, doubtless humbled and frightened by its burgeoning form. The flesh-change was accelerating rapidly as its will asserted itself over the possessed. The armour binding it ruptured and split as a ready flow of scaled feathers burst from within. Its legs extended, transforming into gnarled pinions conjoined to its elongating body by a fleshy membrane. The arms followed, lengthening as talons sprouted from mortal fingertips. Last was the neck, stretching into something long and scaled and serpentine, surmounted by a head that was avian and reptilian at the same time.

The mortals were not fleeing; rather they were mustering to attack.

Engel'saak swept out a desultory claw in the direction of the warriors as their crude weaponry pattered against its skin. As one they sank into convulsions as rapid and violent mutation seized them. In moments, they were little more than steaming piles of blubber, quivering and mewling as their minds surrendered to oblivion.

Another band piled over the dune. They were shouting, trying not to look at the remains of their fellow mortals. Several took up crouching positions and shouldered cannons that blazed with a pellucid light. As the bright beams touched Engel'saak's skin they burned, they actually *hurt* it.

Screeching its hell-cry, the daemon put the warriors on their knees where they clutched their war-helms in agony. Dark fluid seeped between the joins at the neck as they collapsed, one after the other.

So brittle…

Engel'saak wasn't just referring to the dead warriors, for they were not the only ones anchored to mortal flesh. Rivulets of ichor ran from the cracks in its corporeal vessel. Another thought staunched them and re-wove the scaly skin around its body, but the daemon knew it was vulnerable and outnumbered by these lesser creatures.

More were coming. It could smell the tantalising

essence of their soulfires through its flaring nostrils.

Too many to flesh-change.

It spewed a stream of corrupting fire from its beak-like maw, engulfing the summit of the dune and the mortals who were first to crest it. Despite their armour they burned, groping and writhing in the ash of their own immolated bodies.

Charnel-stink on the breeze was invigorating. Such an old familiar odour, Engel'saak revelled in it.

Others shouldered through the flames, hazy silhouettes resolving into solid armoured warriors. Their weapons were levelled and spoke angrily.

Not fear, it thought, tasting with a long rugose tongue, *arrogance.*

These mortals would fight relentlessly, until either they'd killed the daemon or were slain themselves. It could not linger, not here.

Engel'saak threw back its head, emitting a deep and ululating scream. The fleshy membranes attached to its limbs billowed out and became wings…

AGATONE PAUSED IN the killing to gesture at the beast that had just soared from the renegades' ranks and into the air.

'Did you see that?'

Malicant looked skywards. His banner caught on the breeze and made the drake-head icon snap. 'It has wings, but much larger than a dactylid,' he said.

Brother Shen'kar, Agatone's second-in-command, spoke as he released a flamer burst.

'A monster disturbed from the ash-sand, emerged from some freshly opened crevice in the earth?'

Agatone was barely listening.

Since Vel'cona's arrival they'd made good progress through the breach. Nihilan's fodder had been numerous but were close to annihilation now. Agatone had been able to task Scouts from Seventh with shoring up defences and seeing to civilians. Uncounted injured

lined the streets and crowded plazas looking to the Salamanders to deliver them. Agatone remembered lifting
a stricken woman above his shoulders to save her from
being crushed in the mass panic when the sky fell. He'd
done this even though his enemies were all about him.
All the Salamanders did. These were their people, the
humans they'd sworn their lives to protect.

Honorious had been speared through the shoulder
by a xenos blade as he shielded an infant from certain
death. Lok was burned as he threw a man from a renegade's flamer. They'd taken their blows, each and every
one, earning gratitude and scars. Agatone loved his
people. He'd rejoiced to find that echoed in his battle-
brothers.

'With our deeds, raise them!' he'd proclaimed to the
wall before the siege began, in earshot of the huddled
civilians. 'Our courage shall be an example to all. It will
galvanise our people and show them what it means to be
Fire-born. We are Vulkan's shield!'

The great cheer that had followed was gratifying, but
these were words and as such meant nothing without
action. It had been too long since the Third stood in
glory. He would restore them, return honour to their
name, and the long diminished Inferno Guard to pre-
eminence.

Even though he openly refuted such things, he'd once
thought the captaincy of Third to be a poison barb,
cursed to suffer endless ill-fortune. Now he believed it
was a calling. All he had to do to answer it was survive.

The loss of the void shield was troubling and what
Techmarines the captain could spare were already working hard to repair Hesiod's generator. The deep quakes,
the ones that shook the bedrock and had split the Sanctuary's foundation stone, concerned Agatone the most.
He'd experienced the Time of Trial on many occasions
before but this was different, almost apocalyptic, and
now this... this *creature*.

'What is that thing?' he said, scowling at its scaled and

muscular body, its long leathern neck and vast unfurled wings. Old paintings of Terran myth and rumours of the lowest deeps beneath Mount Deathfire arose unbidden in his mind. 'It looks like...'

'It is a *drakon*,' uttered Vel'cona, 'or at least a simulacrum of one.' He was at the captain's side and vanquished a scurrying band of galthite pirates with a torrent of serpentine flame. Their noisome flesh cooked in their armour, their saurian faces ablaze. 'It is also known by other names... *wyvern, felldrake... estragon*. Fenrisians call them *ormr* or *wurm*.' The Master Librarian's inflection was thick with rustic accent, hinting of the campaigns he had fought beside the Wolves. He followed the monster's immense shadow with his eyes until it reached the cloud bank and disappeared. Even then his gaze lingered.

'In ancient days, primitive human tribes worshipped and feared it. They called it *dragon*.'

Agatone slowly shook his head. Through the comm-feed in his battle-helm reports were coming in from the wall sentries that a massed force of Dragon Warriors was marching across the ash-dunes to meet them. There was little time for investigation.

'Whatever name the beast goes by,' he said, 'it tossed those renegades like they were chaff.' He met Shen'kar's gaze. 'What if it is from the deep world, roused in anger at Nihilan's sacrilege?'

Every culture of the civilised galaxy had its tales of monsters, Nocturne more than most. Drakes had many names, not just their given ones that Salamanders had rune-branded on their flesh. There was the *lohikäärme* and the *tulikäärme*. Ancient *sok* and the serpentine *kulebre*. These were old beasts, legends of a forgotten world before even the time of Vulkan.

'No, its aura is malfeasant. Can't you taste the acrid taint of it on your tongue, brother? Like rusted metal and putrefaction. This thing did not come from the earth. It is a daemon, here to lay waste to us all.'

CHAPTER EIGHTEEN

I
Sacrifices

Tsu'gan kept low and fast as he crossed the dunes. He'd scavenged a bolter with a half clip and another spare from the body of a dead renegade half-buried in the ash-sand to add to his chainsword. They were battered weapons, unworthy of a Salamander, but then he reminded himself he was no longer one of them.

Killing his enemies was all that drove Tsu'gan now. Achieve that and he might attain some small measure of peace. He was following the Marines Malevolent's trail when he heard the reverberant screech tear into the air and turned.

Something reptilian and borne aloft on membranous wing had just disappeared into the thick cloud swathing all of Nocturne. He suppressed an involuntary shudder as he realised what this must be. During his incarceration, Tsu'gan had heard mutterings about the 'vessel'. On several occasions, Iagon had goaded him with it, suggesting a loathsome fate for the once-Salamander.

He thought back to the Aura Hieron temple on Stratos. Nihilan had threatened him with daemonic possession,

291

tried to turn him to the renegade's cause. He'd done it
again on *Hell-stalker*. Though his masochism had made
him weak, even fatalistic, Tsu'gan had refused the sorcerer's overtures. He was broken inside but no traitor.
Willingly, he would never betray his brothers.

Iagon, though… he was all too willing. Rage and jeal-
ously were potent nectars for the soulless fiends that
lurked beyond the veil. Such weakness thinned the gossamer membrane keeping mortal and daemon separate.

The monstrous creature was gone for now, lost to the
roiling night above, and Iagon was first amongst its victims.

'I pity you,' Tsu'gan muttered, knowing that if he
returned to where he'd killed the traitor there would be
no bodily remains.

Thunderous impacts shook the earth, signalling the use
of ordnance. Renewed conflict had broken out amongst
Hesiod's sallying defenders and the renegades' second
front. The opening salvos were devastatingly loud and
monstrously destructive. Tsu'gan lost his footing more
than once as he scrambled between flowing lava channels to the summit of a volcanic crag. Lorkar had come
this way. His troops were lying in wait in a ravine below.

Tsu'gan kept down, crouched at the foot of a jutting
rock split in half by the tectonic event ripping into Nocturne. Its broken peak was scattered across the crag's
flanks and basin. It was large enough for him to hide
behind and creep closer to the Marines Malevolent.

One was pointing and Tsu'gan followed the direction
of his outstretched arm to where a vast column of tanks
was rolling into view. His gaze alighted on Tu'Shan,
leading from the front in *Promethean*. The Land Raider
was ancient, its twin-flamers on either sponson clearing
a burning path to the heart of the Dragon Warrior positions.

A squadron of Predator battle tanks, Destructor and
Annihilator variants, rumbled along in its wake. Auto-
cannon turrets and side-mounted lascannons riddled

the static enemy artillery with armour-busting fire.

A missile battery went up in a blaze of fire and shrapnel. The explosion spread to a heavier ground-to-air Bombard, killing its crew and scuppering the war engine. Renegade armour that had been focused on the advancing ground force from the city turned to intercede against the flanking threat.

Tsu'gan watched them gun their track beds in desperate rotational manoeuvres as they tried to bring firing arcs to bear. Ponderous ordnance tanks, the Whirlwinds and Vindicators of Master Kor'hadron's Armoury, laid down suppressing fire from a distance. Rocket bursts chewed up the earth in front of the enemy tanks and split their tracks, slowing their response to Tu'Shan's flanking column. Fat shells spat from the mouths of Demolisher cannons tipped entire vehicles onto their sides where the escaping crew were lit up like burning torches from Tu'Shan's flamestorm side-mounts.

They'd been battered, the Chapter Master and his tank commanders, doubtless come from Themis, but their fury was brazier-hot.

Dragon Warrior tanks ruptured and died in the aggressive cannonade from the forward Predators and Land Raiders. The hulls of some burst apart in the barrage, others merely slowed to an all-stop, billowing smoke.

Tu'Shan rolled over the mechanised outriders, smashing the wrecks from his path and grinding foot troops to paste beneath his iron-shod tracks. In a few short minutes, the artillery was almost totally destroyed and the Dragon Warriors were in retreat. But they were a shadow of the forces Tsu'gan had seen arrayed on the *Hell-stalker*. Nihilan had cohorts and fighting battalions numbering in the hundreds. This was just a fraction of his martial strength.

As he picked his way silently down into the ravine, he wondered what the sorcerer was saving in reserve and why he hadn't committed his entire army. Nocturne was wounded, her blood was evident across the cracked and fiery earth, but she wasn't dead. This wasn't the abject annihilation that Nihilan had threatened.

With the faint scrape of metal against scabbard, Tsu'gan drew his borrowed chainblade as the first of Lorkar's sentries came into view.

What is your purpose, sorcerer? he asked himself, preparing a kill-strike aimed at the Marine Malevolent's back.

An answer of sorts came with the sound of leathern wings flapping on the breeze and a crimson shadow bolting out of the ash clouds. Like a hunter-seeker on an inexorable course, it arrowed towards Tu'Shan.

NIHILAN EMBARKED FROM the belly of the Stormbird to stand upon a vast and yawning crater.

Two of his Glaive followed, taking up position at either shoulder.

Ramlek crouched at the edge, looking down. His boot disturbed a piece of rock that went skittering off into the gloomy depths.

'Deep,' he uttered, a ghosting of fine cinder spilling from his fanged vox-grille.

Thark'n nodded, his thick arms folded across his chest.

'It leads to the heart of Nocturne,' Nihilan told them, 'and our destiny.'

Forged by the fury of the seismic cannon, the bore hole was also wide. It walls were ridged, and descended in molten rings. In the manner of a colossal drill, the energy lance had pierced the many layers of rock and earth between the surface and the magma halls beneath it. Laid open like a wound, Nihilan had but to turn the enemy's eye away and he could walk into this realm unmolested.

'Soon…' he promised, though the intended recipient wasn't listening, at least not in any conventional sense.

Behind them, the shadow of the Stormbird slowly receded as Ekrine guided it above the cloud layer and out of sight. He'd stay nearby but also hidden.

Close to the summit of Mount Deathfire, the air was

acrid and foul with sulphur. Shimmering heat, exuded off the lava tracts and growing magma pools, flaked the paint from their armour. Only the ceramite shielding kept them from burning up.

Banks of pyroclastic cloud ringed the peaks that only Nihilan's witch-sight could penetrate. Far below, he saw the battle raging and the daemon as it descended on Tu'Shan.

'Even if it doesn't end you, there's a second blade with your name on it,' Nihilan promised under his breath.

Though he couldn't see it, all creatures touched by the warp could detect the presence of another. Especially powerful ones blazed like hell-fires.

'Why the worm and not the warrior?' asked Ramlek. He looked up at his lord. 'And why leave its manifestation to chance?'

He was not questioning in the sense that he disagreed, the dutiful hound would never do that; he merely wanted to understand.

'Tsu'gan was more resilent than I thought.'

'Mind and flesh,' Ramlek agreed. He rubbed at his neck where the razor-fan the once-Salamander had thrust him into had severed it.

'Possession was far from a certainty,' Nihilan continued. 'Resistance, or the very least hindrance, could have ruined everything. I needed a pliable vessel. Iagon was perfect, flawed in every way.'

He neglected to say that a part of him respected Tsu'gan, was in awe of his rage and determination. In him he saw an ally, a potential convert. Even now, after everything and on the cusp of achieving his ultimate goal, Nihilan hadn't abandoned the idea of turning the once-Salamader to his cause. But that wasn't for Ramlek to know. Spit on a dog's food enough and soon it will look to find its meat elsewhere, perhaps even the flesh of its master.

Nihilan's eyes narrowed as he contemplated the strands of fate he'd woven to bring about this reality. 'It wasn't chance, Ramlek. It was preordained. The worm, as you call him, hated his old sergeant. Murder was inevitable, and Tsu'gan provided it as I knew he would. After its millennia of yearning, Engel'saak is free.'

A clenched fist suggested Ramlek's barely restrained zeal. 'I would witness its slaughter.' He brandished a hefty power axe in his left hand. 'My blade yearns for the kill. I envy Nor'hak. At least he will face the Firedrakes.'

Nihilan scoffed. 'Don't be so quick to crave blood and death. There'll be plenty to slake your desires, Ramlek.' He gazed down into the swirling smoke. 'I would rather leave Engel'saak with that bastard Lorkar and his cronies. Daemons have no true allegiance, save to themselves. Be glad you are up here and not below with the other sacrificial dogs. Not out of desire, do I bring them to the altar to bare their necks. It is out of necessity and the furthering of our creed. Everything has led to this.'

Ramlek bowed his head. 'Your will is great, my lord.'

'It will need to be greater for what follows.'

Up in the vaults of the world the thunder was louder and the crimson lightning fiercer. A bolt jagged out of the darkness, striking the crater's edge not far from Ramlek's feet. Tiny pieces of rock caromed off his armour but the Dragon Warrior didn't even flinch.

Nihilan lifted his eyes to the sky. 'She voices her displeasure.' The darkness of the crater beckoned.

Ramlek turned his head. 'What is that sound?'

A sonorous mewling echoed from the deeps, resonating off the walls and carried all the way to the surface.

'Drakesong,' answered Nihilan, 'A cry for the dying world. We move now.'

Engaging the ignition stud on his jump pack, Nihilan felt the gout of chemical-blue flame lick from the exhaust-port. Angular vanes attached to the jet engine to assist with trajectory fanned out like draconian wings. Convection vents manufactured into the sides plumed invisible heat vapour. A cruel machine-spirit lurked within, eager to be let loose.

Nihilan obliged it, leaping off the crater's edge and into the abyss.

'Stay close,' he growled against the rushing descent wind. 'There may be defenders we don't know about. Without the daemon to augment them, my powers have lessened.'

The Glaive warriors were as the sorcerer's shadow, ever at his heel down into the long darkness of Nocturne's subterranea.

II
Born of Fire

PYRIEL UNCLENCHED HIS eyes and found he was still alive. Heat radiated off his armour and seized his limbs, despite the psychic shield he'd erected. It was hard to uncurl his body and stand. He felt fused together, as if labouring under a heavy weight that he couldn't throw off.

It took a few seconds for him to realise he was breathing through his battle-helm's internal filters. All the oxygen in the vault had been burned up in the fire. The air blurred with heat haze. It was heady and thick, like moving through liquid.

Fugis was crouched next to him, huddled in a foetal position. Pyriel reached out, snatching his hand back when he realised his gauntlets would likely scald the Apothecary.

'Hold on, brother,' he murmured. His tongue was leaden too, his lips reluctant to function.

Fugis was suffocating.

Staggering, the lactic acid in his knee joints like blade thrusts with every step, Pyriel hit the wall and hammered on the door release.

He called out, rasping, 'Elysius…'

The vault wouldn't open. Its gears protesting, the ancient mechanism whined and growled at the punishment it had suffered. Still sluggish, struggling to stay on his feet, Pyriel said again, 'Elysius!'

Fugis was suffocating.

A crackling shield of energy dissipated from around the kneeling Chaplain. He arose on steady limbs, feeding a jolt of power into his crozius.

'Step aside!' he commanded, swinging the mace around in a blazing arc. The first hit made a dent but the door wouldn't yield. Elysius took the power stave in two hands and swung again. This time he made a crack. It was wide enough for his fingers to get some purchase. For good measure, he made a third strike and opened the crack a little further for greater leverage.

'Now, brother,' he said, 'help me!'

Together they pulled at the door to the vault, Pyriel low and Elysius high, one at either side. Slowly, the two halves of the gate parted and the heat began to escape pushed out by the onrushing air.

Elysius grabbed Pyriel's gorget and pulled him close. His face was a mask of anger but untouched by the flame. 'What was that? What have we done here?'

The Librarian was almost too dazed to answer. He fought for lucidity, but could remember nothing after the conflagration had engulfed them.

'Fire...' he murmured, 'there was only fire...'

Elysius struck him with the back of his gauntlet, hard enough that Pyriel slid a half metre across the floor. Relentless, the Chaplain advanced on him.

'Gather yourself! You mind has been overwhelmed but it will pass.' In the corner of the chamber, Dak'ir's still body was slumped on its side and unmoving. 'I need to know what I have sanctioned.'

Pyriel was coming around, but it was taking time. He looked incredulously at the Chaplain. 'How are you?'

Elyisus brandished his rosarius. 'Faith protects me.' There was a mania in his wide eyes. 'What did we unleash? Tell me, Pyriel!'

The Librarian turned to the corner of the chamber. It

was blackened, the metal scorched. Reduced to a few scattered pieces, the ancient armour from Scoria was no more.

'Dak'ir...'

Fugis had crawled over to the Lexicanum's prone form and was trying to check his vitals.

'Apothecary?' Elysius called from across the room.

Fugis hauled himself up so he was kneeling by Dak'ir.

'Not even warm,' he muttered.

Elysius left Pyriel gibbering as he tried to recover from the psychic storm.

'Our Librarian is gone for the time being, what do you have left?'

Steam was emanating from the Apothecary's skin. Unlike the others, he wasn't wearing power armour but he'd still survived. It seemed a message might not be the only thing he'd brought back from the desert.

His fingers were trembling. Fugis noted the Chaplain's worried expression.

'Just a little nerve damage and some shock. It's nothing.'

He carefully rolled Dak'ir onto his back. It wasn't easy with him clad in full battle-plate, and Elysius had to assist. Then Fugis bent down and leaned in to Dak'ir's chest.

Unclasping his gorget, the Apothecary placed two fingers against the Lexicanum's neck.

'Help me with this,' he said to Elysius. Together they unhitched Dak'ir's plastron and removed it.

Fugis leaned in again, shook his head.

'What did we miss?' said the Chaplain. 'What part of the prophecy did we get wrong?'

'None of it!' snapped the Apothecary. 'Everything is as it should be.'

Elysius threw out his arm, gesturing to the body. 'He is no Fire Sword, brother!'

Returning to a kneeling position, Fugis let his arms fall by his sides.

He sighed. 'You're right.'

Kneeling by the body, the Apothecary looked beaten.

At the entrance to the vault, Pyriel had got back onto his feet and joined them. His expression was grim as he regarded Dak'ir.

'Is he dead?' It came out as a rasp.

Fugis nodded. His face was drawn taut, sharp as a blade. 'Our brother has fallen.'

'By our own hand.' The Chaplain's gravel voice was thick with accusation. He donned his helmet and turned his back on Dak'ir's lifeless body. 'This is over. We make for Hesiod at once and pray to Vulkan that there is some shred of Nocturne left for us to help save.' He stalked from the vault, crozius clenched tight in his gauntleted fist.

Pyriel helped pull Fugis to his feet.

The Apothecary met the Librarian's gaze. Anger and denial warred across his face.

'It should not have been this way. The signs…'

He followed Elysius silently, leaving Pyriel alone with Dak'ir. He bent down on one knee.

Dak'ir's eyes were open but lightless. The red orbs didn't even harbour an ember of life.

'I am truly sorry, brother,' he said, closing the staring eyelids so it looked as if the Lexicanum were merely in repose.

There was no time for any rites or ceremony. They would have to wait. Lying in the vault of the Pantheon Chamber, Dak'ir's body was as safe as anywhere on Prometheus.

Pyriel arose, finding some resolve.

'I failed you, Dak'ir, but I will not fail my Chapter or my people.'

He had not told the others, because they'd had enough with visions and portents. But as the eternal fire burned around him, he had *seen*. The Librarian knew where he must go and what he must do.

Drawing on the latent psychic energies still present in

the room, Pyriel opened up a gate of infinity and was gone.

Fugis looked back to the vault when he heard the eldritch wind of translocation.

'Pyriel is no longer with us,' he said to Elysius.

The Chaplain didn't turn. They were headed for the armoury, for his power fist and a suit of battle-plate for the Apothecary. Without serfs or brander-priests to aid them, they'd need to move quickly.

They passed through the sacred archway to the Pantheon Chamber, sealing the gate behind them. Beyond its threshold, the dampening effect on the feed was lifted. Comm chatter came alive in Elysius's battle-helm. Hangar Seven had been breached. There were xenos abroad on the station.

'He goes to meet his destiny,' he told Fugis. 'We all do.'

CHAPTER NINETEEN

I
Into Hell

THEY BREACHED THE armoured flanks of the *Hell-stalker* to the discordant clamour of vulcan-drills shredding metres-thick starship metal and emerged inside a dingy hangar. Automated pressure seals burst and flung open upon entry and once the boarding torpedo was static. The engines died immediately as a series of access hatches clanged onto the hard metal of the deck. But the incumbents were wise enough to wait before debarkation.

Auto-slaved weapon systems cycled into violent action as secondary holding tubes split apart as if spring-loaded. Droves of missiles sped into the gun decks, ripping into the makeshift barricades erected by the defenders and tearing apart the grisly torture chains draped across its vaults. Bone and metal links cascaded in tune with the *chooming* salvos. Hell-fire chased away the gloom and flash-froze faces by the dozen etched into expressions of horror and imminent death. Dense explosions chewed up weapon teams and hastily scrambled shield-carriers. Frag and hot shrapnel accounted for an even higher yield towards the murder-harvest.

Static Rapier turrets added to the carnage of the Deathwind missile arrays, shredding the packed ranks of canoneers who'd hauled tracked multilasers and wheeled heavy stubbers into firing positions. Hot las and desperate scatter shot pinged off the thick armour of the Salamanders' remote weapon pods but they weathered the counter-fire well. A muted cheer, gritty through their fright masks, from the black flak-armoured defenders greeted the destruction of a Rapier but it was merely a consolation.

The auto-slaved weapons were just a vanguard; the real killers were still awaiting orders to assault.

'In Vulkan's name!'

Praetor stepped out first onto the enemy ship with a roar and raked a lofty gantry where a heavy weapons team was assembling under an overseer's gaze. The heretics died in the bolt storm he drew down upon them. A crate of rocket-propelled grenades went up in tandem with the armsmen and tore the gantry from its mountings. Praetor ignored the screams of those crushed beneath it. His brother Firedrakes were at his back, muzzle flares erupting from their weapons in all directions as they sought to establish a beachhead.

The auto-slaved weapons had thinned the ranks considerably and gave the Terminators vital clear ground to move into and occupy. Resistance was light at first as the reinforcements fell in, consisting of a few hundred armsmen wearing carapace, carrying rudimentary firepower and a few dozen heavier cannon. They were better drilled and equipped – the fodder had been used to soak up the auto-fire – but still woefully understrength to take on warriors in Tactical Dreadnought Armour.

Solid shot pattered off the Terminators like metal-cased rain. It turned the deck into a quagmire of spent ammunition and impotent brass shells. A round smacked against Praetor's left retinal lens and he scowled before eviscerating the shooter and four of his nearest comrades with his return fire.

Scanning the perimeter, cycling through several light spectra until he found one that provided the cleanest visual feed, he isolated cell leaders that were shouting frantic orders for more men.

Lighting these individuals up on the group tac-display was swift; their deaths to the combined fire of several key Firedrake squads were quicker still.

Overseers pressed slave-cohorts into the breach to compensate. These rabid dogs had once been servants of the Imperium from half a dozen different systems or more, but had devolved into crazed wretches. Rabble-rousers daubed in fell sigils and clad in robes of supplication stirred the mob. Some carried thick, broad-handled cutters; others wielded hook-chains and wrenches; most only had their fists and their mania to galvanise them.

While the Firedrakes were hewing down the massed hordes of the unwashed, subordinates in the ranks of the armsmen were slow to assert authority and take control. Troops were being mustered from across the ship. Bulkheads had begun to activate, coming up from the flooring to provide cover or seal off vulnerable areas. It was done without coordination and in a panic.

In the maddening pressure chamber of a boarding action men could be forgiven for losing their resolve and forgetting their purpose. Terminators across the entirety of the Adeptus Astartes were created for such cauldrons, though. They were not *men*, as such, and suffered none of an ordinary man's limitations. Even other Space Marines knew their place in the presence of a First Company veteran. Their very existence allowed for such insane missions to be countenanced, let alone actioned and achieved.

In the close confines of an enemy hulk, reality can take on a different caste. Corridors are smaller, tighter. Sound, especially the hard bark of gunfire, is louder. Muzzle flashes are brighter, and everywhere there is killing. Sweat, piss, the tang of old metal, it fills the air and makes it heavy. The ceiling creeps in as if lowered by a crank and primed to crush what's beneath it to paste. Fear takes root and its tendrils dig deep to the marrow of mere *men*.

During a boarding action, men come to know the truth about the vast floating citadels they are a living, breathing part of. They learn that ships are not ships at all, but that they are tombs, filled to the gunwales with the walking dead.

Ordinary mortals, even those defending the vessels they know intimately, can find themselves suddenly in strange environs, bereft of allies with only death a constant companion. Men flee in such conditions, only to find there is nowhere to run. In a boarding war, there is no back, only forwards. Within, there is heat and blood, noise so raucous it deafens all the senses; without, there is only the void and that cold unforgiving place holds no charity for the gutless.

Terminators knew no such peril. Just as their armour, their spirit was inviolable, their courage unflinching. A warrior with the honour of bearing a suit of Tactical Dreadnought Armour will either stand or advance; nothing else, for he does not know *how* to do anything else.

'Advance, forward and spread,' Praetor called down the comm-feed.

The way ahead was clogged with the grubby remains of bonded-slaves. It chafed to raise arms against once-loyal servants to the Throne but madness and hell had rendered them beyond redemption. Execution was a mercy. 'Fire to cleanse the fore,' he added.

Vo'kar and the other heavy flamers unleashed a furious blaze that turned the sundered corpses into ash.

Slowly, but with purpose, the Firedrakes drove over it and expanded their cordon. Superheated bone cruched to powder underfoot. They fanned out from the breaching point in tight lines, keeping up sustained burst-fire to thin down enemy numbers. Interspersed between the five-man squads were the Dreadnoughts, Amadeus and Ashamon. The two were like titans, the very image of Bray'arth Ashmantle, and laid waste with assult cannon and heavy flamer. Between them they tore up a bulkhead with twin blows from their seismic hammers, exposing a command cohort. Desultory fire from their underslung storm bolters dispatched the enemy officers before a rescue attempt could be made or a counter-attack mobilised.

One with the garb and trappings of a deacon fell to his knees in supplication, muttering curses in the black tongue.

'Your false gods will not save you!'

Ashamon immolated the demagogue in the righteous fires of his heavy flamer.

Soon the enemy dead outnumbered the living as Praetor pressed their shock and awe tactics for all they were worth.

From the postulated schematics he had seen and the proposed trajectory and insertion point for the mission, he believed this to be one of the *Hell-stalker's* gun decks. From here it was a relatively short march to the prow of the vessel and the seismic cannon. Everything depended on destroying the Dragon Warriors' apocalypse weapon. Only the primarch knew what damage it had already wreaked on the surface of Nocturne. It could not be allowed to fire again.

'Rear guard to secure breach point, hold and execute,' he ordered. 'All other Firedrakes are to advance on my lead, in Vulkan's name.'

Amaedus and Ashamon took up sentry positions with four heavily armed Terminator squads to maintain the ground they'd gained and keep the way open for a rapid egress once the saboteurs were done.

The rest continued up the wide avenue of the gun deck, following the veteran sergeant until he came to a halt. Aside from a few scattered and demoralised remnants, the first section of the gun deck was cleansed. At the end of the corridor, a heavy bulkhead gate had slammed into place to prevent further progress. Even now, reeling from the terrifying assault, Praetor knew that the survivors were rallying with reinforcements from the upper decks and planning a counter-strike.

'Apex sergeants, report.'

The squads at the edges of the Firedrakes, control-perimeter sounded in. The message was unified: *All enemy threats neutralised. Zero casualties.*

A glance at Praetor's retinal display informed him that they were missing four squads from the original assault roster.

'Sergeant Halknarr, report.' He cast around the hulking, green metallic ranks behind him and a host of blazing red retinal lenses stared back silently.

He turned to Persephion. 'Find out what has happened to Sergeant Halknarr.'

The Firedrake saluted and went to carry out his lord's orders.

Praetor cursed. Despite the unexpected 'turbulence', he'd thought they'd arrived aboard the *Hell-stalker* with a full complement. There wasn't time to linger but he couldn't just leave the old campaigner to an ignominious death if he could be rescued. He'd already lost too many.

'We should proceed.' He'stan had emerged from the throng and was standing by the veteran sergeant's side.

The Forgefather had fought like a tempest during the initial stages of the breach. Entire battalions of armsmen had fallen to his spear and gauntlet. The warrior-spirit was upon him now, as it was all of them. He was eager to continue and achieve the mission. 'More will be coming.'

'Until I know the whereabouts of our missing brothers, I am staying here, my lord.' There was no hint of truculence in Praetor's reply; it was merely a stating of the facts.

'Don't allow compassion to jeopardise the mission,

brother-sergeant.' He'stan kept his voice low. 'It is war. If Halknarr and the others are lost then it is the will of the anvil.'

Praetor was calling for a Techmarine. They needed to get a better idea of their location and an assault route through the *Hell-stalker's* lower decks. From here on out it would be akin to a labyrinth, one fraught with pitfalls, ambushes and myriad other dangers.

'It was my honour for you to join us on this mission, Forgefather, but this is my command and I will not abandon them if there is a chance they can be saved. Your philosphy may allow for such estrangement from your brothers, but mine unfortunately does not.'

Praetor didn't defy his lord lightly. This was the bearer of the primarch's name, his chosen pilgrim and seeker of the Nine. Even still, he would not condemn Halknarr and the others. It was for the survival of Nocturne they all were fighting. To recklessly discard any of its sons, however dire the situation, was counter to that objective as far as the veteran sergeant was concerned.

He'stan nodded sagely. 'You speak wisely, brother. I have been too long alone on the quest. Leave none behind,' he said. 'Self-sacrifice is one of the greatest tenets of Promethean Creed.'

Though he didn't need it, Praetor was glad of the Forgefather's approval. 'And I mean to enact it to the full.'

Persephion's voice came back over the feed.

'*Brother-sergeant, I have Sergeant Halknarr.*'

Praetor activated the relay-link and Persephion's feed was replaced with that of Halknarr.

'Where are you, brother?' he asked.

'*Good to hear that you're hale and hearty too, Herculon,*' the old campaigner replied.

'The entirety of First rejoices at your survival,' Praetor returned curtly, 'now where?'

Crackling static stalled the response for a few tense seconds.

'*...breached two decks farther out, some kind of ancillary hangar. Looks prepped for receiving ships. Met little resistance so far, but I have wounded from the aborted insertion into the gun decks.*'

'How many are with you? Did we lose any during breach?'

The summoned Techmarine arrived and proffered Praetor a hazing schematic of the *Hell-stalker's* lower decks on a data-slate. The grainy image depicted a vast, sprawling space several kilometres in length that would take time to traverse. It also showed the various junction points between decks. Hardwired into one of the vessel's control consoles, the display kept drifting in and out of resolution as the rogue signal dipped and peaked. It wouldn't last long, so Praetor committed everything he was seeing to his eidetic memory. He'stan did the same.

'*I have nineteen Firedrakes, four of which are injured but still battle-capable,*' said Halknarr. '*One, Brother Karnus, didn't make it.*'

Another sacrificed to the anvil. Its metal flanks must be slick with Salamander blood by now, thought Praetor.

He'stan pointed out a potential point of overlap between the routes of the two disparate groups.

Praetor nodded to him then replied to Halknarr. 'Proceed towards the starboard batteries,' he said. 'There is an intersection between gunports Crucius and Vitriol that will bring you up three decks. Then continue in the direction of the stern. At the end of a mainteinance corridor you should find a freight lifter that will bring you to us on the gun decks. I can locate you with auspex at that point. We are headed to the prow and the primary mission target.'

'*You make it sound like a training mission, brother.*'

'It isn't. Be vigilant.' Praetor heard something behind the crackle of Halknarr's voice, ambient noise coming from the other end of the feed. It sounded like distant gunfire, shouts and booted feet hitting metal. 'What's happening?'

In retrospect, it sounded like an obvious question.

Halknarr was taciturn as he focused his attention elsewhere. 'They've found us.'

'We encountered human battalions on the gun decks,' Praetor replied, straining to hear. The shouting was agitated and coming from the Firedrakes. He recognised at least three of their voices. Sporadic holding fire turned into a sustained barrage from both parties.

'*Not humans…*' Halknarr was moving, distracted as he fought and bellowed orders between reporting to Praetor. '*There are Traitor Astartes down here with us, Dragon Warriors.*'

'In number? Can you break through their ranks?'

'*We are falling back.*'

'Hold and regroup, brother,' Praetor urged him.

A Terminator will only stand or advance – that credo was tested and falsified in the space of a few seconds. Only something that could outmatch the fighting strength of twenty Firedrakes in full Tactical Dreadnought Armour could have forced Halknarr to give ground so easily.

There was a long break, filled with the muffled sounds of combat. Halknarr's chainfist starting up made the feed wretched with static.

A deeper sound like a bellow, but resonant and metallic, overwhelmed the audio and it cut out before returning a moment later.

All Praetor could do was listen.

'*Negative,*' the other sergeant replied at last, '*there are too many of them. Kesare's breath, I thought the bastards were supposed to be on the surface.*'

'Give me your position, brother. I will deploy squads for your immediate reinforcement and egress.'

Again, another long pause laced with vague battle sounds. The bellowing returned; something big, something powerful.

Praetor heard the voices of the enemy. They were deep and guttural, spitting curses at the Firedrakes and offering up their souls to dark and thirsty gods. The metal knuckles of his gauntlet cracked as the veteran sergeant impotently clenched his fist.

'Halknarr, give me your position,' he repeated.

The din of rattling combi-bolters was eclipsed by the roar of heavier cannon. Fell laugher boomed between its staccato shell bursts.

'*Negative. Do not come back for us. Do your duty and destroy the apocalypse weapon.*'

'I will save you, brother. Just tell me exactly where you are.

When Halknarr answered his voice was steady and sorrowful. '*You cannot save us all, Herculon, no matter how much you want to.*'

The fighting intensified. Praetor heard the old campaigner grunt as he took a hit. It was followed by the shriek of his chainfist, audibly gutting the assailent.

'*Don't come back for me, you fool. Praetor, they have Terminators and a mon–*'

The feed died, replaced by static.

He'd lost them, surrendered to the anvil just like all the others.

Praetor bowed his head in a moment of private grief, before he arose again resolute. He gestured to the barrier that had sealed the way ahead.

'Breaching charges on that bulkhead. Meltaguns and chainfists, front and ready. Bring it down. Bring it all down.' He met He'stan's gaze from behind glowering retinal lenses. 'We'll tear the heart out of this thrice-damned ship.'

II
Fire Against Ice

HOBBLING DOWN THE corridor was painful and awkward. Muscles that had partly atrophied through lack of use burned and sent blades of agony through Emek's half-ravaged body. Sweat veneered his brow beneath his battle-helm.

Sweat, for Vulkan's sake!

Ba'ken had been right when he gibed him about his absence from the training cages. Physically, mentally, he was not at his prime.

Emek cast a glance over his right shoulder...

Still nothing...

...and cursed again his decision to go after the Black Dragon. It was rash, foolish and headstrong. It might also prove a fatal one. Beyond the confines of the apothecarion, as he was now, the creature stalking the lonely corridors of Prometheus had him trapped.

Hoarfrost clinging to his shoulder guards forewarned him of the hunter. It crusted the joints, made them crack as he moved his arms. At least he was wearing armour. He'd equipped as soon as the space station was hit, before they knew the extent of the damage or the nature of the attack. A bolt pistol with a full clip sat in its holster, left on the medi-slab in his haste to go after Zartath. At that moment, there had been no threat beyond an escaped patient. Arming himself might have spurred the Black Dragon to violence. But then a moment is but a small piece of time, which can change in the next. Sometimes fatally.

He did have his reductor gauntlet and a surgical paring knife. Not much as far as weapons went, especially given his current situation. A narthecium medical kit came with the armour. It carried various items, coagulant gels, counterseptic, rapid-ossifying sprays, a bio-scanner, chem-ampoules with liquid nitrogen and phials of anaesthetic. Of much higher grade and concentration than human compounds, his medi-kit was designed to prolong and preserve life; none of it was particularly useful in the art of killing.

Cadorian, one of his practitioners, had reached him through his helmet's feed when some of the communications across Prometheus had been restored. Hangar

Seven was reporting a total breach and hostiles in-bound. The nature of the enemy was xenos, classified dark eldar. During his tenure as part of the apothecarion, Emek had done extensive research into the myriad alien races that plagued mankind and knew the thing that was stalking him. It was a wraith-creature, a deadly infiltrator that had slipped the fragile cordons established by Master Argos and penetrated deeper into the station. Scenting blood, the prospect of a quick and easy kill, it had come for him.

Xeno-taxonomers would classify the creature: *mandrake*.

Shadow-skinned, it could appear almost at will and without warning, save for the hoarfrost.

Emek hadn't ventured far from the borders of the apothecarion but far enough to leave him needing to find an alternate route back to the safety of its confines. There, he had augur arrays and visual-spectra devices that could detect the mandrake. He also had a cohort of battle-servitors that could be tasked with its execution or at the very least deter or delay it.

Abroad in the abandoned corridors of the space station, he had nothing but himself. A cripple without bolter and blade, nursing faded hopes would have to suffice. He was still a Space Marine, a broken one but one of Vulkan's sons. If death was to be his fate then Emek was determined he wouldn't surrender easily.

The Apothecary dug deep into what was left of his resolve as he reached the next junction.

The meteor strike had left its mark. A long corridor stretched in front of him, shrouded in penumbral gloom. Halfway down, part of the ceiling was caved in, a welter of broken pipes and cabling spewing forth from the upper deck like spilled intestines. Steam vented dulcetly from a shattered heating duct, the plume white and gaseous. Shallow fires flickered in the distance.

It was one of the approach corridors that led to the apothecarion. At least he was close.

Overhead, jerking lume strips flared into life and cast the corridor in eye-burning monochrome, winked out and then flared up again in a juddering palsy. Tattered strips of insulation plastek hung down in grubby translucent veils, stirred by the stale air-scrubbers, whilst underfoot the deck plates were broken and exposed gaping pitfalls to the maintenance level between decks.

Unafraid but wary, Emek loosened the surgical knife in its calf sheath. His eyes never wavered from the way ahead. His senses were alive to any sound, any sign.

'I know you are here,' he said to the dark, expecting no answer, and started down the corridor.

'*Apothecary*,' Cadorian's voice came abruptly over the feed.

'Hsst!' Emek chided. In the dim emergency lighting, the mandrake could be anywhere, waiting in any alcove. He crouched down, tried to make himself a smaller target. 'I am not alone. Enemy infiltrators have made it as far as the approach corridor. Be quick and speak quietly.'

'*Sorry, but I am to inform you that Master Argos is aware of your situation and has arranged for troops to be sent to your aid.*'

'Negative!' Emek snapped. 'I don't know how many there are hunting me. I haven't even seen it yet, practitioner.' His eyes darted around the corridor at a sudden sound but it was just a pressure valve popping. 'It's too dangerous. Tell Argos to hold the line so there are no further strays for me to deal with. I can find my own route back to the apothecarion unassisted.'

There was a short pause as Cadorian took it all in.

'*Apothecary?*'

Emek was trying very hard to be patient, but his reply was still clipped. 'Yes.'

'*Your sidearm is here on the medi-slab. You are unarmed. Help is not far, I ca–*'

'Did something happen in my absence from the apothecarion, serf? Was I replaced and am simply unaware of the fact that my authority no longer carries weight?'

'No, Apoth–'

'Then do as I order. I know I have no sidearm. I have all the weapons I need. Just keep the injured alive long enough for me to save them upon my return.'

Cadorian sounded disgruntled. '*And if you do not return?*'

Emek cut the link. It was here, in the corridor with him. 'Then you'll be having a different visitor,' he muttered beneath his breath, hoping that the practitioner had as many guns as was feasible aimed at the apothecarion door.

The reductor was a drilling implement attached to his gauntlet. It was noisy but sharp enough to cut through ossmodula-hardened bone. Not a practical weapon but an effective one if used up close. It wouldn't do for the shadow-creature.

There was still the outside chance that Emek hadn't been seen. He didn't want to jeopardise that, so he slid out the surgical knife instead. The *shuck* it made slipping from its sheath sounded loud in the gloom. It was a broad-bladed, saw-edged thing forged of monomolecular steel that could cut toughened Space Marine flesh with ease. Emek hoped it would have the same gory effects on a mandrake.

'Come on then…' He grimaced as he tried to rise. Crouching down was easy. With his damaged leg, it was the getting up again that was hard. Pain brought fresh focus, kept him alert to the patch of shadow drifting towards him that seemed at odds with the light.

Every magnesium-bright flare saw the patch shrink to nothing, stalling its progress as the creature sought the solace and anonymity of the darkness where the lume strips couldn't touch. When the shadows returned it returned with them, moving slowly and silently towards its prey.

THE KILL WAS close. Yulgir had tracked it for a while, savouring the hunt, following the mon'keigh's movements around the dingy tunnels of the crude structure. Its ennui was caustic but he tasted despair and pain exuding from the body of the prey too.

Morsels before the feast, thought Yulgir.

Now it faced him down the corridor, the hulking giant armoured in green, a last act of defiance before the hunt was done. It would not go easy, which only heightened the mandrake's anticipation. These ones didn't feel fear, but they had other chinks in their defences to exploit. Arrogance and hubris for instance. It would fight him in the open. Such creatures were honour bound to do so. They also lasted longer under torture.

Yulgir hungered.

Blades slid into being at the end of the mandrake's wrist stumps. They were gnarled and glowing, like radio-active bone.

He would gorge upon this creature, suck every last iota of agony from it.

Perhaps he would steal its last breath and keep it for eternity as a trophy.

Hnnn… delicious…

It was time to let the mon'keigh see him.

A SHAPE STEPPED out of the shadows, corporealising before Emek's eyes. Skin like shifting oil reflected the Apothecary's image back at him. It was a grotesque simulacrum, twisted by the shimmering fluidity of the mandrake's outer form. Hair the colour of alabaster, lank and gossamer thin, hung past its shoulders. There were glowing sigils cut into its flesh, evil runes that hurt the eyes and promised a hell of eternal suffering.

A mortal man might flee in the face of such an abomination. Certainly, his mettle would be tested in standing his ground. Emek merely wanted to kill it. A smile split his withered half-face as he remembered what it meant to be Adeptus Astartes.

A rime of frost crept across his armour again, intense and paralysing even through the ceramite. It turned

Emek's smile into a grimace. It was as if his arm was vitri-
fying under the baleful effects. His damaged leg and left
side already put him at a disadvantage, he didn't need
another.

'One of your foul kin tried to kill me before. As you
can see, monster, I am still very much half alive. It's all I
need to kill you.'

Emek charged and swung.

Slow, too slow, he thought, berating himself as the
blade missed by a distance.

Or did it? The mandrake appeared to blend around
the attack, so that it actually passed through the surgical knife. He turned quickly, activating the reductor
and using it like a punch-dagger. After three ineffectual
thrusts, Emek was no closer to landing a hit, let alone a
telling one.

'Fight!' he roared, excising some pent up frustration.

The cut to his torso came swift and with a blur of acid-
green light. It brought with it a flare of intense pain.
The glare of the lumen strip seemed slightly darker than
before, as if the presence of the mandrake was somehow
absorbing it.

Emek swung again but just like oil, the mandrake
oozed from the blow, negating it.

It was toying with him, he realised, but he also knew it
was a mistake to play with dangerous things; they had a
habit of biting back and crippled or not, Emek was still
a very dangerous thing.

Like a spectre resolving out of the fog, the mandrake
came again. A downward slash of its glowing blades
cut the Apothecary's forearm and he dropped the knife,
feigning injury. There was just enough time to reach for
an ampoule in his narthecium kit. Attached to the neck
was a small atomiser that Emek triggered like a sidearm.
The liquid contents coned out in a fine spray, vaporising
instantly on contact with the air into a pellucid white gas
which then crystallised.

The mandrake shrieked and recoiled as the liquid

nitrogen compound reacted with its skin. Parts of its body started to freeze solid as it sought the succour of its shadow realm, anchoring it in reality.

Emek lunged with the reductor and this time cut alien flesh, chewing an ugly line that bisected one of the sigils on the mandrake's body. He drove deeper, searching for vital organs, all the while resisting the creature's baleful agony.

'See the dark that's coming?' he snarled. 'That's for you, xenos!' Punching the reductor until it penetrated the mandrake's back, Emek then yanked upwards and out through its shoulder.

There was sheer terror in those once pitiless eyes, the certain knowledge that something even direr than the shadow-skinned monster was coming to claim it.

Emek didn't know what awaited the mandrake beyond the veil, but he was immensely satisfied by its suffering. The creature dissipated into ash and the reek of dead, dank places, leaving behind an ululating scream that carried on long after it was gone.

It wasn't alone.

The realisation, his sluggish instincts condemning him, came too late. Emek turned but the dead mandrake's partner was upon him with its knives poised to plunge in his flesh.

'Vulkan!' He wanted it to be the last word on his dying lips.

A thunderous retort, made louder in the narrow corridor, deafened him and the mandrake disappeared in a welter of flesh, bone and shadowed strips. It didn't have time to scream, only to die.

As the wraith slumped from his eye-line, Emek beheld his saviour. 'I applaud your timing, brother.'

'Saturnine as ever.' Ba'ken, nursing his side and limping with injury, lowered his bolter. He'd fired it one-handed and smoke was still wafting from its muzzle.

'Here...' The hulking brother-sergeant tossed the

Apothecary his holster and sidearm, which Emek caught with his free hand. 'You'll be needing this.'

'What, when I have the mighty Helfist to protect me?' he said, strapping the weapon to his armour.

'You should never have left it, you were... *gnn*.' Ba'ken stumbled and would've fallen if not for the wall. He braced himself, using the bolter like a crutch as Emek hobbled over.

'You are a stupid bastard, Ba'ken,' said the Apothecary, looping his arm around the sergeant's back and supporting him under his shoulder. He wasn't wearing his pauldrons or cuirass, which meant his power generator was absent too. The medi-servitors had removed them during his surgery. He still had his leg greaves, boots and vambraces but it was far from certain protection. He'd also slung a bolter and his piston-hammer around his torso on thick straps.

'And you almost looked like a Space Marine killing that thing.'

They began to stagger down the corridor together.

Emek grunted dismissively. 'Look as us, the cripple and the invalid wounded. Ha! We'll cleanse Prometheus of the dark eldar ourselves.'

'Let us hope—' Ba'ken grimaced at a sudden twinge. There was blood blossoming faintly beneath the bandages binding his torso. 'Let us hope that we find no more of them until we're back in the Apothecarion.'

'That would be a pleasant fiction, brother.'

'I see you have not yet shaken your fatalism,' Ba'ken hit back.

Emek wasn't goaded by the gibe. 'I am a realist, that's all. Aboard the *Protean* was about as real as anything can get.' His head dropped a little as he remembered the ill-fated mission. 'When you have the lightning tendrils of a malicious alien psyker destroying one half of your body and live, *you* try not to become fatalistic.'

A short pause underlined the sudden tension.

The Apothecary lowered his voice. 'But you were right,

though. Some scars do run deeper than others, and they cannot always be seen.'

'We are brothers, Emek, and my shoulders are broad enough for more than just my own burdens.'

The Apothecary was about to make another cutting remark but nodded instead. Despite the danger they were both in, the mood eased.

'We should do this more often,' said Ba'ken, as they were shuffling down the half-lit corridor.

'What? Die slowly together? I think it's more of a once only pastime.'

Ba'ken laughed, loud and deeply. It hurt like the fiery hells of Themis to do it but it was worth it.

Emek's raised hand cut his amusement short. The sergeant's bolter was already aimed down the next corridor.

Shadows lurked there, moving against the light. There were other signifiers too: distant voices, alien in nature and the low scrape of blades kissing against metal.

'Not that way,' said the Apothecary.

'Agreed.'

They had reached a junction point and had to take an oblique route to the Apothecarion that drew them deeper into the heart of the space station.

'We aren't going to make it to your quarters, brother,' Ba'ken said.

'The barricades at Hangar Seven must be breached worse than I thought.'

'Barricades?'

'We are overrun. Whilst Tu'Shan and the Chapter fight for Nocturne's survival below, what's left of the Fireborn must keep Prometheus from being gutted by xenos knives.' Emek's gaze was fixed on the path not taken. 'The Pantheon Chamber is not far behind us. We'll head there.'

The sacred temple was a nodal point on the space station. They could use it as a means of getting around the enemy-held junction.

Ba'ken nodded.

'You were right, too, brother,' he said, as they were retreating. 'I wasn't healed enough. I should've waited.'

'It doesn't matter, Sol. We are here. All that matters is to survive. Watch the way behind us. I will guide in front.'

Panning the darkness with their bolters, the wounded Salamanders headed for the Pantheon Chamber.

'They will find us, brother.'

'Then we had best be ready when they do.'

Behind them, the sound of metal scraping metal grew louder.

FUGIS WAS GONE. It wasn't a particularly fond farewell. Pragmatism overrode sentiment. His years in the desert had estranged the once-Apothecary from his brothers, like a sibling who returns from a terrible war but is changed and no longer the person they were. That was how Elysius saw him now, as someone he didn't recognise and couldn't relate to, a stranger in familiar flesh. His actions in sending Dak'ir to his doom only soured their reunion further.

Fugis had taken the last vessel to the surface, a battered gunship in need of repair. There were no pilots to spare, all were engaged in the void war above, so he took the stick himself and rode it out of Prometheus with engines flaring. The berth was far from Hangar Seven, where the Chaplain was headed.

As he hurried down the empty corridor, the flickering lume strips revealed his way and cast a light upon his thoughts.

Dak'ir's death had shaken the once-Apothecary. He had believed utterly in the sign that had manifested on his Burning Walk. To see it so cruelly disproven to the extent that another Salamander died because of it hurt his resolve.

Elysius knew he could not give in to dismay, and drew deep of his well of faith. He would need it now; they all would. Below, on Nocturne, they had heroes enough.

Up here, in the cold and darkness, was where his flaming torch was needed most.

'*And I shall burn the heretics from my sight, and the alien shall be cast down in my righteous fire.*' The litany tripped off his tongue, fuelling his resolve, readying it for the trials to come. '*I am the flame and it lives within my clenched fist. So am I armoured for war, a brazier to purge the darkness that encroaches.*'

The din of battle was nearing. It grew louder as the Chaplain started to run.

'*It is ruin and it is fury. My heart is molten, incandescent as the blood of the earth. Consume them! Render them unto ash and smoke!*'

Hangar Seven was still relatively distant but the sound of gunfire was close. The defenders had been pushed back, their lines withdrawing. The crozius in his mailed fist blazed into life.

'*The taint shall be cleansed, its perfidy rid from these halls. For I am the flame and it lives within my clenched fist. I am the flame and its conflagration shall bring hell upon the hell-born!*'

He emerged into a blistering firefight. Shard rounds, alien and venomous, impacted against the rosarius field the Chaplain arrayed around him. Like blind insects striking armaglas, the barbs from the dark eldar's chattering rifles fell dead at his armoured feet.

He resisted the urge to crouch down and present a smaller target, instead trusting in his trappings of faith and standing tall.

'Hate the alien with all the canker in your noble veins!' he declared in a stentorian voice. The Salamanders, remnants of Fourth not commited to the void war, redoubled their efforts at the sound of Elysius's dogma. 'Purge them from our midst and cleanse Vulkan's hall of this taint!'

There were humans amongst the throng, who beheld the Chaplain with undisguised awe as he strode into the very heart of the firefight.

'Haul them back,' he urged. 'Take what is yours by blood and breath!'

In his ear, the comm-feed crackled.

'Good to have you with us, old friend.'

Elysius spied the hulking form of Master Argos at the foremost barricade. They were automated shields, a little over waist height. There were several Tarantula and Rapier emplacements slaved to the defence too. Another Techmarine, Elysius recognised him as Brother Draedius, hunkered down behind a barrier in the third rank manipulating the machineries remotely.

Heavy barks of automatic fire spat into a shrieking horde of lithe-limbed aliens wearing segmented armour plate the colour of a deep bruise. Their return salvos were weaker but they were weathering the Space Marines' barrage well.

Elysius reached Argos and crouched down at last.

At such close range, the firefight was almost deafening so they spoke through the feed.

'There are another five hundred metres of shielding I can activate down this ventral corridor,' said the Forge Master, *'Beyond that lies one of the Drake Halls, T'kell's Chamber.'*

'Docking-temple of the *Chalice of Fire*.' Elysius understood at once. The mighty forge-ship he referred to was one of Vulkan's artefacts, restored to the Chapter in an elder age. Without it, the Salamanders' capacity to fashion artificered armour and weapons would be greatly reduced. Not only that, but its destruction would strike a blow to morale that would forever cripple them.

'Amongst other relics, like the Nocturne's Hammer,*'* Argos added. *'We must hold them here and give no more ground.'*

Looking at the xenos hordes, their thickening ranks and the elite warriors waiting to attack behind the fodder using up the ammunition from the emplaced cannons, Elysius saw the anvil. He heard the ring of hammer against metal and knew it was calling to him.

He looked back to Argos and noticed the gaping head wound.

Long ago when they were barely Scouts, he and Argos had served under Captain Kadai. On Ullsinar, much of the Forge Master's face had been burned away by alien bio-acid. The blame lay with Elysius and his over-zealous desire for glory. It had changed them both and seen their paths set: one to the Mechanicus and the other to the Reclusiam. Whilst Argos had reconciled the deed long before, many decades had passed before Elysius could do that. He still wished it could have gone differently, though.

'*I was infected,*' said the Forge Master, '*and needed to excise it at the source.*' He tapped his skull. '*Here.*'

It prompted a raft of further questions in the Chaplain's mind but the sound of heavier troops advancing towards them behind the xenos fodder overrode his need for answers.

The armour-clad warriors parted to let the reinforcements through. These were not dark eldar, though, nor any caste of creature slaved to them. Servitors, grossly mutated and swollen with weapon mounts, lumbered into range of the guns. The first ranks were shot apart; clunks of wet meat and shattered machine parts hitting the deck in a percussion of dense *plinks* and dull thuds.

Argos was on his feet, bolter flaring.

'*From the* Archimedes Rex,' he explained. '*I ordered the hatches sealed but they must have opened them from inside.*'

A missile-tube emerged into being, growing like a corrupted bloom on the arm of one of the servitors that had survived the automated fusillade. A *choom* of displaced air and firing thrusters heralded a burst of small ordnance that ripped up one of the Tarantula guns and bent a barricade out of shape seconds later.

Rattling solid shot erupted in the wake of the explosions. Smoke was still clinging to the corridor in a thick cloud when raking las-fire started scything through the murk.

Armsmen fell quickly as their armoured defences were undone by the sudden barrage of heavy fire. What few

Salamanders held the corridor with Argos stepped up to cover their stations but the line was stretched beyond breaking.

Elysius got to his feet. 'We can hold them here no longer,' he declared, and raised his crozius arcanum aloft.

'*In the name of Lord Vulkan,*' he roared to his brothers.

A chorus of chainswords started up, blades were drawn.

'*Into the fires of battle…*'

'UNTO THE ANVIL OF WAR!' they bellowed as one.

Leaping over the barricades, the Salamanders charged.

CHAPTER TWENTY

I
Last Stand of Broken Soldiers

Ba'ken collapsed for the third time, his legs giving way under his bulk. Bodily supporting him, Emek nearly fell too and was able to lean the hulking sergeant against the corridor wall.

'Leave me here,' he rasped. He was breathing hard and lathered with a feverish sweat. The faint crimson blossom beneath his surgical bindings had become darker and wetter, spreading across his entire torso.

Emek crouched by his side, the effort paining him, and assessed Ba'ken's vitals with his bio-scanner. 'You're bleeding to death. Even your Larraman cells cannot regenerate fast enough whilst your body is being exerted like this.'

'Leave me,' he repeated. Lucidity was fading in his eyes. The fire there had dimmed. 'Just make sure my bolter is gripped in my fist before you do.'

'I doubt you would relinquish it even in death.' Emek cast a glance at the gloomy corridor they'd left behind them. The hunters had their scent now. It didn't matter. Evading them had never really been an option but the prospect of it had got them this far.

A few hundred metres ahead was the gate to the Pantheon Chamber. They could make a last stand.

The sound of scraping metal returned, not as distant as it had once been.

One last look at the end of the corridor, his bolt pistol trained on the junction, and Emek lowered his aim to lean in to Ba'ken.

'We are close, Sol. I would rather die in the Pantheon Chamber than out here in some nameless corridor. Can you rise?'

Ba'ken clenched a fist, using whatever was left of his willpower to get up.

Emek grimaced as he withdrew his hand from his brother's wound to help lift him. It was soaked in gen-hanced blood.

'Who'd have thought you'd have so much blood in you.'

'It's my Themian heritage, we're–' Ba'ken coughed and there was something dark and vital in the phlegm hacked up out of his body.

'One step then another,' said Emek, guiding them the final agonising metres to the temple.

'Are you hoping for divine intervention?' asked Ba'ken as the Apothecary set him down by the opening. It was sealed but not locked. Something had burned away the mechanism. The stench of sulphur and smoke was redolent on the stale air.

'Don't move,' Emek replied, not trying to be humorous. Ba'ken could barely nod. He pressed the activation rune for the gate and it slid open to the screech of protesting gears.

A pall of black smoke escaped from within. The Apothecary stood his ground as it washed over him, scanning the gloom and panning his sidearm across the room until it had dispersed.

There was no fire damage to the Pantheon Chamber itself, though it was clear an incredible blaze had died only recently in the temple. The effect was miraculous and Emek found his first steps across the threshold were tentative.

His eye was drawn to an antechamber at the opposite side of the room to the entrance. Here the smoke and latent heat was thickest.

It was a vault, hidden behind one of the massive obsidian statues that encircled the greater chamber. Emek went closer.

At the cusp of the secret room he paused. The lights were out and showed no signs of revivification. The stench of burning was easily strongest here. This place had been the ignition point. He had a lume-lantern attached to his narthecium pack. Gripping the handle slowly, he pulled it free and pressed the activation stud. An azure glow bled off the hand-held device, grainy in the smoke-laced air. The interior of the vault was blackened to all hell and back. Paint had blistered, ceramite was melted, armaglas vitrified. Whatever had caused the devastation must have been intensely hot.

'Fires of Vulkan...' he muttered, unaware of how apt that was until he noticed the silhouette at the back of the room. It was in the shape of a body, one that had been wearing power armour judging by its bulk and contours. Here the vault was blackest.

Immediately, he was put in mind of one of Zen'de's old philosophies.

'Fire never truly dies. It is merely dormant, waiting for its moment to reignite.'

Those words, spoken years ago in the lectorium, rang especially true in that moment.

Emek approached the strange silhouette, lume-lantern fixed on where it was marked out on the floor. As he reached it he knelt down, extending two fingers to touch the layered ash it was formed of. He withdrew his hand with a mild curse.

It was still warm even through his gauntlet, incredibly so, though the air around it was comparatively cool. There was a draught coming from somewhere. He detected it through his battle-helm's autosenses, a subtle shift in the quality and composition of the re-scrubbed air.

Emek looked up and saw a gaping crevice in the ceiling that led into a ragged tunnel of endless darkness. For the first few metres he could see the inner workings of the between-deck and then the deck above and the one above that. Then there was just blackness, abject and absolute. A gobbet of superheated metal dripped down from the hole and landed on his shoulder guard, sizzling before cooling and solidifying. The entire opening was lined with cooked metal as if something extremely hot had burned through it, like a plasma cutter or meltagun.

The rest of the vault was empty. Any sign of occupancy had been obliterated by the fire anyway. Emek returned to Ba'ken.

The brother-sergeant was still conscious, bolter aimed – and trembling only slightly – towards the end of the corridor.

'What did you find?'

'A mystery to which I don't have an answer. Come on.' Emek hooked his arms underneath Ba'ken and started to drag him.

The scraping and shrieking entered the corridor section the Salamanders were stranded in, announcing the presence of their enemies.

Emek scowled, shaking his hand as he set his brother down again to draw his sidearm. 'Too close.'

'They're coming,' said Ba'ken. 'How many rounds do I have left?'

Emek checked.

'Not enough.' He levelled his bolt pistol in the same direction at the sudden shrieking. No subterfuge this time. The dark eldar wanted them to know they'd found them. 'We'll have to make our stand here.'

A malformed shadow fell across the far end of the distant corridor. It was hulking and gene-bulked, snorting like a mutant bull.

'Not mandrakes,' muttered Emek.

Then there came another and another. A riot of gibbering could be heard emanting from the flesh-hungry pack, and a noisome reek of putrefaction muddied the already wretched air.

'How many do you think?' Ba'ken was having a difficult time staying conscious. He spoke through gritted teeth and stared much too hard.

Emek was belligerent. 'I hope there are hundreds.'

Ba'ken smiled grimly at that. 'I always thought…' He drifted off, before forcing himself back around. 'I always thought I would die in the arena.' His bolter was wavering.

'Not the battlefield?'

'Hasn't killed me yet.'

'Well spoken.'

A horde of lumpen, grotesque creatures lumbered into view. They were stitched-together *things*, bulked-out amalgams of slave stock ripped from the cruel imaginings of their torture-surgeons. Ridged spines split through leathern skin, blood-pink and staked with bizarre chemical tubing; muscle-swollen limbs dragged across the deckplate, their metal talons screeching; mouths wired shut moaned and mewled behind harrowing facemasks. Clutched in flesh-thick fingers, the beasts had massive cleaver-blades and other rending implements. They were nightmares fashioned by some graven tailor, the laboratory progeny of the dark eldar haemonculi.

Ba'ken scoffed. He'd fought these beasts before on Geviox. 'They send their dregs…' His aim dipped until the molten fire coursing through his bloodstream jolted his arm straight. He gasped with the sudden shock, alert and alive.

'What–'

Emek was pulling an injector from the hulking warrior's brawny neck where the veins bulged like cables.

'It's a massive dose of adrenaline. Enough to kill a lesser being, but just the right amount to keep you conscious long enough so you can help me kill these bastards.'

Seeing prey, their scent glands flaring behind leather masks, the wretched horde broke into a loping run.

Ba'ken was already lining up his first kill-shot. 'Why didn't you do it before?'

Alongside him, Emek put a sustained burst into the lead creature, dropping it.

'Because in a few minutes it will overload your nervous system and send you into anaphylactic shock. Your body will then compensate for this trauma by putting you into suspended animation coma.'

'Then be ready to revive me when that happens.'

A raking bolter shot from Ba'ken cut down another of the abominations. Its bloated torso ruptured with multiple detonations, spearing its closest brethren with bone shrapnel as its chest cavity exploded.

'If I am still standing when that happens, brother, you have my solemn oath.'Emek decapitated a third with a headshot, painting the walls either side of it with gore and brain matter. Nothing slowed or deterred them. The dead and wounded were crushed under a stampede of overly-muscled bulk. No fear, no pain – the grotesques lived in torture, they knew nothing else. It had made them immune to such petty concerns as survival. They only wanted to inflict suffering on others.

'We need more firepower...' Ba'ken lurched to his feet. Without the compensators built into his power armour, he had to brace himself as he racked an alternator slide and switched to full auto.

This burst would likely expend all of his ammunition in a single stroke. With one hand under the barrel to steady it, he triggered his bolter and engulfed the corridor in a storm of exploding shellfire. Midway through the salvo, he roared in concert with his weapon and for a few glorious seconds they were of one voice, one purpose. A split second before the hard *chank* of metal announced the chamber was empty, he lifted the barrel.

'I'm out.'

Emek ran dry a few seconds later.

Smoke and blood-scent coloured the air in ruddy grey, a butchered slew of monstrous corpses just visible at the edge of a retreating cloud. Something was definitely still moving further back into the miasma.

'Still not dead.' Ba'ken sounded a little breathless. He drew the piston-hammer from off his back, the metal haft scraping against his vambrace as he hefted it into position. 'I remember when this felt lighter,' he added ruefully.

Emek had his surgical knife and holstered the spent pistol so he could use his reductor like a punch-dagger. The buzzing bone-saw sounded loud and belligerent as it started up.

A few of the beasts, enough outnumber the Salamanders, had survived the barrage and were emerging from the bloodied remains of the dead.

'Hard to kill,' said Emek as the beasts loped slowly towards them.

'So are we.' Ba'ken ran headlong into the mob.

The Salamander ducked a vicious blade-swipe that would have separated head from shoulders, before stepping into the beast's killing arc to stave in its misshapen skull. A downward stroke glanced his shoulder, drawing a spit of blood, but Ba'ken hit again, this time smashing several of the chemical phials seemingly sutured into the thing's skin. A hard blow to the stomach with the piston-driven hammer head caved in its torso and finished it.

The second Emek took in the throat, jamming his knife in all the way to the hilt before the beast could retaliate. He severed its hand with the reductor, stripping skin to flesh to bone in an instant before turning the screaming blade on the monster's face. It died mewling, spitting blood through the tears in its facemask.

A third they killed together, Ba'ken smashing the back of its knee and putting it down before Emek slashed open its throat and let its life ooze away onto the deckplate.

Ba'ken took a hit from the last one. Rib-plate cracked audibly as he was flung across the corridor and smashed into the wall. Still dosed on adrenaline, he was up quickly and dodged a cleaver slash that would've opened him up from groin to sterum. Sparks trailed after the massive blade as it carved up the wall and got stuck as Ba'ken rolled aside.

Emek punched the reductor in the beast's back but the blade wasn't deep enough to reach anything vital. The Apothecary started carving, abandoning his knife so he could curl an arm around the monster's bulging neck. It was like wrestling a sauroch, its strength was incredible. He held on long enough for Ba'ken to smash a hail of two-handed blows into its clavicle, forearm and finally head. With a protracted wheeze, the beast lolled onto its side and died.

Emek was breathing hard when he looked up from the corpse.

'Well fought, brother,' he gasped.

Ba'ken was about to reply when he staggered three more steps and collapsed.

From the depths of the corridor the scraping sound returned.

'Hell-shit...' Emek turned to see three more of the monsters looming. The foremost bleated at him maliciously as it levelled an arcane-looking device attached to its wrist instead of a hand.

Purely out of instinct, the Apothecary hit deckplate as a fount of xanthic spray coursed from the weapon's nozzle. Acid-hiss and the stink of sulphur arrested his senses and he knew his armour was burning.

Pain flared angrily along his left side, not from the acid but from his old wounding, and he struggled to stand. He came as far as getting to one knee when the shadow of the first monster engulfed him and he was suddenly eye-to-eye with the dripping barrel of the liquefying pistol.

For the second time in as many hours Emek faced

death. He closed his eyes, knowing that he had honoured his primarch and his Chapter but wishing his sacrifice could have saved Ba'ken too.

II
Clad in Black

JUST BEFORE EMEK met oblivion, the shadow of something very dark and very fast appeared in his diminishing peripheral vision. The beast shrieked as the pistol barrel was cut open, spraying its arm and torso with flesh-eating intestinal acid. It staggered, skin sloughing like candle wax by the second, then crumpled in a heap of its own half-digested viscera.

Emek had got to his feet as the second monster died. A bone-blade punched through its jugular from behind, spattering the deck with arterial blood. The weapon was *shucked* out a moment later and then hacked across the thing's neck, decapitating it. The Apothecary watched its head bounce wetly against the floor with a dull *thuck* before coming to rest.

The last one lost its forearm and then most of its innards as the shadow figure slashed open its abdomen and spilled everything that was inside, outside. A final blow was delivered with a leap off the second one's cooling corpse and found a way into the beast's shrieking throat, cutting laryx and oesophagus.

Zartath had mounted the monster as it died, straddling its brawny chest, his free hand spearing a pectoral as he rode it all the way to the floor. The metal deck was still resounding to its felling when he climbed off and approached the Apothecary.

The Black Dragon was swathed in blood and scars. This wasn't the ritual scarification practised by the Salamanders, these were war wounds. There were many, an entire colony of injuries that charted his violent past. His skin was pale from being imprisoned on the Volgorrah

Reef for six years. Even without the augmentation of his power armour, he had killed the three monsters like they were children.

Emek backed off a step, trying to gauge the feral warrior's mood. A word he had used to describe the creature returned to him.

Beast.

'Is he dead?' Zartath stopped, and gestured to Ba'ken's supine form.

Emek didn't take his eyes off the Black Dragon, just like he'd never relax his guard around any wild creature.

'Not yet. He's fallen into suspended animation coma. It'll keep him alive, but I need to get him to the Apothecarion.' Emek tried not to balk at the sheer bloody destruction wrought by the Black Dragon. He'd fought alongside tidier Space Wolves. 'Why did you come back?'

'For vengeance. For my dead brothers back on the Razored Vale. To slay dusk-wraiths.' Everything was direct and declarative with Zartath. He knew only one direction: forwards. He bared his spine-like teeth. He'd bitten his own cheek during the killing and they were slicked with dark blood. Zartath's eyes were wide and feral. 'I did not do it to save your skin, flesh-cutter.'

'Regardless, you have my gratitude.' Emek bowed. He was about to rise when he felt a stabbing agony in his gut. Not from his injuries, this was something else. He could barely move, and felt his stomach where the pain was emanating from. His gauntleted fingers came back drenched in blood.

'In Vul–' He lurched up, falling forwards into the Black Dragon as a stream of gore erupted from his chest. It painted the inside of his battle-helm too as he spat it from his mouth, filling it with a coppery stink.

He doubled over again as a second dagger went in, punching through his paper armour.

'Gah…' Words wouldn't materialise. His tongue was heavy, lolling like a fat pink slug in his useless mouth. He struck the deck and realised Zartath had moved aside. Somewhere he heard the Black Dragon shout, but it was a distant and echoing sound. He couldn't pinpoint the exact location. Fog was rolling in across his vision. He felt cold, and then saw the rime of hoarfrost upon his pauldrons and knew what had murdered him.

During the earlier fight, one of them must have escaped. It was watching them, waiting for his guard to lower.

As the last of his blood ebbed from his shattered body, Emek was glad he had found his honour and that he had died a Space Marine.

SKETHE LET THE half-warrior bleed out as he concentrated on the feral one still standing, still lethal. It was fast and seemed to possess some sense of the mandrake, despite the fact it was cloaked in shadow-skin and could not be seen.

The large one was still alive. He'd watched it fall with mild interest. One of several toxins he possessed would bring the hulking mon'keigh around later in pangs of agony. Skethe would savour that. Lyythe's grotesques had failed to claim their fill of flesh, so he would benefit from their deaths instead. Worn down, the genebred warriors were easy meat. Except this last one. The one with the ossified knives jutting from its skin was not so easy to kill.

Skethe jabbed with his blade, the wicked residue from the edge caressing the feral one's armour but not penetrating it. It had weaved aside and fashioned a thrust of its own that Skethe barely evaded.

The nightfiend dissolved into shadow, moving much swifter than sight, and retreated back into the gloom of the corridor. Seemingly possessed, the feral one came after him, spitting curses and swinging with twin ossified blades. Skethe unleashed a blast of bane frost from his distended maw, hoping to bone-freeze the creature and then gorge upon its petrified, still-living body, but the feral one smashed through it and lunged with blades extended.

Skethe slid aside, but was cut along the ribs. He drank in the fortifying pain before turning to apply the killing stroke – but his opponent was gone. It had rolled out of its cleaving dive and was back on its feet, blades bared for another round.

'Wretched spawn,' he cursed in his barb-like language.

The creature muttered something back, mussitating the words of some fate it wished to subject the night-fiend to.

Skethe allowed it a mocking smile and was about to gut the impudent mon'keigh when a voice resolved in his mind. It was just a single word, spoken by the one to whom he had given his fealty. He had known this was coming, that it would be here where the deed would be done.

Now, it said simply.

ZARTATH BREATHED. IT was several minutes since he'd worked his lungs, driven into frenzy by the shadow-thing. But it was gone. The stink of it, so redolent, so obvious, had evaporated like the darkness of which it was made, leaving him alone.

The flesh-cutter was dead. He was lying face down in a pool of his own blood. The shadow-thing had cut him deeply, torn him right open. Despite his belliger-ence towards the Apothecary, Zartath had wanted to kill the creature for that, to exact some small measure of revenge. There were still dusk-wraiths abroad on the space station. He wouldn't need to venture far to find them again. True, the Apothecary was dead but the other one was not. A brother, this one; he'd fought with him and Kor'be on the Razored Vale, killed the hunters.

Suddenly, the Black Dragon found himself at a junc-tion in more ways than one. He knew the route back to the Apothecarion, but would have to go via the empty corridors and not the hidden ways he'd used to escape in the first place. Returning would mean denying his thirst for violence; Kor'be and his slain brothers would remain unavenged. But to leave the hulking warrior to die alone...

Zartath saw the opening to the temple. He knew the sanctity of this place just by being near to it.

'You were brave, flesh-cutter,' he said to Emek as he rolled the Apothecary onto his back and proceeded to drag him into the Pantheon Chamber, 'braver than I credited you for.'

Laying Emek down, he folded the Apothecary's arms across his chest to conceal the wound and make it appear as if he were in repose. After he'd closed the door, Zartath turned to Ba'ken.

'Don't die, blade-brother,' he snarled, heaving the big warrior onto his back, 'or all of this will be for nothing.'

Muttering a curse with every other step, Zartath headed for the Apothecarion.

HE HEARD THE one in black before he saw it. An'scur was letting the flesh-machines of Nihilan's corrupted ship bear the brunt of the enemy's fury before he would commit to the killing. The presence of the one in black had changed all that, though. This was Helspereth's murderer, the lesser creature who had humbled and humiliated her in her own coliseum.

The archon had told himself he was not attached to the wych, that her death was something that intrigued him rather than forced him to despair, but even still. He wanted blood, an equal measure and then the same again to account for the slaying of his favourite concubine. Since Helspereth's death, there was none amongst the coven that could replace her. An'scur had broken a great many in the time intervening; their bleached bones littered the foot of his throne like a mausoleum, their screams were like a requiem to *her*.

His blade unsheathed with a low scrape of cursed metal before he'd even realised it was drawn.

'I want its head,' he hissed to the sybarite at his side.

The blade-hand nodded slowly, eyes glinting in

murderous anticipation behind his flesh-leather hellmask.

An'scur's hand on the sybarite's shoulder made him turn his head.

'I will do it, though,' the archon warned. 'Cut me a path to its neck and my falchion shall part its ugly head from its shoulders.'

The blade-hand nodded again and drew his massive glaive.

IN A FEAT of sheer strength, Argos lifted a corrupt servitor off its feet and smashed it onto the hard deck. Blood and oil spilled from its cracked skull in a sticky pool. He rammed his boot, cracking its chest, before the monster could rise. Another fired a heavy bolter attachment but a bright flare of actinic energy arrested the salvo before it could hit him.

Elysius was shielded by his rosarius and had interceded between servitor and Salamander. The creature was almost point-blank so he only had to swing to stave in its weapon arm. A slew of bolts and broken machine parts radiated from the impact like scatter shot as the Chaplain pressed on, exhorting his battle-brothers.

'Forward for the primarch!' he yelled. 'Purge this taint from our halls!'

'In Vulkan's name, brother,' said Argos, burning through a second servitor with a plasma torch.

The Chaplain nodded, smashing into a pack of the corrupted flesh-machines with his power fist. Broken cyborg bodies were tossed aside like chaff before a storm. He cleaved another with a vicious downward stroke from his crozius, separating flesh from metal.

Argos snapped the head off one with his bare hands. Enhanced by his cybernetics and power armour, the Forge Master's strength was incredible. They would need it. The sentry guns had done all they could. The Rapiers and Tarantula guns had fallen silent, either destroyed or *clanking* on empty mags.

The last remnants of Fourth were putting up stern

resistence too, supported strongly by the armsmen, and thinned down the monstrous servitor horde. The Space Marines were taking the automatons apart, reducing what was left of the *Archimedes Rex's* crew to spare parts.

Elysius knew this was but the beginning. The dark eldar waited beyond. There was no way the xenos would get between the virus-crazed servitors and the Salmanders. Certainly, they would not commit to the fight until–

A lithe figure springing from the embattled throng robbed that thought of its conclusion. Elysius knew this warrior. It was the archon, the one who had tried to kill them all on the Volgorrah Reef. It was An'scur.

With a curt flash of baleful energy, the dark eldar archon cut down a servitor that had lumbered into his path. A second and third fell in quick succession afterwards, split across waist and neck respectively. The blows were florid but economical, he expended no more strength and energy than was needed.

Elysius saw the archon for what he truly was in that moment. A killer.

The Chaplain also realised why the dark eldar lord had entered the fray. He wanted blood, *his* blood. The warrior-witch had been a favoured pet, after all.

The bodyguard An'scur brought with him slashed open a servitor that had reverted to defensive protocols and was actually attacking the xenos. It was not alone. Several of the corrupt automatons started to turn, recognising a threat in their midst. Suddenly, what was meant to be fodder to try and blunt the Salamanders' anger was turning on its xenos allies. A three-way battle erupted in the corridor, the flesh-machines caught in the middle.

'Mon'keigh!' the archon screamed, beheading a servitor and vaulting on top of its corpse to point his sword.

Elysius rotated his shoulder then his wrist; the crozius left a scar of jagged lightning in its wake.

'Whenever you're ready, xenos,' he muttered.

A servitor closed on him but the bodyguard interceded, impaling it on a massive glaive and *shucking* the two halves of its bisected body off the blade.

An'scur dropped down from his grisly perch and walked slowly towards the waiting Chaplain. A burst of bolter fire deflected off the archon's blade, dismissed like an insect.

A battle-brother who'd advanced up the corridor followed up with a drawn gladius but again the bodyguard dashed in. The fight was brief and bloody. It ended with a Salamander sliced from neck to waist. The warrior crumpled, one hand on his chest to try and keep it together; the other firing his bolter. When his head rolled from his shoulders, the desperate salvo was cut short.

Though it rankled to see one of his brothers so cruelly dispatched, Elysius kept perfectly still as the bodyguard advanced on him. Eyes narrowed behind his skull-mask as he watched the warrior's movements and tracked the sweep of the deadly glaive.

A shout from the archon stopped the bodyguard dead and he lowered his weapon immediately in a gesture of subservience.

An'scur was but a few sword-lengths away. His almond-shaped eyes flashed as he regarded Elysius.

'All mine,' he said, the words falling like jagged knives from his lips.

SUCH PAIN WOULD he visit on this lesser being, such utter humiliation he would heap on its bestial shoulders. The hairless apes would learn of their folly in opposing the elder races of the galaxy. An'scur would bathe in their primitive blood.

'Sybarite!'

The blade-hand knew the command tone and began to withdraw.

'Stay close,' An'scur hissed as he passed the warrior. A shallow incline of the blade-hand's head showed he'd been understood.

He focused on his opponent.

The one in black was bulky. One hand ended in a

massive fist, which crackled with actinic ripples. In the other, it clutched a stave devoted to some craven god or another. Death markings characterised its armour. The fire-red eyes glaring from behind its bone-mask were hard and unyielding like stone.

As if they dwelled at the centre of a maelstrom, the battle continued to rage around them. Whether compelled by honour or simply self preservation, none entered the cordon created by the two combatants.

An'scur smiled indulgently behind his daemon-faced helm. He would break this creature. He would cut it down limb by limb, piece by piece, every stroke a bloody devotional to the slain Helspereth.

'You will wish you had not killed her, ape,' he whispered and then struck.

THE WORDS MEANT nothing to Elysius but he knew what they presaged.

The first blow came fast, almost too fast to see. Instinct pulled the Chaplain out of its deadly path, but he felt it cut into his armour plate. He swung in return but was too slow. An overhead with his power fist ended up putting a hole in the deckplate as the archon weaved aside. Elysius managed to parry the follow-up, a chain of eldritch sparks ripping outwards from the impact off the haft of his crozius.

He swiped with the power fist again, but only succeeded in smashing one of the last surviving servitors into paste. Crackling violently, his rosarius field saved him from a certain kill stroke.

Trying to match the archon for technique wasn't working. The dark eldar was faster and more skilled. Elysius had bulk and strength on his side. Trusting to his faith to protect him, he barged into the xenos leaving him open to attack.

AN'SCUR FELT THE crunch of metal as his armour bent inwards. Like a bull, the one in black had thrown itself at him. Pain flashed through his body, hot like quick-silver. A vambrace blade slid from his armour at a twist of An'scur's wrist and he hacked into the mon'keigh's back as he was borne along the corridor. When he was thrown down, he felt something break in his back, possibly a rib, but the one in black was bleeding. Using the pain, An'scur sprang to his feet and launched a flurry of blows with his falchion. They rained against some kind of crude energy shield that the one in black maintained through his incessant muttering. The last blow breached its defences, though, and cleaved deep into its shoulder guard.

With a desperate shout, the mon'keigh fell to its knee.

An'scur smiled through bloodied teeth.

Now, you are mine.

AN'SCUR WAS SAVOURING this. He conducted his symphony of pain with utter devotion, every cut a perfect note, every riposte an exquisite refrain. It would prove his downfall.

'You should have just killed me,' Elysius spat despite the extreme agony coursing through his body. 'Perhaps you can't.' The gibe was indulgent of him. It took all of the Chaplain's resolve to stay conscious. There was some strain of venom on the archon's blade, some dark elixir that was intensifying the pain.

Biting down, Elysius ignored it. He fended off another attack but managed to lock the archon's deadly blade with the haft of his crozius. Pulling the dark eldar in, he swung with his power fist in the same motion and landed a glancing blow. A less agile opponent would have been obliterated, but the archon was merely stunned and staggered back. Dark, alien blood was drooling from beneath his battle-helm.

Elysius stifled a feral grin. He had hurt him.

'Like I said…'

* * *

THIS THEATRE WAS wrong. It was not how An'scur had imagined it. It wasn't supposed to play out this way. The one in black would die by his hand. Its head would be taken as a trophy and defiled upon his return to the Volgorrah Reef. It would mount a spike when his cache of slaves propelled him to High Commorragh and all the prestige he deserved, when a backwater province of the webway was no longer his domain.

The crackling fist had hit him hard, harder than he was letting on.

Better to let your enemy think you are strong when you are not.

It was meant to be easier than this. Why was this one so stubborn?

An'scur didn't let these doubts trouble him for very long. Vengeance could be had vicariously. He had not survived this long without letting others occasionally bloody their hands for him. An'scur was pragmatic as well as a vicious bastard.

He gestured to the stricken ape who was, even now, attempting to stand.

So annoyingly tenacious.

'Sybarite…' He heard the blade-hand rise from a crouching position. 'Kill him for me.'

'As you wish, master…'

There was something in the voice, the tone and the timbre, that made An'scur turn. It had been disguised before, modified somehow. As a veil was cruelly lifted, the archon realised he had never looked his slave in the eye, never deigned to really *look*. If he had he would've noticed a traitor glaring daggers back at him.

The sybarite had removed his flesh-mask and the face of another was revealed from behind it.

An'scur was so utterly shocked he almost failed to parry the blade-hand's first attack.

'Malnakor…'

Blades locked, glaive versus falchion. A dracon he

had once thought dead and forgotten glared across the clashing steel between them.

'Surprised to see me?' Where An'scur was grating and pale, Malnakor was vital and silken. His face was perfect, almost doll-like, as if carved from amber and left statuesque.

'Your problem is, you never concern yourself with the help.' With an angry grunt, Malnakor thrust away from the impasse. A swift double parry, first left then right, the glaive moving like a pendulum with his hands as the fulcrum, negated twin jabs from An'scur.

'Was it Lyythe?' he asked. 'That haemonculus bitch will reap the rewards of this treachery.'

They traded a blindingly fast hail of blows but failed to land anything telling.

Malnakor laughed in a brief respite. 'Of course it was Lyythe, and I sincerely doubt you'll be afforded opportunity to exact any petty revenge.'

'Oh, I doubt that.' An'scur backed up a step, glowering. He gestured to the mon'keigh who was wounded enough to still be down. 'Can't you see I am in the middle of something here, worm?'

'As was I with Helspereth until you tried to destroy me.'

An'scur lashed out. The double-handed blow was so hard it cut the glaive's haft in half.

Malnakor balked at the archon's fury, and staggered. He used the two broken pieces of haft ambidextrously but was hard pressed to defend himself.

'You are no match for me, whelp,' An'scur told him.

'Which is why,' he lunged, opening up his side to attack deliberately, 'I brought help.'

Too late An'scur realised he was done; too late he tried to withdraw from the certain killing stroke that would have ripped the insolent dracon open and spilled him all over the floor. An'scur felt the chilling blades that could only belong to a mandrake slide into his flesh. Armour parted like smoke before them, blood boiled from a particular poison crafted to inflict the maximum agony on him, and him alone.

The archon collapsed, his falchion falling from nerveless fingers as his body began to inexplicably vitrify.

'No...' The voice that came from his slowly crystallising lips was small and oddly resonant.

Hoarfrost swept over his body, filling his veins, converting his flesh.

A shadow resolved in his peripheral vision and he saw Skethe watching his long death hungrily. Betrayed by the nightfiend, betrayed by Lyythe – An'scur cursed his dealings with the sorcerer and the naked ambition that had seen him blinded to a nest of waiting vipers.

With a final agonised lurch of frost-tinged breath, An'scur crystallised completely into ice. Using the bladed end of the glaive, Malnakor shattered him into pieces.

XENOS INFIGHTING WAS of no interest to Elysius but he recognised a coup when he saw one. He gained his feet and buried the head of his crozius into the shadow-skinned creature's back. It was so intent on sucking up An'scur's last shreds of agony that it didn't realise the danger until most of its spine was shattered. Elysius fed a jolt of energy into the weapon, finishing it off.

'I'm still here, lordling,' he growled, stepping over the mandrake's spasming corpse.

Clenching and unclenching his power fist, the Chaplain advanced.

DRACON, NOW ARCHON, Malnakor backed up. Skethe was dead when a moment ago he was a willing ally. At least it meant he wouldn't need to arrange his death later. Killing mandrakes was fraught with all kinds of peril.

His newly acquired troops outnumbered the mon'keigh but the enemy wasn't showing signs of capitulation, even the lesser ones. The kabalite warriors were his now, so too the incubi aboard the *Eternal Ecstasy*. If he didn't return to the ship quickly, the transition of leadership might prove contentious. Malnakor's hand closed around a small ovoid object attached to his armour. It was no larger than a pebble and fashioned of infinite jet, the runes on its surface manifold and bewildering. With the simple manipulation of select surface sigils, he activated the webway portal and a great gulf of darkness tore into reality behind him.

'Return to the ship,' he commanded his warriors, who were cutting down the last of the flesh-machines but otherwise withdrawing from battle. 'An'scur is usurped and I am master in his stead.'

There was the briefest moment of resistance but it passed quickly.

Leaving behind their dead and wounded, the dark eldar retreated into the roiling void of the webway which led to the *Eternal Ecstasy*.

'Your time will come again,' he said to the mon'keigh armoured in black. For now, Malnakor would preserve what he had, return to the Volgorrah Reef and work out how he would hold onto the power he had just seized.

The skull-faced warrior looked back at him, its eyes like burning embers, but didn't move to intercede. All of the armoured giants held the line and watched him and his kabal go.

A reckoning would have to wait.

IN A TEMPEST of eldritch wind, the webway portal collapsed and silence returned to Prometheus.

The quietude persisted until Chaplain Elysius lifted his crozius aloft.

'Glory to Vulkan!' he bellowed, and the halls resounded to the chant of triumph.

'Glory to Vulkan!' he yelled again, exulting in the moment. Even the armsmen and the survivors from Hangar Seven's deck crews took up the cry.

Though most of the Salamanders had survived the assault, there were several dead amongst the human contingent and more still that were wounded.

A labour serf was on his knees trying to push life back into a fallen comrade but to no avail. The armsman died spitting blood.

'So much death…' the labour serf muttered.

Elysius looked down at him.

'It's a heavy price,' he said, 'but one we had to pay. Honour his sacrifice when you mourn him and know he will sit close at the Emperor's hand.'

The labour serf looked up, and at once the Chaplain recognised him. Not a native of Nocturne this one, but he had fought like he defended home soil. Old eyes looked back at Elysius, but from a body that was in its prime. He nursed a gash across his shoulder, a part of his uniform was dark with his blood, but didn't falter.

'Sonnar Illiad,' the Chaplain addressed him. 'I remember you. I owe you a debt of thanks.'

'For what, my liege?'

'For showing me again the depth of human courage.'

This was a man who had lived his life as a freedom fighter on the blasted world of Scoria. It was thanks to Illiad and his men that the relics taken by the Salamanders were there to save in the first place. Elysius had never forgotten that.

'Your example raises us all, liege.' Sonnar Illiad bowed.

'Gather the wounded. Those that can walk must do so. Everyone else is to be carried.' He gestured to two of Fourth, who saluted at the Chaplain's summons. 'Escort these heroes of Prometheus to the Apothecarion. All shall be remembered this day.'

As the pair of Salamanders started to help Sonnar Illiad, Elysius felt a strong hand upon his arm.

'Shoulder to shoulder, the primarch made us strong, as strong as any mountain,' said Argos.

The Chaplain looked down the corridor to the gates of the Drake Hall.

'It was close in the end.'

Argos nodded slowly. 'The sanctity of T'kell's Chamber is preserved.' He averted his eyes from the baroque gate

that led to the relic hall and met the Chaplain's gaze.
'Fighting beside you again brought back memories of
Ullsinar.'

'Has it really been that long?'

'Blade to blade, it has.'

Elysius removed his battle-helm. He wanted to look
his brother in the eye, at least the organic one that
remained. Beneath the metal, the wiring and the cybernetics, Elysius could still see the bio-acid scarring.

'Never to be repeated, not like that. I lost you your face
that day.'

'And the Machine God saw fit to bless me with another.
I do not miss it.'

They clasped forearms, silently renewing old oaths
they had sworn to one another when they had barely
been Scouts.

Elysius could still feel the pain of his injuries keenly
but the work wasn't yet done. The entirety of Prometheus's halls had to be scoured for enemy stragglers. The
dark eldar had infiltrated deeply and not even a remnant of their presence must remain. His expression grew
severe as he thought of the other battles still raging. For
several hours they'd heard nothing from Nocturne or
Captain Dac'tyr.

'I hope the God-Emperor and Vulkan favour our wayward brothers. They will have need of their blessings
before this is done.'

CHAPTER TWENTY-ONE

I
Into the Bowels of Hell

LYYTHE KNEW SHE had been abandoned. How An'scur could've known about her pact with the aspiring dracon was a mystery to her. She was a haemonculus, *the* haemonculus, having progressed from being Kravex's wrack to pre-eminent torture-surgeon of the Volgorrah Reef. Since her master's demise, Lyythe was the only one and she deserved respect. She did not deserve to be cast to these dogs and placed at their beck and call.

'I am not some hireling,' she had cursed when they had taken her to catacombs to await the sorcerer's return. Her slab-armoured custodians had not replied. They had merely taken her to the lower deeps of the ship and left her there. It wasn't fitting. Even An'scur knew that. Lyythe was not blade-hand like the sybarite. Her position in the kabal was a vaunted one.

Sat in the grubby cell-chamber, she felt far from important. On the contrary, Lyythe felt almost sacrificial. To abuse a haemonculus, albeit a fledgling practitioner, in such a way and through her divulge some of the arcane mysteries of the dark eldar… the

Commorite high lords would not approve.

Lyythe wondered briefly, as she had several times over the last few hours, how the archon planned to buy her silence once she was back aboard the *Eternal Ecstasy*. Before giving her over to the mon'keigh, An'scur had given her a device. It was a webway portal but a small one, barely large enough for her lithe, disfigured frame. It was shaped like a tiny, baroque pyramid. The runes on each of its facings had to be manipulated in a precise way to activate the portal. She was tempted to use it now and escape the crude, ugly ship to her laboratory quarters on the *Ecstasy*.

An'scur would kill her for that.

Worse he would throw her into an oubliette until the soul hunger withered her already wretched body and she turned to ash for She Who Thirsts to sate Her daemon's tongue upon.

Thinking of that fate made Lyythe hunger. It had been too long since she'd enjoyed the suffering of others. Even now her parchment flesh, the stitched-together skin, was flaking and cracking. She was soul-starved. Something gnawed at her psyche, just behind her eyes, and she knew with a creeping dread exactly what it was.

Though she had been told to wait, her guard was gone and the ship's iron corridors were empty. Tucking the tiny pyramid back into her filthy leather smock, Lyythe got up and drifted out of her cell. This ship was gorged on suffering. She could taste it in the air. Drawn by the wailing of the damned, she activated her shadowfield and slipped like a wraith into the darkness. Somewhere, she knew, somewhere close, there would be a slave she could feed on.

THE BOWELS OF the *Hell-stalker* were like a labyrinth. The air was cloying and thick, scented with the blood-copper from thousands of sacrifical slaves. Tainted ash muddied armour plate and fouled respirator filters. It was dank and humid, confined and claustrophobic. The gun decks had given way to a network of jagged corridors limned red with visceral brazier fire.

After breaching the bulkhead gate, Praetor had unhooked his thunder hammer and storm shield. Close confines demanded close and deadly weapons. He led with the latter, glaring through retinal lenses over the shield's edge, the Firedrakes tramping loudly in his wake. According to the schematic provided by the mission's Techmarine they were not far from the weapon chamber.

A more direct route to the seismic cannon was denied to the Firedrakes by a barricade of debris and slamming bulkhead doors that even melta weapons and chainfists could not penetrate. Huge sections of the ship, parts of its actual superstructure, had been demolished and set up to impede them. A seemingly overlooked access duct had led the Terminators to the maze of maintenance corridors they were now traversing.

Besides the intermittent screaming of the damned coming up through floor vents leading down into the *Hell-stalker's* catacombs and dungeons, they had met nothing in the way of resistance. Wherever the overseers and their hordes had gone, it was not here.

'*Why does it feel like we are being herded?*' he heard Persephion remark over the comm-feed.

'Because we are,' Praetor replied curtly. 'Be ready.'

Vulkan He'stan stayed quiet, just beside him. The Forgefather scanned the shadows, every alcove, every nook and choke point as if something was about to happen at any moment.

The wait was not prolonged.

Through a combination of his autosenses and finely honed instincts, Praetor detected the booby trap a few vital seconds before it went off.

'Down!' he roared, moving into a squat, braced position, shoulder behind his storm shield.

The other Firedrakes responded instantly, hunkering behind him, heavier shoulder armour turned towards the threat as fiery shrapnel washed over them in a blistering wave.

The trap was only intended as a distraction, not to actually wound or kill. What followed it would do that.

'*Enemy contacts*,' Persephion said down the feed.

Power-armoured silhouettes loomed in the red-tinged darkness. A second later a host of muzzle flares erupted from their bolters, ripping into the shadows and revealing the renegades in their full panoply.

'*Dragon Warriors*,' another Firedrake clarified above the din of mass-reactive rounds hailing their Tactical Dreadnought Armour.

'Engage, engage,' Praetor snapped, rising to break into a heavy, lumpen charge. 'Target and eliminate. Death to the traitors!'

A plasma bolt struck the skull boss of his shield and rocked him. Servos protesting in his leg armour, he pounded into the shell storm being unleashed by the renegades. 'Hell and flame!' he bellowed.

A burst of superheated promethium from Vo'kar's heavy flamer roared through the tightly packed corridor, burning the leading squad of Dragon Warriors down.

Praetor and He'stan were in amongst them quickly.

Like a bull-sauroch, the veteran sergeant barged the plasma gunner to the ground before he got off a second shot. Stepping forwards he smashed a flame-wreathed warrior with his thunder hammer, shattering ceramite and crushing shoulder and neck. A shield smash that bit into the deck also beheaded the one he had just floored.

Snatches of the wider combat through his retinal lenses revealed He'stan spearing one warrior as he unleashed the Gauntlet of the Forge on another squad readying heavy weapons.

Brother Or'vo took a lascannon beam in the chest, which felled him. A succession of storm bolters put his slayer down soon after.

Praetor was killing freely now, using his strength and aggression to bully the renegades out of position. His hammer moved almost automatically, reacting to the nearest threat and dispatching it before finding another. He fought like a crusader of old, thrusting with his shield and bludgeoning with his hammer. Chainsword teeth met adamantium hammer haft and started spitting sparks. Praetor drove his elbow into his attacker, shattering the Dragon Warrior's nose cone and breaking the deadlock. A punch from his hammer head crushed the renegade's sternum. A slash from his shield's rim did the rest. The names of the fallen, the Firedrakes he had lost whilst leading the First, were on his lips as he slew.

'Nu'mean and Hrydor,' he intoned, crushing in a warrior's flank with a heavy swipe; 'Kohlogh and Gathimu,' another collapsed with a split skull and battle-helm; 'Tsu'gan and Halknarr,' he choked a third in his gauntleted fist, letting the thunder hammer hang by a lanyard around his wrist.

It was not enough. It would never be enough.

'Retribution and death,' Praetor hollered over and over again until the corridors echoed with his voice 'In Vulkan's name!'

Sustained bolter fire nearly drowned him out, but the last part was amplified through his helmet-vox.

Traitor Astartes were tough fighters. They had once been loyal Space Marines and carried all of that training, all of their genetic enhancements, and fused them with the mania of Chaos. They were changed things, these warriors. Even encased inside power armour, Praetor could feel the creeping taint of Ruin running through their veins. Barbed and hooked, festooned with chains and scraps of incarnadine scale, horned and reeking of sulphurous ash, the Dragon Warriors were black-and-red-clad nightmares come back from hell.

But against Terminators, they were outmatched.

Renegade fatalities easily outstripped that of Praetor's First. Subconsciously, he checked the schematic arrayed on his right retinal lens as a stream of combat data scrolled by on the opposite one. They were getting closer. According to the schematic, there was a large vent ahead. Some kind of cooling chamber, it would lead them up to the prow of the ship and the seismic cannon.

It took another three minutes of intense corridor fighting before Praetor breached into the cooling chamber.

'Secure and fan out,' he ordered. The room was immense, a vast octagonal chamber set with massive spinning fans that pushed ice-laced air into a web of generatoria far above. Halfway up the long tunnel, industrial jets squirted gouts of liquid nitrogen into the manufactured atmosphere. Upon contact with the air, the jet streams vaporised and veneered the lower sections of the generatoria in a chemical frost.

Praetor could think of only one thing that would require such excessive methods to cool it. Above them was the apocalypse weapon. They had but to climb the vent to reach it. Between them, the Firedrakes had enough charges to cripple a battleship. Get close enough to attach them to the seismic cannon and it would be silenced permanently.

The edges of the octagonal chamber were largely flat and made of metal. There was maybe just over a hundred metres to the mesh underfloor of the chamber above. Burn through that and they had a clear assault vector to the cannon. A series of gated ancillary shafts bled off from the main spine but they were all closed. By mag-locking their boots to the walls, they could march all the way to the top. Praetor found the audaciousness of it all appealing.

Perhaps Halknarr was rubbing off on him. Putting the old campaigner from his thoughts, he gestured to three of the squad sergeants: Kabok, Festar'on and Vorpang. A steady bolter storm was thrashing away at the entrance, keeping the Dragon Warriors pinned.

'Heavies and officers are to stay here at ground level,' he told them. 'I need three of your boarding assault troops each, loaded with explosives.' Praetor arched his head as far back as it would go and pointed up the sprawling shaft. 'I'll lead them, through that mesh ceiling and then into the weapon chamber located in the ship's prow.' As he looked down again he met the collective gaze of the listening sergeants. 'If the primarch is with us, we will destroy the seismic cannon and regroup with our forces at the insertion point. In Vulkan's name.'

Each sergeant nodded, slamming a gauntleted fist against his plastron in salute and producing a resounding *clang* of metal before heading off to assemble the demolition teams.

Praetor was re-checking the rack of melta bombs he had locked to his wargear when he noticed He'stan kneeling in the middle of the chamber, the Spear of Vulkan across his lap.

'What are you doing, Forgefather?' he asked.

He'stan kept his head bowed. He was utterly still. 'Preparing for the trials,' he said.

Praetor was nonplussed. 'We have them stymied. Those traitors in the corridor won't breach our lines.'

'Not them…' said He'stan, looking up into the shaft. The sound of something cumbersome and massive crawling up one of the ancillary tunnels boomed through the walls. 'Did you think they would let us come in here and destroy what we wanted without significant opposition?'

The strange acoustics made the sound hard to pinpoint. Praetor could only liken it to a heavy scuttling, emanating from every direction simultaneously.

He hefted his thunder hammer, scanning the upper reaches of the shaft. His voice darkened. 'Nihilan knew we were coming. He knew we would go for the cannon.'

He'stan was rising.

'The pacts he has made with daemons and their masters have granted him foresight none of us could have predicted.' He held the spear tip-down, ready to be shouldered and thrown. 'Look to your weapons, sergeant.'

Praetor's gaze never wavered.

'I am ready.'

He was not alone. At a sub-vocal command, the Fire-drakes not defending the entrance to the chamber turned their storm bolters skywards.

With a shriek of ruptured metal, one side of the shaft tore open and a creature dredged from the depths of the Eye itself crawled out.

The noisome thing stank of raw warp sorcery. The air around it was formed of a crackling miasma that shimmered like heat haze. It was immense, easily the size of a Land Raider, possibly bigger. The lower half of its body consisted of six insectoid limbs, engineered by some insane techpriest. Mechanised parts met daemon flesh in an unholy fusion where its abdomen and torso joined. Here it was red as blood-fire, sinous and over-muscled. It was not unlike a grim, daemonic centaur, only more horrific, an engine merged with the physical essence of a warp-fiend. An ululating, metallic roar belted from its spined-toothed mouth. Pipes jutting from its back vented hell-smoke in sympathetic empathy of its tangible anger.

Praetor scowled, fighting the revulsion in his gut at the mere presence of the thing. This was the monster that had killed Halknarr and the others, the one the old campaigner had tried to warn them about. He levelled his thunder hammer like he was pointing the crooked finger of death itself.

'Slay it!'

A crescendo of bolter fire rang out as the Firedrakes tried to put the monster down before it could reach the ground and begin setting about them.

The shells seemed to ripple against its skin as if striking a molten barrier that was robbing them of all potency. It was like rain hitting glass, and just as effective.

'Use your blades and hammers,' shouted He'stan, hurling the Spear of Vulkan as the monstrous thing descended. He ran to the outer edge of the chamber as the daemon-machine came thundering down, crushing one of the Firedrakes beneath its bulk. It bleated angrily, trying in vain to dislodge the spear that was burning its rune-engraved skin.

He'stan unleashed a burst from his storm bolter. Like all of the Forgefather's trappings, this was no ordinary weapon. It was blessed by the hand of Vulkan and fashioned to smite the denizens of eternal hell-realms.

'It is a creature from the Soul Forge,' he said. The hallowed shells from his first salvo detonated brightly against the monster's daemonic torso. The wounds were white against its hell-red flesh and flared with a righteous flame, but did little to slow let alone kill the thing. 'It is a Soul Grinder,' He'stan told him, 'and I will know its name.'

Though the Firedrakes surrounded it, chipping at it with hammers and blades, the Soul Grinder was far from outmanoeuvred. It lashed out, snapping a warrior in two before it seized upon another with a hideous mechanised claw and butchered him. Heavy rounds thundered from a cannon fused into one of its arms, chewing up another of the indomitable First.

Praetor cried out in anguish as his brothers were slain so cheaply. He moved aside as a Firedrake was battered back and slammed into the wall of the shaft.

'This beast was abroad on the traitor's ship?'

How Nihilan could've tamed such a thing was beyond the sergeant. He came face-to-face with it and stood his ground, a mortal before a daemonic hell-engine. The Soul Grinder towered over Praetor, dwarfing the noble Salamander lord who brandished his hammer like a threat.

'See this? I shall use it to smash you to paste.'

The names of the fallen passed his lips like a mantra, before he roared out a challenge: 'Back to the void with you, hell-beast!'

The Soul Grinder bellowed. A blast of foetid air gusted from its maw as it slashed down with a hot and glowing blade. Daemon whispers coursed off the edge of the weapon like vapour, promising torture and destruction.

Praetor charged to meet it but was borne to the ground and out of harm's way by something heavy slamming into him at speed. The daemon-blade bit into the deck-plate, shredding it with the baleful energies oozing off the sword.

He'stan helped return him to his feet. The Forgefather was immensely strong but it was only for the fact of the Tactical Dreadnought Armour's suspensors that he was able to lift the prone sergeant at all. Then he pointed. 'Your fate is up there, destroying that cannon,' said He'stan. 'Mine is here with the beast.'

There was no point in protesting, the Forgefather was right. Praetor nodded and went to rally the demolition teams.

'All incendiary carriers to me,' he ordered over the feed. 'We ascend, brothers!'

He cast a brief look back at He'stan. At the edge of his vision, he also noticed the Soul Grinder had just managed to release its wedged blade.

'Keep that thing occupied for as long as you can,' he said.

He'stan was already running at it, shouting clipped orders to the other Firedrakes to slowly encircle it. 'I intend to kill it, brother-sergeant.'

The beast was massive but so too was the chamber. While He'stan drew it off, Praetor was able to begin the climb relatively unmolested. The mag-locks were powerful and adhered to the metal shaft with a resonant *clang* but held his boots in place. Despite the fact it was only a short distance it was slow going, each footfall having to be placed precisely and carefully. By the time they'd reached halfway up the vertical, Praetor was feeling the pressure. He could only hear the battle below, caught snatches of it over the feed. He focused on the way ahead, on heading up, and instructed his warriors to do the same.

They'd reached just over fifty metres, when three more ancillary hatches opened. This time they gusted with pressure release and a narrow platform extended from the doorway that was created.

Hulking forms lumbered from the darkness onto these reinforced gantries. They wore red and black, and their helms were horned. Though scarred by the claws of things best left consigned to nightmares, and reeking of old blood, the design of their armour was not so dissimilar to the Firedrakes'.

Traitor Terminators.

To a warrior, they laughed as a hail of fire came withering down at Praetor and his brothers.

'Defend yourselves!' he cried. He couldn't reach his mag-locked storm bolter so he raised his storm shield instead and weathered the salvo.

II
Dead End

LYYTHE WAS GETTING closer to the source of agony and torture she had scented on the breeze. She had found a few scraps along the way, huddled slave-things barely worth her efforts. Their lives had been short, their endurance limited. She derived little sustenance from their deaths; her hunger demanded more. Lyythe could feel the presence of She Who Thirsts. It might have been imagined paranoia but she was in no position to test that theory. She pressed on.

Something wafted stronger up ahead, the slightest tremor of pain and remorse. It was faint but getting stronger. It could not be far. This sensation felt a little more substantial than the slave-things. Perhaps one of her armoured custodians was gravely injured and crawling to find help. Lyythe smiled, pulling at the stiches in her patchwork face.

That would be perfect.

* * *

HE'STAN SAW ONE of the climbing Firedrakes fall. His brother hit the ground thunderously like a comet, hurt but not dead. Adapting to the surprise attack, the rest were holding. Praetor was even driving upwards slowly. Rounds *pranged* off his shield. Discarded shell casings clattered against He'stan's armour like brass rain. A third force had ambushed them. As he ran around the scuttling Soul Grinder, he saw the retinal lenses of more traitors glowing evilly in the gloom above.

'As the storm gathers around us, so must we keep hold the purifying fire to banish the shadows.' The litany had sustained him many times over during the long isolation of the Quest. It was only now, as he fought for his life and the lives of his brothers, side-by-side with his Chapter, that He'stan realised the toll the Nine had taken upon him. It had made him a recluse, severed him from the bond of brotherhood. He revelled in this, the line reforged in battle as Vulkan had always taught them. If this was to be death, then at least they'd meet it together.

He needed the spear. It was still lodged in the beast's back. From there he could plunge it into the Soul Grinder's black heart and end the daemon, but only if he could reach it.

He'stan had lost count of the monsters he had slain. The Quest had taken him to the farthest reaches of the galaxy. He had been to places for which there were no maps and fought things that defied reason. This beast was no different. But during those battles, he had only needed to think of himself and not his brothers. The trail of dead and wounded was already beginning to tell on the Firedrakes. Those who could do so had edged to the periphery of the octagonal arena and engaged the traitor ambushers; the rest tried to fight the beast with hammer and blade. He'stan watched as one brave soul was bludgeoned into the wall. Another, attempting to saw into one of the Soul Grinder's legs, was crushed.

Like Praetor, he felt every death, every wounding keenly. Through Volgorrah and now the assault on the

Hell-stalker, he had become attached to the Firedrakes. Long lost, his connection to the Chapter had been restored through them. It was a link in danger of being broken.

'Fall back and support your brothers!' he yelled down the feed. Using its pincer, the beast had dislodged the spear and cast it aside. It clattered noisily to the deck-plate and stayed there, waiting. Vulkan He'stan eyed it keenly, between scuttling, mechanised legs. 'I shall fight this beast alone,' he said to himself. He sent a gout of flame into the Soul Grinder's midriff. Blessed, burning promethium seared up the creature's torso. It recoiled from the fire's purifying touch, rearing like some massive arachnid. It gave the Forgefather the moment of opportunity he needed. Barrelling between the beast's upraised forelimbs, he burst through to the other side and snatched up the spear just as it began to turn.

Enraged, the Soul Grinder unleashed a storm of shells from a weapon fashioned into the flesh of its pincer arm. The fusillade struck one Terminator and brought several others to their knees.

'Here!' shouted He'stan. He slammed his chest, hefted the Spear of Vulkan high so the beast could see it. 'Here is your prey. Face me, daemon.'

'Pilgrim...'

So it had a voice, this thing from the hell-depths. Not only that, but it seemed to know who stood before it and what he represented.

'Oh, you are a good dog, aren't you?' He'stan replied.

A stream of warp flame burst from the Soul Grinder's mouth, forcing He'stan to dive aside or be immolated by it. He barely had time to spring to his feet when a second burst engulfed the deck behind him. The metal squealed and spat as it was malformed under the warp fire's terrible influence.

He'stan kept running. Dim memories returned of corralling giant bull-sauroch of the Arridian Plain. Hacking into the beast's trailing leg, he drew off a chain of sparks that cascaded from the wound where ichorous oil was leaking like black blood. The Soul Grinder shrieked and cleaved down at the Forgefather with its blade.

'Hurts, doesn't it?' He only narrowly avoided the hellish sword. Baleful residue hissed against his armour plate like acid.

It swung again. He'stan had not time to avoid the blow so he had to meet it with the hallowed spear's glaive-like tip. Such power was levelled in the blow that He'stan staggered but stood his ground.

The sheer strength of the Soul Grinder was incredible. He'stan clung to the spear haft with both hands but was still pushed to one knee. The monster knew he was weakening. It came close, baring its spine-like fangs and opening wide for a final burst of warp flame.

'*Pilgrim…*' it drawled, hungrily.

'Vulkan…' He'stan pleaded, and hoped the primarch was listening.

LYYTHE FOLLOWED A trail of carnage all the way to a narrow chamber in the bowels of the ship. She judged she was close to the prow. Not far above her, she could hear the sounds of a furious battle taking place. She felt residual pain and suffering exuding from the iron walls, seeping down to her like blood-stink from a corpse, but her prey was ahead. There was a dark line of something wet and vital amidst all the wreckage. It didn't take a torture-surgeon to know what that substance was and what it meant.

Wounded.

Lyythe shuddered excitedly at the thought of it. She would gorge herself on this morsel of suffering.

Still, she cautioned herself, it might have some fight left in it.

Lyythe delved within the confines of her skin-tight leather robes and impossibly pulled forth a claw-like glove. It was hard like leather, but pieced together from scraps of skin and stitched with sinew. With the flesh gauntlet, the haemonculus felt bolder and pressed towards the silhouette she had just seen slump down in the corridor ahead.

Wraith-like and silent, Lyythe got within a few metres of her prey. She was already drinking in its palpable agonies when the sound of something heavy and metallic slotting into place caused her some alarm.

The voice that came out of the darkness at her was old and thick with phlegm.

'Heard you coming from way back,' it said, and discharged the round in its weapon.

The haemonculus shrieked as the high-velocity, mass-reactive shell came at her. Only through the artifice of her trappings was she able to narrowly avoid the flaring salvo as it lit up the corridor in harsh monochrome.

Not prey at all this one, but a hunter like her.

It was on its feet.

Not really wounded, not badly.

It was firing again. Fleeing madly, she'd put some distance between them but the shadow was tenacious. Lyythe could hear its monstrous footfalls as it gave chase. Suddenly the flesh gauntlet seemed woefully inadequate for her needs.

Death surely imminent, Lyythe had no choice but to risk the wrath of her lord; whoever that might be. She grasped the pyramidal object An'scur had given her and hurriedly activated the runes. It was only as the last sigil was sliding into place and a dark light infused the device from within, bleeding from its joints, did Lyythe consider she had made a mistake.

An'scur was not about to become beholden to a haemoculus. She *had* been abandoned. More than that, she had been consigned to execution.

As the dark light burned Lyythe's wretched hands into skeletal claws she enjoyed a final, tragic moment of absolute agony before the concealed void mine exploded and her soul was cast to the feet of ravening daemons.

A TREMOR RIPPLED through the underdeck, so heavy it
forced He'stan and the daemon apart. Released from
the terrible pressure he'd been under, the Forgefather
backed off from the Soul Grinder's lethal attentions.

'Something you should know about me, daemon...'
He'stan spun the Spear of Vulkan around until the tip
was facing down and he had the haft in a backhand
grip. He lifted the primarch-forged weapon to rest on his
shoulder. 'I never miss twice.'

Like a spit of purifying flame, the relic blade coursed
through the air and pierced the Soul Grinder's fell heart.
It was a throw of peerless strength and accuracy, a death-
blow powerful enough to kill a daemon. Disbelieving,
the beast lurched back from the imperious Forgefather.
It staggered on mechanical limbs, convulsing like some
kind of hideous spider in its death throes.

He'stan yelled to the Firedrakes. 'Finish it!'

A host of waiting chainfists and thunder hammers
smashed the vile creation back to the abyss until there
was nothing left of it but broken machine parts and an
ichorous residue.

Halknarr and his warriors had been avenged, but it
wasn't over. He'stan looked up the shaft. A brutal fire
exchange was taking place between the Firedrakes on the
ground and halted on the walls, and the Dragon Warrior
Terminators assailing them both.

Praetor was close. He had almost reached the mesh
ceiling of the shaft and was reaching out with a breaching charge when a second wave of armoured figures
appeared at the summit. A reaper canon spat out from
the shadowy throng, catching the veteran sergeant in the
chest and hurling him down.

BEFORE HE HIT the ground, Praetor knew it was over.
Nihilan had them outmanoeuvred and outgunned
before they'd even boarded the *Hell-stalker*. He had kept
his best warriors aboard and in number. The sorcerer
had even unshackled a monster to cull the Firedrake's

ranks. So many had the brother-sergeant lost. He had led them to their dooms. It was numbing and he barely felt the jolt as he smashed into the deckplate, buckling it.

With a tenacious death grip, Praetor held on to his shield and hammer. The breaching charge went skittering away in the darkness, lost and useless. On the walls, the Firedrakes were being beaten back. The sheer amount of fire gave them little choice. Retreat and live; hold and die. A Salamander's creed was to be indomitable and unyielding but they were also pragmatic.

Guns lined the summit of the shaft now, chewing through the mesh and pouring down fire onto the First. Heavier weapons were allied to the barrage of twin-linked bolters. Through the cracked resolution of his retinal lenses, Praetor recognised the telltale muzzles of reaper cannons and heavy flamers. Dark, smoke-edged fire rippled through the remains of the mesh and turned the base of the shaft into a cauldron.

Vision hazing from the heat and the damage to his battle-helm, Praetor barely saw He'stan striding through the flames. In his salamander mantle, he was all but impervious. The sergeant struggled to his feet for a second time.

As the fire began to die, the reapers started up. A bark of heavy shells became a roar. Plasma and melta bursts came in the wake of the ammo storm, thickening the air with actinic heat.

'I stand at your shoulder, brother,' He'stan shouted above the deadly crescendo.

Praetor hunkered behind his shield as he reached for his mag-locked storm bolter.

'What you did to that monster,' he said, fighting against the din of the storm. No ordinary Space Marine could've survived for long in such a battle. Even Terminators would be sorely tested. 'I have never seen such bravery.'

'Then we shall both die as heroes,' He'stan replied.

'I am sorry, my lord.'

'For what, brother?'

'For signing your death warrant with this mission.' Praetor slipped the end of the storm bolter's barrel against one corner of the shield and started shooting.

By now, there were no Firedrakes on the wall. Any who could fire were doing so. The rest fell back to the corridor to repel the Traitor Terminators coming from that direction. From the reports in the feed, Praetor knew they were surrounded and out of options.

There was no escape.

'You must call me brother, Herculon Praetor,' said the Forgefather, 'or Vulkan, as that is my name.'

'I'm sorry, lor– Vulkan.'

'It is not an ending, Praetor,' said He'stan, 'for the Circle of Fire does not end.'

Praetor nodded. 'Then I am glad to be here fighting at your side.'

'As am I, brother, as am I.'

The storm intensified. Several of the Firedrakes had already fallen. Against such an intense levelling of firepower, those who were left would not last much longer.

NOR'HAK STOOD UPON one of the gantries, laughing loudly as he rained death upon his hated enemies.

'Die, die, die!' he repeated like a mantra, neither elegant or inspiring. He just wanted to kill. It was the only time the tremors ceased, when whatever corrupt fuel filled his veins was stilled. Through the jagged eyeslits of his tusked battle-helm, he watched a Firedrake jerk behind the flare of his canon's muzzle flare. Spent shell casings spat from the weapon's breach at an almost mesmeric rate, Nor'hak's finger clenched perpetually on the trigger.

He laughed again, an ugly, booming sound filled with malice.

'Stop them, Nor'hak, that's all I need you to do.' Those were Nihilan's words when he was put in charge of the

Hell-stalker. Not Ramlek, the dog, but him, Nor'hak.

'*Do that and they will die on this ship. All of them, including the pilgrim,*' Nihilan had said.

'It will be done by my hand,' he said, reaching for a
fresh mag with a trembling gauntlet. He so wanted to cut
them, to plunge a knife into the pilgrim's heart whilst he
was still screaming.

Nor'hak was considering the drop when a blazing
heat manifested above. His autosenses were crazed with
temperature readings. Unwilling to pause in his manic
fusillade, he didn't see the vaulted ceiling glowing red
and the burning line etched in the kilometres-thick
metal.

CHAPTER TWENTY-TWO

I
Heavenfire

DAC'TYR WAS NOT one given to pessimistic thought but
when he had lost contact with Praetor and First, he considered the worst had happened.

There was precious little time to mourn the death of
the Firedrakes, an entire company, the Salamanders vet-
erans no less, lost on a single mission. It was desperation
to believe they could have penetrated the enemy ship,
neutralised its host of defenders and destroyed its prin-
cipal weapon system in one single move.

As Lord of the Burning Skies, Dac'tyr was not given to
capitulation either and as they coursed towards the *Hell-
stalker* he summoned his helmsmaster.

'Plot an impact course with the *Hell-stalker*, and give
me all power to the forward shields and port weapons.'

The response was strained and betrayed the helmsmaster's injuries. *'My lord, that is–'*

'Suicidal. Yes, I know. I prefer to think of it as a noble
sacrifice. We have no choice. Praetor and the First have
failed. We are Nocturne's last hope.' He opened up the
bridge-wide feed and then broadened the comms-relay

further so that it rang through the ship.

Multiple weapon impacts from the *Hell-stalker* and the other enemy ships still engaged in the void-war registered on the tacticarium display alongside streams of damage data that Dac'tyr ignored. Ahead, the main occuliport was awash with laser bursts and silent torpedo explosions. The front shields rippled and bloomed, dangerously close to being overloaded, and it would only worsen the closer they got to the enemy flagship.

'All crew, as we are flung headlong into the yawning darkness, heed my words. That sound you hear, the chiming of metal upon metal, the shriek of adamantium steel and the lofty thunder beyond our walls is the anvil. Make no mistake, the time of our reckoning is at hand.'

The bridge was shaking violently. Fires were breaking out across all stations as servitors and human crew battled to keep the *Flamewrought* void-worthy long enough for it to strike a crippling blow.

'You have fought for me, you have fought for this ship and for that I will be eternally in your debt. Men and women of Nocturne, Vulkan calls you now. Hold on until the anvil is done with us, hold on and fight with your blood and breath for one last time. This is Captain Dac'tyr, Master of the Fleet and Lord of the Burning Skies. For glory and for Vulkan.'

He couldn't hear the cheers of defiance above the noise. It was deafening on the bridge. Dac'tyr had to clutch the arms of his command throne just to stay seated.

'Hold the course,' he roared above a chain of explosions from the ventral hull that were felt all the way to the prow.

His teeth were gritted so hard he thought they might buckle and snap under the pressure. That was when he saw the flame. At first, as he saw it blaze across the black vista of space on the occuliport, he thought it was a comet or some celestial body that had chosen that precise moment to manifest. Only when it didn't follow a prescribed trajectory, when it dodged around and

through the debris of sundered vessels did he realise it
was something else.

It was climbing, this flame, this spear of fire, and
headed for the *Hell-stalker*.

'Helmsmaster...' Dac'tyr leaned forwards in his command throne as he tried to get closer to the occuliport.
He consulted the tacticarium display but the readings
were indecipherable. The sheer speed of the flame spear
was incredible. It was like no spacefaring vessel he'd ever
seen, but then this wasn't a ship; it wasn't a ship at all.

'Magnify that image and reduce power to all engines.
Half impulse on the plasma drives. Pull us out of this
collision. Do it at once.' He relayed coordinates through
the tacticarium and a section of the occuliport was
brought to extreme magnification as the mighty Salamanders flagship slowly began to course-correct.

Broadsides opened up on the *Flamewrought's* flanks
as its aspect changed and it came abeam of the *Hell-
stalker*. Shield power was diverted to the starboard side
to absorb the retaliatory cannon fire from the enemy
ship's gunners. Scrambled fighters wove and jinked into
a maelstrom of bright tracer, seeking out the torpedo
spread vented from the *Hell-stalker's* tubes.

All of this and Dac'tyr was transfixed by the flaming
spear. His eyes widened and he wept openly, realising
what it was he was seeing.

'In Vulkan's name...' he whispered.

The flaming spear widened at its tip, spreading into
a fiery blade that burned in the void despite the lack of
oxygen. Brighter than the sun, it struck the *Hell-stalker*
with the force of a god and sheared it in half.

FIRST PRAETOR FELT an overwhelming sensation of heat
and then he saw a crackling wall of flame. It passed
through the hull of the enemy warship, cleaved through
it like a welding torch cutting through metal. He lost
sight of the Traitor Terminators in the heat haze, though
he heard their screaming. Depressurisation came in the

fire's wake, the chill of the void rushing into the shaft as the *Hell-stalker's* prow simply fell away and parted from the rest of the ship.

Its occupants were jettisoned at once. Praetor's world became a tumbling, incoherent mass of sound and images as he fought to cling to whatever was left of the crippled ship. Nothing he knew of, no weapon ever fashioned by man could inflict that sort of damage. It had cut the the prow from a capital ship, devastated it and the seimic cannon in a single catastrophic blow. It was impossible.

Warriors were being cast into the void, armour flash-freezing, bolters pumping out rounds slowly with rigid determination. Praetor saw one of the vented Dragon Warriors struck by an errant shell. The brass casing burst against the renegade's armour, like a metal bloom opening and fragmenting in slow motion. Most of the Firedrakes were still mag-locked to the deck and fought to hold their ground, but the pull was incredible and tore the deck from under them.

He saw Vo'kar, and wanted to reach out. The heavy flamer bearer was sucked from the shaft and spat out into the darkness.

Explosions were rippling throughout the *Hell-stalker* as the rest of the ship started to come apart. The gun decks went up in a silent flare of incendiary red, felt through the bucking of the abused hull.

Praetor was clinging to an exposed strut, its ragged end molten and hot. His gauntleted fingers drove furrows into the cooling metal as the void sought to claim him. There were dozens of figures out there now, Dragon Warriors and Firedrakes both. Some had become locked in deathly embraces, fighting tooth and nail even as the cold web of space closed in around them.

Dozens became hundreds as the wretched serfs and armsmen from the upper and lower decks were ripped out, disgorged like the innards from some mighty space-borne beast. They froze upon contact with the harshness of the void; the blood crystallised in their veins, their limbs super-hardened. Several bounced off chunks of floating hull and broke apart on impact. Others shattered into tiny flesh-frozen fragments. Only the superhumans in power armour and the Terminators were capable of surviving in the void, but even that wasn't indefinite. Stay with the ship as it slowly disintegrrated into a dead and floating tomb or let go and be lost to the vageries of space.

Praetor considered his lack of options.

'*Ferro Ignis, brother.*' He'stan was talking to him through the comm-feed. The Forgefather sounded almost jubilant.

Despite the incredible forces trying to rip him into the abyss, Praetor managed to turn his head. He'stan was alongside him, hanging on to a different piece of strut ribbing. A few other Firedrakes had achieved the same feat. Precious few, Praetor noted.

'*The Fire Sword,*' he said. '*The prophecy.*'

A fiery glow was dying below Praetor as the wall of fire descended to the surface of Nocturne.

Praetor could barely believe the truth of it as he watched the flame-red aura fading. '*Dak'ir?*'

With a lurch of shrieking metal, the strut sheared away and he was cast into the darkness.

FUGIS BATTLED AT the controls of the *Incendar*. It was perhaps insanity to take such a damaged gunship out into a void war, but there was little choice in the matter. Reaching the hangar had taken time through the damaged sub-corridors of Prometheus. The once-Apothecary had considered going with Elysius but his place was on the surface with Captain Agatone. He was still a part of the Inferno Guard, albeit one whose place had not been filled for some time.

It was a stupid act, and one born out of the despair he'd felt at Dak'ir's death. He had been so sure he was right. Amidst the fury of death-riddled space above

Nocturne, it seemed a much lesser concern than it had.

'Bank and turn, thrice-cursed ship!' he raged, tugging hard on the controls to pull away from a vast piece of looming debris. Fluid glittered in its wake, icy and shining with the glow of distant nebulae. Engines squealing, Fugis fought the gunship under his control amidst further curses. His supplications to the machine-spirits were indelicate to say the least. It wasn't so much the threat of enemy fire that posed a serious danger to Fugis breaching Nocturne's atmosphere intact – unless engaging another ship directly, he could go relatively unnoticed into the maelstrom – but rather the immense chunks of floating wrecks and other jetsam that floated in the void. One slip, a single lapse in concentration and the ship would be crushed, him with it.

Fugis coursed through a jagged hole in a frigate's hull, narrowly making the gap and scraping the *Incendar's* outer armour. Within, the vessel was black and silent. Fugis decreased engine speed, slowed so he could see what was ahead and brought up the frontal lamp arcs. Dizzying, pellucid white scorched into the darkened chambers of the dead ship. Bodies, frozen solid, drifted around in the shadows, one half inside an environment suit. They bounced morbidly against the hull as Fugis drove through a floating graveyard. Despite the crusting of ice, the rapid degradation of tissue from void-exposure, the once-Apothecary recognised the uniforms of the dead serfs. They were Nocturnean. He was passing through the sundered guts of a Salamanders ship.

Muttering the litany of the Emperor's mercy, which was taught to all Apothecaries via the wisdom of the Codex, Fugis shut his senses to the dead and rode on.

The *Incendar's* lamp arrays detected a point of egress ahead, describing a much larger gash in the frigate's flank that it could pass through more easily. From the curious stillness of a floating, tomb-like world, Fugis was thrust back painfully into the void war.

Only seconds after emerging from the destroyed

frigate, he was confronted by the slab-sided remains of another ship, only much bigger. This leviathan seemed without end as Fugis wrenched *Incendar* into a sharp and almost vertical climb. Running a gauntlet of exploding turrets and venting blast doors, he came to the apex of the massive ship debris at last. It was a jagged spike of broken ship's spine, naked struts jutting from the wound like broken ribs. It had been severed, and molten edges of the metal superstructure suggested it was something phenomenally hot that had done it.

A false dawn was dying off to the gunship's port side, slightly obscured by the hulking wreck. Fugis caught a distant glimpse, like a spear, like a setting sun falling to earth. At some instinct, for just a moment, he dared to hope.

'The Fire Sword, the Unbound Flame...'

He was almost caught off guard during his reverie. A chunk of broken deck was hurtling at him with gunship-crushing impetus. Boosting the engines, he slammed the *Incendar* into a dive and tried to find an opening where he could slip through. Portholes came and went, flashing by too fast to change course or too small to fit the gunship into. The slab of deck was getting closer, the glacially slow suddenly hellishly quick and immediate, when Fugis found his escape route. He passed into a wide and open deck. Corpses were here too, hooked on iron chains or shackled to columns. Slaves, the lost and damned.

Something up ahead, picked out in the magnesium white of his frontal arc lamps, got the once-Apothecary's attention. He checked twice to make sure he wasn't seeing things. It was a living being, someone that had survived the death of the ship. Fugis did not need to remind himself this was a traitor vessel. Evidently, one of the garrison had proven tenacious enough not to die.

Flicking the manual trigger lever for the heavy bolter mounted in the gunship's nose, Fugis intended to rectify that. A second away from blasting the clinging figure to oblivion, he stayed his hand.

Scaled armour, draconian pectorals, the faceplate of a snarling creature of the deep earth – he knew this figure, or at least what it represented.

'Firedrake.'

Fugis could scarcely believe it. He realised the wreck he was piloting through must be the *Hell-stalker* and this one of the warriors sent aboard to scupper it. Thoughts of elimination turned to rescue in his mind as he sought out a place to land. A plateau appeared out of the gloom, framed by the gunship's lamp array. He set the *Incendar* down a few metres from the stricken Firedrake's position and opened up the comm-feed.

'Get aboard. Be quick about it, brother.'

With his boots mag-locked to the crippled deck, the Firedrake was painfully slow in reaching the gunship's rear embarkation hatch. Fugis had already sealed off the crew section and launched again as soon as the instrument panel indicated the hatch was closed and repressurisation in progress.

He opened up the internal vox to the troop hold behind him.

'You are fortunate I did not shoot you,' he said, leaning in to the receiver cup.

'*Had I a flare,*' said the passenger, '*I would've set it off.*'

'Are you alone, brother? Are there others nearby?'

'*All slain. To my shame, I survived.*'

'Who are you?'

'*Brother-Sergeant Halknarr of the Firedrakes. And you?*'

'Fugis, once of the Apothecarion.'

They were finally reaching the end of the deck. The opposite end was wide open, several times larger than a hangar door.

'*I have heard of you, brother,*' said Halknarr. '*Though I must confess, I thought you were dead.*'

Fugis scowled. 'Lucky for you that I am not.'

He guided them back into the open void. For a few moments the dark skies were clear. Then he saw the wrecks. Ship after enemy ship littered the void, burned and blackened by incendiary fire, broken and bleeding. They'd emerged into utter carnage. It had swung the favour of the battle to Dac'tyr's fleet and the Salamanders.

Fugis didn't need to see it to know the spear of flame he'd caught a glimpse of earlier had done this, had reduced an enemy flotilla to rags.

So in awe of this terrible miracle, he didn't notice the host of gunships arrayed around them until it was too late.

II
Tome of Fire

IT WAS DARK in the deep caverns of the world. As he drifted down into the chasmal crater, Nihilan cycled through his optical spectra until he found a filter that provided the cleanest visual acuity. Other than crags and drifting ash there was little to see, but the ridged edges of the bore hole were treacherous. One scrape could puncture a vent, disable his jump pack and send him falling to oblivion in the fuliginous depths below. The seismic cannon had cut a wound into the molten core of Nocturne, close to its heart.

Sulphur palls drifted upwards from the distant basin of the crater, buoyed on rising magma thermals. There was a strong stench of burning in the air, and an acerbic tang invaded Nihilan's nose and throat despite his battle-helm. It brought back memories, that smell, of his Lexicanum training with Pyriel, of the days when they had fought as allies.

Smoke and heat cascaded across Nihilan's retinal lenses, occluding his remembrances and fouling the visual signal. Despite the interference, he had seen an opening ahead. He increased the burn in his engines, thumbing just a little more power into the vents. Then he waited silently in the shadows, jump pack eating fuel with a dulcet burr, keeping its wearer aloft and relatively still.

Below them, much deeper into the crater, the blood of the earth cracked and spat. The heady drifts of burning air were thicker here and wafted up from a ruddy pit; the smoke was so dense it obscured the belts of magma boiling at its nadir, reducing them to an umber glow. Soon, it would swell and burst. Mount Deathfire would crack and open. She would bleed to death and drown the world in hellfire.

Nihilan eyed the dark a moment longer.

Nothing stirred, no guardians, no monsters of the deep world opposed them – the way was open. Everything and everyone was on the surface, defending Nocturne. They did not realise their true enemy was below, that the vaults and bastions they thought safe were not.

With such a massive beam, the margin for error with the seismic cannon was large but it was still quite a feat to have homed in on almost the precise incision point Nihilan needed.

Hearts drumming in his chest, he thumbed a burst of power into the engines and glided through the shadow-darkenened corridors to the edge of the crater. His retainers followed. Before them was a chamber, sliced open as if in cross section by a surgeon's knife. The vault's massive, artificered gate was cleaved almost in two. A molten arc where the beam had cut into it still glowed. The aperture left behind was easily wide enough for the three Dragon Warriors to enter abreast.

'I am shaking, Ramlek,' Nihilan confessed to his dog.

'It reeks of Salamanders, this place,' he snarled.

Thark'n merely nodded as the three passed through the shadow of the broken gate.

Low-burning braziers, those not destroyed by the passage of the seismic cannon, described a sparse shrine. The flickering torches picked out an obsidian plinth. Upon it was a book.

Nihilan landed gently onto the floor of the shrine room. It was webbed with cracks and smaller stress fractures but, even beneath the armoured bulk of the three Dragon Warriors, felt solid enough. As the sorcerer approached the plinth, his warriors stayed behind to guard the mouth of chamber. It was like a cave hewn into the side of the mountain, its threshold utterly flat.

'Nothing moves,' said Ramlek, surveying the darkness both above and below.

Thark'n slowly panned his reaper cannon around, and grunted much the same.

Nihilan wasn't listening. His hands were trembling, almost close enough to touch the ancient tome.

'Vulkan buried you here, didn't he,' he whispered, as if expecting the artefact to respond. 'He discovered something during his time on this world, something from the Old Ways, something forbidden and proscribed.'

Nihilan scowled behind the faceplate of his battle-helm.

'A jealous father protecting his secrets,' he hissed, 'but *I* know, *I* see what is within...' He gripped the edges of the book with gauntleted fingers, holding it up carefully to the light as if at any moment it might crumble. 'Simple drake-hide, bound with a gilded clasp,' he muttered. 'Who would believe the revelations you possess... life, resurrection.'

Engel'saak had told him of the *corpsemancers*, of the fell men of ancient Nocturne and their dark mastery of the earth. Only a daemon was old enough to remember such things, but it had been all too willing to divulge its secrets for Nihilan to give it flesh again. For the simple promise-price of a vessel, he would possess the means to return life to the dead.

'For my lord,' said Nihilan, his voice cracking. 'For Vai'tan Ushorak.'

His reverant mood was interrupted by a shimmering heat haze materialising towards the back of the shrine. Nihilan felt it before he saw it, as a prickling of his psychic senses. A jagged line of fire tore into reality and expanded. From within its smoke-filled confines, a figure wearing the blue power armour of the Librarius stepped forth and into the chamber.

Pyriel was wreathed in psychic fire as he emerged from the gate of infinity. The force staff in his clenched fist crackled with trapped power.

'Have you come alone, brother?' Nihilan sounded surprised, even a little insulted. He was also still holding on to the book.

Smoke drizzled from the Librarian's armour in a flood. He appeared unperturbed.

'For now.'

'That was foolish, very foolish, especially after such a difficult ritual. Did you cast you body and soul all the way from Prometheus?' Cerulean fire flashed in Nihilan's eyes. 'You look tired.'

'Do I?'

A plume of white flame arrowed from Pyriel's outstretched fingertips, spearlike and incandescent. Nihilan blocked it with the palm of his hand, deflecting the fire bolt into Thark'n who was about to rake the shrine room with his reaper cannon. Struck in the chest, the Dragon Warrior was pitched from the chamber and into the chasm below.

There was no scream, but Thark'n was most certainly dead.

'Slay him!' Nihilan snapped, backing off to protect the book.

Ramlek broke into a loping run, power axe swinging. Pyriel threw the hulking warrior aside with a burning column that spiralled with the heads of chasing serpents and crashed the Dragon Warrior into the chamber wall. He tried to get up but Pyriel hit him again with a blazing hammer that left Ramlek's armour cracked and trailing smoke. Out cold, the Dragon Warrior didn't rise again.

'Just you and me, brother,' he said, turning to face his nemesis.

Nihilan had his staff in his hand and was describing arcane sigils in the smoke-drenched air with its tip. 'You failed to defeat me on Scoria. What makes you believe you can do anything other than die this time?'

Pyriel's eyes flashed cerulean blue in the gloom. 'Because now you are without your daemon's crutch.'

Nihilan laughed, his blood-red armour lit by the fiery convocation his old fellow acolytum was summoning. A ribbon of flame wrapped around Pyriel's body, fending off a hail of black talon-darts.

The psychic castings cancelled each other out but the Librarian had kept something in reserve.

'Do you remember much of those days, Pyriel?' asked Nihilan as a surge of flame-red lightning crackled impontently against the dark sigil he'd fashioned in the air. The sigil became a daemonic mouth, drawing the lightning in and swallowing the psychic storm whole.

THERE WAS BLOOD in his mouth. Behind his faceplate, Pyriel licked at it where it rimed his clenched teeth. A taste of copper came back on his tongue, warm and vital. That and the throbbing at the back of his skull told him he was losing.

He drew in a long, steadying breath. It felt as if his lungs were lined with razor blades. He exhaled, shuddering.

Vulkan's blood… One of the black darts had bitten through his armour. Pyriel imagined it moving parasitically through his body, intent on his heart. It wasn't real, though, just a psychic manifestation. His mind made it real. His will alone could excise it like a splinter from the wound. Gasping another knife-edged breath, he pushed the dart out.

The mental rigours of the duel were wearing him down. Pyriel knew when he had come here, when he had realised what Nihilan was about to do, that he was the lesser psyker. Though he tried to deny it, the 'sending' from Prometheus *had* weakened him. Even at full strength, this was always going to be difficult. Nihilan was formidable. He always had been and that was part of the problem, for Nihilan knew it too. This wasn't some revenge-crazed renegade, or some blood-lusting warlord thrown from the Eye intent on carnage. Those threats were easy to counter and then vanquish. The weaknesses of such obvious men were exploitable. The 'chinks', Pyriel called them. Every opponent he had ever faced had one. Nihilan was different. He had no chinks. Even when they had trained together as Vel'cona's acolytes Pyriel had seen it. Nihilan was frighteningly pragmatic to the point of ruthlessness, and, before Dak'ir, the most gifted psyker Pyriel had ever met. His powers might already outstrip Vel'cona and here Pyriel faced him, alone.

Every strategy, every piece of psychic alchemy and shred of prescience led the Librarian to the same conclusion: he was going to die. Capitulation wasn't in his nature.

Even outmatched, he had to try.

'It's a pity the master didn't destroy you when he had the opportunity,' Pyriel said.

'Pity, was it? No. It was weakness that stayed Vel'cona's hand, consigned me to the null collar and the bloody ruins of Lycannor!' Nihilan carved a blackened blade from the raw material of the ether, gave it solidity and hacked at Pyriel.

A chain of fire wrapped around the smoking edge of the warp blade, snaring it, slowing it. By the time the glowing links had been broken, the black sword had dispersed into ethereal smoke.

The effort of creation nearly staggered Pyriel but he could not show weakness before his enemy.

'You made your own fate, a Lexicanum with ambition beyond his knowledge. You were warned of the danger–'

'I sought only to enhance my strength. Mastery of knowledge was our credo, if you remember.'

'Your tastes verged on the heretical, brother.'

Pyriel was stalling, trying to marshal his power. Amidst the furore of his thoughts it was hard to focus. He hoped his voice had been heard in the ether and not devoured by some hungry, half-spawned sentience.

Nihilan smiled. The gesture was obvious in the timbre of his words. 'I knew you were tired.'

'I tire of your rhetoric.' Pyriel's bones felt like powder, filled with agony. His muscles cramped as lactic acid threatened to burn them from the inside out. He tried to summon the mantras he needed to fortify his mind but failed.

I am fading.

Nihilan strode around the chamber, like a predator that had trapped his prey. His eyes never left the Librarian. Behind the battle-helm slits, Pyriel saw them narrow.

'Are you gathering your strength for something impressive, Pyriel? I liked the psy-hammer, by the way. It's not easy to put Ramlek down.'

'He died a traitor's death,' he spat, 'no different to any other rabid dog.' Pyriel brought his staff across his body in a warding gesture, watching the sorcerer's every step. It took all his efforts just to keep it steady.

Nihilan tilted his head as he considered that.

'You are at least partially right,' he conceded.

Bored of the taunting, he grew serious.

'I only craved wisdom, and Vel'cona sanctioned me for it. Brutally! He stripped me of my power, humiliated me in front of my brothers.' The derision in his voice created the impression of Nihilan's sneering face in Pyriel's mind. 'You speak of the anvil and how we must all be tempered by it. I see only a bastard's tool, a convenient excuse to condone negligence. It is blind acceptance. If it is the will of the anvil then it is just, Vulkan had decreed it.' He clenched his fist. 'I spit on Vulkan!' he declared, and brandished the book. 'This is the only facet of his legacy worth anything and it was hidden by earth and metal.'

'What is in those pages that you were willing to sunder a world to attain?' Pyriel asked.

A sudden and disturbing calm possessed Nihilan, as if the truth within the tome were the only salve to his anger.

'The means to reverse entropy, brother.' A flash of fire lit his eyes behind the retinal lenses of his battle-helm.

'Explain it to me.'

Sadness tinged the sorcerer's reply. 'You would never understand.' He put the tome away, shackled it with a dead penitent's chain to his armour. 'Enough prevarication. I truly wish I could spare you, brother, but the Fire-born walk a treacherous path that will ultimately lead to their deaths.'

'And you walk a devil's road, paved to damnation. Were those the demagogue's words? Is that how he turned you on Lycannor?'

Nihilan was shaking his head. The voice emitted from his battle-helm was rasping and full of malice again. 'No... Ushorak opened my eyes, but it wasn't until your beloved captain burned off half my face and more in the crypts of Moribar that I was truly enlightened. That is when I turned, when I embraced Chaos.'

The braziers around the room guttered violently.

'That is when I knew I had been truly abandoned and consigned to death by my own brothers!'

Pyriel snarled. His anger was galvanising. 'You spat on your Chapter and threw it into disrepute by your hubris. You shamed us all, but it will end now!' Smashing the butt of his force staff into the ground, Pyriel unleased a roiling belt of conflagration that grew into a vast wall of fire, crested by a score of roaring drake heads.

Nihilan sank to one knee. His staff was braced across his body like a breaker when the flame hit him, impeding its flow and spilling it aside. He weathered the firestorm and stood, shimmering with heat haze but otherwise unscathed.

He scoffed, letting the bile rise in his throat. 'Is that the best you can do?' Nihilan thrust out with a bladed hand.

Pyriel described a psychic shield of drake scale to repel the next attack but found the casting had dissipated before it was properly formed. Cold was flooding through his chest, spreading to his neck and limbs. A spike of white-hot pain followed, focused on his solar plexus. He looked down.

A lance of writhing warp energy had impaled him, extending all the way from Nihilan's talons. It bulged with the tortured faces of the soul-damned, twisting like some hellish drill into Pyriel's broken defences as if they were nothing.

They *were* nothing, he realised. Nihilan had just been humouring him, debating whether or not to spare his life. All the training, the many long hours spent in psychic meditation suddenly felt cheap. The sorcerer could have ended it at any time.

'You were always such a petty little pyromancer,' Nihilan said, 'but I did love you, brother.' With an aggressive thrust, he drove the soul-lance deeper as the cerulean light in Pyriel's eyes died forever.

CHAPTER TWENTY-THREE

I
Summoning Fire

EVEN THROUGH THE rebreathers in his battle-helm, it was the smell that assailed Tu'Shan first. Pervasive and noisome, it carried the reek of spoiled meat. It even overwhelmed the tang of ash and sulphur on the breeze. If the stench was a warning, then the fat beat of leather against the air and the shadow eclipsing the sun described the nature of Tu'Shan's enemy.

Daemon. Standing in the *Promethean's* lofty cupola, he lifted his gaze to the blood-red sky.

It was dragon-kind, or something that had moulded itself to look like one. Such things had been consigned to myth aeons ago, the wicked kin of the nobler and most ancient drakes as recounted in Promethean lore. Like all Nocturneans, Tu'Shan had been taught the legends of the ancient wars between the monsters of the deep earth and the towering mountain crags. It was before the coming of men. Few remembered it, or cared to. Like so much history, it was lost and forgotten, unimportant. The beasts of that singular age had been titans. This one, albeit an ersatz version, was immense.

Gunning their engines, a pair of Predators went to engage it, turrets booming. Autocannon shells exploded harmlessly off the daemon's scaled hide. In retaliation, it spewed a torrent of warp fire that reduced the tanks to molten slag and their crew to ash.

In front of Hesiod's walls the battle had reached a crescendo and was still being fought furiously despite the unfolding cataclysm, but several warriors had stopped the killing to witness the terrifying creature.

'Stay back!' Tu'Shan shouted down the armoured column's feed, knowing that he would be sending his Fire-born to their deaths if they got involved. Despite his orders, an armoured Rhino strayed too close to the daemon and was immolated. Another, slewing on its tracks to drive clear, was smacked aside with a sweep of the creature's tail. It rolled, spitting fire and frag before crashing to a halt on its roof. Side hatches were kicked open and what was left of the crew and occupants staggered out.

The creature needed a distraction before it destroyed the entire tank company. Tu'Shan called down to the Land Raider's driver.

'*Promethean*, forward!'

If he must sacrifice his life to stop this thing, then so be it. The anvil would temper or break him. It was time to test the strength of the Chapter Master's forging.

He had to bellow above the scream of the engines to be heard but Tu'Shan's voice carried well enough, 'Hell and flame!'

Both side sponsons erupted as the flamestorm cannons were unleashed. Purifying promethium washed over the daemon and it was lost in haze of heat and smoke.

'Pour it on!'

The fire intensified as the flamestorm cannons were pushed to their critical limits.

A silhouette writhed in the fiery maelstrom and for a moment Tu'Shan dared to hope... but a beast of the abyss, a true daemon-kind, was not so easily banished.

On unfurled wing, the creature sprang from the conflagration. It trailed fire and smoke, emitting a screech
of hellish anger. It was hurt, but far from dead.

Tu'Shan grimaced as the daemon-dragon smacked
into the Land Raider's hull. He got off a desultory burst
from the pintle-mounted storm bolter before the battle
tank pitched onto its nose and the Chapter Master was
thrown clear of its negligible protection.

Tu'Shan skidded across the ash-sand but used the
momentum of the fall to spring quickly to his feet.

The dragon-daemon had crushed the front of the *Promethean*, squeezed its armour in its talons like it was
parchment and left it buring. The venerable battle tank
had fought in countless wars and now it was reduced to
wreckage. Tu'Shan's anger fed his resolve like a furnace
but the daemon's sheer presence battered him back so
he had to stand braced against it or be pushed to his
knees.

Tu'Shan pulled out *Stormbearer* and held it up like
a talisman. The thunder hammer glowed with a faint
light, lent strength to his limbs.

Serpentine eyes regarded him curiously, as if the daemon was putting an identity to the mortal challenging
it.

A MORSEL OF anxiety fluttered through Engel'saak as it
felt again the bite of sanctified steel that had sent it
from the material plane. The daemon easily suppressed
the tremor of half-buried horror from its host. Too late
had the vessel realised the folly of its compact with
the daemon. It was beneath Engel'saak's notice. This
mortal, the one bearing the burning bright hammer,
had its undivided attention. After the demi-god had
banished it, Engel'saak had drifted along on the warp
tides for millennia, with only its anger as sustenance.
It had been weak, vulnerable and prey to the greater
intelligences that swam those ethereal seas. Returning
had not been easy.

Vengeance would not be swift for this mortal, Engel'saak decided, but it would be painful.

'RECOGNISE THIS?' TU'SHAN said, then muttered under his breath, 'You do. You're an old bastard, aren't you?'

An answer of sorts was forthcoming. Rising up on its hindquarters, the beast extended a long, sinuous neck to its full height and released a storm of hell-fire.

Tu'Shan roared, and brandished his hammer like a shield as the flames washed against it. Rreaching around his back, he gripped the edge of his drakescale cloak and threw it around in front of him. No fire existed that could penetrate salamander hide and Tu'Shan's had come from one of the oldest and most venerable beasts. It provided a better barrier than *Stormbearer* but after a few seconds, the heat was intense.

'How much fire is in you, hell-kite?' he spat, hunkered down against the barrage.

Instinct made him move, and the slightest suggestion of the blaze abating. The daemon slashed with a massive talon, carving furrows into the earth in Tu'Shan's wake. Lava plumed from the gash in Nocturne's flesh, scalding the creature and drawing an avian shriek from its foul, distended maw.

Tu'Shan smiled grimly. His land, his heartblood – it had risen to the defence of its Regent. While the daemon still recoiled from its wounding, he struck it hard across the foreleg and was rewarded with an audible crack of bone.

His second blow never fell. The daemon fended Tu'Shan off with a beat of its colossal wings, buffeting him back so he had to regain his footing. Like ash carried off by the wind, he'd lost his advantage as soon as it was gained and was back on the defensive.

Parrying a lash from the daemon-dragon's barbed tail, Tu'Shan staggered. His guard opened up to a raking talon that would rip apart his artificered armour and spill his lifeblood over the ash-sand.

Vel'cona's lightning shield saved the Chapter Master's life. It flickered and spat as the creature's warp essence touched it, reacting like a refractor field does when exposed to rain. There was a hiss of static then the stink of ozone and the shield collapsed.

Not waiting for a riposte, the Master Librarian threw a psychic storm against the daemon, feeding arcs of jagged, azure lightning into its neck and torso. It was badly burned. Fat slabs of scale hung off the daemon by immaterial threads and an ugly, black scar marred the bloody shimmer of its hell-skin but the daemon still came at them.

'Back!'

Tu'Shan obeyed without question, falling back as Vel'cona thrust his open hand towards the ground. As he brought his hand back up, stiffened into a grasping claw, the surface of Nocturne was wrenched up with it.

Tendrils of dust and debris trailed off a vast, metres-thick wall of earth. For a few seconds even the daemon-dragon was obscured from sight. The clatter of crumbling stone presaged its return as the creature crashed through the elemental barricade.

It was relentless. Pain, fatigue, fear; these concepts held no meaning for the denizens beyond the veil. Mortal limitations did not apply to its kind.

Vel'cona dug deeper, dredged up the bedrock Hesiod had been founded on. With a psychic sculptor's hand he fashioned a prison of sanctuary stone around the creature, encasing it within the fortified heart-rock of Nocturne.

It barely held.

'That cage of stone won't trap it for long,' he said.

Tu'Shan could hear the tiredness in the Master Librarian's voice, though he betrayed no outward sign.

'Then we'll take our chance to smite it now,' he said. 'Can you reach the *Flamewrought*?'

Vel'cona's eyes narrowed. 'It should be possible. What are you thinking, my lord?'

'If psychic lightning and sacred hammers can't kill this thing, we need to use something bigger.'

THE VARKONAN BROKE up with a satisfying chain of explosions along its starboard side. Incendiaries in the prow cooked off in the resulting blast and finished off the cultist-cruiser in a spectacular supernova. By the time the light flare of the *Varkonan's* death faded, it was sinking into the void like a headless shark, bleeding gas and crew.

Dac'tyr watched another icon blink out on the tacticarium and looked for the *Flamewrought's* next target.

'Frigate, abeam, port side,' he spoke into the bridge-vox. 'Give it a volley of the broadside laser batteries.'

A few minutes later and the already damaged enemy frigate was no more. In the final stages of the battle they had racked an impressive tally of kills. Dac'tyr committed each and every one to memory for the brander-priest to score his flesh with later.

Other concerns were at the forefront of his mind at that moment, and it wasn't the swathe of ships he was cutting down with impunity either. Dac'tyr knew the *Flamewrought* and trusted it with his life. It had never lied to him, never let him down in any way, and yet he still found it hard to believe what the tacticarium had described when he'd been locked on a suicidal ramming run against the *Hell-stalker*.

He should be dead. They all should be.

Despite Dac'tyr's best efforts, the Salamander fleet had been facing certain defeat, outnumbered and outgunned by a superior foe. The Lord of the Burning Skies was a superlative captain, he knew this without a shred of arrogance, but even he could not have achieved victory in such a scenario.

A trailing torch of fire had intervened. Everything changed in the space of a few heartbeats. It had torn the enemy flagship into pieces and crippled several others. The balance of the scales had tipped, and in Dac'tyr's favour. He meant to make the most of it.

Though he didn't have many functioning vessels left, those he did have were being put to good use. With the flame's intervention, it was now a matter of destroying the enemy ships above Nocturne that were either too tenacious or too stupid to flee into the warp. The dark eldar were already long gone. They'd quit the void-war much earlier for some inexplicable reason. Some of the more belligerent war-spheres of the kroot remained. A broadside barrage raked one that had appeared through the debris field left by the destroyed frigate and been seen via *Flamewrought's* main occuliport. There were a handful of smaller renegade cruisers too, cult ships and hell-barges brimming with fanatics. Such creatures as these didn't know how to retreat. They couldn't. Dac'tyr and his fellow captains punished them without mercy.

The death of the *Hell-stalker* had signalled the defeat. It was the first unpicked seam upon which the enemy's plans unravelled, but a crucial one. The massive capital ship was reduced to a floating wreck, listing in the blackness and broken into three disparate sections. Venting fuel, vapour and men, it was a cold carcass ripe for later plunder by the void's carrion-eaters. Dac'tyr was content to let it drift.

Like a belt of tiny signature flares, the Firedrakes spilling from the shattered hull had appeared brightly on the *Flamewrought's* augur arrays and sensorium. Dac'tyr had dispatched his entire complement of gunships and fliers with any troop capacity to pick them up. The surviving Dragon Warriors disgorged at the same time were gunned down. Two ships, a Caestus and a Thunderhawk, had fallen prey to the renegades, hacked apart as they collided and latched onto their hulls, but the rest engaged in the rescue mission were successful.

Flocks of the lighter vessels were already bound for Nocturne, descent jets blazing. Communcation with the surface had still not been re-established, which meant the ground war was still being waged. Reinforcement from the First would make a difference to its outcome. After everything, victory was within reach.

One gunship amongt the vast squadron was not in Dac'tyr's original roster. The *Incendar* was being piloted by a Brother Fugis. The name was known to the captain as belonging to an ex-Apothecary he'd thought dead. Brother Fugis had gruffly corrected him on the falsehood of that in no uncertain terms when the *Flamewrought* had made contact.

Unlike the other gunships, the *Incendar* was headed back to Prometheus after a belligerent warrior, the Black Dragon survivor of Volgorrah, Zartath, demanded the presence of an Apothecary on the space station. Dac'tyr didn't ask about the fate of Brother Emek, who he knew was supposed to be manning the Apothecarion, and instead sent a single Thunderhawk escort with the *Incendar* as it went against the tide. Word had come via Master Argos that Prometheus had sustained casualties but was secure, Vulkan be praised. Fugis's return was timely, then.

As the gunnery captains unleashed the *Flamewrought's* broadside salvos, Dac'tyr reviewed the damage reports and crew fatality lists. It was hard reading. Both ship and men had taken a severe beating. The bridge itself still carried the scars of the battle. Several bodies were still awaiting transfer but had to make do with being shawled by silver hypothermic blankets for now. Already, Dac'tyr had begun to formulate a programme of repair and refit for the broken fleet. It was methodical and exacting, as was to be expected from a Salamander. As soon as the void-war was won they would return to Prometheus, to whatever hangars and docking spikes were operational, and rebuild. Dac'tyr wanted to revel in victory, to excise some of his grief in cathartic retribution, but practicality would not allow it. Let the rest of the crew vent their anger. They needed it.

Dac'tyr was in the process of evacuating and sealing off several damaged areas of the battle-barge when a keening sensation split his skull like an axe-blade. He gripped the tacticarium for support, stumbling from his command throne as he lurched forwards in agony.

'My lord?' ventured the bridge's practitioner. At his order, a pair of nearby medical servitors began to approach, bio-scanners drawing data from the staggered captain, but he waved them off.

Dac'tyr clenched his eyes tight. His hands were balled into fists pressing on the tacticarium display. Then he relaxed, exhaled a breath and opened his eyes again. His voice was thick and laboured as he summoned the attention of the helmsmaster.

'Have the gunners power the prow-lances,' he said, wiping a line of blood from his mouth, 'and prepare a firing solution to the surface.'

'That's an orbital strike, my lord,' confirmed the helm, reviewing the coordinates.

Dac'tyr had almost recovered. An intense ocular migraine still blurred his sight, worsened by the chromatic aberrations in his peripheral vision, but at least he could see again. The sensation had not been a pleasant one and if the war on Nocturne was won he intended to have serious words with a certain individual.

'It is. Be precise.'

II
Redemption

A MINIATURE SUN was born in the bloody sky above them, magnesium white and growing by the second. Static electricity crackled the air, presaging a flurry of dry lightning strikes. Vel'cona fended off one with his outstretched palm; another he earthed to his force staff.

'We should retreat to a safe distance,' he said. His cerulean gaze never left the stronghold of rock he'd forged around the daemon. Small stones were already skittering down its rugged flanks, along with rivulets of displaced grit.

Tu'Shan gestured to the *Promethean*, lying crushed on its side.

'What about tank armour for cover?' he suggested.

Vel'cona didn't need to look. He dare not. 'Good enough.'

Together they reached the wreckage of the Land Raider as a tiny targeting beam pierced the oily clouds above.

As if waking from a dream to a sudden and terrible realisation, the look on Vel'cona's face made Tu'Shan turn.

'What is it?'

'I have to leave. Immediately.'

In less than a minute the lance strike would hit the surface.

'Right now?'

'Nihilan is inside the vault.'

'Beneath Deathfire?'

Vel'cona nodded.

Tu'Shan's gaze strayed back to the cage of stone where the Master Librarian had trapped the daemon.

'Whatever his goal, he must be stopped. I can finish this thing myself.'

'With respect, you cannot, my lord.'

'You've been wrong before.'

'Rarely.'

'Then pray this is one of those times. Find Nihilan. Stop him.'

Vel'cona didn't argue. He disappeared in a flash of cerulean light, bound for the nadir of the world just as a blazing white light filled its heavens.

LORKAR SHOUTED FOR his warriors to take cover as the orbital lance strike came down. It hit the earth with an ear-splitting *boom*, the shock wave billowing out as far as the ravine where the Marines Malevolent sheltered. It was bright, incredibly bright and the after-flare was slow to recede from the sergeant's retinal lenses.

A pall of debris washed over them, flung from the

impact point. Hard grit caught up in the eddying swirls of dust *plinked* against the sergeant's armour. Sulphurous smoke was pooling in the deep basin too, running off the mountains. In the dirt-smog, Lorkar's vision worsened further.

'Harkane!' He summoned the Techmarine, knowing the visual filters in his bionics could penetrate the murk.

A whirring, clanking shadow knelt down beside his sergeant. It sounded like Harkane's machine parts were in need of re-sanctifying. Manipulating a series of dials embedded into the mechanical part of his skull, his ocular bionic implant ground noisily into focus.

'Ordnance, fired from deep space,' he asserted.

Lorkar racked the slide on his bolter impatiently. The gloom was still too thick for him to penetrate. 'I know that. Tell me what just happened down here.'

Harkane's bionic clicked three stages to the right, one back to the left as he refocused. The dirt cloud was extremely dense. Without rebreathers, a non-augmented human would choke to death in it. Grey soot veneered the Marines Malevolent's chipped yellow armour from the disturbed ash-sand.

'The Chapter Master of the Salamanders is down. Not dead.' Harkane adjusted again, his optics relaying a low intermittent hum as they zoomed in on the target. 'Cursory wreckage analysis suggests he was thrown by the blast. Currently, he is trapped beneath a section of a battle tank that has flipped onto its side.'

'Any rescuers?'

Harkane panned around. The aperture of his bionic expanded and contracted as it continually refocused and adjusted.

'Negative. The lance strike has isolated him from the rest of the fighting. I can detect no heat signatures or electronic returns within five hundred metres. The density of the surrounding dust cloud suggests visual recognition would be even less than that.'

Lorkar smiled, muttering, 'So we have our opportunity.'

He was almost salivating at the prospect of the Salamander's Chapter Master pinned and helpless. 'And the creature?' They'd seen it soaring overhead before it engaged the Chapter Master and his witch. Lorkar had no desire to become the subject of its attention. His mission was very specific.

There was a short pause as Harkane gathered more data before he answered. 'Inconclusive. The blast radius suggests the Chapter Master was thrown beyond its immediate path.'

'And into ours,' Lorkar concluded. The dirt cloud was thinning. He could finally see the prone Chapter Master sprawled on his back, trying in vain to push the massive battle tank off his trapped leg.

IT WAS JUST like Stratos all over again. He was back inside the Aura Hieron temple with Kadai at the mercy of the traitors. Dark memories returned of his captain facing off against the warp spawn, an assassin lurking in the shadows, the melta beam ending him forever...

'Never again,' Tsu'gan swore, closing silently on the warrior below him.

'STAY ALERT,' LORKAR told his troops. 'This is still an active battlefield.' He was about to order the advance when a fire-red glow scorched overhead.

As one the Marines Malevolent crouched down and aimed their weapons skywards. It was fast, so fast Lorkar couldn't detect its origin.

'Anyone get a bead on that?' No one replied. 'Harkane?'

The Techmarine shook his head. 'Negative.'

It moved erratically, like a hunter-seeker missile, only it was ablaze.

Vathek gestured with his well-worn chainblade as the flame disappeared somewhere in the distance.

'There! What is it?'

'A fight we want no part of,' muttered Lorkar. He was looking through the magnoculars. Putting the scopes down, he shook his head, 'All I can see is fire.'

Karvak, the Apothecary, was conducting a cursory analysis with a battered auspex. 'I'm reading intense thermal spikes on a vast scale and holding.'

Harkane confirmed.

Not far beyond the wreckage site where Tu'Shan was struggling to free himself, the air shimmered with haze.

'I can actually *smell* the heat coming off that thing, even from here,' said Vathek.

Lorkar scowled. It was a risk, anything unknown always was. The others had slowed. As their sergeant, he needed to get them moving again. The *voices* gave him focus, boosted his resolve and determination. Vinyar's orders... weren't they, recalled from deep conditioning? He could almost feel certain sections of his salvaged armour contracting against his skin, reminding him of his mission.

I will not fail you, lord.

'Not our concern. We are presented with an opportunity. This is what we came here for. Seize it! With me. Now.' Lorkar leapt a shallow barrier of rock, slipping from the ravine as Vathek glanced to the ridgeline behind them. Gorv's silhouette was barely visible in the dispersing dust cloud. The sentry appeared to stumble.

'What about Gorv?'

'I can see no sign of Vogan, either,' said Karvak, following Vathek's gaze.

Lorkar barked into the comm-feed, static adding unneeded grit to his voice, 'Forget them. They will have to catch us up. Move!'

He had never abandoned men before. Ever. Something was wrong. Lorkar knew it. He had known it ever since they had left the *Demetrion*. Only now he no longer possessed the desire to care. The mission was all that mattered. Salvation was all that mattered. Head low as he ran through the dirty smog, he only hoped they had not left it too late.

* * *

Tu'Shan had enough self-awareness to realise he was injured. This was not a flesh wound, like the countless minor injuries he had sustained through the course of being a Space Marine; this was genuinely debilitating. Warriors died from such wounds. Not because of the wound itself. It wasn't life threatening. They died because they were weakened, and an enemy will always seek out a weakened opponent to put him down. Tu'Shan had no intention of dying to an executioner's blade or a point-blank shot to the side of the head. He would fight. So, he heaved against the Land Raider with all the strength he had.

That he had survived the blast was testament to his endurance, but his leg was trapped beneath the tracked section of the tank. He blessed Vulkan's mercy for that. Under the hull and he'd require a bionic replacement. As it was, he could drag the limb loose and need an Apothecary rather than a Techmarine in order to walk again.

Dark spots blossomed intermittently in front of his eyes, but it wasn't through his failing consciousness that he had lost sight of the daemon. Tu'Shan hoped it was dead. The lance strike hit harder than he'd expected. He knew the risks. The pressure wave had lifted the wreckage of the *Promethean* off the ground, him with it. For a few crucial seconds he'd blacked out. By the time he'd come round again, he was on his back in the dirt with a massive battle tank sat on his leg.

Stormbearer was lashed securely to his wrist, the only reason he still had the hammer. He gripped the haft and swung, deciding to smash the track apart instead. The first blow went a little wide, splitting off a few chunks of metal tread. Too cautious. The second put a crack in one of the Land Raider's track rollers. Tu'Shan didn't swing a third time.

He felt the presence of warriors gathering around him and arched his neck so he could look behind him. One of the Marines Malevolent he'd met aboard the *Purgatory* stalked into view. Smoke was rolling in from the venting calderas in the mountains, muddying the view, but the warrior wasn't trying to hide. It didn't even occur to Tu'Shan to question why this warrior was on Nocturne. His posture and determined gait told the Chapter Master all he needed to know. From a prone position, the warrior was upside down and had drawn a short combat blade. That confirmed it.

'I knew you were a bastard, Lorkar, but I didn't think you were also a traitor.'

'I'm flattered you remember me.'

'I never forget a bastard.'

'You can't goad me, Tu'Shan. I'm not one of your whelps.'

'Are you here to try and kill me then?'

'If that were my intention there would be no *try*.' Lorkar thumbed the activation stud on his grip and the combat blade buzzed into motion. 'I merely wish to part you from something.' He looked around theatrically. 'Seems your brothers have abandoned you.'

Tu'Shan suspected the rest of the Salamanders were close, maybe even looking for him, but he'd been carried far from the main battlezone. For now, he was on his own.

'Save the histrionics. I need no help in besting the likes of you,' he said, then smiled mirthlessly. 'I could do it with one leg crushed beneath a tank.'

Lorkar nodded as three of his cohorts appeared behind him, brandishing their blades. 'Just as well.'

Tu'Shan immediately lashed out but to his blind side, crippling the Marine Malevolent trying to outflank him. The warrior's knee plate buckled, the bone too as it was pulped by *Stormbearer*. His assailant collapsed and screamed in agony, clutching at his shattered limb.

Lurching onto his elbow, Tu'Shan swung across his body and caved in the chest of a second ambusher. He fell back and didn't move again.

'Two down,' he snarled, 'sure you don't want to even the odds some more?'

'No,' said Lorkar, shutting off his combat blade and

sheathing it. The three warriors behind him had drawn bolters and levelled them at the Chapter Master. 'I think we'll just shoot you instead.'

'Always thought you were a murdering dog, bereft of honour.'

Lorkar beat his fist against his plastron. 'I am no murderer,' he snapped, before recovering his lost composure. He gestured with his bolter's serrated bayonet at *Stormbearer*. 'But I will take that hammer.'

Tu'Shan's face creased with angry confusion. 'Trophy hunting? I thought you Malevolents only cared for scrap.'

And that was when Lorkar revealed the truth.

'I need it. *Need. It.*' He ordered the others to lower their guns. 'Something happened to us, aboard a ship.'

'The *Demetrion*,' said one of the warriors, a Techmarine judging by his trappings.

Lorkar nodded to him. 'The *Demetrion*.' He unclasped part of his vambrace armour. It was an old piece, battle-scarred and scorched by fire. It detached from a larger section that sat beneath it. An unpleasant musk escaped into the air as this second layer of plate was revealed. It was pitted, rusted at the edges and fused into Lorkar's flesh.

Tu'Shan had seen the tainted armour of traitors before. He knew how it could mould to the wearer, become a symbiotic part of them.

'Vulkan's mercy, you *have* turned. You just don't realise.'

'It was not…' Lorkar faltered, 'intentional.'

Tu'Shan was dour. 'The path to damnation never is.'

Lorkar let the bolter swing loose on its strap and drew his blade again, his mind in obvious disarray. 'I am sorry, but I need that hammer. I can break it…' he said, breathless. 'I can break it apart, become who I was.'

Tu'Shan shook his head slowly. 'No, brother. You can't.'

There was a gleam of madness in the sergeant's eye. 'We shall see.'

The four Malevolents attacked together. Tu'Shan blocked the chainsword of one with his haft. Another he punched in the face as he lunged. Lorkar rammed his vibro-blade into the Chapter Master's armour, between the pectoral and shoulder guard. Tu'Shan cried out as the churning teeth met flesh.

'Give it up,' Lorkar snarled.

The fourth warrior, the Techmarine, had wrapped a gauntleted hand around the *Stormbearer's* haft.

'Not even when I am slain,' said Tu'Shan, feeding a jolt of power into the hammer and severely electrocuting the Techmarine who was flung back several metres and landed in a quivering, smouldering heap.

Lorkar drove his blade deeper. 'So be it.'

The chainsword came down again, the attacks from its wielder frenzied. Tu'Shan parried a couple of blows but one got through his defence and ground against his rerebrace. The one whose face he'd punched was back up too and keen for retribution. Looking through the frantic melee, Tu'Shan realised the warrior's helm and face were one. Skin and metal were conjoined.

'This is madness,' he spat. 'The hammer will not achieve what you want it to.'

'It will cut me free of this nightmare,' said the helmet-headed one, drawing a sidearm and pressing it to the Chapter Master's temple as he struggled.

An executioner's blow.

The others pinned him, Lorkar no longer caring if he had Tu'Shan's blood on his hands.

'I can separate you easily enough,' promised a voice behind them.

Helmet-head half-turned, bringing the bolt pistol around, but was stopped by the chainsword cutting through his neck and decapitating him.

'See?' said Tsu'gan, running through another, tearing up his innards until they were red mulch inside his tainted armour.

Lorkar swung wildy at him. 'You were dead,' he

protested, as the other sentries he placed around the ambush site started to return.

'No, *brother*. Your troops, those fools you left on the ridge, *they* are dead. I am very much alive.' He blocked the sergeant's overhead cut, punching him in the gut with his free hand. Lorkar recoiled and went for his bolter.

Tsu'gan saw it coming and severed the weapon through stock and barrel.

On the ridge at the edge of the blast crater, reinforcements were looming. Tsu'gan gripped the bolter hanging off his shoulder on a strap and put down the first Malevolent to appear.

Return fire juddered from the dust and smoke in a series of dull muzzle flashes. Tsu'gan clipped another and then strafed right as the ground was chewed up in his wake. Between bursts, he saw Lorkar fall back to his own ranks and scowled with disdain. Shots were *pranging* off the Land Raider's impregnable hull as he slammed against the tank's underbelly next to Tu'Shan.

'Let's hope they don't have anything more substantial in their arsenal,' he said. The Chapter Master's eyes were penetrating as he took in his rescuer's ravaged face, his borrowed armour. 'Are you afflicted like them too, brother?' he asked.

Tsu'gan's voice darkened. 'No, not like them.' He squeezed off a few rounds of snap fire to keep the Malevolents pinned.

Tu'Shan was close enough to the edge of the tank to peer around it into the smoke.

'They're widening their spread,' he said, 'trying to encircle us.'

Letting off another desultory burst, Tsu'gan rolled behind the improvised barricade. 'We need to move.'

'Agreed. Can you lift a Land Raider, brother?'

Tsu'gan regarded the point where the track had Tu'Shan pinned. 'Not above my head, but...'

As the rain of fire continued to batter the tank, he got

his fingers under the piece of half-wrecked track and heaved.

'We thought you'd perished in the warp,' said Tu'Shan, realising what Tsu'gan was attempting and forcing the long haft of *Stormbearer* under the tiny aperture he had made.

'In a way, I did.'

Together they pushed down on the thunder hammer, using it as a lever.

'Get ready to move that leg,' said Tsu'gan. The shots smacking the hull were getting closer.

'Whatever you have done, you can be redeemed,' Tu'Shan told him, seeing the emptiness in his eyes. Hauling his leg out from under the *Promethean*, he grimaced but didn't cry out.

'No I can't. Not yet.' He helped the Chapter Master to sit up, got his back braced against the underside of the tank.

'You saved my life, Tsu'gan.'

Tsu'gan paused, about to sneak a glance around the edge of the Land Raider. It wouldn't be long before Lorkar had them surrounded. 'You might still die yet, my lord.'

A voice called through the smoke and dust behind them, 'Lord Tu'Shan!'

It was Agatone.

'Here come your saviours now, liege.'

The closing bolter fire striking the hull receded as Lorkar chose discretion over valour.

'Stay,' said Tu'Shan, eyeing the retreating shadows of the Marines Malevolent even as those of Agatone and the Third materialised at the edge of the crater. 'Stay with your Chapter and–'

He was talking to the air. Tsu'gan was gone, lost to the ash and smoke.

CHAPTER TWENTY-FOUR

I
Broken by the Anvil

STRANDS OF GOSSAMER-THIN unreality shredded before Vel'cona as he passed through the flaming infinity gate and into the vault. A battered and crippled Pyriel was sliding to his knees as he arrived, the gaping hole left in his chest by the warp lance raw and mortal. He had trained the acolytum, seen in him something great and the promise of legacy. None of that would ever come to pass. Nihilan had seen to that.

The Dragon Warrior sorcerer reacted immediately to the Master Librarian's presence, unleashing a storm of darkness. Vel'cona fashioned a hasty defence of protective sigils described in the air with his force staff but was too late to negate the deadly summoning.

'Hell has come to you, master,' roared Nihilan. Vel'cona barely heard the taunt above the terrible tumult of the cloud. Inhuman voices, deep and guttural, smothered all thought and reason. He felt their malign will pressing against him as tangible as any blade.

There were *things* writhing in the blackness. Vel'cona felt them slither against his armour plate, pallid tentacles of sentience that left burn marks in the ceramite. Horror lived here in this cloud and it wanted to pick him clean of flesh, bone and soul.

Bowing his head, Vel'cona shut his eyes as he struggled to maintain his focus. Mental strength, the endurance of will was all that a psyker had. It was what kept him alive against the predations of the warp, against the very conduit through which he siphoned his power. Vel'cona had spent many hours, long years in fact, in psychic meditation, learning to manipulate and interpret the vagaries of the warp, channelling and honing his powers. He needed every second of that dedication to his art during those moments when the black horror was all about him.

Vel'cona sank to one knee as the coiled tentacles lashed, retreating to a molten core within himself. Here was his fortress, his refuge against dark forces. He had forged it with his own psychic hands, raised and nurtured it. Pain made him jerk and spasm, reminding him of the immediacy of reality. Threat of taint kept him awake. Nothing must disturb his serenity. A beacon of light shone in his mind's eye, just a flicker at first but growing swiftly to a roaring pyre. Vel'cona regained his feet, wrapped himself in armour of fire. Where it touched him, the hellish cloud became ablaze. Its myriad sentience shrieked as it was put to the flame, turning to scraps of ephemera that burned away like parchment before being reduced to ash.

Emerging from the fading darkness, Vel'cona fed a lightning arc through his palm that struck Nihilan in the shoulder. The Master Librarian called down a second strike that cracked his chestplate then a third, hammering the Dragon Warrior as he tried to rise.

Nihilan earthed a fourth bolt with his staff, using it like a lightning rod. He was halfway to his feet when Vel'cona clenched a fist to split the ground beneath him. Foundering in the cracks, Nihilan threw a wayward spit of hell-flame that the Master Librarian repelled easily with a dismissive gesture.

'Weak, sorcerer.'

'So was your apprentice.'

Pyriel's body lay inert on the floor of the vault, blood-less and still. During the momentary distraction, Nihilan summoned a lance of darkness that would strip his old master's soul from his flesh and leave the rotting husk in its wake.

Vel'cona threw up a spear of his own, an arcing line of flame that met the blackness of Nihilan's warp sorcery and held it.

Fire warred against shadow. The vying psychic conjurations expanded as more power was fed into them by their wielders, becoming a miniature event horizon that slowly filled the vault and everything in it.

Within the boiling morass of warp energy, Vel'cona percieved his avatar as a roaring drake, thick-scaled and tusked; whereas Nihilan had fashioned one of the dragon-kind, a blood-red, winged beast scarred by old wounds. The monsters clashed, gouging and clawing, tearing hunks of scale and flesh with their fangs, giving physical form to the mental struggle.

Slowly, the drake began to assert its dominance. It grew larger even as the dragon diminished.

'Pyriel shall not die unavenged,' Vel'cona promised as his monstrous avatar bit down on the other's neck and tore off its head. The fountaining gore became motes of sundered warp energy, dissipating in a violent explosion that threw Nihilan across the vault.

Vel'cona heard the sorcerer's spinal column crack as he hit something hard and unyielding. In the far reaches of the chamber, obscured by shadow, was an anvil. It struck Vel'cona that despite the time he had spent in the vault he had never seen this anvil before. It was old, colonised by rust. There was something ancient, slightly anachronistic about it. It was a black-smiter's tool but one left unused for many years, even millennia. Nihilan had been broken against it.

But he wasn't dead. Not yet.

The cerulean fire in Vel'cona's eyes dimmed to faint

embers. Despite his better judgement, he put his force
staff away. Nihilan's was snapped in two, far from the
sorcerer's agonised gasp.

'I'll choke you with my bare hands for this,' Vel'cona
promised. 'It will not be quick.'

It wasn't for his staff that the sorcerer was reaching.

A blast of fire smashed into Vel'cona. Like a tank had
rammed him in the flank, the Master Librarian hurtled
across the vault. In spite of the pain, he was on his feet
within seconds of being downed.

Ramlek was badly burned, his armour hung in scraps
across his body, but he was healing. Puckered flesh reknit
and smoothed over. Bloody gashes sealed themselves
up as if an invisible thread was stitching them together.
Bones re-set with an audible crunch. In moments he was
whole and vital again.

'Impressive trick,' Vel'cona conceded.

The renegade dog glared. 'Death to the Salamanders,'
he growled, and spewed gouting fire from his mouth.

Vel'cona sheltered behind his drakescale cloak and let
the flames smother him. After he'd endured the worst of
Ramlek's conflagration, he threw the mantle off, ready to
kill them both, but found the vault was empty.

His enemies were gone, and they had taken the tome
with them.

Allowing the lightning arc he was marshalling to fade,
he was about to focus his powers in pursuit when he
heard Pyriel's choked voice.

'*Master…*'

Incredibly, he still lived.

Vel'cona went over to him. He had to hold up Pyriel's head to keep it from falling. 'I am here. Be at peace,
brother.'

'*I am sorry, my… lord.*'

The words did not come easy for the Epistolary. He
had hung on this long, but the fire was calling and
would soon consume him.

'For what?' Vel'cona asked.

There was a gaping chasm in Pyriel's torso from where the soul lance had gutted him. Though the hell-fire had cauterised the wound, it had left it black with taint and destroyed the majority of his organs. Only his will had kept him alive this long. With no Apothecary at hand, this was the end of Pyriel's legacy, and for that Vel'cona was truly remorseful.

'*For my defiance at the council, for… trying to kill Nihilan myself.*'

'He was beyond us all in the end, brother, but you need not apologise to me. It is your strength of will that was always your greatest asset.'

'*Perhaps it is… ironic that this is what saw me dead.*'

'Perhaps, but I take no solace from that.'

'*Did you finish him, lord?*'

Vel'cona's expression darkened. 'No. Nihilan escaped with the book, one of our most sacred relics.'

'*He means to resurrect Ushorak with… the proscribed lore within its pages.*'

'I should have foreseen this.' Vel'cona looked into the darkness as if prying an answer from its depths. None were forthcoming. 'My thought was bent solely on the prophecy. I was blinded, Pyriel and for that *I* am sorry.'

There was no reply.,

'Brother, did you hear–' Vel'cona looked down but Pyriel was already dead. He let out a long and rueful breath. 'I will bear you to the mountain myself.'

The vault was devastated and the tome's sacred temple defiled, not that it mattered now. At least Nihilan had been made to pay a price of sorts. The anvil had broken him, it had…

Vel'cona could not find it. He searched in the darkness but the vault was empty, just as it had been when he'd first entered. The anvil, if it had ever truly been there, was gone.

WHEN AGATONE FOUND the Chapter Master slumped against the underbelly of the wrecked *Promethean* he was quick to signal for reinforcements.

The smoke had begun to clear at last and a bright, bloody-hued sun glared down on them from an oppressive sky. To Agatone, it was the most beautiful sight he had ever seen.

'Promethean sun...' he breathed, descending into the basin and taking it as an omen from Vulkan.

Sporadic bolter fire erupted from distant engagements as warriors of the Third made the site secure. Beyond that, the last throes of a larger campaign were being fought and won. News of the *Hell-stalker's* destruction and the defeat of the enemy fleet, along with their general's sudden absence, had reached the ground troops. Apart from the Traitor Astartes who still fought doggedly, the rest were all but routed.

Reports were coming in rapidly on the comm-feed. Captains Mulcebar and Drakgaard had made contact. Heliosa and Aethonion were secure; the few enemy forces that had reached their borders were unsupported and swiftly crushed. Units from the reserve companies were en route to Hesiod to help round up any recalcitrant enemy formations that still remained.

Gunships, squadrons of them, were landing in the Pyre Desert. Straight from the victorious void battle, the Firedrakes were deploying in force and cutting off the Dragon Warriors' retreat. Between hammer and anvil the enemy would be crushed. The war wasn't over yet but the Salamanders had the tactical and numerical advantage. Surely, it was just a matter of time.

'He is here!' Agatone cried out, rushing to Tu'Shan's side. 'Can you walk, my lord?' he asked, dispensing with any preamble. Tu'Shan nodded. He was weak, and spoke through clenched teeth.

'Tsu'gan,' he said, 'did you see him?'

Agatone was trying to assess his Chapter Master's injuries. The right leg was badly crushed and there was another wound to his shoulder and torso. Without an Apothecary, he couldn't be certain of their severity.

'I saw no one leave this basin, my lord,' he replied.

Malicant and Shen'kar, survivors of Agatone's Inferno Guard, were close by and keeping a watchful eye. They had encountered renegades on the way in to where they had found Tu'Shan.

'*We are clear for extraction,*' crackled the voice of Honorious through the feed.

Agatone turned from the Chapter Master for a moment, showing his profile as he put a gauntleted finger to an ear-bead.

'Contact Brother Hek'em and get the *Fire-wyvern* to this position immediately. Our Lord Chapter Master is injured.'

'*In Vulkan's name, brother-captain.*'

Agatone cut the link.

'He was here,' said Tu'Shan. 'Tsu'gan,' he clarified, 'he saved my life.'

Lowering his bolter, Agatone helped Tu'Shan to his feet, supporting him on his wounded side like a crutch.

'I saw no sign,' reasserted the captain. 'We must get you back into the city and then to the Apothecarion on Prometheus.'

Tu'Shan was barely lucid. He kept drifting in and out of consciousness, enhancing Agatone's concern further.

'You'll get me to Hesiod where I'll stay until this war is won.'

'It is not safe, my lord. We must–'

'Am I not your Chapter Master?' snapped Tu'Shan, though his anger was fleeting because of his injuries.

Agatone reluctantly conceded. 'To Hesiod then, under my protection. There are human medics in the city. Not as versed in Space Marine physiology as a practitioner, but even still.'

Tu'Shan shaped to protest but Agatone was quick with a rebuttal.

'In this there will be no argument.'

Now it was the Chapter Master's turn to nod and concede. They had reached the edge of the basin and were hobbling out of it to higher ground as two squads from Third forged a protective cordon around them.

Shen'kar was setting up the signal-beacon for the Thunderhawk when a shadow flitted across the sun. It was winged and jagged-edged, bringing with it the stench of spoiled meat. Guts churning, Agatone set the Chapter Master down and crouched with his bolter aimed at the sky.

'Bolters high!' he warned.

The two squads forming the cordon followed the captain's example, as did Shen'kar and Malicant.

The air became still and thick, the company banner a lifeless piece of cloth attached to its bearer's standard.

'It is the creature, the drakon.' Malicant used Vel'cona's word for it. 'I can sense it.'

'As can I,' muttered Shen'kar. The veteran's flamer would be of little use against an aerial target so he concentrated on acting as spotter for his brothers instead. Several of the squad warriors muttered much the same. Even soaring high above them, the presence of the creature was palpable.

'Didn't we just level an orbital lance strike against that thing?' said Malicant. They had seen the magnesium flare from the main battlefield.

Shen'kar nodded, scouring the smoke-laden sky for any sign.

'Stand ready,' Agatone told them. 'Stay behind me, my lord.'

It was a daemon, this thing. No one had described it thusly but Agatone knew enough of such creatures to recognise one in his midst. And it was old, this one. Venerable. Even with squads from Third and his retainers, he knew he couldn't kill it.

Tu'Shan was unconscious, having reached the limits of his endurance. Suddenly vulnerable, Agatone and his men would have to safeguard the Chapter Master's life. Nothing else mattered.

From imminent victory to dire peril in just a few

heartbeats, no war was ever truly won until the last enemy was killed. This one, the creature prowling the skies above them, eclipsed all others. Its shadow passed over again, closer this time. It was circling.

'Hek'em?' Agatone reached the *Fire-wyvern's* pilot and tried to keep his voice calm and level.

'*Inbound, captain,*' was the clipped reply.

'Make it swift. We are not alone out here. And watch the skies, brother.'

Static foiled Hek'em's immediate reply. '*I see it, captain, aloft on pinioned wing.*' There was another short delay as the pilot convened with his crew. '*It has seen us! Engaging!*'

'No, brother. Evade!' Agatone searched the skies desperately but knew he was impotent to do anything on the ground for Hek'em.

The feed stayed live. Muffled shouting and the low bark of heavy bolter fire filled the background.

Agatone listened. Warning sirens suddenly forced their way to the forefront of the feed. The *Fire-wyvern* was in trouble.

'*Vulkan's blood...*' Hek'em's reply was broken, only half-focused as he concentrated on not dying. '*There is... I can see something... fire. Captain, I see fire.*'

'What in the hell-pits is he talking about?' asked Shen'kar, who was listening in.

The sky was suddenly ablaze as if all of the air in the upper atmosphere had turned to fire. It was roaring, incandescent... devastating.

The sensation in Agatone's guts faded, supplanted by awe and a desire to kneel down in supplication.

Moments later, the descent jets of a Thunderhawk gunship could be heard as *Fire-wyvern* made its landing on the plain. It was burned. The wingtips and fuselage were black. Talon marks scraped the troop hold but it was still operational. The glacis plate disengaged with a hiss of released pressure and Hek'em stood up in his pilot's position in the cockpit.

'Get him aboard now,' he said. His tone was urgent and without ceremony.

Agatone knew better than to question. He turned to Shen'kar as he lifted the unconscious Chapter Master back onto his shoulder. 'Help me, brother.'

Shen'kar took the other arm and between them they half-dragged, half-carried Tu'Shan to the *Fire-wyvern's* lowered embarkation ramp.

Agatone used the feed to speak to Hek'em.

'We are aboard, brother. Close the ramp and get us into the air.'

Powering turbo-fans obscured the pilot's affirmative reply. The embarkation ramp was still lifting as the Thunderhawk soared into the air. Through the slowly closing gap Agatone saw the sky. It was an ocean of fire, boiling and churning a few metres above them. He caught a glimpse of something arrowing through its waves. It was carrying a heavy burden, a monstrous thing with splayed wings unable to resist the fury of the fire tide that bore it away towards the mountain. This spear of flame that Agatone saw, it looked very much like a man.

'Did you see that?' asked Shen'kar, as the ramp closed and pitched them briefly into darkness.

Crimson hold lamps flickered on as Agatone replied, 'I did, but do not ask me what it was, brother. For I have no words for it. None at all.'

II
Saviour and Destroyer

Burning, ever burning. The flame was incandescent, like a supernova given form in a human host. It had torn the metal ships from the endless night like they were nothing; less than nothing. Like a blade of fire it had ripped through them and cast them screaming into the void. It was infinite as an ocean, endless as time. It was the flame and its power was without limit. All would burn. Everything would be as ash before its rage was spent.

DAK'IR WAS ONLY partially self aware. A significant part of him was given up to the fire coursing through and over his body.

I must be anchored, he thought, struggling to channel the roaring psychic energies within. More than a hundred sentiences crowded inside him. Their animae and subsumed memories were fuelling him. He knew he was no Unbound Flame, whatever that even was. He was not a relic given the form of flesh. He was a conduit.

Upon the throne of Scoria, Gravius had held onto the psyches of his former brothers and it had driven him to insanity, burned him from the inside out. But Gravius was no psyker, his mind was untrained and unready for the burden of legacy he placed upon it. He was merely a vessel, a means of harbouring that power until the right host came along. Dak'ir *was* the Ferro Ignis, the Fire Sword, and he had emerged from the ashes of war to smite Nocturne's enemies.

This beast from the blackest pit, this hell-spawned thing he fought across the blood-soaked heavens was pre-eminent amongst them.

It raked him, scoring deep rents in his fiery armour, as they struggled. Dak'ir carried a burning blade, literally a tongue of sharpened fire made solid and white-hot by his psychic will. He hacked into the beast, ignoring the damage he was sustaining to its talons. Only when it bit his shoulder, seizing upon it with long, serpentine jaws, did Dak'ir cry out.

He lashed at it with a burning gauntlet, cracking its scales and tearing at its flesh. Hammer blows that would have crushed battle tanks rained against the daemon. His sword-arm effectively pinned, Dak'ir battered at its neck, dug his flame-wreathed fingers in and gouged until it shrieked in agony. Wounded, the beast recoiled. Beads of molten lava bled from Dak'ir's armour as he was released, cauterising and sealing his damaged shoulder.

It was fighting him, fighting against the flame that would bear them both to Mount Deathfire. Belatedly, the daemon realised its peril. It felt the heat of Nocturne's oldest and greatest volcano. Embattled, they soared to the mountain's summit, bursting though dense banks of pyroclastic cloud, surging beyond thunderheads of dry, crimson lightning. Sulphur wreathed the breeze, so thick and corrosive even the daemon's unnatural scales began to blacken.

The daemon struggled, but the flame was stronger. Dak'ir let it take another shred of his will and conscience, fuelled it into bearing the daemon to the edge of Deathfire's caldera.

'Dak'ir,' it said, 'please... brother.'

He knew that voice. It *was* his brother, but a distant, traitorous one. He blinked and it was a Salamander in his clutches, a warrior of his Chapter and blood.

'Iagon.' Dak'ir didn't recognise the resonance in his reply at first; it took him a moment to realise it was him that had spoken. The word crackled as if it too were ablaze. Whorls of smoke escaped from his parted lips.

'Save me, brother. You were always the compassionate one, Dak'ir. I knew I should have followed you, trusted you. I was betrayed, led to this devil's bargain, but you can redeem me. You can–'

Pitiless, fiery eyes regarded the daemon-Iagon as Dak'ir saw the ruse for what it was.

'Still the serpent, still the traitor,' he said. 'You are going to burn for all you've done, monster.'

Desperation gave the daemon a last rush of strength. Iagon's pleading mouth grew into a distended smile. It opened, revealing dragon's teeth, and threw black fire against Dak'ir. For a moment, he was engulfed. Blinded, choking to death on the warp fumes, his mind awash with images of burning worlds, Dak'ir lunged and trusted to instinct.

A scream was torn from the daemon's throat, the creature's true name.

Dak'ir spoke it loudly, the words unutterable in any mortal tongue but passing from his lips as easily as breathing. The black fire receded, withering away to nothing. The burning blade in Dak'ir's hand had become a lance. It pierced the daemon's ribbed belly and transfixed its heart.

Then it fell, still wearing Iagon's form, and Dak'ir fell with it, over the edge of the crater and into Nocturne's fiery heart.

The daemon was devoured, its physical form burned up and consumed by hungry, vengeful lava.

Dak'ir felt his strength and will fading. He had fallen far, deep into the lifeblood of the mountain. He needed to rise. Deathfire tried to pull him down, to swallow the flame. It was draining, bleeding away the power that had made him capable of sundering starships. With the last of it, he climbed. Every effort was bent towards escaping the endless lava sea. Like a sword reborn from the forge's fire, Dak'ir breached the surface of the caldera. Blind, weakened by the battle, he soared erratically across the heavens. Too weak to stay aloft, he plummeted like a fallen comet into the Pyre Desert, burning a great furrow into the earth.

When Dak'ir opened his eyes again, he was on his back and staring into a bloody sky. He didn't know how long he had been lying there. The fire that had coursed through him was dying out. Just a few stray embers remained. His time as the conduit for whatever power had infused him was ending.

'Saviour or destroyer,' he rasped through cracked, fire-blackened lips. His armour hazed with heat, partly molten from the influence of the flame. It cracked as it cooled, a forbidding sound that make Dak'ir think of his bones.

The daemon was dead, banished back to the Eye. Nocturne's armies were victorious. All the doom-laden prophecies, the vision he had seen during the burning. None of it had come to pass. He lived and so too did his world.

'Saviour…' he decided.

Dak'ir was about to rise when he felt a surge of heat within him. A fiery core of something he had thought extinguished was suddenly reignited. Despite his injuries, he struggled to his feet. In the distance, enemy troops were retreating from a force of Firedrakes. Gunships were taking to the air. Even further away, he could see his brother Salamanders reinforcing Hesiod's walls. A blackened Thunderhawk touched down on one of the city's landing pads.

He looked to the sea, to the endless desert, to the mountains, and imagined the other Sanctuaries. Victory cries would fill their mouths, songs would be sung, tears of sorrow and relief would be shed. Life, despite everything, would continue on this hell-world.

Unless…

Dak'ir tried to harness the flame, to bring it under his control, but it was beyond him now.

I have to die, he realised. He needed to sever the conduit at its source. He *was* that source. *I have to die.*

The burning blade was gone and Dak'ir could not make it manifest. He carried no other weapons and so could not even fall upon his sword. He wanted to call out even as the fire around him began to grow. First it would infuse his fingertips, then it would wrap around his body, then burn the desert, burn so hot the sand would turn to glass. The fire would expand, more destructive than a payload of atomics. It would burn and consume, overwhelming the cities until all that remained was ash.

'I cannot stop it…' The realisation was cold, in sharp contrast to the heat, and terrifying. Glaring at his fire-wreathed fists, Dak'ir was not even sure he wanted it to stop.

'Then let me.'

The first blow across his back put Dak'ir on his knees.

He snarled, trying to find his attacker, but a second blow doubled him over. He lashed out blindly, hit something hard that fell back. On his feet, Dak'ir saw the face of his enemy.

'I'll beat the fire out of you,' said the scarred warrior wearing a renegade's armour, his bottom lip curled down in a snarl. '*Ignean*.'

Tsu'gan advanced on Dak'ir, the teeth on his chainsword blurring. He smashed Dak'ir across the chest, cutting a deep groove in his armour, and then struck again, hard across the shoulder guard.

Impelled by its need for survival, the burning blade started to materialise in Dak'ir's hand but Tsu'gan just hit him again and the weapon faded to smoke. The blow should have killed, but Tsu'gan had only managed to put a crack in Dak'ir's armour.

'Trying to marshal your strength, to burn us all to hell and back,' Tsu'gan spat, landing a punch across Dak'ir's jaw.

Dak'ir was staggered but parried the chainsword with his vambrace, letting the teeth drag and spark against his battle-plate. He smashed Tsu'gan in the torso and threw him back. Burning ovals where Dak'ir had placed his fingertips blackened Tsu'gan's armour.

'I heard you were lost to the warp,' said Dak'ir. 'I knew it could not be true. I *felt* you were still alive.'

'I did die. I just came back to kill you.'

'We are still brothers, Tsu'gan.'

'You are no brother of mine, *Ignean*,' he snapped, then lowered his voice a moment. 'None of you are any more. Like I said, I died.'

'How did you even find me?' Though he tried to conceal it, Dak'ir was struggling to keep the flame at bay. In his mind's eye, his fingers clutched the floodgates but he was slipping.

Tsu'gan smiled, at least one half of his face did. The other was too badly burned to form expression. 'I was hunting different quarry when I saw your burning trail in the sky. I knew it must be you,' he sneered, 'the one of the prophecy, the doom or salvation of Nocturne. To me, *Ignean*, you were always just an aberration.'

'You are the one armoured in the trappings of a renegade.'

'Aye,' said Tsu'gan with a hint of melancholy as he brandished the chainsword, 'and I shall use them to dispatch you.' He swung the weapon around, relieving some of the tension in his wrist. 'Now, bare your neck to the blade and I'll end this quickly. I always despised you, Hazon, but you killed that thing Nihilan dredged from the abyss. I don't understand how, but you did and tore the bastard's fleet to ribbons too. For that, I'll grant you a merciful death but death it must be.' He gestured to the sand in front of his feet. 'Now, kneel.'

'Zek, I...'

'Just kneel. Do it quickly.'

Dak'ir nodded but didn't kneel. Instead, he thrust a hand around Tsu'gan's throat.

'*I am the flame,*' he said, in a resonant voice akin to his own, as the skin held beneath his gauntleted fingers began to smoulder.

Tsu'gan screamed.

'*Everything must burn. Even you, brother.*'

Tsu'gan met his gaze and over four decades of resentment poured from his eyes as he croaked through gritted teeth, 'Not this day, *Ignean*...' He rammed the still buzzing chainblade into the crack he'd made in Dak'ir's armour, shoving it into his body all the way to the hilt.

Dak'ir gasped and released his grip.

Tsu'gan let the chainblade go, left it buried and churning. He collapsed to his knees, clutching at his ruined throat but determined to watch as Dak'ir staggered.

The vessel for the flame, its psychic conduit, had been breached. Fire was leaking from the grievous wound, spilling from Dak'ir's eyes and mouth in a glutinous flood. Ablaze, burning inside and out, he threw back his head and screamed.

The flare of burning light that roared out of him was brighter than a dying sun.

Tsu'gan didn't bother to defend himself. It was pointless. He closed his eyes, thought of Captain Kadai and let the blast wave take him.

VAL'IN WAS ON the wall with Exor, ministering to Master Prebian, when he saw the explosion in the desert. It looked like a fireball, burning and expanding rapidly until it collapsed under its own mass and dissipated.

Below them, the Salamanders and the citizens of Hesiod had seen it too. Shoulder to shoulder, Fire-born and human alike stopped to witness the event. None amongst them knew what had happened. Few would even recognise the names Zek Tsu'gan and Hazon Dak'ir. They would never know of the sacrifice that had been made and the legacy that had brought it about.

Exor had been working with a field kit, dressing Prebian's wounds, when the flare had made him look up.

'What in Vulkan's name was that?' he asked.

Val'in couldn't tear his eyes away. 'Victory and death, brother.'

'And ending?'

'No. The Circle of Fire never truly ends.'

CHAPTER TWENTY-FIVE

I
Sons of Vulkan

'IS THIS ALL that was left of him?'

Tu'Shan was sitting on his throne with his right leg fixed in a brace. The armature had been fashioned by Master Argos to assist with the Chapter Master's recovery, but also meant he was confined to quarters on Prometheus.

According to Fugis, who had taken over responsibility for the Apothecarion after Emek's death, the wound would heal given time. Not many warriors, even Space Marines, could expect to walk after being crushed beneath a Land Raider, let alone be able to fight, he had reminded the Chapter Master.

Tu'Shan was looking at a pict screen that showed an image of an armoured silhouette burned into the ash-sand.

'We scoured the desert for days on end and in every direction,' said Agatone.

'With how many?'

'As many as the repairs to Hesiod and the other Sanctuary Cities could spare.'

'And Tsu'gan?'

Agatone shook his head sadly. 'No sign, my lord. It seems he perished in the fire.'

'No Salamander can be burned by fire,' Tu'Shan countered.

'It was no ordinary blaze, my lord.'

Tu'Shan stared at the pict and tried to make sense of everything that had happened. Barely a few weeks ago, Nocturne had been under siege and close to destruction. Prometheus was in ruins and overrun by xenos. His Chapter was brought almost to its knees and eradicated. It had taken this long to sift through the wreckage.

Now, the traitors were dead or fleeing, cast to the warp like the craven dogs they were. The deserts and mountains had been purged of any lingering enemies. The hostile environs of Nocturne would deal with any that had fled deep enough to avoid the Salamanders patrols. According to seismographic beacons Argos had instructed planted in the deep deserts, the planet was tectonically stable for the moment. How long that state would last was not known. Prometheus was partly restored and functioning as a space port again, albeit with a reduced fleet until extensive repairs to Dac'tyr's damaged ships could be made, and Vulkan's Eye was operational under Kor'hadron. But Tu'Shan still had questions, lots of them.

'He is gone, my lord.' Vel'cona stepped out from the chamber's penumbral gloom and into the flickering brazier light. 'They both are.'

Tu'Shan looked up and met his gaze. 'As is Nihilan, if I'm led to believe correctly.'

The Master Librarian nodded humbly. 'He escaped with the Tome of Fire, a piece of it at least.'

'Bent on resurrecting Ushorak, is that right?'

Vel'cona betrayed no emotion. 'Those were Pyriel's last words, yes.'

'What is to be done about that?' asked another.

It was the first time Elysius had spoken since the

assembly. The Chaplain looked tired, despite his rigid posture. Restoring the faith and resolve of the Chapter had been at the forefront of his many duties since the invasion. Learning of Dak'ir's supposed apotheosis and eventual fate had also seen him retreat to the Reclusiam for hours, even days at a time. He had only recently returned from one such castigatory session.

Tu'Shan let out a long, weary breath and leaned back in his throne.

'Nothing can be done, not yet. We cannot hunt the traitor, nor can we prepare for an old enemy resurrected.' He glanced at the Chaplain. 'For now we rebuild, gather our strength. The Emperor's wars must still be fought. The crusade has not ended for us.'

He regarded his captains, all of those who had fought in Nocturne's defence. Only two were absent, Mir'san of Second who was fighting the wars the Chapter Master had referred to, and the captain of Seventh. More than ever, the custodian of the Scouts was needed. Tu'Shan's gaze fell on Praetor last of all. The veteran sergeant had lost many aboard the *Hell-stalker*, though the survivors numbered well over half and included the Dreadnoughts Ashamon and Amadeus.

He knew Praetor felt the losses keenly. More would be needed to swell the ranks again. In fact, a list of battle-brothers had been provided that were considered worthy of commendation.

'We live, so too does Nocturne and our Chapter,' Tu'Shan told his officers. 'The anvil has tempered us, forged us stronger.' He allowed a pause, gauging the mood of his warriors during the short silence.

Beaten but resolute, battered yet enduring.

It would suffice, for now.

'That is all. Go to your duties,' he added, 'in Vulkan's name.'

Their reply echoed him in unison as the Salamanders officers departed. Some were bound for galactic war far from Nocturne's orbit; others would remain to bring about the rebuilding Tu'Shan had spoken of.

'Masters Vel'cona and Elysius,' he said. The Master of the Librarians was always the last to leave and lingered behind as the throne room emptied. The Chaplain knew this was coming and had not stirred.

Tu'Shan dismissed the Firedrakes too, ensuring the three of them were alone.

'Is it possible?' he asked simply once the throne room was empty.

'Is what possible, my lord?' asked Vel'cona.

'Please don't be evasive, Master Librarian. You know of what I speak.'

Vel'cona nodded, contrite. 'Ancient and proscribed rituals can achieve many things, but I have never heard of one returning life to the long dead.'

'And what do you say, Brother-Chaplain? You have told us all that you witnessed a miracle on Volgorrah. Are such things even feasible?'

'Are you asking me if I *believe* it can be done, that the disparate spirit can be reunited with the body and the body itself restored at the same time?'

Tu'Shan didn't answer. He waited.

'Ushorak was a bastard and a zealot. I have *never* seen a Chaplain of his like before. Ever. He inspired devotion with a will of iron and a brutal ethic as far as punishment and righteous fury were concerned. There are few of my order that ever caused me disquiet, but he was one of them. If all it takes to crawl from the worm-infested earth is will then he is already clad in armour and clutching his crozius as we speak. Thankfully, that is not the case.'

'You failed to answer my question, Elysius,' said Tu'Shan.

'That is because it has no answer. I cannot say whether I believe it or not. Dak'ir arose from death, *from death*, and became something which defies definition. Now he is gone and with him any answers he might have had, though I doubt he knew any more than we did.'

'The Unbound Flame,' Tu'Shan said to Vel'cona. 'Was

he an artefact made flesh, one of the Nine?'

The Master Librarian had no answer, either.

Tu'Shan turned and glared into the darkness at the very edge of the throne room.

'Can you tell me, Forgefather?'

Vulkan He'stan had entered silently and emerged from the shadows at the chamber's door.

'No, Dak'ir was not the Unbound Flame.'

'Is that it? All of your wisdom and that is all you have for your Regent?'

'Should I lie to you, Lord Tu'Shan? Should I break the solemn bond of brotherhood we forged just to salve your mind?'

Tu'Shan looked about to retort but then sagged in his throne. 'No. Of course not,' he said. His voice was low, tired. 'Forgive me, brothers. I am weary. I want answers where there are none to be found.'

'I am leaving,' said He'stan, apropos of nothing.

Tu'Shan nodded, knowing this would happen.

'I am glad you were with us for this long.'

He could see the sadness in the Forgefather's eyes, his desire to stay warring with his honour. The Nine were his masters. Perhaps with their acquisition, some measure of truth could be found that would explain everything.

Somehow, Tu'Shan doubted it.

'As I fought the daemon and Nocturne burned around me, I felt something,' he confessed. 'As if I were not alone.'

'In the vault, I felt it too. I think it even broke the traitor's back,' said Vel'cona.

'It was alive in all of us, brothers,' said Elysius.

He'stan didn't need to speak his evidence to show he had experienced it too.

'His strength was in my arm. I saw it in the courage of us all,' Tu'Shan went on. 'It has made me consider whether he is truly dead.'

He'stan smiled. It was a strange expression to see on one usually so taciturn and enigmatic. 'He is not dead, my lord.' He opened up his arms in an expansive gesture. 'I see him before me now. He lives on. We are, all of us, his sons.'

Tu'Shan nodded. There was determination and strength etched upon his face as if it had been branded there by the priests.

'Vulkan,' he said.

'Vulkan,' answered the others.

II
Legacy

THE PRACTICE SERVITOR exploded in a shower of sparks. Oil and pseudo-plasma was spewing from its severed cabling, smoke spilled from its machinery. It was a heavy-duty variant, armoured up and fashioned to absorb punishment.

Ba'ken had split it apart with a single blow.

As he yanked the chainblade free with a grunt of effort, he became aware of someone watching him.

'Emek's notes suggested you preferred to train in the Themian hell-pits.'

Ba'ken turned around and sheathed the sword in a nearby weapons rack.

'I believe a great many scorpiad and gnarachnid were disturbed during the earthquakes. You could have your pick of the fiercest,' Fugis concluded.

The Apothecary was wearing his power armour, although he eschewed a battle-helm. He paused at the entrance to the training cage, observing.

'Looks good on you, brother,' said Ba'ken, indicating the armour.

'Feels heavy, somehow.'

'The armour?'

'No, not the armour.'

He meant Emek and the void left by the previous Apothecary.

'I feel it too,' Ba'ken confessed.

'The burden of leadership, you mean?'

As soon as Ba'ken had been able, Prebian had handed over the mantle of captaincy of Seventh. The Master of Arms had returned to his old duties and to tend his own wounds.

'Yes, and the fact that my two closest battle-brothers are dead and gone.'

Fugis stepped into the training cage. He picked up a power stave from the rack, gauged its heft and indulged in a few practice swings.

'Your technique needs some attention.'

'Aye.' The Apothecary restored the stave to the rack. 'But I'd wager there's no one can touch me at spearing sauroch.'

They laughed but their humour died quickly.

Dak'ir was gone. Emek was dead. Many others had also lost their lives in the war. Brothers. Allies. Friends.

Fugis turned his back, considering his next words. 'You know, Ba'ken, I could tell you that as Salamanders we must endure. I could quote the Promethean Creed and discuss the nobility that comes with self-sacrifice.' He faced him, and his expression was stern. 'I am not Elysius. I won't do that, so if you're looking for a catechism to bolster your battered faith or some esoteric scrap of scripture to salve your grief then seek it elsewhere. I am concerned with bones and blood, your body not your soul. You are strong, brother, but do not make the mistake of leaving this battle cage until you are ready.

'Emek is dead and I will take over his duties from here on out. Dak'ir is gone, also likely dead. Vel'cona has other acolytes to fill his place. You and I, we live, we go on. If I can give you a single piece of advice, it's don't dwell in grief. Become strong. Hone your aspirants and make them strong too. We shall need them.'

'I feel alone, Fugis.'

'You are alone,' snapped the Apothecary. 'We all are. Deal with it.'

He left a short pause to allow the message to sink in.

'I will have need of you soon, so I would suggest finishing up in here and joining me in the Apothecarion.'

'Val'in and Exor?'

'Yes, they are to receive the black carapace. It's the beginning of a bold new legacy for the Fire-born. You should be there to witness it. Oh,' Fugis added, 'Zartath has been added to your list of responsibilities also.'

'The Black Dragon?' The tone of Ba'ken's voice suggested this was anything but good news.

'It might be some time before he can be reunited with his Chapter. If he's to be useful, he will need indoctrinating into our ways of war. I cannot think of anyone better for this task than the Master of Recruits.'

Fugis turned his back and was walking out of the cage when Ba'ken called out to him.

'You really are a hard-faced bastard, Fugis.'

The Apothecary didn't turn or slow down, he merely said, 'I am a pragmatist, brother. No more, no less. Be swift, your former aspirants are already prepped for the final stage towards apotheosis.' He stopped a few metres beyond the cage entrance and turned. His eyes flashed red in the gloom.

'I trust you will be ready.'

Fugis walked on until he was lost to the darkness.

Ba'ken nodded slowly. He felt the strength in his arm. His entire body radiated with power.

'I will be ready,' he promised to the shadows. 'The Salamanders will rise again.'

EPILOGUE

THE SIGNAL BEACON blinked three times in quick succession on the viewscreen, paused for a second and then blinked again three times.

Leaning over to the receiver cup, the Thunderhawk pilot spoke into the vox.

'Mechanicus facility detected and in range.'

The message was relayed through to the troop hold. As he finished, he switched back to the emergency rebreather he was using for oxygen.

It was dark in the troop hold. Most of the lume arrays were down and what sporadic crimson light there was did little to alleviate the gloom. It did describe the melta-sealed sections, the ragged industrial solder lines. It also cast a grim, visceral light on the rows of the wounded. There were several.

Lorkar had known the danger when he'd accepted Nihilan's offer but he had not realised the full cost. Of the thirty men he'd entered Nocturne with, only four were battle-ready and one of those was the pilot. The rest, those he and his able-bodied brothers had managed

435

to drag from the blood-soaked ash-sand, numbered in single figures. Barely a squad had survived.

He glanced at Harkane before he answered the pilot.

'Then get us to a landing zone quickly.'

The Techmarine was keeping them aloft, deep in supplication and ritual to the machine-spirit as he worked to ensure the turbo-fans kept turning.

Lorkar still couldn't quite believe they had escaped the vengeful Salamanders ships. They'd fled through the debris field of stricken vessels, under fire. They'd taken several hits but managed to limp to the orbit of a Mechanicus station at the edge of the system. Had the Salamanders' fleet not been so badly damaged during the battle, he felt sure they wouldn't have reached this far.

As it was, they now had a chance.

Karvak was knelt over one of the fallen, muttering.

Lorkar watched him unsheathe his mono-molecular blade and shove through the warrior's gullet, up into his brain. Then he went to work with the reductor.

'We are a dying breed,' he said to the Apothecary.

Karvak was drilling noisily through super-hardened bone carapace, and pretended not to hear him.

Lorkar became quickly distracted, scratching at the infected armour plate fused to his arm. There was another piece attached to his back, a section of cuirass that was also irritating him.

'What fate for the Marines Malevolent now?' he mused, 'What fate for the damned?' One of the wounded stirring caught Lorkar's attention.

He shuffled over to the warrior, bracing himself several times whenever the damaged gunship bucked and pitched. The pilot and his gunner up in the cockpit had a difficult task ahead of them to bring the limping vessel in but were at least prevailing so far.

'Be still, brother,' Lorkar whispered. The warrior was muttering something under his breath. He was badly burnt. The upper portion of his armour was scarred black and half-melted from heat.

'Be still,' Lorkar repeated, pressing a hand reassuringly to his chest. 'We are nearing salvation.'

The wounded warrior grimaced. He might have snarled. It was hard to tell in the gloom and with his facial injuries. Lorkar realised he was trying to speak, to impart a message.

Lorkar leaned in close. 'Tell me, brother. I will answer if I can.'

He heard the tension in a gun trigger being slowly squeezed and when he realised what the wounded warrior was saying, knew his critical error.

'Salvation does not exist for the likes of you.'

The wounded warrior's right hand was moving. Lorkar seized on it, pinning the bolter carried in it to the deckplate. When the combat blade in the other hand was sunk into the meat of his neck, he knew he was dead.

Lorkar met the fierce gaze of his killer, but could only rasp, 'Brother...'

'Brother-sergeant?' Regon barked urgently down the vox when he'd heard the dull boom of bolter fire coming from the hold.

'Brother-Sergeant Lorkar.' Still no response. The pilot looked to his gunner.

Vakulus pulled his sidearm and went to cover the door. He had almost reached the reinforced column surrounding it when the cockpit hatch burst in with an explosion of incendiaries.

Vakulus went down under a short staccato of mass-reactive shells. He was only wearing half armour and the usual protection afforded by a full suit of battleplate was absent. He died as his internal organs were pulped by the shells detonating inside his body.

A Marine Malevolent stepped over the twitching corpse, but Regon was powerless to intervene as he was locked in at the controls.

'Kill me and we will crash land,' he warned, straining to align their flight trajectory.

Klaxons were sounding and impact runes were flashing across the control console. Through the glacis plate, the outer atmosphere of the repair facility bled by in a polychromatic swathe. Structures loomed through the industrial fog and smeltery clouds. From one of them there jutted a landing dock.

'I can bring us in,' he snarled. Regon assumed one of his brothers had gone insane, been finally driven to homicidal madness by the *voices* they all shared.

'So can I,' the other warrior whispered into Regon's ear. His breath reeked of ash and burning.

He aimed the bolter's muzzle at the pilot's head and removed it with a single explosive shot.

The gunship was locked into a landing vector but not a perfect one. Unclipping the pilot's harness, the warrior shoved him aside, took his seat and prepared to crash land.

He closed his eyes before the Thunderhawk hit the landing platform and breathed, 'In Vulkan's name.'

'On the Anvil of War are the strong tempered and the weak made to perish, thus are men's souls tested as metal in the forge's fire.'

ABOUT THE AUTHOR

Nick Kyme is a writer and editor. He lives in Nottingham where he began a career at Games Workshop on White Dwarf magazine. Now Black Library's Senior Range Editor, Nick's writing credits include the Warhammer 40,000 Tome of Fire trilogy featuring the Salamanders, *Fall of Damnos*, the Space Marine Battles novel and his Warhammer Fantasy-based dwarf novels and several short stories.
Read his blog at *www.nickkyme.com*

FALL OF
DAMNOS

NICK KYME

UK ISBN: 978-1-84970-040-5 US ISBN: 978-1-84970-041-2

An extract from Fall of Damnos
by Nick Kyme

LIKE THE THUNDER-SMITE of a storm god, the drop pod touched down and sent impact cracks webbing across the surface of Damnos. It was one wound amongst many the planet had suffered.

A pneumatic pressure hiss preceded the exit ramp slamming down. Seconds later Sicarius was bounding through it, cape flaring, Guilliman's name on his lips.

He speared a necron warrior, half-cooked by the drop pod's incendiary flare. Another nearby had rapidly self-repaired and was advancing with automaton-like implacability. Sicarius pummelled its torso with a blast from his plasma pistol. Breaking into a run, he got close enough to behead it. The green bale-fires in its eyes guttered and died.

Behind him, the hard chank-rattle of bolters sounded as Daceus and the others opened up. Energy beams, viperous and emerald green, streaked through the smoke before Sicarius's retinal scanners could resolve a better view. A gauss-beam scudded over his pauldron, stripping it back to naked ceramite with the barest touch.

The necrons' bale-fire eyes appeared in the gloom like dead stars. The few they'd destroyed around the drop pod were just part of the vanguard.

More were coming.

THE THANATOS FOOTHILLS loomed in the distance like bad omens. The drop pods had got them as close as they could.

The ground running up to the snow-crested mounds was over three kilometres of debris-choked mire. Fanged by ice shards and dotted with arctic sink-holes, it was treacherous.

Scipio Vorolanus ate up the metres eagerly, his 'Thunderbolts' keeping pace alongside him and in spread formation. He checked the dispersal on his retinal display. A series of ident-runes showed good separation and fire-arc discipline.

'Move!' he said into the comm-feed, spurring his warriors as one.

Through the smoke-fog and the dust palls from the sundered refinery complex, shapes were moving ahead of them. They strode, slow and purposeful. Whickering emerald gauss-beams preceded them.

A grunt of pain, an armoured silhouette crumpling to Scipio's extreme right signalled a hit. Brother Largo's rune went to amber as the tac-display in Scipio's helmet registered a serious injury.

Just a few more metres...

A long line of silver-grey, flecked with pieces of ceramic, opposed them. The necron fire was a relentless barrage now. Another Ultramarine battle-brother fell to its fury.

+*Halt!*+

Scipio was stunned into obedience by the figure running just ahead of him. The word resolved in his mind rather than his comm-feed, a psychic impulse that could only be defied by one with sufficient will.

Varro Tigurius dropped into a crouch, gauss-beams

flashing against a kine-shield the Chief Librarian had raised around him.

'Get to cover. Hunker down!' Scipio ordered, slamming behind a shattered wall in the gutted remains of the half-destroyed refinery.

The place was a grim mortuary, littered with the bodies of Damnosian labourers and indentured Imperial Guard troopers. There'd been a battle here, a hard-fought one that had ended badly for the human natives.

Scipio barely gave them a second glance. It had not always been so. Black Reach and the many hard years that followed had changed him.

Fifty metres of spar-studded, wire-drenched courtyard stood between the Ultramarines and the necron firing line. Tigurius had brought the Space Marines to a sudden stop behind a ragged barricade before the final charge.

Peering through the gauss-laced haze, Scipio engaged the comm-feed. 'Specialists to point, on Vorolanus.'

Brothers Cator and Brakkius moved up, crouch-running, a few seconds later. Scipio clapped Cator on his shoulder guard. 'Plasma and meltagun at either end, brothers.' Both nodded as one, taking position at the edges of the wall.

Chips of rockcrete and semi-flayed plasteel slivers forced Scipio to duck.

'What are we waiting for, brother-sergeant?' asked Naceon.

Scipio had his eyes on the courtyard – there was more than merely war-churned earth beneath its shattered flagstones – and didn't look back.

'For thunder and lightning.'

Telion had taught him when to wait and when to strike; the Master Scout's expert tutelage and influence, presently engaged in other war zones, would be missed on Damnos. Scipio gestured towards Tigurius, a couple of metres ahead of them. 'Watch and be ready.'

A coruscation of electricity suddenly wreathed the Librarian's ornate battle armour and he pressed one gauntleted palm to the ground. Instantly, the azure energy banding him leapt into the earth and ripples of psychic force went searching through the no-man's-land.

Like gruesome marionettes jerking to horrific un-life, the necron 'flayed ones' sprang from their ambuscade. They'd been buried just beneath the surface of the earth, poised to attack the Ultramarines as they charged. A minefield of sorts, but one littered with an animate and deadly enemy rather than merely explosives.

Two of the ghoulish creatures juddered and expired from Tigurius's lightning arcs, the flayed human skin draped across them like cloaks and cowls burning off in a noisome flesh-smoke. Several more came on, having lost the element of surprise, but slashing with razored finger-talons anyway.

Scipio roared, 'Space Marines – unleash death!' The flare of his bolt pistol framed the hard edges of his crimson battle helm in jagged monochrome.

A plasma bolt took one of the flayed ones in the chest, annihilating mechanical organs and processors. The necron collapsed in a heap, quivered and then phased from existence as if it had never even been there.

Another sloughed away under the beam of Cator's meltagun. Despite the rapid self-repair engines of the necron's advanced mechorganics, the damage was critical and it too was teleported away.

Naceon had leapt the barricade, full-auto adding thrust to his battle cry. 'Ultramar and the Thunderbolts!'

Impact sparks riddled the onrushing necron, jarring but not stopping it. Naceon saw the danger, bringing his bolter's combat-bayonet low to block, but was too late. Finding the weak points of Naceon's armour joints, the flayed one punched several fatal wounds into the Ultramarine before slicing open his gorget.

Naceon's head rolled like a dud-grenade into the dirt.

'Guilliman and the Temple of Hera!' Scipio invoked a blessing as he cut into the metal clavicle of Naceon's killer. The chainsword bit deep and jammed.

An expressionless silver rictus, stained with blood, reared towards the sergeant. A bolt pistol burst took off the necron's left claw-hand before it could slash him. Scipio then butted it, snapping the creature's neck so its head lolled at an unnatural angle. He thumped his chainsword's activation stud again, muttering a quick litany to the machine-spirit within, and it churned to life. Dropping his pistol, Scipio drove the blade two-handed clean through the flayed one's body and out the other side. As he stepped back, ready to strike again, the two mechanical halves slid diagonally and fell in opposite directions.

Scipio had barely recovered when a second necron was advancing upon him. Without his bolt pistol, he adopted a rapid defensive stance.

The flayed one exploded before it could engage, sparks and machine-parts flying like frag.

A pair of hard eyes, glowing with power and set in an ice-carved face, regarded him.

+*Take up your arms*+

Scipio gave a curt nod of thanks to Tigurius, his soul ever so slightly chilled by the Librarian's gaze, and retrieved his bolt pistol.

There was little time. The flayed ones were vanquished, Brakkius and Cator were finishing the wounded at close range, but the line of gauss-flayers remained.

Scipio waved his squad forwards after Tigurius. Catching the Librarian's battle-signal on his retinal display, he opened up the comm-feed again.

'Squad Strabo. Bring fire from heaven.'

Hidden behind the wreckage of a refinery tower, ten bulky figures arrowed into the air on plumes of fire. The roar of their ascent jets made the necrons look skywards. Half of the creatures switched their aim, but the gauss-stream was too late and not nearly enough.

Hit from the front by Tigurius and Squad Vorolanus, and from above by Assault Squad Strabo, the necron firing line disintegrated leaving the Ultramarines the victors.

In the aftermath, Tigurius eyed the distant Thanatos foothills. The forbidding arc of necron pylons and the long noses of gauss siege cannon blighted the horizon line. Sustained particle whips and focussed energy beams bombarded the city of Kellenport relentlessly.

'They will be well guarded,' counselled the Librarian, without acknowledging Scipio's presence but answering his question before he'd even asked it.

'We'll need a way to breach their defences,' Scipio replied. Behind him, his squad and that of Sergeant Strabo secured the battle-site.

'A dagger rather than a hammer,' said Tigurius. 'But not one wielded by the hand of a Space Marine,' he added cryptically, turning his attention onto the sergeant. 'Does something trouble you, Brother Vorolanus?'

Scipio shifted uncomfortably in his armour, wishing he hadn't removed his battle helm.

'No, my lord,' he answered, truthfully. *Nothing, except your psyker's interrogation.*

Tigurius smiled and it was, at once, a deeply incongruous and unsettling gesture.

'Perhaps it should be,' he said, and left Scipio to plan the next stage of the assault.

Brother Orin was at the sergeant's shoulder before he could reply.

'We've secured the battle-site, my lord.'

Scipio re-donned his helmet. 'Retrieve Naceon's body and replenish ammo. We advance,' he replied, left to wonder at Tigurius's meaning.